CREEKE

CREEKE

RONALD SAVAGE JR.

Ronald Savage Jr.

Acknowledgements
Thanks to God, family, friends, and supporters.

In Loving Memory
'Grammi' Diana Askew Thorne
(1949-2021)

Part 1:
Derrick Harrison

Chapter One

If Creeke had a definition it would be, 'a small town with a church at its center founded by Abraham Creeke'. Abraham begat Nathaniel and Laverne; Nathaniel died young while Laverne married Franklin Harrison. Franklin begat Lionel; Lionel married Judith Morris. Lionel begat me, Derrick Jermaine Harrison.

Like most of my family, I was dark-brown with a carefully maintained afro. But the part of me seared into the towns' minds were my muscles. They were the source of many nicknames for me, and they even had their own nicknames. My personal favorite for them was T n' T. Abraham's legacy to my family was Creeke Church, which the men in my family had pastored since its founding. When Papa retired, I would be the next head pastor. Until then, I was his soon-to-be-eighteen preacher's son that played football and taught Sunday school.

"Today we're going to talk about honoring our parents," I said to a room full of children one cold, February morning. "God gave us to our parents for a reason, and it's our jobs as children to respect that. Does anyone know why we have to do that?"

"Because God said so," one child answered.

"Correct. How many of us here have had our parents tell us to do something and when we asked why, they told us 'Because I said so'?"

I raised my hand along with everyone else.

"See?" I pointed around the room. "We've all heard it, even me. Keep your hand up if you get annoyed when your parents say that because you still don't understand why. Be honest."

I left my hand up, and so did everyone else.

"What if I told you that when we get annoyed with our parents' instructions, God gets upset with us?"

A collective gasp rose from the children. The horror of God being upset with them flooded their faces.

"Everyone, go with me to Deuteronomy chapter five and verse sixteen." The sound of rustling pages followed my instruction. "In this verse, Moses tells the Israelites what God wants them to do when they go into the Promised Land. Read that for us, Damian."

"Honour thy father and thy mother, as the Lord thy God hath commanded thee," one of my best friends, Damian Lee Parker, read.

"Stop!" I said as I put my hand up. "Read that part again."

"Honour thy father and thy mother, as the Lord thy God hath commanded thee."

"As the Lord thy God what?" I held my hand up to my ear.

"Commanded thee."

"See? The Israelites had to honor their parents because God said so. Just like us. Listen to this next part because this is where God tells them why. Keep reading."

"Honour thy father and thy mother, as the Lord thy God hath commanded thee," Damian reread, his dark-brown eyes darting across his Bible from behind his big wire-framed glasses, "that thy days may be prolonged, and that it may go well with thee, in the land which the Lord thy God giveth thee."

"Okay, some of you might be confused by these big words here but that's okay because I looked them up in the dictionary for you. God told the Israelites to honor their parents so they would live long lives in the Promised Land where he was taking them. Now if we go to Ephesians six, we'll see that Paul says the same thing. Damian, read please."

"Children, obey your parents in the Lord: for this is right. Honour thy father and mother; which is the first commandment with promise; That it may be well with thee, and thou mayest live long on the earth."

"There it is again: obey your parents because it's right, and if you do, you'll live a long life. We all know Pastor Derrick loves God and football. Think of us as God's football team, and life is the big game of the season.

God is our coach, and honoring our parents is one of His plays. It's our job to run the play how God wants, so we'll win, and He'll be pleased with us. Honoring our parents means that we're honoring God. If we don't honor our parents, then we don't honor God, and that makes him upset with us. Do you know who else honored their parents?

"Who?" the children asked.

"Jesus," I said. "I'll prove it right now. In Luke Chapter two, Jesus was with his earthly parents in Jerusalem. When they were supposed to leave, Mary and Joseph lost Jesus. They found him three long days later in the temple, and this is what Jesus did when they found him. Damian, read Verse fifty-one."

"And he went down with them, and came to Nazareth, and was subject unto them."

"Stop!" I held up my hand. "Jesus was in God's house, and He could've thrown a fit about leaving. But he didn't do that. He chose to obey to his parents and leave with them. By obeying his parents, He obeyed God, which means He didn't sin and continued being perfect. Even Jesus obeyed his parents and when we obey our parents, we're being like Jesus. That's why it's important to honor our parents: because it makes us like Jesus."

After the lesson, Damian and I escorted the children back to their parents. Cool morning air nipped at my face as we walked along the side of the gray church building with beautiful stained-glass windows. The second half of the main church service would start soon.

"That was a good message," Damian said.

"Thanks."

"If only Leonard were here to hear it."

"When have you ever known Leonard Calvin Brown to come to church?" I laughed.

"It would do him some good. He and his parents stay cooped up in their house, driving each other nuts."

"Well, that's their business. Besides, Leonard visits me every Sunday after church so it's not like he doesn't know what I'm teaching."

"I still think he should come to church." Damian crossed his arms across his pudgy body. His light-brown cheeks were rosy, and he had stuffed his curly black hair into a knitted cap.

"How's your folks?" I asked, changing the subject.

"They're fine. They took in another baby since I'm on my way out."

"Another one? Taking you in wasn't enough for them?"

"I guess not." Damian answered, smiling at my playful jab. His 'parents' were his aunt and uncle. They'd taken him in from a relative when he was a baby.

"What's the baby's name?"

"Arthur Lee. He's got lots of energy just like a certain linebacker I know."

"So, I'm an active person." I protested. "It's not my fault I like being alive."

"Well, Arthur is lucky to be alive at all," Damian muttered. "Someone dumped him on our doorstep with a note telling us his name and asking us to take care of him! It's a good thing I heard him crying or else he'd be a human popsicle."

"That's horrible," I said. "But at least we both know he's in good hands with your folks."

"Yeah, you're right," Damian sighed.

I pushed open the church's brown wooden doors and released the children to their parents. Damian followed me to my seat in the front pew. He used the handkerchief in my suit pocket to clean his glasses.

"So, what's your plans for your birthday this weekend?" he asked.

"I don't know. Maybe I'll have a small party at my house."

"Who all is going to be there?"

"You, Leonard," I listed off. I scanned the room and noticed a pair of girls sitting together. "Marianne and Thelma."

"Marianne and Thelma?"

"You know Marianne's dad is best friends with Papa, so she'd probably be there anyways."

"And Thelma?"

"Why not Thelma? She's my friend too."

"I know...," Damian said as he scratched the back of his neck. "It's just... she does this weird thing with her eyes whenever she talks to me."

"Don't look at her eyes then. I'll go invite them right now."

I marched over to the girls with Damian in tow. Marianne Solomon Jones was thin, dark-brown, and had warm brown eyes that captured anyone who looked in them. Thelma Reid was healthy-sized, medium-brown, and was the sweetest girl I'd ever met. They were always together.

"Hi Derrick," Thelma said. She looked past me and lowered her chin so that her brown eyes were just beneath her eyelids. "Hi Damian."

"H... hi Thelma." Damian avoided Thelma's eyes and looked at the floor.

"Ladies," I said as I clapped my hands in front of me.

"Oh Lord," Marianne giggled. "He's got that smile on his face Thelma, which means he done cooked something up and he's going to drag us down with him."

"Aw, come on Marianne," I whined. "I just came to ask y'all a question."

"What do you want? A cherry pie?"

"Now that you mention it..." My mouth watered at the mention of my favorite pie flavor.

"Alright," Marianne sighed. "I'll make you one but only because your birthday is coming up."

"Yes." I pumped my fist. "You can give it to me at my party this Saturday."

"Party?" Marianne raised her eyebrows. "What party?"

"My birthday party. It won't be too many people there. Me, Damian, Leonard and you guys if you want to come."

"Will your parents be there?" Marianne asked. "Because you know my dad won't even *consider* letting me go unless both your parents are there."

"Why wouldn't they be there?"

"Alright. I'll see if I can go."

"Sounds like it'll be fun," Thelma said. She smiled at Damian, causing him to blush and look away again.

"We'll leave y'all alone now then. Come on, Damian."

I led Damian back to my pew. When we were out of earshot, he latched onto my shoulder.

"You see what I mean?" he whispered in my ear. "She does that every time I talk to her!"

"Tell her to stop then."

"What if she can't help it though? I don't want to hurt her feelings."

"I guess you'll have to deal with it."

Grandpapa Franklin cleared his throat. It was his way of telling us to find our seats because service would start soon. Damian left, and I couldn't help but chuckle at him. Sometimes, he could be so dense.

Leonard came over to visit that afternoon like he did every Sunday. He was a scrawny, dark-brown boy. His brown eyes were hard and mean, but sometimes they held a sadness too. Most people avoided Leonard and his strange family, but I saw him as he was: a lonely boy that needed a friend.

"You think Damian will ever figure out Thelma likes him?" I asked.

"You know he's simple."

"Don't say that about him."

"I don't know what Thelma sees in him anyways. She needs a real man. Someone strong and tough–!"

"Like me!" I flexed my biceps next to my head.

"I said tough not goofy."

"You also said strong." I placed my elbow on the table with my hand in the air. "I don't think Thelma would take you with those spaghetti noodles you call arms."

"We can't all be baby-oiled barbarians with no facial hair like you." Leonard set his elbow on the table and closed his fingers around my palm. I nodded, and our arm-wrestling match began. "Besides, I don't even like Thelma."

"A baby-oiled barbarian?" I chuckled, ignoring what he said about not liking Thelma. I knew his real crush was Marianne. Every time he saw her, he looked at her the way a dog did a piece of meat. "That's what I look like to you?"

"If the... shoe... fits," Leonard grunted as he struggled to push my arm.

"You know what I think of you, Leonard?"

I relaxed my arm a little and allowed Leonard to drive my arm toward the table.

"What?" Leonard asked. He licked his lips at the sweet taste of victory.

"I think you should spend less time being mean...," I said as I wrapped my fingers around Leonard's hand. I twisted his arm and banged it on the table. "...And spend more time being nice."

"Ow!" Leonard hollered. He rubbed his hand and glared at me. "Why do you always do that?!"

"Because it's funny."

"Man, you ain't nothing but a big bully."

"Derrick Jermaine 'Big Bully' Harrison." I framed my fingers in front of my face like a sign. "Man of God. Linebacker. Barbarian. I like how that sounds. Thanks Leonard."

"You would like that," Leonard sighed with defeat. "Always nick-naming stuff."

"What was that noise?" Momma asked as she hustled into the kitchen, a frown etched into her medium-brown face.

"Me whooping Leonard in arm wrestling again."

"Boy, how many times have I told you about slamming stuff on my table?" Momma placed her hands on her hips. She lowered her body until her light-brown eyes were level with mine. "You break my table and I'm going to break your butt. You hear me?"

"Yes ma'am." I placed my hand over my mouth and giggled when she turned around.

"You need an ice pack for your hand, Leonard?" Momma asked as she opened the freezer.

"I'm fine, Mrs. Harrison."

"Okay." Momma closed the freezer and eyed me. "Play nice."

"You know my birthday's this Saturday, right Momma?" I said as I watched her open the oven to check on dinner.

"How can I forget when you mention it every time we talk?"

"Well, I was wondering...," I stalled before blurting the rest of the sentence. "...if I can have a party here?"

"A party?"

"It wouldn't be too many people. Just a few friends."

"Derrick," Momma groaned as she rubbed her face. "I wish you'd mentioned this earlier."

"Why? What's wrong?"

"Your father and I are going out of town this weekend. He's preaching at another church."

"Oh."

"Sorry son." Momma patted my head on her way out of the kitchen. "You'll be alright."

"We can still celebrate your birthday," Leonard said with an impish grin once Momma was gone.

"How? I can't have a party if my parents aren't here."

"Who said anything about celebrating at your house?"

"What are you getting at?"

"Listen." Leonard leaned in and lowered his voice. "I know this place in the city. It's got great music and lots of dancing. You'll love it."

"Are you crazy?" I cried.

"Shhh!" Leonard covered my mouth. "Do you want the whole house to hear you?!"

"We can't go to a place like that!" I whispered when he uncovered my mouth.

"Why not?"

"Because my parents will have a fit if they find out!"

"Your parents won't be here. Nobody will know except us."

"Leonard, the Bible says to honor your parents." I wagged my finger at him. "You'd know that if you came to my lesson at church today."

"Here you go with that Bible crap again," Leonard complained. He hated when I talked about the Bible. "It also says not to provoke your children to wrath. But no one ever talks about that part."

"Do your parents provoke you to wrath?"

"Is that any of your business?"

"You brought it up."

"I was making a point."

"What was the point?"

"That everyone only follows the parts of the Bible they like. That's why I don't like being around church folk because they're hypocrites."

"See, this is why I'm going to be a preacher one day. So, I can talk about the parts nobody likes."

"Shoot, you do that and maybe I'll come to church."

"You mean it? You'll come to church when I become a preacher?"

"I mean, I guess I could attend a service."

"Let's shake on it." I said as I rubbed my hands together.

"Do we have to?"

"Of course we do! This is a big deal!"

"Fine," Leonard grumbled as he held his hand out.

"Do it right."

"We haven't done it that way since we were kids!" Leonard whined.

"Leonard," I growled.

"Man, you *are* a big bully," Leonard huffed as he put his hand to his mouth and licked it.

"You're sure it's only dancing?" I asked as I licked my hand.

"Dancing and a good time. You can't say no to that. Harrisons are always down to have a good time, right?"

"I'll go then."

We locked our spit-covered hands together in a handshake, sealing my fate. I hoped I wouldn't regret this.

-

Chapter Two

That Monday, the aroma of bacon filled my nose as I put my school uniform on. It was another typical weekday. Momma cooked breakfast, while Papa read shocking stories from the morning paper to us. He greeted me with the latest one when I entered the kitchen.

"Now, listen to this, Derrick," Papa said. "A Black girl was threatened and beat up by White students at her school after winning class treasurer. And the school claims to not know who the culprits are even though they've been 'monitoring the situation'. What kind of mess is that?"

"Where was this?" I asked.

"Up the street in the city!" Papa huffed. "These people hate integration so bad they're willing to let a young girl be bullied for no reason!"

"Lionel, please don't get yourself worked up so early in the morning," Momma pleaded.

"I can't help it, Judi!" Papa ranted. "As a preacher, I naturally empathize with people! Don't even get me started on how the city treats Preston High!"

"Don't even mention them," I grumbled.

"I know, I know," Papa said. "You're still sore about losing to them back during football season. But Preston is the only predominantly Black high school out there, and those kids are given scraps compared to the other high schools."

"I'd rather focus on my own high school," I said.

"As you should," Momma agreed. "Leonard should be here any minute to scoop you up."

As if on cue, Leonard honked his car horn from outside. He was the only one of my friends with a car. It was his father's car, but his father didn't drive anymore so Leonard drove it instead.

"There he is now," Momma said.

"I'll see y'all later," I said as I took a piece of bacon with me.

"Bye," Papa said as he flipped to the next page of the paper. "Have a good day."

"And don't get in any trouble," Momma added.

"I won't!" I called.

Creeke High School was the place where dreams went to die. Our school colors were maroon and gray, and our mascot was the cowboy. It was a bleak prison full of rules and restrictions I couldn't wait to be free of when senior year ended. As I walked to homeroom with Damian and Leonard, I noticed a poorly covered bruise on Damian's neck. I stared at it until my curiosity got the better of me.

"What happened to your neck?" I asked him.

"Nothing...," Damian uttered as his cheeks grew red.

"It doesn't look like nothing," I said as I pulled his collar down. "It looks like a hickey."

"Why are you all up in my neck?!" Damian snapped, swatting my hand away. "I told you it's nothing!"

Damian hurried away from me and Leonard.

"What's his deal?" I huffed.

"You know he's sensitive about everything," Leonard grumbled.

We rounded a corner and saw Thelma kneeling on the floor while Marianne stood face to face with a teacher.

"Miss Jones, are you refusing to adhere to the rules?" The teacher asked as he tapped his yardstick into his hand.

"I'm just asking why I have to do a skirt check when my skirt is clearly below my knees," Marianne said.

"Just do it, Marianne!" Thelma urged. "You're going to make us late for class and *my knees are starting to hurt!*"

"We wouldn't be late if people used common sense!" Marianne argued. "Do you really think my father would let me out the house in a skirt above my knees? Better yet do you think I'd even *own* a skirt that short?"

"Will we be making a trip to the principal's office today?" A smirk appeared on the teacher's face before his eyes flicked to me. "Mr. Harrison, your hair is too long."

"It is?" I asked.

"Yes." The teacher placed his hands over his own afro. "Afros should be this length or shorter. Anything outside of that is against the rules. You could always slick your hair down like Mr. Brown's to meet the requirements."

"Who died and made you king of the afros?" I muttered under my breath. Leonard's hand flew to his mouth to stifle a laugh.

"Seems you'll be joining Miss Jones and I on our trip to the principal's office today."

"This is ridiculous," Marianne ranted as we sat on the bench outside the principal's office. "Girls already can't wear pants to school. We have to kneel to check our skirts when we change classes, but they also can't be *too* long or we'll get in trouble for that too. What can we do?"

"I want to know how my hair is too long," I grumbled. "I've had my hair this same length all schoolyear long and no one's said anything about it."

"This is what I mean!" Marianne threw her hands up. "They just make stuff up as they go! We're in the seventies not the seventeen-hundreds!"

The door to the principal's office flew open. His short stature stood there, gripping the doorknob with his medium-brown hands. A vein throbbed in the forehead of his long, stern face as his eyes pierced the veil of his dark expression.

"Miss Jones," the principal stated in his deep, gravelly voice. "Come in."

Marianne entered the principal's office. She wasn't in there long. Before I knew it, she emerged rubbing her behind.

"How many times did he whack you?"

"Twice," Marianne said as she gathered her books. "It was either the paddle or call my parents. And if you think I'm giving up what little freedom I have over a *skirt*, you are sadly mistaken."

"Mr. Harrison," the principal called for me next. "Come in."

"I'll see you in class," Marianne said with a grin.

I entered the principal's office. He sat behind his long wooden desk with his hands laced together in front of him.

"What seems to be the issue?" he asked.

"The teacher said my hair was too long."

The principal glanced at my head.

"It is."

"With all due respect sir, I disagree."

The principal removed a binder from the shelf behind him. He placed it in front of me and opened it to the school's dress code.

"Read this line for me, please," the principal requested as he pointed at the section on boys' hair.

"*Hair must have a cleanly edged neckline* – which I do." I motioned to the back of my head to emphasize my point. "*...cannot go below the ear* – which it doesn't – *and cannot be unnecessarily long or distracting.* I don't believe my hair is unnecessarily long or distracting."

"What *you* believe doesn't matter. What matters is what *I* believe. And *I* trust my staff's judgement when they say your hair is too long."

"Why is this the first time someone has told me about it then?"

"Tell me, Mr. Harrison." the principal said. "As Bishop's son, would you say you have a firmer grasp on God's word than most of your peers?"

"I'd say I have an understanding of it."

"Then can you remind me what verses thirteen and fourteen from First Peter two say?"

"Submit yourselves to every ordinance of man for the Lord's sake: whether it be to the king, as supreme," I rattled off. I couldn't count how many times adults forced me to quote these scriptures growing up. "Or unto governors, as unto them that are sent by him for the punishment of evildoers, and for the praise of them that do well."

"Don't you think it would be better to do as *The Lord* says and submit to my authority, rather than argue with me?"

"Yes sir," I mumbled.

"I mean, you must be aware how it looks that *Bishop's son* is in my office. Arguing with the staff over hair? That's not very becoming of a future preacher who claims to follow the Bible, is it?"

"No sir, it's not."

"Cut your hair." The principal picked up a long wooden paddle with holes drilled into it. "And as for your little comment to the staff..."

That night, I ate dinner with Momma and Papa. The teacher had called Momma and told her all the gory details. Momma told Papa, and his reaction went as I expected.

"They paddled you... for hair length?" Papa scrunched up his face.

"They paddled him for mouthing off to a teacher," Momma corrected Papa while cutting her eyes at me.

"Oh," Papa said with a wince. "Son, you can't mouth off to your teachers."

"Yes sir."

"Still," Papa said as he scratched his head. "Your hair has been this length during football season, through the holidays, and now it's February. Why are they just now saying something?"

"That's what I said!" I exclaimed. "But apparently what I think doesn't matter."

"You're right," Momma said as she cleared the table. "As long as you're at that schoolhouse, what you think doesn't matter. You should only be thinking during your schoolwork because what matters is getting that diploma. Once you graduate and you're grown, you can have all the opinions that you want. Understand?"

"Yes ma'am."

"Get your coat on, boy," Papa commanded. "Let's see if we can get something done about this hair."

Papa drove me to Graham's barbershop. It was owned by Mr. Riley Graham, the only barber in Creeke. He'd cut my hair since I was a little kid.

"Tell Riley you want your hair cut shorter," Papa said as he handed me the money for my haircut. "And make sure you give him the change as a tip."

"Papa, we do this every time I get a haircut. I know the routine by now."

"I'm just making sure you remember. I'll swing back around to get you in about half an hour. You should be done by then."

I exited Papa's car and watched him drive away. It was ridiculous to waste his money over a stupid school rule the teachers enforced when they felt like it.

"Well, if it ain't my star linebacker!" Creeke High's head football coach Elmer Tucker grinned at me as I entered the shop. He was having what was left of his gray hair trimmed. Coach Tucker looked at Mr. Riley through the mirror and said, "You know I call him my little Samson, right?"

"Only every time you brag about him," Mr. Riley sighed. "What are you doing in my shop so late, Derrick?"

"I need my hair cut."

"I just cut your hair last week."

"I need it cut again."

"Oh, I see." Mr. Riley winked at me. "You want that special birthday haircut. I'll get to you once I finish with Elmer here."

I sat in a waiting chair and glanced at the magazine covers next to me. A cute Black girl with plump lips smiled at me. The magazine predicted she'd be a big star that year. When I finally got a girl on my arm, I'd want her to look like that girl and be smart, funny, and kind.

'Show some skin' read another cover. It was an old summer issue from the previous year. A bikini-clad woman lay next to a man wearing the shortest pair of shorts I'd ever seen. I was doomed if showing skin was the way to get a girl's attention. Even if I thought it looked cool, my parents wouldn't let me do something like that. If only my birthday would hurry up so I could be a man already.

I settled on reading the sports magazine. An ad for the army was the first thing I saw, and several grinning faces stared at me as I read the list of benefits they offered. One benefit was having most college costs covered. It was something to consider since I needed schooling to be a preacher, and my parents didn't have money to pay for it. There were many cigarette and alcohol ads. I'd never smoked or drank before, but I couldn't help but notice how manly it made the men in the ads look.

"I'm ready for you, Derrick," Mr. Riley announced as I was halfway through one of the stories about a new basketball rivalry. He flapped a smock through the air a few times and placed it around my neck when I sat in the chair

"What's this I heard about you mouthing off to a teacher today?" Coach Tucker asked. He always hung around the shop to talk after he finished getting his hair cut.

"Boy, I thought we talked about you acting up at school," Mr. Riley griped as he pulled my head back until his amber eyes met mine. "Kids these days. Y'all do stuff we wouldn't even *think* about doing back in my day."

"We disagreed about my hair."

"What's wrong with your hair?" A scowl crossed Mr. Riley's dark-brown face. The obvious black rinse in his hair shined under the shop's lights. "They don't like the way I cut or something?"

"They said it's too long."

"See that?" Coach Tucker said as he pointed a medium-brown finger at me. "That's why I told you back during the season to cut your hair short like how I have mine. You see anyone complaining about my hair? But you want to be hardheaded and now look at you. In trouble because your hair is too long."

"I can't wait until I'm grown so I can wear my hair how I want," I muttered.

"There's a lot of responsibility that comes with being a grown man, Derrick," Coach Tucker said. "It's not all about doing what you want."

"Yeah," Mr. Riley agreed. "Lots of bills to pay and mouths to feed. Riley Jr. learned that the hard way when I kicked his lazy butt out my house."

"How's he doing by the way?"

"He went into the army. You better hope you don't get drafted, Derrick. Then you'll have to cut all your hair off."

"What a nightmare," I said.

"This whole war is a nightmare," Coach Tucker grumbled.

"A real nightmare that I hope we'll wake up from someday," Mr. Riley said as he finished my hair. "Tell your father to offer up a prayer for my Riley Jr., will you?"

"Sure thing, Mr. Riley," I answered. I handed him his payment and said, "Keep the change."

"If you insist," Mr. Riley said with a smile. "No more arguing with your teachers, boy."

"And don't eat up all your father's food either," Coach Tucker added. "You don't need to grow anymore."

"Alright," I laughed as I exited the barbershop.

Saturday came, and my parents left for their trip. My friends agreed to celebrate my birthday, but only Leonard knew where we were going. I decided to wear a red button-up shirt with some jeans and my brown leather boots. Damian came over to my house to get ready and was full of skepticism.

"Is he sure this place is safe?" he asked.

"He said it'll be fine," I answered as I rubbed body oil on my arms.

"But what if something bad happens?"

"Nothing bad is going to happen."

"How do you know?"

"Because I trust Leonard's judgement."

It was nice to see Damian act like himself for once. He'd acted weird and even skipped some classes that week, which was something he'd never done before. I stopped buttoning my shirt when I reached my chest. I'd seen some of the other guys wear their shirts half-buttoned. They strutted around town with their chests exposed to the world, and I thought it looked neat.

I traced my finger down the middle of my chest before deciding to button the rest of my shirt. It didn't matter what I thought. People would gossip about me if I did something like that, and the last thing I needed was a ruined reputation. Damian pulled off his shirt behind me, and his reflection revealed scratches all over his arms and back.

"What happened to you?!"

"What do you mean?"

"You're covered in bruises and scratches! If someone's picking on you, let me know and I'll handle them for you."

"No one's picking on me."

"Then why is your neck and back all torn up like that?"

"It's... nothing. I'm okay. Really."

Damian covered everything up under a white knit turtleneck. It didn't sit right with me that he walked around like that. But I couldn't do anything if he chose to keep quiet. A car horn honked outside, and I looked out the window to see Leonard waiting for us.

"What took you guys so long?" he griped when we got in the car. He smoothed out a wrinkle on his green shirt.

"We were getting dressed," Damian said. He glanced at me, silently begging me not to say anything.

"Yeah," I sighed. "We were getting dressed."

"Well, if it took you guys this long, I can only imagine how long the girls will take."

We drove to Thelma's, and Leonard repeated the same routine he used to summon us. Thelma appeared in the doorway, her head swiveling left and right as if she were a lookout. She nodded to herself and disappeared back inside.

"What is she doing?" Leonard complained.

Thelma reappeared with a trench-coat-clad Marianne. They rushed to the car, and Thelma shoved Marianne into the backseat before getting in behind her.

"Hey," Marianne said. "I'll have your pie tomorrow, Derrick."

"What's with the trench coat?" Leonard asked.

"I didn't want anyone to see what I had on."

"Scared someone might see you and squeal to daddy?"

"Yep." Marianne pulled her trench coat open, and all eyes fell on her legs.

"Where'd you get pants from?" I blurted.

"I bought them."

"Your parents let you buy pants?" Damian uttered.

"Nope."

"Then how...?" Leonard whispered.

"Drive the car, Leonard." Marianne looked at her compact mirror and tousled her hair. She clamped it shut and rolled her eyes at us "Y'all act like y'all ain't never seen a girl in pants before."

"We haven't," I said. A new thought sprang to mind. "How did you get your dad to agree to let you come out?"

"I'm spending the night at Thelma's."

"You lied to him?!"

"I didn't lie," Marianne said. "When we get back, I'm spending the night at Thelma's. Her mom has to work late tonight, so no one will know about this unless one of you squeals."

Minister Gabriel Ray Jones was not the one to play with. He was the music minister at Creeke Church with a horribly short temper. Papa called him his 'Gangster for Christ'. I'd heard rumors about Minister Jones' past, and I wasn't interested in finding out if they were true. It amazed me how Marianne tried her dad's patience. She was his only child, and he ruled their household with an iron fist.

It took half an hour to get to the nightclub. Leonard parked the car, and we went inside. It was packed.

"You were right, Leonard," I said with a smile. "This does look like fun."

"Told you." Leonard beamed with pride about being right.

The sea of people on the dance floor swept me into their waves. As I grooved to the music, a girl floated up beside me. She was a few inches shorter than me, with dark-brown skin and big brown eyes. We danced together, her eyes focused on mine, until the current of the crowd pushed us apart. I kept dancing, but the girl remained on my mind. Thelma sat alone against the wall, so I went and sat with her.

"Tell me the truth." Thelma looked at the dance floor. "Does Damian... like Marianne?"

"I'm not sure. Why do you ask?"

"I saw him with her and... something's changed about the way he looks at her. It's the same way that girl has been looking at you all night."

"What girl?"

"The girl you were dancing with earlier. She's over by the restrooms looking at you right now."

My head swiveled toward the restrooms. Sure enough, the girl stood there looking at me. She looked away when she saw my head turn toward her. I wanted to go and talk to her, but I didn't want to leave Thelma alone while she was feeling down.

"I..."

"It's okay." Thelma put on a brave face. "Go ahead. I'll be fine."

I patted Thelma on the arm and walked over to the girl.

"Uh... hi..." I stammered as I approached her. "I'm Derrick. Derrick Harrison."

"Kiana Barnett," the girl said. "Um... do you play football?"

"I might." I leaned against the wall behind her, my body towering over hers.

"I knew I'd seen you before. You're one of the linebackers at Creeke High."

"How did you–?" I backed away from her.

"Relax," Kiana giggled. "I'm a cheerleader at Preston."

"Oh," I sighed, relieved.

"So, what are you doing out here?"

"Celebrating my birthday. What about you?"

"I'm friends with the guy whose parents own this joint. He let me tag along to check the place out."

"Is he around?"

"Somewhere. He's not as cute as you are though."

"You think I'm cute?"

"Cute enough." Kiana looked around the room. "It's getting pretty late…"

"You can't call me cute and run off," I whined. Papa's advice to always carry a pen came in handy. I wrote my number down on her hand. "Call me sometime."

"I'll think about it."

Kiana left, and Leonard stumbled from the bathroom laughing his head off.

"What's funny?"

"Something I saw." He wiped a tear from his eye. "You ready to go?"

"Yeah."

"I'll get Damian and Marianne and meet you at the car."

"Alright." Leonard was acting weird. On the way home, he kept laughing to himself. I got curious and asked him again, "What's so funny?"

"It's personal," Leonard giggled. "If I have a son, I'm naming him Jeremy."

"Why?"

"Because my dad hates that name. He says it sounds like the word 'germy.' What about you, Damian?"

"Huh?" Damian said.

"What are you going to name your son?"

"My son?"

"When you have one."

"I don't know."

"What about you Marianne?"

"Why are you asking me this?"

"I want to know."

"I'll name him Micah. Happy?"

"Very. I would ask Thelma, but she doesn't look too happy."

"Leonard please," Thelma groaned. "It's been a long night."

"Oh, it definitely has." Leonard was never this excitable. I tried to see if anyone else was weirded out, but only Thelma would look at me. Damian and Marianne blushed and avoided meeting my eyes. Leonard looked at me and said through a grin, "Wouldn't you agree, Derrick?"

"Yeah... are you feeling alright?"

"I feel great! Why do you ask?"

"You're a lot... happier than normal."

"I had a great time!"

I let the conversation go. Leonard dropped everyone else off, leaving only us two in the car.

"What was with all those questions?" I asked.

I wanted to mess with Damian," Leonard chuckled. "He pretends to be so innocent."

"What do you mean 'pretends'?"

"Give it some time." Leonard winked at me. "It'll make sense soon enough."

As we neared the church, I focused on the bullet hole in the stop sign next to it. Directly across the street was Marianne's tan-colored house she lived in with her parents. A great tree sat on the front lawn, its leaves scattered across the yard. It was a beautiful house, but something about it was off.

"Where's Minister Jones' car?" I whispered as I stared at the house. I looked at my watch and saw it was almost midnight. Minister Jones should've been home.

"How should I know?" Leonard asked.

"He doesn't go anywhere after eight. His car should be there."

"Maybe he had something to do."

"On a Saturday night?"

"Why are you so worried?"

"If Minister Jones catches me out this late at night, I'll be in trouble."

"Man, Minister Jones doesn't care what you do."

"Easy for you to say. Your father isn't best friends with him."

"You worry too much."

Leonard dropped me off at home. The front door was slightly open, and I swore I'd closed it before I left. Only one thought raced through my mind: someone broke into the house. As I neared the porch, a loud thumping noise caught my attention. A black cat made itself comfortable on the hood of a car. Relief washed over me only to be replaced with panic when I realized it was Minister Jones' brown station wagon. If he was inside, the intruder could've attacked him. I raced to the door and pushed it open.

"Who's in here?!" I yelled into the darkness, being sure to add more bass to my voice. If there was an intruder, they didn't bother answering. I stepped inside and shut the door.

I had the wind knocked from my lungs as I was pushed to the floor. Something leathery repeatedly stung my backside. My legs scrambled to stand, but I was forced back to the floor. The attacker inflicted their punishment on me, and I was at their mercy. When they finished me off, they lifted me to their face by the collar of my shirt.

"He...Hey Minister Jo...Jones..."

"Where've you been, boy?" Minister Jones rasped. He wore a scowl on his light-brown face, and I'd probably added another gray hair to his already graying black afro.

"I..."

"*I* advise you to think long and hard about your answer," Minister Jones said through gritted teeth. He tightened his grip on the belt he'd just beat me with.

"I was out celebrating my birthday..."

Minister Jones let go of my shirt and I tumbled back to the floor. His stocky frame towered over me as I dragged myself to my feet and faced him.

"Your father told me to come over here and check on you because you wouldn't answer the phone," Minister Jones explained as he put his belt back on. I knew better than to talk back to him when he was angry.

"Get to bed! Because if you think you're missing church tomorrow you've got another thing coming! Do you understand me?"

"Yes sir," I said as I averted my eyes to the floor. Minister Jones left. I went to my room and went to sleep, my butt still stinging from being whooped.

Chapter Three

"Ow, ow, ow." I hobbled into church after Sunday school ended. Every step made me wince as I went to my seat. When my butt landed on the pew, I sighed and said, "Okay."

"What's wrong with you?" Granny Laverne asked.

"Nothing Granny," I said, smiling through the pain.

"You sure?"

"Yes Granny, I'm sure."

"If you say so."

"Gabriel got you good, didn't he?" Grandpapa Franklin said as he sat beside me. "I guess you could say, he got his birthday licks in."

Granny hid her dark-brown face behind her church fan. I sat mortified as my grandparents laughed at my expense. It was only a matter of time before Papa and Momma knew too. Minister Jones sat at his organ preparing for worship. He looked at me and shook his head. No one could get away with anything with him around.

"Boy what were you thinking?" Grandpapa asked.

"I wanted to celebrate my birthday."

"You couldn't think of any other way to do that?" Granny fanned at her eyes to dry the tears that had formed there.

"It was Leonard's idea."

"If Leonard jumped off a bridge, would you jump too?"

"No Granny, I wouldn't."

"Then why would you follow him to go out when you know your parents wouldn't approve?"

"I wanted to have fun."

"I see," Grandpapa said. He stood up and left.

"Did I say something wrong?"

"No." Granny patted my shoulder. She smiled a knowing smile and said, "If I know Frankie, he's got something up his sleeve."

I looked at Grandpapa as he disappeared into Papa's office. Church began and went as usual. We worshipped, gave our tithes, and heard the church announcements. Then Grandpapa started his word.

"As we all know, Lionel and Judi are out of town, so I'll be filling in for today," he said after his introduction prayer. "I have a question for y'all: Do y'all know where you're going when you die? Because I know where I'm going! Straight to Heaven!"

"I know that's right!" someone yelled.

"But some unfortunately aren't on the path to Heaven. Some are headed straight for Hell." Grandpapa paused for dramatic effect before continuing. "I want to talk to those people today. Is that alright with y'all?"

"Yeah!"

"Alright!" Grandpapa cheered as he clapped his hands together once. "See, some people believe that God isn't fun. And since God 'isn't fun', y'all are going out in the world looking for fun in all the wrong places."

I shrank in my chair.

"But that 'fun' is leading you straight to the pit of Hell!" Grandpapa shouted. "A horrible, fiery place that's full of nothing but wailing and the gnashing of teeth. Is that really where you want to go?"

"Amen!"

"How long ye simple ones will ye love simplicity?" Grandpapa cried. "How long will your hearts deviseth wicked imaginations, and your feet be swift in running to mischief? Drinking, partying, on drugs, sleeping with this one and that one because they're 'cute'."

The word 'cute' caught my attention. I wondered if Kiana was at church too, being targeted by a sermon like me.

"All that riotous living is leading y'all astray like the prodigal son."

Grandpapa was rubbing salt into an already bleeding wound. He would center his sermon on the prodigal son of all the people in the Bible.

"The prodigal son," Grandpapa laughed as he shook his head. "Boy, did he get himself into some stuff."

I zoned out of the sermon. The prodigal son wasn't new to me. He wasted all his money on partying and then returned to his father's house when he was broke. My concern was whether Papa would be upset with me or be like the prodigal son's father who was just happy his son was safe.

"We as Christians are fighting a spiritual war!" Grandpapa preached. "We can't allow ourselves to be influenced by the opinions of others under any circumstances."

"Preach Bishop!" someone encouraged.

Grandpapa was laying the conviction on thick with this one. He finished reading the passage and looked at the congregation.

"It's not too late to turn your life around and get right with God," Grandpapa said. "Because if you don't, you could make things real bad for yourself."

"Yes Lord!"

"Do you know where you're going?!" Grandpapa hollered.

After service, Grandpapa took me home, I cleaned the house to make it look as presentable as possible for Papa and Momma when they returned. I wouldn't give them more reasons to be upset with me. Papa called after he finished preaching to let me know what was happening.

"We'll be back this evening."

"Okay."

"And Derrick?"

"Sir?"

"Try to be in the house when we get there."

"Papa, I–!"

"I don't need to know what happened. I'm sure Gabriel will give me all the gory details. Just be home when we get home. Alright?"

"Yes sir."

"Alright, I'll see you tonight. Bye."

"Bye." I placed the kitchen phone back on the hook. Before I could move, it started ringing again. I picked it back up and said, "Harrison residence."

"Hi, can I speak to Derrick?"

"That depends." I deepened my voice, trying to imitate Papa. "Who's calling?"

"Kiana."

"Kiana?" my voice cracked. I didn't expect her to call so soon. Keeping up my charade, I asked, "Kiana who?"

"You do know your voice just cracked, right?"

"I'm aware," I groaned, giving up the charade. "So... how are you?"

"I'm good. How about yourself?"

"I'm good," I said followed by an awkward silence. "So... you think I'm cute?"

"I said it, didn't I?"

"Yeah but... it was dark."

"I've seen you before...?"

"Oh yeah," I chuckled. "I forgot."

"Ah," Kiana sighed. "You're a meathead."

"*A meathead*?!" I gasped as I clutched my chest. "I'll have you know I have good grades."

"So, you're a cute meathead with good grades. Glad we've established that."

"What does that make you then?"

"A gorgeous, sophisticated lady... talking to a cute meathead with good grades," Kiana giggled.

"So... you called me to insult me?"

"I called you because you gave me your number."

"Are you always like this?"

"Only with people I like. Do you have a girlfriend?"

"Do you think I'd give you my number if I had a girlfriend?"

"Wouldn't be the first time it's happened to me."

"No, I don't have a girlfriend."

"Someone as cute as you isn't taken? Why not?"

"You sure do ask a lot of questions. Why don't you tell me about yourself first."

"What's left to tell? You already know I'm gorgeous and sophisticated. I'm eighteen and I have two younger sisters. My mom's a maid, my dad works in a warehouse, and once I graduate, I'm going to be a seamstress."

"A seamstress?"

"Aht, aht," Kiana stopped me. "You have to tell me about yourself now."

"I'm a handsome and strong eighteen-year-old only child that plays football and teaches Sunday school. My dad's a pastor and when I graduate, I'm going into the army."

"The army?! Why?!"

"Aht, aht, you have to answer my question first. Why a seamstress?"

"Because I need a job and I can sew," Kiana rushed through her answer. "Why are you going into the army?"

Before I could answer her, someone knocked on the front door.

"Hang on, there's someone at the door."

"Of course, there is," she huffed.

I set the phone down and answered the door. Minister Jones stood on the porch still in his church suit.

"I brought pie." He said, holding a dessert up in his right hand.

"You made me a pie, Minister Jones?" I teetered from side to side on my feet as I eyed the dessert he held.

"*Marianne* made you a pie for your birthday. But since she's grounded, I'm delivering it for her."

"Tell her I said thank you," I said as I accepted the treat. "What kind is it?"

"I think she said it was cherry..." Minister Jones put a finger to his lip.

A small, excited laugh escaped from my lips as I danced around with the pie in my hands.

"Now, don't eat it all at once, boy. Lord knows you'd swallow the thing whole if you could with the way you eat."

"Yes sir." I regained my composure. Only Minister Jones would spank you one day, then give you pie the next like nothing happened.

"Tell your father I'll see him tomorrow," he called over his shoulder as he walked to his car.

"Okay." The pie's sweet aroma wafted up my nose as I took it inside. I stopped myself from tearing into it, remembering Kiana was still on the phone.

"Sorry about that," I said as I picked the phone back up. "Someone was dropping off a late birthday present."

"You have to promise to come back."

"I do?"

"Yeah. We can't get to know each other if you're dead."

"I'll come back."

"I'm holding you to it."

Chapter Four

A giant tree stood over me, its branches intertwined at the top with another tree. As I touched the tree, it rotted. Rot spread to the other tree, then to the ground. Everything rotted, including me.

"AAAAHHH!" I screamed as I watched the skin melt off my bones.

My blood seeped into the earth, mixing itself with the dirt and roots of the tree above me. The blood and dirt formed into a man clothed in the roots of that rotten tree. His skin was like mud, and his hair was an afro formed from the tree's dead leaves. He sat before me and looked at me with dull, lifeless eyes. Every time I moved, he moved. I opened my mouth to speak, and so did he.

"Wake... up!" he yelled. "Ricky! Wake up!"

I awoke in my college apartment. My roommate, Richard Anderson, looked down at me through tired blue eyes.

"Good grief," he sighed as he ran a suntanned hand through his blond hair. "I didn't think your nightmares were *this* bad."

"Sorry." My cheeks burned with embarrassment as I avoided his eyes. Nightmares plagued me since my time in the army. "What time is it?"

"Three in the morning."

"Ugh," I groaned. "I'm sorry, Rick."

"It's alright." Richard pointed at my sweat-drenched sheets and smiled. "At least you didn't pee this time."

"Thanks," I grumbled, acknowledging his attempt to try and cheer me up. "Maybe I'll head home this weekend since we don't have a game..."

"Whatever floats your boat, kid," Richard yawned. "I'm heading back to bed. These eight a.m. classes are going to be the death of me."

"Alright," I chuckled. "Goodnight."

"Goodnight."

He left my room. I turned on a light and sat at my desk. Another sleepless night awaited me.

"Gosh darn it, Anderson!" the university's head football coach yelled as he threw his clipboard to the ground. Richard had messed up one of his kicks again. "My six-year-old kicks better than that!"

"Sorry Coach!"

"Don't apologize!" the coach screamed hard enough that he'd turned red in the face. "Kick better!"

"Yes sir!"

"Harrison!" the assistant coach called my attention back to him. "I'm only going to explain this once, so pay attention."

"Alright," I agreed.

After I left the army, I went to college in the city. I joined the football team as a twenty-two-year-old freshman walk-on player. Benefits covered my tuition, but I still needed someone to cover half the rent in my off-campus apartment. Richard was an eighteen-year-old freshman walk-on player that needed a place to stay when campus housing was full. He'd grown up in the city but wanted to live closer to the school. Within weeks, Richard became my closest friend on campus.

"I hope I don't mess up at the game next weekend," Richard groaned as we walked through the parking lot after practice. "Or else Coach skin me alive."

"I'm sure you'll do fine."

"Hey, you!" someone called from behind me. I turned around in time to catch Kiana as she leaped into my arms. We'd been dating for a few months, and she always visited me after practice when she got off work. She buried her head into my uncovered chest and snuggled against me. "You smell so good."

"I smell like outside."

"I like when you smell like that," Kiana said before turning to look at Richard. "Hey Rick."

"Hey...," Richard whispered. "I'll... be on my way."

Richard left us to ourselves.

"What's up with him?" Kiana asked.

"Rough day."

"Oh." Kiana nodded with understanding and then ruffled my hair. "How's my favorite meathead today?"

"I'm fine."

"You don't sound fine." Kiana released me and placed her hands on her hips.

"I had another nightmare, that's all."

"Again?" Kiana asked with a hint of concern in her voice.

"Everything I touched rotted in this one."

"Did you pray about it?"

"Yeah."

"Then leave it in God's hands." Ever since we'd started dating, she'd become more serious about her relationship with God. "He'll take care of it."

"Alright." Kiana always knew what to say to lift my spirits.

"So, are you still good to have dinner with my family tonight?"

"Of course. I wouldn't miss it for the world."

"Great." Kiana played with my half-buttoned shirt. "Make sure *this* is buttoned all the way when you come."

"You don't like the way I wear my shirts?"

"Do you want to explain 'Samson'?" Kiana referred to the tattoo above my heart.

"Alright, I'll close my shirt. But only because you asked nicely."

"Thank you." Kiana kissed me on my cheek. "I'll see you tonight."

Kiana ran off while I went in search of Richard. I found him sitting on the tailgate of his truck. We climbed inside the vehicle and took off for home.

"Why were you being all awkward back there. You act like you've never met Kiki before."

"Some of the guys on the team." Richard avoided my eyes. "The ones that went to school with her. They've been saying things about her when you're not around."

"Like what?"

"Just some stories..."

"How long has this been going on?"

"Since she started visiting the practices."

"And you're just now telling me this?"

"It's embarrassing."

"Don't pay them any mind, Rick. They're just a bunch of block-heads who've got nothing better to do but gossip about others."

"Alright..."

Kiana lived in a small house in the city with her family. She was named after her mother Kimberly and her grandmother Ana Barnett. Her father, Barry Barnett, was Mrs. Ana's only child with her late husband, Bartholomew Barnett. Mr. Barry had wanted to name Kiana 'Danette' but agreed to make that her middle name instead when Mrs. Kimberly and Mrs. Ana overruled him. Paulette and Nancy were Kiana's two younger sisters. Altogether, six people lived in Kiana's house.

"Danette, pass the salt please," Mr. Barry said.

"Yes sir." Kiana passed the salt to him, and he sprinkled it over his food.

"So, Derrick, how's school?" Mrs. Kimberly asked me. She looked like Kiana but older.

"It's going well."

"What are you studying for?" Mr. Barry asked.

"I'm getting a Master of Divinity."

"What's that?" Paulette asked. She was the reserved middle sister that was two years younger than Kiana.

"A preacher degree," Kiana answered Paulette's question.

"You have to get a degree to be a preacher?" Nancy gasped. The vibrant baby sister four years younger than Kiana, one heard Nancy before they saw her.

"Depending on where you preach," I said.

"It makes me so happy to see our young folks do what we couldn't." Mrs. Ana welled up with tears. "Going to good schools, working better jobs than we could. I wish Bartholomew were here to see it."

"So, you're studying to be a preacher and playing football?" Nancy asked.

"Yeah."

"When do you have time for Danette, then?"

"Nancy," Kiana whispered.

"She's got a point," Mrs. Kimberly said. "You and Derrick have dated for months, and this is the first time you've brought him here as your boyfriend and not as your friend."

"Mommy don't encourage her," Kiana whined.

"They're only curious, Danette," Mr. Barry said. "This *is* the first time you've brought a boy home to meet us in years. Granted, we already know Derrick but still."

"Has she ever dated a football player?" I asked. I wondered if those gossiping scoundrels on the team were jealous ex-boyfriends.

"Not that I know of," Mrs. Kimberly said.

"I've always wondered," Paulette said. "How did you two meet?"

"We um... well..." Kiana stammered. Paulette was trying to help by changing the subject, but it only made things more awkward. We'd never told our families how we met.

"We met in town," I answered for Kiana. "She kept staring at me while I was hanging out with my friends because she recognized me from my high school's football team."

"Kiana, what have I told you about staring at folks?" Mrs. Ana fussed.

"Sorry Nanna." Kiana shrank in her chair. When no one was looking she gave me a thankful smile, and I mouthed the words 'you owe me' back to her. She nodded her agreement, and we carried on with dinner. Once things had settled down, Kiana slipped out the front door, and I helped Mrs. Ana wash dishes

"Do you know I raised Barry in this house?" Mrs. Ana said as she scrubbed at one of the plates. She was a short, plump light-brown woman who was adamant about helping around the house.

"You did?"

"I sure did. Bartholomew died in a work accident when Barry was still about sixteen."

"I'm sorry to hear that."

"Yep. After that, Barry dropped out of school and got a job to help out because my wages as a maid weren't enough."

"Nanna!" Nancy called as she skipped into the kitchen. "Can I use some of your lipstick for work tomorrow?"

"What happened to yours?"

"I gave it to Danette, and she lost it. And you know I have to look presentable since I'm a waitress."

"Go on girl," Mrs. Ana grumbled. "I can't wait for y'all to get married and get out my house so I can have some peace."

"Thanks Nanna!" Nancy laughed as she ran from the room. "Love you too!"

"Where was I, Derrick?"

"Mr. Barry dropped out of school."

"Oh yeah. He's worked in that warehouse for all these years. Then he showed up one day with Kimberly. Next thing I knew, they were married, and I had a whole new family to feed under my roof. Thankfully, Kim turned out to be a good and useful woman."

"Nanna," Paulette said as she entered the kitchen. "Can I use some of your thread? My sweater has a hole in it, and I need to mend it."

"Go ahead."

"Thank you, Nanna."

"As you can see, these girls run me ragged," Mrs. Ana sighed once Paulette left. "I guess what I'm trying to say is, please be a good man to Kiana because once y'all are married, I don't want her coming back unless it's to visit."

"Yes ma'am," I giggled.

"That's all the dishes." Mrs. Ana dried her hands. "I'm sure you're tired of listening to an old woman complain."

"Of course not! You can complain to me all you like."

"You're such a sweet boy," Mrs. Ana laughed. "But you didn't come all the way out here for me. Go spend some time with Kiana."

I did as Mrs. Ana said and went outside to be with Kiana. She was sitting on the porch steps gazing up at the stars.

"Thanks for saving me in there," Kiana said.

"Yeah, I'm going to collect on that favor now."

"Already?"

"Yep." I sat down on the porch next to Kiana. "Rick told me some of the guys on the team have been talking about you."

"Oh boy," Kiana groaned. She gave me that glance, letting me know she knew exactly what Richard meant. "What'd they say?"

"He wouldn't go into detail, but I'm sure we both know what's up."

"I guess this is it then," Kiana sighed. "This is the part where you break up with me, right?"

"After all that work I did to get you to date me? I need *at least* four years' worth of a relationship for my troubles."

"Why bring it up then?"

"I needed to know."

"You don't just ask a woman about something like that! What if I brought that up to you?"

"I don't have anything to tell. Even if I did, it wouldn't change how I feel. Who cares what those blockheads on the team think?"

"You're such a meathead."

"Listen to me." I cupped Kiana's face. "I don't care about anything that happened before we got together. All that matters to me is our present and our future."

"Future?"

"Yeah. I want to marry you one day."

"*Marry me?*" Kiana's eyes bulged.

"You thought I was dating you for fun? I plan to steal you away from your grandmother's house for good."

"I'll tell you what." Kiana patted my back. "I'll marry you after you graduate."

"That could take up to four years!"

"You said you wanted four years' worth of a relationship for your troubles, right?"

"Me and my big mouth," I grumbled.

"And so you know I mean it…"

She ran into the house, leaving me outside alone. A car drove past, and a few gnats circled the porch light. I looked up at the sky and realized I couldn't see the stars as clearly here as I could in Creeke. Faint excited screaming came from Kiana's bedroom, and I could only assume she'd told her sisters what I'd said. Once the cheers died down, Kiana returned with a Bible in her hand and flipped through the pages.

"*I am my beloved's, and his desire is toward me,*" Kiana read from Songs of Solomon Chapter seven, Verse ten. She blushed as she continued our tradition of flirting with each other by using Bible verses. "That's what my next note was going to say. If you're serious about marrying me, then I'll wait for you."

"*I am my beloved's, and my beloved is mine,*" I quoted Songs of Solomon Chapter six, Verse three. "I'm serious. I want to marry you."

"Then all that's left is for you to graduate," Kiana said as she wrapped her arms around my neck. "And get a job. And buy a house. And propose."

I kissed her.

"Oooooooh!" someone yelled from inside. I opened my left eye and spotted Nancy and Paulette giggling in the window. As I pulled Kiana closer, Nancy ran off singing through the house, "Derrick and Danette! Sitting in a tree! K-I-S-S-I-N-G!"

Kiana chuckled at her sister's immaturity as our lips parted. I couldn't imagine my life without her in it. She was who I wanted to spend my life with for better or for worse.

-

Chapter Five

Creeke hadn't changed since I'd last been there during the summer. Marianne and Damian were married with two kids and seemed happy together. Their oldest son Terrence was born nine months after my eighteenth birthday. He was the answer to Leonard's weirdness that night. Two years later, they had a daughter named Ruth-Anne. Damian took the skills he gained as a military cook into a career as a cook in the city. Thelma worked as a seamstress at the same shop as Kiana.

Nobody knew what Leonard was up to. I hadn't seen him at all over the summer. Rumors circulated that he'd moved out on his own, but I wasn't sure how true they were. As I waited for the ride Papa arranged to take me home for the weekend, I wondered if I would see Leonard at all during my visit.

"Well, if it ain't the future Pastor Harrison." A man with black sunglasses pulled up in front of me. The car was Leonard's car, but the man didn't look like Leonard. He was dark-brown like Leonard, but he was also muscular and had a bushy mustache.

"Who... who are you?" I tensed up.

"Seriously?!" the man hollered. He snatched his sunglasses off. "I can't have changed that much!"

"Leonard?!" I gasped. He exited the car, and I hugged him. "You grew up on me!"

"Aw man." Leonard giggled as his cheeks turned red.

"Man look at you!" I looked Leonard over. "You look good! What happened?"

"I got a girl."

"You did? Do I know her?"

"Yep."

"Who is it?"

"You'll find out soon enough."

"Come on Leonard," I whined. "Tell me who she is."

"You have to wait." Leonard picked up my suitcase and put it in the trunk of his car. "How are you?"

"I'm fine," I said as I got into his car. "What have you been up to, man? I ain't seen you since before I left for the army."

"Well, no wonder! You came home in spring, hid in the house for half the summer, then left for school without saying anything."

"I needed time to myself."

"It is what it is man." Leonard turned the radio until he found something he liked. "Listen, how about I stop here at the corner store, get us something to drink, and we have a good time."

"I don't drink anymore."

"Big Bully Harrison drank alcohol, and I wasn't there to *see it*?! You've got to drink something tonight! I have to witness this for myself!"

"I'd rather not." Too many things could go wrong if I was drunk. I needed to be alert in case trouble arose.

"Alright fine. You can watch me drink. I'll even invite Damian over for you and it'll be like old times."

"You're always getting us into some mess," I chuckled.

"It's what I'm best at."

Leonard had moved into a three-bedroom house closer to the church. I figured he planned on moving his mystery girl into it one day. He and Damian were drunk out of their minds that evening. I'd expected it from Leonard, but Damian surprised me. Damian wasn't the type to go so hard with alcohol. But I could tell something was bothering him.

"I have to tell y'all something," Damian said after downing another glass.

"What's up?" I said.

"Marianne and I are divorcing."

"What?!" I gasped.

"That's too bad," Leonard said before guzzling his drink down. He didn't seem as shocked as I was by the news.

"Are you sure you want to do this? The Bible says–"

"I know what it says, Derrick," Damian interrupted me.

"Here you go with that biblical crap again," Leonard grumbled as he poured himself another drink. "Can't we have one night without you bringing that mess up?"

"I wanted to spend time with her when I returned home back in the spring," Damian explained, leaving us to infer what he meant. "She was pregnant."

Leonard choked on his drink.

"You alright?" Damian cut his eyes at Leonard.

"Yeah," Leonard coughed. "I wasn't expecting to hear that."

"Marianne's pregnant?" I asked.

"Seven months now." Damian's face was a mixture of heartbreak and anger.

"Who's the father?"

"He knows who he is," Damian growled. His eyes flicked between Leonard and me. "And after the baby comes, he can have them both."

Two months later, Marianne had her third child and Leonard was the father. They named the baby Jeremy-Micah and married almost immediately after Marianne's divorce was finalized. It left a bad taste in my mouth, and I quietly removed myself as a friend from them both.

Fourteen years passed in Creeke. During that time, I got my degree a year earlier than expected, and Kiana married me like she said she would. We moved back to Creeke, and I worked at the Anderson's construction company. Richard was being prepared to take over his father's business one day. My parents had retired from the church and left it in my hands. Kiana and I were the new Pastor and First Lady of Creeke Church.

My grandparents died during those fourteen years, and Kiana gave me two sons. Our oldest son was ten-year-old Marlin Trevor Harrison.

Marlin had a habit of picking with people that I hoped he'd stop. He'd proven to be a decent brother to our one-year-old, Malcolm Drew Harrison, though. Being a father was interesting.

"I'm serious," Richard said over the phone one summer Sunday evening. "I have to come down there and hear you preach sometime. This is a bigger deal than the time I kicked that winning field goal freshman year."

"You were so worried you were going to miss it too."

"I sure was. But I pulled it off. Just like I'm sure you'll pull off being a great pastor, kid."

"It always tickles me that you call me 'kid' considering I'm four years older than you."

"That's what makes it fun," Richard laughed. "Besides you earned that title when you took me in freshman year."

"I was just being helpful. Besides, you're the one who put up with me interrupting your sleep for three years."

"I'd take sleep deprivation with you any day over the guy I roomed with during my last year," Richard sighed.

"Sorry," I chuckled. "I wanted to get married."

"I'll bet you did."

"But unto Cain and to his offering he had not respect," Marlin read. "And Cain was very wr... wro... Dad, how do you say this word?"

"I have to go, Rick."

"Bye."

"Sound it out, son." I told Marlin as I sat with him at the kitchen table.

"Why do I always have to sound it out?"

"Because I said so."

"Urgh," Marlin grumbled. He hated when I made him sound things out. "Wr...oh...th."

"The o makes the "ah" sound, Marlin."

"Why didn't you say that earlier then?!"

"Don't yell at me, little boy!"

"Hmph!" Marlin crossed his arms and pouted.

"I finally got Malcolm to sleep, so don't make too much noise," Kiana whispered as she entered the kitchen. She stopped and took in the scene in front of her. "What's wrong?"

"Dad's being mean."

"Why are you being mean?"

"Why do you instantly take his side?" I whined. "For your information, I asked him to sound a word out, and he caught an attitude with me."

"You know he doesn't like doing that."

"I don't care what he doesn't like doing," I argued. "What happens when he's an adult, and he can't do anything because you kept handicapping him?"

Kiana knelt in front of me and put her hand on my knee.

"Can you do me a favor, meathead?" she spoke. "Can you never question how I parent my sons ever again? Can you do that for me?"

She turned on her feet and faced Marlin.

"And you. You can't get an attitude with Daddy. If Daddy asks you to do something, you do it and you don't get an attitude. Okay?"

"Yes ma'am."

Kiana stood back up and looked at me.

"Satisfied?"

"Marlin, keep reading." I ignored Kiana's sarcasm.

As Marlin picked up from where he left off, the phone rang. Kiana answered it, and I watched as her face went from normal to concerned. She motioned for me to come over to the phone.

"Keep reading," I repeated to Marlin. I walked over to the phone, and Kiana handed it to me.

"It's Damian," she told me. "He sounds upset."

I took the phone from Kiana. She sat at the table with Marlin, and I lifted the corded phone to my ear.

"Hello?"

"Derrick," Damian whispered. His tone was disturbingly calm. "I'm going to kill Leonard."

"Where are you?"

"I'm at home."

"Stay there. I'm coming over."

I hung up the phone and grabbed my keys.

"Where are you going?" Kiana asked.

"I'll explain later," I called as I ran out the door. "Watch the boys!"

Damian seemed to be doing better since the divorce. He ushered at the church, was dating Thelma, and shared custody of his kids with Marianne. Leonard hadn't interacted with him since the affair came out. It confused me why he was suddenly going to 'kill Leonard'. When I arrived at his house, what I saw horrified me. Terrence had a busted lip, and bruises were forming all over Ruth-Anne's arms and legs.

"What happened?"

"I'm going to kill him," Damian muttered. He had this wild look in his eye I'd never seen before.

"Thelma, can you take Damian to his room, so I can talk to the kids?"

"Yeah." Thelma grabbed Damian's hand and led him away. "Come on, Sugarbear."

"I'm going to kill him."

"Tell me what happened," I said as I sat on the couch.

"It's all my fault!" Ruth-Anne sobbed.

"No, it's not Gracie," Terrence grumbled.

"If I had been watching Torrance–!" At the mention of her younger brother's name, Ruth-Anne's eyes grew wide. She looked around wildly. "Torrance! Where's Torrance?!"

"I... Isn't he at home?" I asked.

"No!" Ruth-Anne cried. "You have to go get him!"

These kids were traumatized. And the way Ruth-Anne acted, it might not have been only them. Something needed to be done. A loud thump came from Damian's room, followed by Thelma yelling at him.

"He did that to my children!" Damian hollered when I entered the room. A fist-sized hole sat in the wall opposite him. "I want to kill him!"

"You're sure it was Leonard?" I asked. Although I'd stopped speaking to Leonard, it didn't seem like him to do this.

"Yes, I'm sure!" Damian shot up from his chair. "I want my kids out of that house now!"

"How about this?" I proposed. "How about I take Terrence to go get their stuff while you stay here and tend to Ruth-Anne? Okay?"

"Whatever," Damian grumbled as he sat back on the bed. "Just as long as my kids are out of that house!"

"Okay," I agreed. "Thelma, please make sure he doesn't do anything rash."

"I'll try," Thelma said.

I took Terrence and drove to the Brown household. There weren't any cars in the driveway, and none of the lights were on.

"Brown isn't here," Terrence referred to Leonard. He unbuckled his seatbelt and opened the car door.

"Do you want me to come with you?"

"That's alright. It won't take too long."

Terrence was gone for fifteen minutes. Marianne and Leonard had two more kids after Jeremy-Micah: Marie and Torrance. Jeremy-Micah was the loud goofball, and Marie was the shy sweetheart. Torrance was the same age as Marlin, and he always seemed sad. I wondered if they'd also been abused. Although the evidence was in front of me, part of me still didn't want to believe Leonard did this. When Terrence came back, he had two suitcases in his hands.

"That's everything?" I asked as he put the suitcases in the backseat.

"Most of our stuff is at Dad's house," Terrence answered as he got back in the car. "Torrance was sleep and I didn't want to wake him."

"Is he okay?"

"Looked like it." Terrence twiddled his fingers. "He's not Dad's, so we can't take him with us."

"What happened in there?"

"I don't want to talk about it."

"Okay," I whispered.

I returned to the Brown household the next day. After what I saw, I needed answers about how all five children were being treated.

"What are you doing here?" Marianne asked when she answered the door.

"I came to talk to Leonard." Behind Marianne, I spotted Torrance peek out from behind a wall. He had an eyepatch on under his glasses over his right eye. "Is he here?"

"He's out."

"Why does Torrance have an eyepatch on?"

"He fell against a table and had to get stitches." Marianne scratched at her forehead as she answered, being sure to avoid my eyes. Her body language said it all. Leonard had hurt these children. It angered me that he did this, and Marianne didn't stop him.

"Is he alright?"

"Clearly."

"Tell Leonard something for me."

"What?" Marianne crossed her arms.

"Tell Leonard." I said with a smile. "Whatever he does to these kids, I'm going to do to him. Times ten."

"I didn't know pastors threatened people," Marianne scoffed.

"I didn't know mothers let people hurt their children. Guess we both learned something today."

"My children are *my* business." Marianne pointed her finger in my face.

"My flock is *my* business, and these *children* are part of that flock."

"You don't have to worry about us," Marianne argued. "We're good over here."

"Are you really?"

"You know what, get off my porch!" Marianne snapped. "Asking me all these questions like you're the police!"

"Forget you too then!" I snapped back. "I was trying to help you out!"

"I don't need your help, Derrick!"

"Clearly you do if three of your kids end up injured on the same day!"

"Ooooooh I–!" Marianne fumed before slamming the door in my face.

I walked off the porch madder than I was when I came. Something was going on in that house, and it wouldn't stay hidden forever. The truth always came out.

-

Chapter Six

After arguing with Marianne, I didn't bother talking to her or Leonard anymore. Damian took Terrence and Ruth-Anne to live with him, and the rest of the kids seemed okay. Four years passed, and I spent that time focused on my sons. Marlin had become a little bully around town, and I wanted to curb that behavior before it got worse. The best way to do that was to turn his focus to something more productive.

"Alright Marlin," I called one Saturday morning as I threw my old football between my hands. "Give it all you got."

"Okay," Marlin yelled back.

I gave him the signal, and we ran towards each other. Marlin watched me and got low as I neared him. He hesitated before deciding to lunge at me. It was enough time for me to lower my shoulder and knock my fourteen-year-old son off his feet.

"Oof!" Marlin grunted as he landed on his back. He sat up and glared at me. "What the heck Dad?!"

"You hesitated." I held out my hand to help him up. "What have I told you about hesitating?"

"Don't," Marlin grumbled. He got on his feet without accepting my hand.

"Exactly." I crossed my arms. "The time you waste on hesitating is the time your opponent uses to take you down."

"Let's run it again."

Marlin was following in his old man's footsteps and going out for the freshman football team at Creeke High. It was a welcome change for him. As I prepared to run the drill with Marlin again, the back door to the house flew open. Kiana ran out waving her arms and screaming like a madwoman.

"Derrick!"

"What is it?"

"Marianne called! You need to get to the hospital now! Something's wrong with Leonard!"

"Why would Dad care?" Marlin snorted. "He doesn't even like him."

"Hush boy!" I snapped. "Go inside and watch your brother!"

Marlin skulked inside. No matter how much I tried to fight it, I still cared about Leonard enough to not want anything bad to happen to him. Kiana couldn't tell me anything other than he'd been in the hospital since the day before. I would have to ask Leonard myself what happened.

"What are you doing here?" Leonard complained as I entered his hospital room.

"Doing my duties as Pastor," I said as I sat in a chair beside his bed. "What are you doing here?"

"What does it look like I'm doing here, Derrick?!"

"Well, it looks like you're lying in a hospital bed, but nobody knows why."

"I had an accident." Leonard clenched his jaw and turned away from me.

"An accident, huh?"

"Just pray over me like you came to do and get out!"

"Do you always have to be so hostile? I was your best friend once, you know."

"Yeah, until you chose to side with Damian over me."

"What'd you expect me to do?"

"I expected you to be neutral. Marianne didn't want to be with him anyway. She wanted a real man by her side."

"And real men do what you did, Leonard?"

"You would've done the same thing if you had the chance. Shoot, look at who you married."

"What do you mean by that?"

"That you're a hypocrite. Because you're Pastor now, you act like you're so innocent and perfect. But you know if you had the opportunity, you'd be with Marianne too."

"No, I wouldn't. I don't have a jealous spirit like you."

"Here you go again with that biblical crap. Every time someone tries to confront you with the truth, that's the first thing you run to."

"Because it's the *real* truth. You're a jealous man, Leonard Brown. Everywhere you go and everything you touch is destroyed because of your jealousy."

"Why don't you go worry about those wild banshees you call sons and leave me alone?" Leonard grumbled.

"Alright, I will," I said as I stood up. I leaned over Leonard's bed and looked him in the eye. "Let me make one thing clear though. I'm not a bully and I don't like hurting people. Especially people that are scared of me. I know you can't relate to that. But if you ever insult my wife and kids again, this little 'accident' you had will be nothing compared to what I'll do to you."

"Get out."

I left Leonard's room and went home. Kiana kept trying to get me to tell her what happened, but I wouldn't budge. If Leonard wanted to play dirty, then so be it. Sunday morning, I had a message that would shake the church up.

"I'm not going to talk about football today, I promise," I joked as I began my message. A few laughs rose from the congregation. "My message today instead... it needs to be said."

Murmurs filled the room as I paused to let my words sink in.

"The Bible says my gorgeous, sophisticated wife is many things," I listed off the adjectives Kiana used to describe herself. She giggled at the joke only we understood. "Proverbs eighteen and twenty-two calls her a good thing, while Mark ten makes it clear that together we are one flesh that no man shall put asunder."

Kiana smiled at me with a hint of confusion in her eyes.

"Proverbs twelve and four says that a virtuous woman is a crown to her husband." The smile faded from my beautiful wife's face. "I'd say our wonderful first lady here is a crown to me. Don't y'all agree?"

A series of yeses, amens, and even a few whistles rose from the congregation. None of it placed the smile back on Kiana's face.

"Now, I won't pretend our marriage is perfect. But I can say that I've been blessed with a truly good thing. However, some of you have forsaken this blessing and that's what I want to talk about today."

Kiana sat up in her chair and crossed her legs into a different position.

"Ephesians five is clear on the roles and responsibilities of the husbands and wives in a marriage. Wives submit to their husbands' leadership the same way the husbands are submitted to The Lord's leadership. And husbands love their wives the same way Christ loves us. But some in our world have chosen not to follow this. They step outside of their marriages. Or they don't marry at all and instead sleep with this one and that one and create families all over the place. Then they wonder why their children and their lives are out of control."

Some members yelled out their agreement to my message while others had guilt written all over their faces. Kiana herself shifted around in her seat at the mention of people sleeping around. All eyes were on me, but the ones I felt the most were two separate sets of dark-brown eyes. One set sat in the back row opened wide behind thick wire-framed glasses. The other set glared at me from the front row as two of their owner's five children sat on the other side of the church with their grandfather.

"Proverbs twelve and four says that a virtuous woman is a crown to her husband: but she that maketh ashamed is as rottenness in his bones," I said. "Let me restate that for y'all in a way y'all understand. A woman who cheats on or leaves her husband for someone else, or takes someone else's husband, is like a rottenness in his bones."

I glanced at Marianne. Her eyes burned with anger as I preached my message.

"Matthew five and twenty-eight says that whosoever looketh on a woman to lust after her hath committed adultery with her already in his heart. Men, if you thought you were off the hook from my message, you're not. If you cheat on or leave your wife for someone else, or take someone else's wife, you're wrong too. Adultery and fornication are wrong, and Hebrews thirteen and four says that God will judge fornicators and adulterers."

"Amen!" someone yelled.

"The Lord shows us the consequences of adultery in Proverbs seven, starting at verse six," I preached. "It reads 'For at the window of my house I looked through my casement, and beheld among the simple ones, I discerned among the youths, a young man void of understanding, passing through the street near her corner; and he went the way to her house, in the twilight, in the evening, in the black and dark night'."

I paused and looked up at the congregation.

"Some of y'all look lost already," I said. A few laughs resounded through the sanctuary. "Let me make it simple. A young unsaved man is walking amongst under unsaved people to a woman's house at night. Now we all know what the Bible says about what's done in the dark."

"Amen!"

"Verse ten, 'And, behold, there met him a woman with the attire of an harlot, and subtil of heart. She is loud and stubborn; her feet abide not in her house: Now is she without, now in the streets, and lieth in wait at every corner.' So, this young unsaved man has met a prideful young woman on a street corner at night. Now I don't know about y'all, but my momma always said ain't nothing open after midnight except–!"

Momma's face stopped me mid-sentence. Her crossed arms and raised eyebrows dared me to finish the rest of the sentence in The Lord's house.

"Y'all know how the rest goes," I said. Momma didn't care if I was a forty-year-old pastor with a wife and two kids. She'd still pop me in front of everybody for embarrassing her in public.

"Speak on it, Pastor!"

"Y'all trying to get me in trouble," I laughed. "Verse thirteen. 'So she caught him, and kissed him, and with an impudent face said unto him,

I have peace offerings with me; this day have I payed my vows. Therefore came I forth to meet thee, diligently to seek thy face, and I have found thee.' Basically, she went up to the temple, gave her sin offering to repent for her sins, and then came out at night to find this man so she could kiss him and seduce him on the street corner. Doesn't that sound suspicious to y'all?"

"Sure does!"

"Verse sixteen. 'I have decked my bed with coverings of tapestry, with carved works, with fine linen of Egypt. I have perfumed my bed with myrrh, aloes, and cinnamon. Come, let us take our fill of love until the morning: let us solace ourselves with loves. For the goodman is not at home, he is gone a long journey: He hath taken a bag of money with him, and will come home at the day appointed.' So, this woman has prepared for a long night of passion with this man she's not married to. Her husband is out handling business to take care of her, and she's at home cheating on him. Ain't that some mess?"

Damian's eyes flicked to the back of Marianne's head. She sat seemingly unbothered by what I was saying. At this point, everyone knew my message was about her and Leonard.

"Verse twenty-one, 'With her much fair speech she caused him to yield, with the flattering of her lips she forced him. He goeth after her straightway, as an ox goeth to the slaughter, or as a fool to the correction of the stocks; Till a dart strike through his liver; as a bird hasteth to the snare, and knoweth not that it is for his life'. This young man allowed lust to lead him astray and it's leading him to death. The young woman is cheating on her husband and causing someone else to stumble. She doesn't realize she's going to share in his consequences because she thinks she's good since she gave a sin offering. What she failed to realize was her sin offering doesn't matter if her heart isn't in the right place. There's no point in repentance if you continue to behave wrongly."

"Yes!" One of the elders proclaimed.

"Verse twenty-four, 'Hearken unto me now therefore, O ye children, and attend to the words of my mouth. Let not thine heart decline to her ways, go not astray in her paths. For she hath cast down many wounded: yea, many strong men have been slain by her. Her house is the way to hell, going down to the chambers of death'. The consequences of adultery and fornication is death. True repentance and obedience to Jesus Christ is the only way to make it right."

I closed out the service and dismissed everyone. Marianne left without speaking to anyone. I'd called her out in front of everyone, hoping she'd understand I didn't approve of what she and Leonard did. Usually, Damian told me his thoughts on my messages, but he just hugged me goodbye and left. Kiana wouldn't come near me and chose instead to tend to Malcolm. Papa was the first person to tell me his feelings.

"Son." Papa pulled me aside. "Are you sure The Lord told you to preach that message that particular way?"

"I..." There had been some reservations leading up to my sermon, but I'd steeled myself against them. "It needed to be said, Papa."

"I understand that, but it seemed too... personal... like it was coming from a place of hurt." Papa took my hands in his and squeezed them. "Just remember that the goal is to lead people *to* Christ and not *away* from Him."

"*I know*, Papa."

"I'm only reminding you. Your heart has to be in the right place when you preach. You're not only representing yourself up there, but also The Lord. And He can knock you down as quickly as He lifted you up."

"I understand."

"Okay." Papa released my hands and smiled at me. "I won't hold you any longer. Enjoy the rest of your Sunday, son."

I hugged Papa and went to find my family. Marlin was talking to Torrance, which I wasn't used to seeing. Usually, they'd be trying to fight each other. My curiosity got the best of me, and I wandered over to listen to their conversation.

Torrance still wore an eyepatch. He refused to be seen in public without it. I could only imagine what he hid underneath it. It angered me that Marianne allowed it to happen to him. She needed to hear that message and understand the consequences of her actions.

Torrance's face changed into a scowl. Whatever Marlin said upset him, and he made it clear by raising his voice. The apple hadn't fallen far from Minister Jones' tree when it came to having short tempers. Things would only get worse. I arrived in time to catch the beginning of Marlin's next sentence.

"It's not my fault your mama doesn't know who–"

My body reacted before my brain finished processing what I'd heard. The whole church grew silent as they looked in our direction. Torrance's uncovered eye was wide with shock as Marlin held his hand over his mouth. I wiped my spit-covered hand on my pants. Marlin glared at me like he wanted to kill me right there and then.

"Fix your face before I fix it for you," I told him.

Marlin stayed quiet as I dragged him from the church. Everyone was silent on the way home. Nobody said a word when we entered the house, and I sent Marlin off to his room. It wasn't until after Kiana put Malcolm down for his nap and started dinner that she spoke to me.

"Derrick," Kiana said as she boiled water on the stove. "Did you really have to pop Marlin in the mouth in front of the whole church?"

"Where you act up is where you get beat up. I bet he won't get slick at the mouth again."

"Hush!" Kiana snapped. "I don't know what's going on with you, but you've been mean ever since you saw Leonard in the hospital."

"I have not!"

"So, you're going to sit here and act like your whole sermon wasn't targeted at Marianne?"

"All I did was tell the truth."

"But is that how God wants the truth told? By publicly shaming people?"

"I'm a pastor. It's my job to encourage people away from their wicked ways and direct them to God."

"You make it sound like you're perfect," Kiana snorted.

"I'm not perfect. But I know I'm right."

"Well since you want to talk about fornication, I wasn't exactly the perfect angel when you married me," Kiana complained. "And you told me that didn't matter to you, and you loved me anyways. A lot of people already think I'm not fit to be First Lady because of my past. I can't help but wonder if you think that too."

"Why would even think like that?"

"Because I was Marianne at one point." A few tears rolled down Kiana's face. "When you talk about her and what she's done, it feels like you're talking about me. It hurts my feelings."

Kiana's actions during the sermon suddenly made sense. She saw herself in Marianne. The version of herself still being used against her by the town although she'd grown and changed. And I'd led the charge against her like a blind idiot in my witch hunt to shame Marianne. I'd hurt my best friend.

"Oh Kiki." I hugged Kiana. "I didn't mean to hurt your feelings. I'm sorry."

We sat like that for a while. Me holding Kiana as she cried in my arms. After she got done, she told me she needed time to herself. So, I went for a walk. I figured I'd use the time to clear my head and talk with The Lord alone.

The afternoon sky was the clearest it'd ever been as I walked along the road that my house was on. Bugs of all shapes and sizes crawled on the ground and buzzed through the air. Heat filled my lungs while the summer sun beat down on my head. A pickup truck packed with rowdy teenage boys barreled down the opposite side of the road.

"Stop the truck!" one of them yelled to the driver. The truck skid to a stop beside me, and Jeremy-Micah Brown waved at me to get my attention. He gave me a big silly grin as his deep voice bellowed out, "Hey Pastor! What are you doing out here in this heat?"

"Praying," I answered. "I didn't see you in church today."

"About that...," Jeremy-Micah laughed nervously.

"You're going to sleep through your blessing one of these days."

"I know..."

"Where are you going?"

"Me and some of the boys are headed down to the creek to swim." Jeremy-Micah had Marianne's eyes and Leonard's nose. His dark-brown arms glistened with sweat as he leaned against the edge of the truck.

"Trying to have as much fun as you can before you head off to college, huh?"

"I guess you could say that."

"Well, don't have *too* much fun," I said. "The last thing we need is another lecture from Minister Jones."

"Yes sir." Jeremy-Micah slapped the side of the truck and saluted me as the truck drove away towards the creek. The boy was adventurous to be Leonard's son. It wasn't his fault that he was born from an affair. He was an innocent victim in a mess far greater than him. A mess I might've made worse.

"Lord, I really messed up," I sighed. "Please forgive me for taking an opportunity to encourage your people and using it instead to hurt them."

A cool breeze blew against my face. I kept walking and praying, allowing my feet to wander wherever. When I looked up, I saw they'd led me to Damian's house. Damian sat on his front porch eating a snack. His face met mine, and my stomach twisted in knots as I approached him.

"Hey Damian."

Damian looked at me as he shoved a handful of peanuts into his mouth.

"I'm sorry," I said. "I shouldn't have put your business out there like that."

Damian set down his can of peanuts and stood up.

"Arty!" Damian yelled.

"Yeah?" Twenty-year-old Arthur appeared behind the screen door. He was beige with oval-shaped eyes, a flat nose, and loosely curled light-brown hair.

"I'm going out. Make sure my house stays intact, okay?"

"It's only me and you here, Damian."

"You are a force of nature on your own."

"I won't break anything this time. I promise."

"You said that the last time."

"I mean it this time."

"You said that the last time too."

"Have a little faith in me."

"Just don't break anything."

Damian motioned for me to follow him off the porch. We started walking up the road together.

"Arty's really grown up, hasn't he?" I said.

"Yep." Damian rubbed his temples. "Grown up and working my nerves. You know he wants to be a teacher?"

"What's wrong with that?"

"Nothing... except you have to go to school to be a teacher."

"Give him some time. I'm sure he'll figure it out."

We walked along the path to town in silence.

"I'm sorry too," Damian spoke. "I shouldn't have made you feel like you had to pick sides."

"You didn't make me do anything. I made my own decision."

"Yeah. But now more people are involved."

"Like who?"

"Our children for one," Damian mumbled. He always thought of the children. Damian loved kids, and he took pride in being a father. I felt bad about how things turned out for him. "Your sermon really made me think when it came to my relationships. What made you want to preach about that?"

"I was upset with Marianne and Leonard," I admitted. "I went and saw Leonard in the hospital yesterday it... didn't go so well."

"He has no one but himself to blame for that." Damian's demeanor hardened as he shoved his hands in his pockets. "You know that idiot called himself leaving Torrance on my doorstep last Friday?"

"He did?"

"I'm getting ready for work, right? Tell me why I look out the window and see Leonard dragging Torrance up to my door with a suitcase. Mind you, I still haven't bashed Leonard's face in for what he did a few years ago because I'm trying to stay right with The Lord. This man left Torrance on my doorstep and just left. I had to call out from work because I didn't know where Arty went and I'm not leaving Torrance by himself in an unknown place. Derrick, come to find out this man has Torrance believing that I'm his father and tried to pawn him off on me."

"What?" I scrunched my face up. "Why?"

"I don't know!" Damian threw his arms up. "After a few hours, Minister Jones came and picked Torrance up. Then the next day I hear Leonard is in the hospital."

"Where was Marianne when all this happened?"

"Who knows?" Damian grumbled. "That woman ain't never around for nothing when it comes to her darn kids!"

By the time Damian finished ranting, we'd reached Brewer's grocery store in town. Marianne emerged from the store, and her eyes locked onto me. She charged over to me like an enraged bee ready to sting its target.

"You have some nerve!" Marianne poked her finger in my chest.

"Marianne, I–!"

"Save it!" Marianne cut me off. "I would never do to you what you did to me today! Embarrassing me in front of the whole town like that, Derrick?! Really?!"

"Now wait a minute!" I argued. "I admit I was wrong for how I addressed things. But that doesn't change the fact that you were still wrong for what you did."

"It's been eighteen years!" Marianne yelled. "I've moved on, Damian's moved on! Why can't you?"

"Because you're still making stupid decisions that affect the community, and as pastor, it's my job to help this community any way I can."

"I swear all you church men are the same!" Marianne screamed. "Always looking down on others like y'all aren't doing wrong yourselves! You're a jerk, Derrick Harrison and I hate you! I'll never forgive you for this!"

Marianne stormed away.

"I really mucked things up this time," I groaned.

"Don't be too hard on yourself." Damian patted me on the back. "We all make mistakes."

I returned home feeling even worse than I had when I left. Laughter filled the air as I walked up the path to my house. Marlin swung Malcolm around in circles by his arms in the front yard.

"Boy!" I hollered as I ran over to them. "Put your brother down!"

Marlin stopped spinning and set Malcolm back on the ground.

"What are you doing?!" I yelled.

"I'm playing with Falcon," Marlin answered using the nickname we'd given to Malcolm.

"That's not how you play with him!"

"He was having fun."

"I was a superhero, Daddy!" Malcolm cheered.

"That's great, son." I rubbed Malcolm's little head. I scowled at Marlin as I told him through gritted teeth, "Pick a different game."

"Why don't you play with him then!" Marlin complained as he mean-mugged me. "Always tripping and being mean for no reason!"

"Boy I–!" I snatched Marlin up by his shirt and pulled him close to my face. I'd had enough of his disrespect and glared into his hard brown eyes. "Keep trying me, Marlin! Keep it up!"

Marlin was strong-minded, but it was as much a curse as it was a blessing. Sometimes he was like a stubborn horse that refused to be broken. I let his shirt go, and he took a few steps back.

"I hate you!" Marlin declared as he pushed the wrinkles from his shirt.

"What else is new?"

"I mean it! You're the worst father ever!"

"That's fine." I shrugged my shoulders at him. "As long as you're fed and clothed, I could care less whether you like me or not. And if you get smart with me again, I'll show you just how mean I can be."

Marlin shook with rage and stormed into the house. He slammed the door behind him, ensuring that he'd have two parents mad at him instead of one.

"Is Marlin having a doll lettuce again?" Malcolm asked. His little brow furrowed with worry as we watched Kiana yell at Marlin through the screen door.

"Yeah," I confirmed. "Marlin's having adolescence again."

Chapter Seven

Marlin hated me. I felt it when he looked at me with his cold brown eyes. His voice conveyed it when he spoke to me with no emotion. The way his body tensed up every time I came near him and relaxed when I moved away from him. If I could, I would take back what I said about not caring how he felt about me because I did care. He hated me, and he wanted to get away from me. It's the only explanation for why he would marry one of those Perry girls right out of high school.

The Perrys were saditty. They lived a lavish lifestyle funded by the father, Mayor Bernard Perry. He was about five years older than me, and he owned several car dealerships in the city. His wife Sophia was a kept woman nine years younger than him, and she'd trained her two daughters to be the same way. Soriah was the older daughter with medium-brown skin. Like her mother, she'd married well and didn't work.

Soleya Perry was the younger daughter Marlin was engaged to. They'd dated for some time and even won prom king and queen together. I couldn't understand what Marlin saw in her though. She was pretty, and that was it.

"She seems like a nice girl to me," Kiana told me one afternoon during lunch. Marlin's wedding was a few weeks away, and she was trying to make a case to me on Soleya's behalf. "A little bougie but that's alright. I'm sure she'll be a good wife for Marlin."

"Perrys don't marry to be good spouses." I sipped my lemonade. "They marry for money and status."

"Well, it certainly isn't money," Kiana laughed. "The Perrys are already the richest family in this town. And Marlin isn't anybody to be marrying for status so…"

"My dear." I sat down my empty glass. "You've got to look at this through the eyes of someone born and raised in Creeke."

"Sir, I've lived in this town for almost two decades now," Kiana stated as she carried my dishes to the sink.

"That's true. But you still look at things from that city girl perspective of yours. Remember how I told you my great-grandfather founded this town and the church?"

"Yeah."

"Well, that still matters to the people here in Creeke. The church is the pillar of this community. And since the church so far has been passed down from generation to generation in my family…"

"Are you telling me that Soleya is marrying Marlin because she thinks he might take over the church?" Kiana asked as she paused from washing the dishes.

"Like I said, Perrys marry for money and status. Even if Marlin doesn't take over the church, he's still a Harrison. That means the Perrys will be added to what I would say is the most influential family in this town. And something like that would do wonders for Mayor Perry's credibility."

"Boy, what kind of mess did you bring me into?" Kiana shook her head as she returned to washing the dishes. "I ain't sign up to be small town royalty."

"You signed up when you called me cute," I teased as I moved toward her. I wrapped my arms around her waist and began nibbling on her ear. "I warned you not to arouse my love unless you meant it."

"Stop it!" she giggled as she pulled away from me. "I'm trying to clean these dishes!"

"I'm just trying to love on you," I whined.

"You are such a *needy meathead*!" Kiana sighed as I snuggled my head into her shoulder. "I've never met a man who needed so much attention in my life."

"I like being around you."

"Lord, please get your son so I can finish these dishes." Kiana looked up at the ceiling.

The phone rang, which meant The Lord was still in the prayer answering business. I ripped myself away from my wife to get the phone.

"Harrison residence," I grumbled as I answered the phone.

"Hello? Dad?"

"Marlin?"

"Yeah, it's me. Listen, Soleya and I want to take you and Mom out for dinner today."

"Take us out for dinner? What'd you do?"

"Why does there have to be a catch for me to take you out to eat?" Marlin complained.

"I was just asking."

"Look, be ready at six, okay?"

"Wait, what should we wear?"

"Something casual. Six o'clock."

"Alright," I said before hanging up the phone.

"Who was that?" Kiana asked.

"Marlin. He and Soleya are taking us to dinner at six."

"Six? What about Falcon?"

"My parents can watch him. He likes playing with that Monique girl that lives over there anyways."

"Well alright then." Kiana dried her hands. "I'll go get him ready."

"Have fun."

"I will."

Papa and Momma's house still looked the same as it did when I moved out. Tan carpet expanded across the floor as lemon-themed drapes hung over the windows. Soft yellow flower-themed wallpaper filled the spaces between the Christian and Black art on the walls. The smell of spaghetti wafted up my nose.

"Lord have mercy," Papa laughed. He still had the same goofiness about him in old age. "Judi, look what the cat dragged in!"

"Hey son!" Momma exclaimed as she rushed out of the kitchen. Her hair had grayed over, and her soft skin had gained a few wrinkles. She threw her arms around me and hugged me. "It's so good to see you!"

Momma let me go and looked down at Malcolm.

"Boy, you sure are growing fast!" she beamed as she looked at him. "How old are you now?"

"Nine." Malcolm grinned as he held up nine fingers.

"Nine?!" Momma gasped. "Already?! Time is flying by. Have you eaten today?"

"No ma'am."

"You're not feeding my grandbaby?" Momma asked as she glared at me.

"He ate earlier," I said.

"Come on, Falcon." Momma led Malcolm to the kitchen. "I'll get you something to eat. That way you know at least *somebody's* willing to take care of you."

"What's new?" Papa asked as I sat down on the couch next to his chair.

"I need advice."

"Advice?" Papa scrunched up his dark-brown face. "About what?"

"Marlin."

"Oh Lord," Momma sighed as she returned from the kitchen. She sat on the sofa next to me. "What's he done now?"

"Nothing...," I paused to think about my answer and continued with, "That I know of. He's taking me and Kiki out for dinner later."

"So, what's the problem?" Papa asked.

"I'm concerned about him," I groaned. "He hasn't been the easiest to raise and now it's like he's going off on his own with seemingly no plan."

"You weren't the easiest to raise either," Papa chuckled.

"I wasn't that bad!"

"Son, you had the biggest mouth I'd ever seen on a child in my life," Momma giggled. "Couldn't take you nowhere."

"Not to mention, you used to play too rough with the other kids," Papa added. "I was always getting complaints about your behavior."

"And let's not forget what you did the night you turned eighteen." Momma wagged her finger at me.

"Had our and Gabriel's pressure all the way up that night!"

"I don't even want to imagine the trouble you would've gotten in if a girl was involved." Momma rubbed her temples. "I'm so glad The Lord sent someone like Kiana to keep up with you."

"More like he has to keep up with her. You know she's smarter than him. And that's a feat considering the degree he has."

"Alright, I get it." I threw my hands up. "I made some mistakes. But I was nowhere near as bad as Marlin is."

"That's the point, son," Momma said with a smile. "You were *a lot* for us to raise. But look at you now. Pastoring a church and with a family of your own."

"And being stressed out by his own son now." Papa laughed before settling down to look at me. "Son, Proverbs twenty-two and six says, 'train up a child in the way he should go: and when he is old, he will not depart from it'. We trained you up and you went in the right direction. Trust Marlin to do the same."

"Okay," I sighed. I put a smile on my face to brighten the mood. "Was I really that bad?"

"Let's just put it this way," Papa said. "You're our only child for a reason."

Marlin picked us up in his new silver car at six like he said he would. The car was impressive, and Marlin knew it. He'd leaned his seat back and drove with one hand, hoping to show off for anyone who might recognize him. It had wood trim on the doors, leather seats, and automatic windows.

"This is a nice car," I said.

"Daddy gave it to us as an early wedding gift," Soleya bragged. "He said it's the latest model."

"Oh wow," Kiana gasped. "That's nice of him."

"So where are we eating at?" I asked.

"This place called Seaweed's," Soleya said. "It's this seafood place I've been dying to try, and Marlin finally agreed to take me."

"Oh Seaweed's!" Kiana lit up. "I haven't had that in forever."

"You've been there before?" Soleya turned around to look at Kiana.

"I went there once before I moved to Creeke. It was expensive then so I can't even imagine the prices now."

"Oh, I'm not worried about the price," Soleya declared as we arrived at the restaurant. As I helped her out of the car, I realized her definition of casual was different from mine. Kiana and I had put on t-shirts and jeans. Marlin wore a tracksuit, which was the latest trend among the kids. Around his neck was the gold chain he'd bought with the money he'd earned from his job. But Soleya wasn't dressed like any of us.

"Thank you, Mr. Harrison." Soleya smiled at me as she placed her manicured hand in my outstretched hand. She stepped onto the pavement in expensive-looking black heels.

"Oh my!" Kiana exclaimed as she came around the car with Marlin. "Don't you look nice and pretty tonight."

"Thank you." Soleya blushed at the compliment.

Kiana was right. Soleya did look nice and pretty. Everything about her was sleek and presentable. From her dark-brown skin gleaming under the moonlight, to her black dress, and even her hair. It seemed like all eyes were on her from the time we stepped into the restaurant to the time we were seated.

"So, Soleya," I said to start the conversation. "What do you have planned now that you've graduated?"

"I'm going to open a hair salon and a new barbershop in Creeke," Soleya explained. "Mother doesn't like the idea of me running a business, but I feel like this needs to happen. Graham's died with Mr. Graham, and all the men in this town have been looking rough ever since. Plus, there's never been a place for women to get their hair done in Creeke and that needs to change."

"I know that's right," Kiana agreed. "Don't you agree, dear?"

"What do you mean 'the men have been looking rough'?"

"No offense Mr. Harrison, but some of y'all cannot cut hair at all. I'm tired of the homemade cuts."

"Does that mean your dad looks rough too?"

"Of course not," Soleya said. "But that's only because he gets his hair cut out here in the city. In fact, we all get our hair done out here and that's my point. Why drive all the way out here when I can open a place in Creeke?"

"You'll have to excuse my husband, dear," Kiana said as she squeezed my leg. "He can be a bit ... aggressive at times."

"That's alright." Soleya excused me. "I get to see for myself where Marlin gets it from. He can ask me all the questions he wants. It's not like I haven't heard them all before."

"Okay. What made you want to be with Marlin?"

"I like him." Soleya placed a hand on Marlin's arm. "He's a good fit for me."

"What makes him a good fit?"

"I think his loyalty and reliability is what attracted me to him the most."

"Loyalty and reliability," Kiana echoed. "Those are important in a relationship. I'm happy that he's found someone as smart and strong-willed as you are."

"So...," I said. "About the wedding..."

"Daddy's offered to pay for everything," Soleya informed us. "All you'll both have to do is show up."

"That's generous of him," Kiana said.

"Yes," I agreed. "Very."

"He settles for nothing less than the best."

"Dad, come with me." Marlin suddenly stood up. He led me away to the restroom. As I followed him, I wondered if I'd upset him somehow.

"What's up?" I asked when we were alone.

"I wanted to talk. Just the two of us."

"What about?"

"Just something with the wedding." Marlin twiddled his fingers.

"You don't want me there or something?"

"What?" Marlin's voice got high. "Why is that the first thing you go to?"

"Why else would you be so nervous?"

"Because I...," Marlin started, then stopped. He dismissively waved his hand. "Forget it. I'll figure it out myself."

"Don't be like that, Marlin."

"Why do you always assume the worst when it comes to me?" Marlin crossed his arms. "You don't do that with Falcon."

"Trouble seems to find you more easily than it does him," I chuckled. "You have a fighting spirit that you need to work on."

"I only fight with people that are disrespectful."

"Really?" I stroked my chin. "Is that why you and Torrance keep going at it?"

"I don't mess with him as long as he doesn't mess with me. If he messes with me, then we fight. Simple."

"Y'all are both eighteen. How long are y'all going to keep this up?"

"Why do you always take up for him? *I'm* your son, not him."

"Because I hold you accountable. I've told you several times to leave him alone and you haven't listened. Therefore, in my eyes it's your fault."

"Man." Marlin sucked his teeth. "I hate you."

"Do you really?" I said, my mouth forming into a frown.

"Do I really what?"

"Hate me."

"No, I don't really hate you. I'm just talking mess."

"You don't?"

"I said I didn't, didn't I?"

Normally, I would've popped Marlin in the mouth for being smart. But I was so overcome with joy that I let it slide. It felt like a weight lifted from my shoulders. My son didn't hate me after all. I hid my face as the tears started falling.

"What are you crying for?"

"You don't know how happy it makes me to hear that you don't hate me."

"Dad, wipe your face." Marlin handed me a paper towel. "Forty-four years old and crying over something like that."

"So?" I sniffled as I wiped my face.

"Let's just get back to the table."

"Okay."

My son didn't hate me and that's all that mattered to me.

-

Chapter Eight

Torrents of rain washed down the kitchen window as thunder rumbled outside. My fourteen-year-old son and I sat silently in the dark as the storm passed over our heads. A bolt of lightning pierced the dark clouds of the afternoon sky and seemed to touch the ground in the distance.

"How long do we have to sit like this?" Malcolm whined as he shook in his seat. "I hate thunderstorms."

"Until The Good Lord above finishes whatever he's doing," I told him. "There's nothing to be afraid of."

"But you're shaking too."

Malcolm held my shivering hand up. I hated thunderstorms as much as he did. Loud noises frightened me, and thunderstorms were the worst when it came to that. But I couldn't let my son know I was scared.

"Let's just let The Lord finish working."

"Okay," Malcolm sighed. He was more relaxed than Marlin, and I never had complaints about him.

Someone knocked on the front door. Monique Evans stood on my porch in the pouring rain. The umbrella over her head barely held on as the strong wind blew against it.

"Monique?" I asked. "What are you doing out in this storm?"

"Pastor, I need to talk to you," Monique whispered. I could tell something was wrong by the look on her medium-brown face. "Can I come in?"

"Of course." I let her in. "What's going on?"

"I don't know how to say this but...," Monique paused to take a breath. She put her hand over her stomach and looked at me through teary eyes. "I'm pregnant."

"Oh...," I choked. "Does your mother know?"

Monique shook her head and looked away.

"I see. You haven't told her yet."

"Pastor." Monique closed her eyes. "My baby ... your son is the father."

Another flash of lightning filled the sky. The revelation sunk in, and I realized Monique was serious.

"Marlin?" I whispered.

"No... no." Monique waved her hands. "You...your other son..."

At first, I was relieved. Then, a new feeling washed over me. I only had two sons. And if Marlin was not the father, then...

"*Malcolm*?" I gasped.

Monique sobbed.

"Don't panic," I told myself. "Don't panic."

I took a few deep breaths to collect myself.

"Monique, I thinks its best you go home now," I said. "Have your mother meet with me after church tomorrow and we'll tell her together."

Monique nodded between her crying. I saw her out of the house and returned to Malcolm in the kitchen. He had some explaining to do.

"Malcolm, I need to talk to you," I said as I returned to my seat.

"But The Lord's still working." Malcolm looked at me. My heart wrenched as I looked into those warm brown eyes of his. The image of my innocent little boy was shattered.

"He'll understand," I told him. "Are you aware... of how babies are made?"

"Can we let The Lord finish working please?" Malcolm squeaked as he looked at the floor. "I don't want to talk about this."

"Monique just came by..."

"She did?" Malcolm asked. A slight smile crept onto his face. "Is she still here?"

"No, she left." I grabbed his wrist before he could get up. "She told me she's pregnant."

"Oh." Malcolm deflated. "That sucks."

"Malcolm... have you ... and Monique ... been... you know..."

"What?" Malcolm's voice got high the way it did when he was nervous. He wore the same look Kiana did when I asked her the same question before we were married. "Why would you ask me that?"

"She told me you're the father of her baby."

Malcolm looked at me with horror. His reaction told me everything I needed to know.

"Fourteen-year-olds can't have babies," he laughed. It was a nervous laugh.

"Fourteen-year-olds can definitely have babies."

The smile faded from Malcolm's face. It slowly contorted into a frown.

"I'm going to have a baby?"

"It looks that way."

"What am I going to do?"

"Raise it and take care of it."

"I don't know how to take care of a baby!"

"You knew how to make one. If you can make one, you can take care of one."

Malcolm looked out the window.

"Do you think Mom will get super upset?"

"We'll cross that bridge when we get there," I patted his shoulder. "For now, just go to your room."

I was not looking forward to telling Kiana about this. The storm outside had calmed down. It was the proverbial calm before the real storm began.

"Hey," Kiana greeted as she walked through the front door that evening. She kissed me and set her purse down on the counter. "You won't believe what happened to me and Thelma at work today."

"What?"

"We got a raise!" Kiana cheered.

"That's great," I sighed. "I need you to sit down."

"Okay." Kiana sat next to me. I grabbed her hand and squeezed it. "What's going on?"

"Monique is pregnant."

"Really?" Kiana gasped as her eyes went wide. "She's only seventeen!"

"And Malcolm is the father."

Kiana stared at me with a blank expression and started laughing.

"Derrick, stop playing," she said. Her glee decreased as she noticed I wasn't laughing with her. "You're playing, right?"

"I wish I was."

Kiana began shaking her leg up and down.

"Are you telling me ... that my fourteen-year-old son ... got a girl pregnant?"

"Yeah..."

Kiana lifted her face as she tried to hold back her tears.

"Why would he do this?" she whispered.

"Kiana, breathe."

"Why would he do this?!"

"Kiki, calm down."

"NO!" Kiana shot up from her chair. "MALCOLM!"

She ran to Malcolm's room, yelling his name. A commotion arose in the room, and Malcolm was on the floor when I arrived.

"Mom, why did you slap me?!" Malcolm cried as he held his face.

"You got a girl pregnant?!" Kiana ranted. "What is wrong with you?!"

"It was an accident!" Malcolm whined.

"How do you accidentally get a girl pregnant?!" Kiana argued. "What are you even doing having–! Ooooooh breathe Kiana breathe..."

Kiana paced back and forth, taking several deep breaths to calm herself down. Malcolm got up and sat on the bed.

"This is what you've been doing when you go over to your grandparents' house?" Kiana accused him when she was calm. "Messing around with Monique?"

"Mom I–!"

"Uh, uh." Kiana held her hand up to shush Malcolm. "You're fourteen! You can't drive, don't have a job, but you want to have a baby? What do you know about raising a baby?"

Malcolm avoided Kiana's eyes.

"I asked you a question, didn't I?"

"I don't know anything about raising a baby."

"Exactly!" Kiana exclaimed as she threw her hands up. "Why are you having one then?"

"It just happened."

"It just happened," Kiana mocked him. She turned and glared at me. "You're not going to say anything?"

"I'm just here to make sure you don't kill the boy."

"I need to get out this house," Kiana declared as she pushed past me to leave the room. "Because if I don't, a father and son will die up in here today! And I ain't going to jail over y'all!"

Kiana slammed the front door as she left the house. An hour later, I received a call from Thelma about Kiana's location.

"Would you like to explain why your wife is on my couch crying when we just got a raise at work?" she asked.

"No..."

"What did you do?"

"For once, it wasn't me. That's all I can say. You'll have to ask your best friend for the rest."

"Can you like... do something...?" Thelma whispered. "Because y'all's drama is affecting my time with my Sugarbear and you know he leaves my house at sunset because he doesn't want to be tempted."

"He wouldn't have to worry about that if you two got married already."

"Derrick!" Thelma whined. "Come get her!"

"Okay, okay," I sighed.

I found myself in front of Thelma's house. Damian was standing on the porch, and when he spotted me, he ran over to me. He moved rather fast for us both to be forty-nine.

"What did you do?" Damian asked.

"I didn't do anything!"

"All the stuff we've been through, and you can't tell me why your wife flew up here like the police were after her and she needed a hide out?"

"Malcolm got into some big trouble..."

"See, this is what happens when you make Rick the godfather instead of me."

"You're Marlin's godfather though..."

"And look at how he turned out," Damian bragged. "Back on the right track after a few bumps in the road, and all it took was one summer working with me in the city. That's all the proof you need that I'm the better godfather."

"Whatever helps you sleep at night, Damian."

I entered Thelma's house to find Kiana on the couch.

"Kiki," I said.

"Leave. Me. Alone."

"You can't run away from this forever."

Kiana looked at me.

"Is this what I deserve?" she complained. "To be reminded of my mistakes through my children?"

"This is not your mistake," I said as I knelt in front of her. "This is Malcolm's mistake."

"But if I'd done a better job–!"

"Sometimes, we do everything we're supposed to, and stuff still goes wrong," I told her. "That's life. You can't control it. What you can control is whether you'll give up or keep going."

"I can't believe this," Kiana said.

"Look, I'm going back home," I said. "You don't have to come with me, but you can't stay here."

"I'm coming," Kiana sighed. A giggle escaped her mouth as she wiped a tear from her face. "You're not very good at encouraging people."

"You got the message, didn't you?" I laughed. "Now, somebody help me up. I'm too old to be doing all this kneeling and stuff."

Kiana and I met with Monique and her mother after church the next day. Monique wore a light blue dress and a bun on top of her head. She resembled her mother, Etta Evans. Etta was a single mother, having divorced her husband some years ago.

"Hello, Pastor. First Lady," Etta greeted us as she settled into her chair. "What's this about?"

"The floor is yours Monique," I gestured for Monique to speak. All eyes fell on her.

"Ma," Monique said, leaning as far as possible from her mother. "I'm pregnant."

A few emotions swirled around in Etta's eyes. She leaned back in her chair and laughed.

"This is what you brought me in here for?"

"Yeah..."

"Who's the father, girl?"

"Malcolm..."

"OH!" Etta laughed harder. She looked at Kiana and me with a sly smile. "I see why we're here now. Y'all want us to handle it, right?"

"Handle what?" I wrinkled my face up.

"Getting rid of the baby."

"Are you crazy?!" Kiana snapped. "We're here to figure what we're going to do after the baby is born!"

"I don't need to figure out anything," Etta said. "Monique wanted to be grown, so she can figure it out herself. I hope y'all got a spare room because I ain't raising any babies."

"So, that's it?" Kiana crossed her arms. "You're going to throw her and the baby out on the street?"

"I ain't raising any babies, First Lady."

"Then I guess there's nothing else to discuss," I said.

"Derrick!" Kiana protested.

"We'll see y'all when the baby's born." I said. "Have a blessed day, ladies."

Etta and Monique left the office.

"Why would you do that?" Kiana argued when we were alone. "That girl can't raise a baby on her own! She needs help!"

"I know that. But Etta's already decided she's putting Monique out when the baby is born, and we can't stop her from doing that. We need to figure something out because my grandbaby's not sleeping on the street."

"I guess you're right," Kiana sighed.

"Plus, we have a bigger problem. The church might turn on us when they find out our fourteen-year-old son is having a baby."

"I didn't think about that."

"Our time as leaders may be coming to an end," I muttered.

"Don't say that. I'm sure everything will turn out alright."

I looked at my wife. She still had that same kindness in her eyes. My spirit lifted as I understood that we were in this together, for better or worse.

"Let's keep this amongst ourselves for now," I said. "I don't want this affecting Malcolm or Monique any more than it already has."

"Okay."

This was our secret. One we'd have to hold onto together until we couldn't hold it anymore.

That afternoon, Marlin and Soleya dropped by with their kids to visit. They'd been married for five years and lived in the Perrys' guest house with their two sons, Matthias Jamal Harrison and Deidrick Aaron Harrison. I'd nicknamed them Matty and Cornbread. Marlin worked as a garbageman in the city, while Soleya worked toward opening her salon. Her plans had been halted, however, because she was pregnant with her third child.

"I have some news!" Soleya cheered. She looked between Kiana and me excitedly before blurting out, "The baby's going to be a girl!"

"That's wonderful dear," Kiana said as she hugged Soleya.

"You guys don't seem all that excited," Marlin said as he chowed down on the food Kiana made.

"We're excited," Kiana said. "It's just... well..."

"Falcon's having a baby too," I said.

"He's what?!" Marlin choked.

"You know that Monique girl that stays over by your grandparents?" Kiana asked.

"Ain't she messing with like three other dudes?" Marlin asked. "Y'all better make sure that's his baby."

"Way to be gentle, son," I grumbled.

"I'm serious." Marlin bit into his food again. "Those other dudes she's messing with ain't got anything going for them. She might be trying to pin the baby on Malcolm because she knows y'all are the best option for it."

I watched as three-year-old Matthias rolled his toy car across the living room. Two-year-old Deidrick was asleep on the couch. Soon, two more babies would be added to the mix. But with this new information, the question of paternity would always surround Malcolm's child. Marlin was right. We needed to know this baby was Malcolm's before we accepted it into the family.

Chapter Nine

I took Marlin's advice and checked out the other boys Monique had been with. One was her ex-boyfriend that dropped out of school to run the streets in the city. The other two were older boys with nothing going for themselves. Marlin was right. Malcolm *was* the best option for her baby.

Life went on, and Monique became six months pregnant. School started, and rumors filled the hallways about who her child's father was. It didn't take long for those rumors to reach the parents. From there, it spread like wildfire across Creeke that Malcolm was a potential father. The church elders called a meeting to get everything sorted out.

"Pastor," one elder squeaked as he blushed with embarrassment. "We've learned your son has gotten into a bit of ... trouble."

"Let's get to the point," I said as I rolled my eyes. "It's true: Malcolm got a girl pregnant."

"Pastor!" another one exclaimed. "Have you no shame?"

"Being ashamed won't change the fact that a baby will be here soon."

"Trifling."

"Didn't you–!"

"Derrick." Papa held his hand up to silence me. I sat back in my chair and crossed my arms. At forty-nine, I still knew to shut up when Papa wanted me to.

"Pastor Harrison," another elder addressed me. "Your time as pastor has been a mess. You've intimidated members of the community, used sermons to attack others, and now your house is out of order."

"How have I intimidated members of the community?"

"Pastor, you of all people should know how fast word spreads in a small town like Creeke."

"So, you're going off gossip?"

"We're going off eyewitness reports of you arguing with residents on their front porches in broad daylight," the elder argued. "Smacking your own child in front of the whole church? Remember that?"

"Disciplining my son is an issue now?" I snorted.

"Even now you argue with us when the Bible clearly says that the younger should submit themselves to their elders," the elder complained. "And you come in here with this nonchalant attitude and look on your face like you could care less. Then you wonder why we want you removed. You haven't done a good job leading this flock, Pastor. The majority has–"

"Majority?" I asked.

"Yes, majority," the elder grumbled. "As I was saying, the majority has decided that you are not fit to lead the church. We ask that you vacate the office of pastor immediately and Lionel resume pastoring the church until we find a suitable replacement."

"Okay."

They wouldn't get the satisfaction of seeing me upset. Seeing me brokenhearted over the loss of something I loved. Creeke Church was the lifeline of the community, and it had been in my family since its creation. I spent countless hours preparing to lead the church for it to end with nothing. Pastor Harrison was gone. Only Derrick Harrison was left.

After the meeting, Papa, Minister Jones, and I were the only ones left in the room. Minister Jones looked rough, and it was clear his health wasn't what it used to be.

"Why are you always the odd one out, Gabe?" Papa laughed.

"I am not without sin; therefore, I can't cast a stone." Minister Jones said as he shrugged his shoulders. He was the only one to vote against my firing. "Especially after everything that's happened in my life."

"Your life is one for the books."

"And yours isn't?" Minister Jones coughed. He released a few more coughs before continuing with, "You've been on the Earth longer than I have."

"We're not that far apart in age, Gabriel! Shoot, we're ... we're ... um ..."

"Five years apart, Papa," I sighed. "You're seven-eight and Minister Jones is seventy-three."

"Seventy-eight?! I'm old! How long have we been friends, Gabriel?"

"I'm not doing all that counting. All I know is I moved to Creeke when I was fourteen and we became friends a week later."

"Oh yeah... didn't you move here because you shot someone in your hometown?"

"Those rumors were true?!" I said.

"Gabriel stayed in some mess," Papa groaned. "He's the one that put that bullet hole in the stop sign outside the church."

"You and your son are just alike," Minister Jones complained. "Can't hold water for nothing."

"Well, you and your grandson Torrance are just alike," Papa teased. "Short-tempered and always yelling at folks. And I'll bet his son, Drake, will be the same way too."

"So?" Minister Jones fussed. "If y'all would do right, I wouldn't have to yell at y'all!"

"Sure Gabe. Whatever helps you sleep at night."

I watched as Papa joked around with Minister Jones. Papa didn't let on easily about his feelings as Minister Jones did. He'd always been easy-going and preferred to make everyone smile, but I wondered how he really felt about the situation.

"What happened?" Kiana asked when I got home. Marlin and his children had visited again.

"We've been fired," I sighed.

"This is some bullcrap!" Marlin yelled, causing Deidrick to flinch. Unlike Papa, I didn't have to question how Marlin felt. It was the first time he'd been clear with his feelings toward a situation.

"Now Marlin...," Kiana said.

"No Mom! Dad's cared for this community for years and look how they treat him!"

"It's my fault, son," I admitted. "I should've made better choices."

"How were you supposed to know what that idiot was doing behind your back?!"

Malcolm gave Marlin a dirty look before shuffling into the kitchen.

"It's not just about this," I said. "There are other decisions I made as pastor that I shouldn't have made."

The issue with the Browns was taking a toll on my personal life. But I couldn't stand by and let them think what they did was okay. Their actions affected everyone in this town. I would hold them accountable for it, pastor or not.

"Well, if you're not the pastor, I'm not going to the church anymore!" Marlin declared.

"Oh yes you are!" Kiana argued. "We're not going to stop going just because we're not leading anymore. Forget what everyone else thinks."

"No. They're making an example out of Dad and I don't like that. I'm not going and that's final."

"Marlin!" Kiana called as Marlin stormed from the house.

"Let him go," I told her. "He just needs time to calm down."

"I don't want to go anymore either," Malcolm announced.

"What?!" Kiana cried. "Why not?!"

"Those people talk about me behind my back!" Malcolm ranted. "Their kids treat me like I've got a disease. It hurts my feelings."

"Oh son," Kiana sighed as she hugged Malcolm. "Don't let those people get to you. What they think doesn't matter."

"I still don't want to go," Malcolm said. He skulked off to his room, leaving Kiana and me alone with our grandkids.

"Everything's just falling apart," Kiana sighed.

"We'll get through this." I took her hands in mine. "Maybe things need to fall apart."

"What are you saying?"

"I'm saying maybe The Lord is doing something new and we need to trust him. He makes all things work for our good, remember?"

"You're right," Kiana agreed. "He makes all things work for our good."

Although I tried to keep the family's spirits up, I felt horrible on the inside. I needed to talk to someone who didn't have any bias in the situation. Thankfully, I knew just the person to call.

"Anderson residence," a girl answered the number I dialed.

"Hi," I greeted. "Can I speak to Richard, please?"

"Just a minute," Richard's daughter, Kaitlyn, said. "Daddy! Phone!"

A few seconds passed.

"Hello?"

"Hey Rick."

"Ricky!" Richard cheered. "Hey man! How are you?"

"Not so good," I sighed.

"What happened?" Richard asked, the excitement leaving his voice.

"I had to take an early retirement from pastoring the church."

"No!" Richard cried. "I never got to come hear you preach!"

"I know man."

"What happened?"

"Well..."

I filled Richard in on everything that happened since we'd last spoke.

"What a mess," Richard complained when I finished. "I can just hear Damian now: *this is why you don't make Richard the godfather over me*."

"He actually did say that when he found out."

"I told you! What happens to the church when your dad can't preach anymore?"

"I guess they'll find a new pastor."

"Just like that? Your great-grandfather's church just goes to someone else?"

"I made my bed and now I have to lay in it."

"That sucks, Ricky. How about I tell you something that'll cheer you up?"

"I could use some good news."

"Due to your level of education, you're overqualified for your job now. I'm going to have to let you go from that position."

"How does this cheer me up, Richard?"

"Because kid," Richard chuckled. "Our company manager retired, and we need a new one. It pays a lot better than your old job, you won't have to do backbreaking work, and you're the only person I trust to promote to that position. Say yes and it's yours, no questions asked."

"Man, you play too much," I groaned.

"*I* play too much? You're the king of playing around too much."

"Man whatever."

"So what do you say? Want the job, kid?"

"Yeah. Thanks Rick."

"No problem. If you ever need anything I'm a phone call away."

"I know."

"I'm just making sure. We can't have Damian out here thinking he's the better godfather."

"I'm not getting in between that," I laughed.

"One day, you're going to have to pick," Richard warned. "It'll come down to that."

"That day's not today."

The future looked bleak. But I had to go through it. Like I told Kiana, everything would turn out alright. It had to.

Chapter Ten

Soleya's baby came first that year. It was late September, and Soleya's parents weren't in town when she went into labor. Her only family at the city's hospital were us, her sister, and her seven-year-old nephew, Marcellus. We all waited as Soleya delivered my third grandchild into the world with Marlin and Kiana by her side.

"I can't believe Leya is having a third baby," Soriah gawked as she applied lip gloss. She was two years older than Soleya, and her make-up looked frosted onto her face. "I only had one and that was enough for me."

"I think she just wanted a girl," I said as I watched Matthias and Deidrick play a game with each other in their chairs.

"Yep." Soriah popped her plump lips. "A little girl she can parade around town like a princess. Just like Mother did to us."

"You know, Soleya doesn't talk much about Sophia."

"I don't blame her."

"Mommy, I'm hungry," Marcellus whined. He looked like Soriah.

"Boy, you just ate."

"I'm hungry!"

"Come on...," Soriah sighed. "Should've left you with Quincy back in Creeke..."

She grabbed Marcellus' hand and led him away. Marcellus turned back to us with an impish grin on his face. I looked at Matthias and Deidrick, who looked back at me.

"I better not catch you acting up in public like him," I warned them. "Do you hear me?"

"Yes sir," they both said.

The double doors to the hospital split apart, and Nancy and Paulette came running inside.

"We came as fast as we could!" Nancy panted. "Did we miss the baby?"

"Nope," I said.

"Good," Paulette sighed. "I wanted to be here when we finally got to see her."

"Well, you just missed Soleya's sister," I told them. "She went to get her son a snack."

"Every time Soleya has a baby that boy gets hungry," Nancy joked. "But you know who doesn't get hungry? My cute little nephews!"

"That's because you only see them twice a year," I teased Nancy as she hugged the boys. "Those boys are human vacuums. Especially Cornbread."

"You leave my babies alone!" Nancy shushed me. "You're probably the one that eats everything and blames it on them."

"Why would I do that?"

"We've seen the way you eat," Paulette added. "You have a bottomless pit in your stomach."

"Soleya needs to go ahead and push this baby out so y'all can go back home."

"Don't try to rush us away." Nancy wagged her finger at me. "I'm not leaving until I see my very first niece."

We all sat in the waiting room. Eventually, the doctor told us we could go back and see Soleya and the baby.

"Look at my little girl," Soleya sobbed as the nurse led us into the room.

"Look at her little face!" Nancy cooed. "She's so adorable!"

"You want to hold her?" Soleya motioned to Kiana.

"Can I?" Kiana grinned as she reached for the baby. She took the baby in her arms and the three women crowded together.

"What's her name?" Paulette asked as she doted on the little girl.

"Allison Queen Harrison," Soleya yawned.

"Queen?" I smiled. "Then I'm going to call this one, Queenie."

"Whatever you like," Soleya sighed as she closed her eyes.

Marlin had fallen asleep in his chair. I crept over to him and draped my jacket over him.

"You've done good, son," I whispered to him. "I'm proud of you."

That November, we were back at the hospital for the birth of Malcolm's son. Monique opted to have only her mother in the room.

"I want to name him after you, Dad," Malcolm told me as we waited in the waiting room.

"After me?"

"Yeah. Derek Drumaine Harrison."

"Drumaine? What kind of name is that?"

"It's our middle names combined. Like how mom's name is a combination of two names."

"Oh." I put my finger to my chin. "Do you know what Monique's decided to do?"

"She said she'd tell us her decision after the baby's born."

"We still need to test the baby to make sure it's yours."

"I know."

"And I know you and Monique haven't been getting along lately but y'all need to pull it together for this baby if it is yours."

"All that matters to me is being a good parent to my son."

Soon, Monique finished delivering the baby, and we could go back and see him.

"Here," Monique said. She shoved the baby into my arms.

"Hey!" Malcolm chastised. "Don't hand my son off like a football!"

"Whatever," Monique muttered. "Wouldn't even be here if you'd handled yourself like a man."

"No, you wouldn't be here if you'd handled your business as a woman," Malcolm argued.

"You know what–!"

I tuned out their argument as I looked at the baby in my arms. The little tyke sparked many changes in my life, and each change worked out for my good. One look at his sleeping angelic face ended my doubts.

This was my grandbaby, and I didn't need a test to prove that. As I held little Derek in my arms, I only had one thought: *Who would this baby be?*

Part 2:
Torrance Brown

Chapter Eleven

It wasn't clear who my father was. Mama's first husband, Mr. Damian Parker, fathered my oldest brother and sister, Terrence Lee Parker and Ruth-Anne Grace Parker. Her second husband, Leonard Brown, fathered my other older brother and sister, Jeremy-Micah Kyle Brown and Marie Denise Brown. I was Mama's youngest child, and my last name was only Brown because it was Mama's last name. Brown didn't claim me as his son because I wasn't as dark as him.

"That's not my baby!" he'd yell. "That's Parker's baby! He looks just like him!"

"He looks like my daddy!" Mama would scream back.

Terrence claimed Brown used to be nice and would still be if I hadn't been born. He told me that when I was six and he was fourteen. The only kids Brown treated well were Jeremy-Micah and Marie. Since they looked like him, he was sure they were his. Brown tried to pit them against us, but Grandpa wouldn't allow it.

Grandpa Gabriel was the closest thing I had to a father. He lived by himself across the street from the church. Grandma Mavis died when I was seven, so Grandpa spent all his time working on music. His biggest wish was for my siblings and me to sing with him, and one day he got it.

It was a summery Tuesday when Terrence was seventeen, Ruth-Anne was fifteen, Jeremy-Micah was thirteen, Marie was ten, and I was nine. We were all at the church with Grandpa, who taught us one of the choir's songs while he gave Marie and me piano lessons. Marie sang in a soft, whispery voice, while Jeremy-Micah's voice was vibrant and loud. Ruth-Anne's voice was sweet and soothing, while Terrence's was plain and dull. According to Grandpa, my voice was still high enough to reach the notes Jeremy-Micah couldn't.

"I think I'll have y'all sing this with the choir for tomorrow's service," Grandpa said.

"In front of the whole church?" Marie whispered.

"Yes."

"That's scary, Grandpa."

"You can do it, Marie," Grandpa encouraged her. "The boys will sing with the tenors, Ruth-Anne with the altos, and Marie with the sopranos."

"Grandpa, I can't sing that high!" Marie whined.

"I've been hearing a lot of 'I can't' from you today, young lady." Grandpa looked above his glasses at Marie. "What does Philippians four and thirteen say?"

"I can do all things...," Marie mumbled.

"I can't hear you."

"I can do all things through Christ who strengthens me."

"And who are you singing for?"

"The Lord."

"I want to hear all y'all say it. Who are you singing for?"

"The Lord," we all said.

"Exactly. You're singing for the Lord. Not for me, not for the people in this church, not even for yourselves. You sing for the glory of the Lord and its Him who gives you strength to do it. Understand?"

"Yes sir."

"Good," Grandpa said as he positioned himself behind the organ. "Now, let me hear you sing something."

"But you just said we're not singing for you," Jeremy-Micah joked.

"Little boy." Grandpa glared at him, and Jeremy-Micah looked down. "I want to hear everyone sing together."

"Grandpa, I can't reach those high notes." Marie whined.

"You hear how high your voice is when you talk?" Grandpa asked. "If you can talk that high, you can sing that high. Now sing."

Grandpa pressed a note on the organ and looked at Marie. She took a deep breath and sang. Marie reached those notes like Grandpa said she would. We all sang, and our five voices melted into one. For the first time in our lives, we were unified.

"Perfect," Grandpa sighed with a smile. He was always happiest when we sang with him. Making Grandpa happy made me happy.

Chapter Twelve

Mama could only do so much with a man like Brown as her husband. She worked all day as a secretary at one of the local businesses, then came home to cook and clean. Brown worked at a factory in the city and didn't do anything at home except boss us around since he was the 'man of the house'. I didn't know if Mama loved Brown how he loved her, but she stayed with him.

Since he couldn't turn our siblings against us, Brown resorted to separating Terrence, Ruth-Anne, and me as much as possible. The three of us couldn't eat any meals until 'Brown's family' finished eating. We shared one bed in the smallest room, and we couldn't go on family outings either. Terrence and Ruth-Anne at least got to escape to Mr. Damian's house every weekend. But I remained trapped in Brown's house every day year-round.

Grandpa kept my hopes up by telling me The Lord would reward me if I did what was right. So, I behaved, hoping one day I'd be free from Brown. Everything changed when Ruth-Anne talked to Arnold Green on the last day of school.

"I was walking home along the dirt road when Arnie came out of nowhere," Ruth-Anne explained to Mama one night when it was our turn for dinner. "He walked with me all the way to the house and then asked me out for a date on Saturday. Isn't that something?"

"Gracie, I hope you told him you couldn't go," Mama said as she wiped the counter.

"Why would I tell him that, Mama?"

"Because you're supposed to watch Torrance this weekend, re-member?"

Brown was taking 'his family' to spend the weekend at his parents' house. Since Terrence would be at work, Ruth-Anne agreed to stay and watch me instead of going to her dad's. Although I was ten, Mama didn't want to leave me at home by myself because she feared I'd break something.

"Oh no, I forgot." Ruth-Anne slapped her forehead. At sixteen, she could be forgetful at times. "I already told Arnold I would go with him."

"Well, tell him you can't go."

"Alright." Ruth-Anne's shoulders drooped.

I carried my glass and plate over to the sink. The glass slipped from my hand, and Mama caught it before it crashed into the floor. She set it on the counter next to the sink.

"Be careful, Torrance Dean!" Mama whispered. "I don't want to hear Leonard's mouth tonight all because you broke a glass."

"Sorry, Mama," I said. I looked at the glass, thankful she'd caught it.

Saturday came, and Ruth-Anne and I spent the whole morning cleaning the house. By noon, we lay sprawled on the living room floor, listening to the radio. Someone knocked on the front door, and Ruth-Anne got up to answer it.

"Arnie?" I heard her ask. "What are you doing here?"

"Well, you had to cancel the date so you could watch your little brother, right?" Sixteen-year-old Arnold answered. "So, I brought my little brother and thought maybe we could watch them together."

I got up and went to the front door. Arnold's brother, Alfred, stood behind him, tossing a football up and down in the air. All I knew about him was that he was thirteen and played sports.

"I don't know," Ruth-Anne said as she bit her lip. "I don't think it's a good idea to have anyone in the house while Mama and Brown are out."

"That's okay," Arnold said. "We can sit outside."

"Well…," Ruth-Anne said before looking at Arnold's light-brown face. He raised his bushy black eyebrows, and Ruth-Anne gave in. "Okay. But we'll only sit outside."

"That's fine by me."

We spent the whole afternoon outside in the front yard. Ruth-Anne and Arnold talked on the porch while Alfred and I played catch with his football. Soon, I got thirsty and took a break.

"Ruthie, I'm going inside to get some juice," I said.

"Okay but drink it in the kitchen."

"Alright."

I went inside and poured myself a glass of red fruit juice. Ruth-Anne and Arnold continued talking, but I could barely hear them. The only way I could hear was if I went into the living room, and that's what I did.

"Why do you always wear those floor-length skirts?" Arnold asked when I was closer. "Don't you get hot under them?"

"Because Brown wants me to wear pants like every other girl," Ruth-Anne giggled. "Mama gets annoyed with me because she hated wearing skirts when she was my age. But it's worth it to me if it means I don't have to listen to Brown."

"So, by that logic, if I asked you not to be my girlfriend would you do the opposite?"

"I'd say we need to get to know each other a little better first."

"That's better than no."

I could see Arnold through the black bars of the screen door. He and Alfred had their black hair shaped into neat boxes on their heads. His smile and personality were nice. I imagined him as a prince in a fairytale that came from a faraway kingdom.

Prince Arnold rode on his trusty steed toward the evil castle, ready to slay anything in his way. He was on a mission to save Princess Ruth-Anne from the clutches of the evil King Brown.

"Arnie!" Princess Ruth-Anne cried from her tower. "Save me!"

"I'll save you, Ruth-Anne!" Prince Arnold declared.

"You fool!" King Brown laughed. "The princess belongs to me now! You'll never have her!"

"I'll save her if it's the last thing I do!" Prince Arnold said.

Prince Arnold and King Brown battled with their swords. Sometimes it seemed like King Brown would win, but Prince Arnold always found the strength to keep going. In the end, he drove his sword into King Brown's chest.

"AHH!" King Brown yelled, dying on the sword.

Prince Arnold freed Princess Ruth-Anne from the tower. He let the princess' family come live with him too, including King Brown's children. They all lived happily ever after.

My daydream over, I turned to go back to the kitchen and fell. One of the living room table's legs had tripped me. Fruit juice covered my shirt and Brown's favorite rug. If the cup had landed a few inches further on the wooden floor, everything would've been alright. But since it didn't, we were going to get in trouble.

"Ruth-Anne!" I cried as I ran to the front door.

"Torrance!" Ruth-Anne gasped. "What happened to your shirt?"

"I spill my fruit juice."

"That's it?" Ruth-Anne sighed. "We can clean it up."

"I spilled it on Brown's rug."

The color drained from Ruth-Anne's face. She stood up and grabbed my hand.

"Arnold, I think you should go now," she whispered.

"Is there anything I can do to help?"

"No, there's not," Ruth-Anne said. "Thanks for coming by."

Ruth-Anne led me past the bars of the screen door like a prisoner to a jail cell. Our fun was over. We scrubbed at the rug for hours, praying the juice would come out.

"Why were you even in here in the first place?!" she yelled. "I told you to stay in the kitchen!"

"I wanted to hear what you and Arnie were talking about."

"So, you were being disobedient and nosy?!"

At some point, Terrence came home. He looked at us and got on the floor to help.

"It's no use!" Ruth-Anne sobbed. "It won't come out!"

"Gracie!" Terrence grabbed her shoulders and shook her. "Calm down! Everything's going to be fine."

"No, it's not! Brown is going to kill us."

"It'll be fine." Terrence pointed at the light stain in the rug and said, "Look, you can barely see it."

He looked at me, urging me with his eyes to say something.

"I'm sorry, Ruthie," I said. That's all I could say.

Grandpa knew something was wrong that Sunday at church, but none of us said anything, so he stopped asking. After church, we went home and found Brown's car in the driveway. Brown stood above the stain with a belt in his hand when we entered the house.

"What happened to my rug?" he asked.

None of us answered. Jeremy-Micah and Marie stood in a corner with fear on their faces. Mama stood behind them with a blank expression, like a mannequin. Brown moved closer to us, his eyes burning with rage.

"What. Happened. To. My. Rug?" Brown forced each word out through clenched teeth. His grip on the belt tightened. "I won't ask again."

"I... I spilled juice on it," I admitted.

Brown's fiery gaze fell on me. Terror seized me as he moved toward me.

"Leonard, stop!" Mama screamed. It was the last thing I heard before I found myself waking up in a hospital room. My head hurt as the bright lights blinded me for a bit. Jeremy-Micah sat in the chair beside my bed looking at me.

"What happened?"

"Dad slapped you and you fell and hit your head on the table near the front door," Jeremy-Micah whispered as he looked at the hospital room door. "But Mama said if the doctor asks, you *tripped* and hit your head on the table."

"She wants me to lie?"

"Your left eyebrow is split open and you're going to need stitches. If you tell them the truth, they'll take you away and we'll never see you again."

"But won't The Lord be mad at us for lying?"

Jeremy-Micah dug his fingernails into his upper arm as he crossed them. He didn't like the idea of lying either.

"If we don't do this, Dad will get mad at all of us," he said. Jeremy-Micah squirmed in his chair and looked at the wall. "I've never seen him so angry before..."

"Where's Terrence and Ruthie?" I asked him.

"They're at their dad's."

"Did Brown hit them too?"

"Yeah."

"Mama?"

"He'd be in the hospital too if he did. She tried to stop him, but he wouldn't listen."

"So, only the people he doesn't like..."

Jeremy-Micah looked at my face again and left the room. The doctor came in alone and stood next to me.

"Hello, Torrance," the doctor said with a smile. "Can you tell me what happened?"

"I fell into a table at home."

"What caused you to fall?"

"I tripped."

"No one pushed you or made you fall into it? No one hit you in the head with anything? You fell on your own?"

"Yes," I said. It made me sad to lie, but I didn't want to get taken away.

"Okay," the doctor sighed. "I'm going to bring your mom in so we can talk about fixing this, alright?"

"Okay."

After our conversation, the doctor gave me stitches above my eye and an eyepatch to cover them. When I got home, Marie wouldn't answer any of my questions. All she could say was Brown had scared her.

Terrence came back that night. His feet shuffled into our room, and I felt his eyes on me. I didn't feel like listening to him blame me again, so I pretended to be asleep. He opened the closet and left. The next morning, Mama came in and woke me up.

"Where's your brother and sister?" she asked.

"I don't know," I yawned.

"They never came back from Damian's?"

"Terrence did," I said as I picked the crust from my eyes. "I heard him open the closet door and then he left."

"He opened the closet and left?" Mama asked as she opened the closet. She looked inside and said, "All their clothes are gone."

"They are?" I got up from the bed and stood next to Mama. Sure enough, only my clothes were in the closet.

"Your brother didn't tell you where he was going?"

"No ma'am."

"Go wake your brother and sister up," Mama ordered. Her eyes flicked back and forth, which meant she was worried.

Jeremy-Micah and Marie didn't know where Terrence and Ruth-Anne were either when I woke them up. We went into the kitchen and saw Mama had made Ruth-Anne's favorite: pancakes with sausage and scrambled eggs. Brown strode into the room in his pajamas and yawned. I got comfortable on the couch to wait my turn to eat when a hand rested on my head.

"You're eating with us today," Brown told me.

Brown placed me in the chair next to his at the table and fixed me a plate. His being nice to me was weird, but I didn't want Brown to get mad and hit me again, so I went with it. Jeremy-Micah kept glaring at Brown throughout breakfast, and Marie wouldn't look at him at all. Then Grandpa stopped by. He greeted us and before I knew it, had lifted Brown from his chair by his throat.

"If you *ever* put your hands on one of my grandchildren again," Grandpa threatened. He squeezed Brown's neck. "I will kill you."

"Okay, okay," Brown coughed as he grabbed at Grandpa's hand.

Grandpa let Brown go and left. Brown left the house after breakfast, shaken up. When we were alone, I asked Mama if Grandpa would really kill Brown.

"I don't know," Mama answered. "I wouldn't put it past him though."

"You wouldn't?"

"Nope. Your grandfather told me he ran with the wrong crowd before he got saved. He told me some of the things those people did, and it wouldn't surprise me if he did them too."

"What'd they do?"

"Things that aren't suitable for little ears," Mama said as she pinched my ear.

Someone knocked on the door, and Mama went to answer it. I peeked out from behind the kitchen wall and spotted Pastor Derrick Harrison talking with Mama. Pastor Harrison was a funny man, but he was always mean to Mama and Brown.

"Are you really?" he asked Mama.

"You know what, get off my porch!" Mama snapped. "Asking me all these questions like you're the police!"

"Forget you too then!" Pastor Harrison yelled back. "I was trying to help you out!"

"I don't need your help, Derrick!"

"Clearly you do if three of your kids end up injured on the same day!"

"Ooooooh I–!" Mama slammed the door in Pastor Harrison's face and stormed back into the kitchen. "I can't *stand* him!"

"Why not Mama?"

"Because he always thinks he's better than somebody!"

"He's always nice to me..."

Mama looked at me, and it seemed she suddenly remembered I was in the room.

"Boy, get out my business!" Mama left the kitchen in a huff, leaving me to wonder what I'd said wrong.

Later that day, Mama took me with her to visit Grandpa. His house had wood flooring and many religious paintings on the white walls. Grandpa's big 'family Bible' sat on the living room table. It had beautiful decorations on the front and big letters on the inside. I sat at his feet, flipping through his personal Bible while he chewed Mama out.

"Marianne, sometimes you don't have the sense The Good Lord gave you!" Grandpa complained. He lifted the eyepatch from my face and looked at my stitches. "Look at my grandson's face!"

"Daddy, what happens in my house with my kids is my business."

"Your business is walking around town looking like a pirate," Grandpa argued. "My granddaughter is wearing sweaters in the heat to cover bruises on her arm, and my other grandson has disappeared to God knows where."

"He's at Damian's house."

"Grandpa!" I exclaimed as I landed on a colorful page in Second Samuel.

"What is it, Torrance?"

"What is this highlighted part?"

Grandpa took the book from my hands. I watched as his face turned sad for a moment. He flipped the page and handed the book back to me.

"It's nothing. Find something else to read."

I did as Grandpa said and kept flipping through the pages. He was already upset at Mama. The last thing I needed was for him to be upset at me too.

"Mark my words," Grandpa said. "If Leonard does something again, I'm taking the children to live with me."

Mama begged Brown not to hit me again after she talked with Grandpa, and Brown agreed. Brown mentally and emotionally tormented me for three years instead after that.

"If it weren't for your mother, I'd throw you out on the street right this second!" he told me when I was eleven. "Every time we argue it's over you! I can't believe she has me feeding another man's child!"

"Come with me to the ice cream truck," he said to us kids later that same day when he heard the jingle.

"And get all of them whatever they want too," Mama said. "Don't be stingy."

"Yeah, yeah," Brown huffed. He bought us our favorite ice creams. Mine was vanilla. Jeremy-Micah and Marie thought nothing of the action, but I knew he did it to make up for what he said to me earlier.

"Why do I have to pay for these when you're not even mine?!" he complained when I was twelve and needed glasses. "Maybe if you took that stupid eyepatch off, you could see something! All it does is make you look uglier than you already are anyways!"

"I'm taking you to see a movie at the drive-in tonight so we can put your new glasses to the test," he declared that same day. It was once again to make up for his earlier complaints. "I need to see if they were worth buying."

"Isn't that sweet?" Mama gushed.

By the time I was thirteen, I was used to Brown's emotional tug-of-war. It was always the same routine with him. He'd say something horrible when Mama wasn't around because she went off on him whenever she heard him. Then he'd do something nice in front of Mama to make up for his mean words and trick her into thinking he treated me well. But he never hit me again. Grandpa had scared him straight. In fact, Grandpa scared everyone in Creeke, including Pastor Harrison.

Pastor and First Lady Harrison held youth Bible study at the church every Tuesday night. They separated us by gender into two different rooms. I sat alone at Bible study because most of the boys didn't talk to me besides Alfred. That Tuesday, Pastor Harrison preached the passage from Second Samuel I'd seen highlighted in Grandpa's Bible. It was from chapter twelve.

"Let's review," Pastor Harrison said. "What's the first thing David did wrong?"

"He watched a hot girl take a bath," Sixteen-year-old Kasey Ferguson joked. Kasey was Marlin's lanky, light-brown, football player best friend at Creeke High with a lopsided fade haircut and mischievous hazel eyes.

"Really Kasey?" Pastor Harrison griped. "You couldn't find a better way to say it?"

"It's true though," Kasey said. He smiled with a mouth full of braces at Pastor Harrison.

"Anyways," Pastor Harrison sighed. "What's the next thing David did wrong?"

"He slept with Bathsheba," Sixteen-year-old Zackariah Graham answered. He was the youngest grandson of the town's barber, Mr. Riley Graham, and Marlin's other best friend. Zackariah was medium-brown with crooked teeth, waves on his head, and rolls throughout his back.

"Thank you, Zack," Pastor Harrison said. "Why was it wrong for David to sleep with Bathsheba?

The answer was David disobeyed God, slept with a married woman, and got her pregnant. But no one would say it.

"Anyone?" Pastor Harrison said.

More silence. I got fed up.

"Because Bathsheba was married to Uriah, David knew it, and he got her pregnant," I griped. "It's not that hard."

"Why didn't you say it the first time then, Brown?" Marlin said.

"Stop it," Pastor Harrison commanded. "Marlin, you answer the next question: How did David make things worse?"

"He tried to convince Uriah to sleep with Bathsheba so he could pin the baby on him, and when Uriah didn't agree, David had him killed and married Bathsheba," Marlin grumbled.

"And what was David's punishment?"

"He lost the baby," Sixteen-year-old Alfred answered.

"And what did God do after David repented?"

"He gave David a new baby and they named him Solomon," Alfred said.

"And what's the moral of the story."

"Don't lust," Marlin muttered. "Can we go home now?"

"Yeah, when the girls get done," Pastor Harrison said.

"Ugh," Marlin sighed.

I wasn't sure why Grandpa had that passage in his Bible highlighted. He always acted weird about it when I brought it up to him. If anything, the passage matched more to Mama's life than it did Grandpa's. The only similarity in the story I saw to Grandpa's life was that he'd given Mama the name Solomon as her middle name. As we waited for the girls to finish, I approached Pastor Harrison with the question that had been on my mind the whole night.

"Are you scared of my grandpa?" I asked him.

"Am I scared of Minister Jones?" Pastor Harrison chuckled. He stopped laughing and looked me in my thirteen-year-old eye. "Minister Jones is the scariest man I've ever met."

"He's not *that* scary."

"You don't know him like I know him, Torrance."

"What makes him so scary?"

"You sure do ask a lot of questions," Pastor Harrison said. He pointed at my black eyepatch. "I have a question for you: what happened to your eye?"

"I... I tri...tripped and...and fell," I stammered out the lie. It never felt right saying it. Although I didn't need an eyepatch anymore, I still wore one in public to cover the scar through my eyebrow.

"You tripped and fell?" Pastor Harrison asked the question in a way that sounded like he didn't believe me.

"Yes sir."

"Is someone picking on you? Because if someone's picking on you, let me know and I'll handle it."

I was tempted to tell Pastor Harrison about Brown. But if I told, I could be separated from my family. Pastor Harrison looked at me for an answer.

"Um...," I uttered as I looked around the room. My eyes landed on Marlin. "Marlin's picked with me before."

"I thought I told him to cut that out," Pastor Harrison said through his teeth. "I'll talk to him again. If he keeps picking on you, let me know."

"Yes sir."

Marlin *had* picked with me before. He'd started after I told on him for kicking a kickball at my face in second grade. It was clear he never liked me before that though, and I didn't know why. Pastor Harrison snatched Marlin up by his ear in front of his friends.

"Ow, ow!" Marlin yelped. "Dad, what are you doing?!"

Pastor Harrison led Marlin away to his office. Despite what I told Pastor Harrison, Marlin hadn't picked with me in a while. What I'd done might've made things worse between us.

Chapter Thirteen

Three years after leaving Brown's house, Terrence worked to become a police officer and helped Grandpa run choir practices. Ruth-Anne attended college to become a nurse and married Arnold at nineteen. Making music with my family became the highlight of my life. It brought me closer to my siblings. People started calling us the Brown Family Band, and our rising popularity made Grandpa happy.

"This is great," he told us when we visited him on a Friday evening. "More people will hear about how good The Lord is."

"Some of the church members don't like that we're becoming known," Terrence said. "They think you're using us for popularity."

"If I paid everyone's opinions any mind, no one would get ministered to," Grandpa said. "I work for The Lord, not them. He knows my heart and will judge me accordingly."

"Grandpa, are we still going to that gospel concert in the city tomorrow?" I asked.

"We're more than just going," Grandpa laughed. "Y'all are singing up there."

"We are?" Marie whispered.

"Don't you start that shy mess, Marie," Grandpa warned her. "I don't have the time or patience for it. Y'all are going to minister two songs up there. Understand?"

"Yes sir," Marie sighed.

"I want us all to wear black tomorrow," Grandpa said. "And don't eat any chocolate or peanut butter, and don't drink any soda."

"You want us to starve, Grandpa?" Jeremy-Micah joked. Grandpa cut his eyes at him, and Jeremy-Micah shrank back in his chair. "Sorry Grandpa."

"We're leaving at five o'clock on the dot," Grandpa declared. "Don't be late or you will get left."

"You hear that, Torrey?" Ruth-Anne teased. "That's for you."

"Shut up, Ruthie," I grumbled.

"You shut up."

"Both of you shut up," Terrence griped. "Don't nobody want to hear all that."

"Took you long enough," Grandpa said before sipping his drink. He sat his mug back down and said, "I won't have any arguing tomorrow either. We've got too much to do. Am I clear?"

"Yes sir," we all said.

"Good."

The next day, Grandpa picked me, Jeremy-Micah, and Marie up at five in the evening. Grandpa's car didn't have air conditioning, and he refused to let us roll the windows down. Jeremy-Micah sat up front with Grandpa, and Marie fell asleep next to me. As we flew up the highway, I imagined us on the church's pulpit that evening.

Every seat in the sanctuary was filled. There were five microphones for each of us and one at the organ for Grandpa. We stood up there in our all black, the lights shining down on us. I looked over at Grandpa, and he smiled back at me. He said something, but I didn't catch it. His smile faded, and he spoke again.

"Torrey, can you answer the man please?" Jeremy-Micah asked.

"Huh?" I said. I realized I'd been staring at Grandpa's face through the rear-view mirror.

"Is my hymnal back there?" Grandpa asked.

"Yes sir, it is," I said.

"Okay. Clean your ears out better."

Terrence, Ruth-Anne, and Arnold were waiting for us in Terrence's car when we arrived at the church. Grandpa reached behind his chair and grabbed his hymnal.

"Come on," he said. "We don't have all day."

Grandpa led us to the back row of the packed church. Although it was a Saturday, everyone wore the bright colors of their Sunday best.

"Grandpa, I feel like I'm going to throw up." Marie whispered as she held her stomach. "This is a lot of people."

"Marie Denise Brown, you're fourteen! If you don't stop acting scared and act like you have some sense! Who are you singing for?"

"The Lord," Marie mumbled.

"And what does he do?"

"Gives me strength to do all things."

"Exactly. Stop focusing on everything else and focus on what you came here to do, which is to sing for the Lord."

"Yes sir."

We sang our hearts out that night. My shoes were too big because Mama said I'd grow into them, and I got too excited and accidentally kicked one off. When the concert ended, Arnold took a picture of us on the church's steps. It was for his job at the Creeke Courier, but Grandpa also used it on the cover of the CD he had us record. He used a connection to get us into a studio. Some of our songs got played on the local radio station. Things were going great until Brown spoke up.

"I don't want them performing anymore," he argued with Mama one night. I listened to their conversation from my room.

"Why not?" Mama asked. "It's not like it's hurting anyone."

"It's one thing if they want to waste their time in that church choir up the street. But I'm not about to have my children going to Timbuktu to sing to a bunch of strangers."

"I don't see nothing wrong with it," Mama protested. "Besides, it makes Daddy happy and gets him out of my hair."

"I don't care what makes that man happy!" Brown exclaimed. "Clearly, you don't either or you'd watch what you eat like he raised you to. You've let yourself go."

"Say that again and I'll bring this skillet down right on your head!" Mama threatened. "Because I know full well, you're not talking about how I look when you've got a beer gut and a receding hairline! If anyone's let themselves go it's you! Plus, you said you liked my heavier size when we first got together, so don't start singing a different tune now!"

"Whatever," Brown grumbled. "He needs to stop giving Torrance solos. That boy is thirteen but still sounds like a little kid when he sings! Give me a break!"

"I thought you said you weren't going to listen to their 'little' CD, Leonard."

"I can listen to what I want."

I stopped listening and went to Marie's room to tell her what I'd heard.

"Brown doesn't want us to sing with Grandpa anymore," I said as I lay at the foot of her bed.

"Why not?"

"He said he doesn't want his kids traveling to Timbuktu to sing to a bunch of strangers."

"Oh," Marie said. "Oh well then."

"That's it? You don't care?"

"I like singing with Grandpa but singing in front of people makes me nervous. Plus, Dad's scary when he's mad and I don't want him getting mad at me."

"Well, I don't care if he gets mad at me," I declared. "What's he going to do? Hit me again?"

"He might."

"Not unless he wants Grandpa to kill him," I laughed. "I'm not going to stop singing."

"That's your choice."

Marie was right. It was my choice. I wouldn't stop singing, even if Brown said I sang like a little kid. At least that's what I thought. The more I thought about Brown's words though, the less I wanted to sing in front of people. By the time I was fourteen, I stopped singing publicly. Terrence and Ruth-Anne were too busy to sing with us anymore anyways. Jeremy-Micah would leave for college soon, which meant Marie and I would be the only children left. Brown got what he wanted. We didn't sing together anymore. But it wasn't enough for him. Every day, Brown stared at me and muttered to himself. He made his move one Friday in the summer.

Marie and I walked home from the store when Brown drove up next to us, and told us to get in. My suitcase was in the backseat. When we got home, he let Marie out but told me to stay in the car. Once she shut the door, Brown sped off. I didn't know where we were going. Brown stopped the car in front of Mr. Parker's house.

"Get out!" Brown yelled as he grabbed the suitcase.

I did as he said, and he dragged me by my arm to Mr. Parker's doorstep. Brown banged on the door and ran back to his car. He drove off as Mr. Parker ran from the house.

"Torrance, what the heck is going on?" Mr. Parker asked.

I shrugged, too scared to talk.

"Get in here," Mr. Parker groaned. He grabbed my suitcase and led me inside.

Mr. Parker lived down the road from Pastor Harrison on the edge of town. His house didn't have much furniture or decorations, except for a few photos of Terrence and Ruth-Anne on the wall. From what I could tell, Mr. Parker wasn't married. I picked at the ham and cheese sandwich he made me while he talked on the phone with Ruth-Anne.

"What should I do with him, Gracie?" Noah's at work, you've left for school, I don't know where Arty is, and Marie said Marianne isn't home," Mr. Parker spoke into the corded phone on the wall. He looked at me and put his hand over the bottom end. "Torrance, eat your food before it gets stale."

I nibbled on some of the chips and took a bite of the sandwich.

"Well," Mr. Parker sighed as he sat down next to me. "Your sister said she's going to call your grandfather to come get you, but it might be a few hours."

I nodded as Mr. Parker watched me chew the sandwich bite.

"Is something wrong with your sandwich?"

"There's no mayonnaise," I whispered.

"I knew I forgot something." Mr. Parker put his hand to his head the same way Ruth-Anne did when she forgot things. "Is that why you've been staring at it this whole time? Because its dry?"

I looked down at the table.

"Why didn't you drink the water then?" Mr. Parker motioned at the glass in front of me. "That's what it's there for."

"I didn't want to get in trouble."

"You sound just like my knucklehead son." Mr. Parker threw his hands up. "I'm not going to punish you for drinking water before you finish your food."

I grabbed the glass of water in front of me and chugged it down.

"Torrance, do you have any idea why Leonard would bring you here?"

I looked at Mr. Parker, and for the first time, I noticed how beige he was. He looked identical to Terrence and Ruth-Anne. The light-brown skin, the black curly hair, the dark-brown eyes. They all matched each other.

"Torrance, did you hear me?"

I held my hand up to the side of his face. It was darker than him.

"We're not the same color," I whispered.

"Did you think we were?"

"Brown always says I'm light like you."

"You're not that light," Mr. Parker laughed. "You're definitely a bit lighter than your father. But I'd say you're smack-dab between your mother and your grandfather. A nice caramel color."

"Who's my father?"

"Leonard," Mr. Parker said like it was common knowledge.

"He says he's not my father."

Mr. Parker sat up straight and wrinkled up his face how Terrence did.

"Who does he think is your father then?"

"You."

Mr. Parker's eyes grew big, and he started laughing. He laughed so hard his face turned red.

"It all makes sense," he said as he wiped a tear from his eye. "Torrance, do you have any homework?"

"It's the summer."

"Oh yeah…"

If I could choose a father, I'd choose Mr. Parker because he was nicer than Brown. Maybe if I called myself Torrance Brown-Parker, everyone would be happy. We spent the whole afternoon together playing games and telling stories. Mr. Parker had lots of stories.

"Do you have a girlfriend?" I asked.

"Not right now."

"Why not?"

"The woman I was dating said she needed time to figure things out," Mr. Parker sighed. "You'll understand when you're older."

"You were dating Ms. Thelma, right?"

"Yeah, I was dating Thelma."

"Why do you, Mama, and Ruthie call Terrence, Noah?" I asked, changing the subject. Talking about Ms. Thelma seemed to make Mr. Parker sad.

"Because when he was younger," Mr. Parker said as he tried to hold back laughter. "I used to read him and Gracie bedtime stories from the Bible when they would stay over. One night when he was around six, I read to them about Noah. The next morning it rained, and the street was a little flooded. Terrence took all of Gracie's stuffed animals, put them in the bathtub, and locked himself and Gracie in the bathroom. He was scared the Earth would flood. Apparently, he fell asleep and missed the part where I said The Lord created rainbows as a promise to never flood the whole Earth again. Ever since then, I've called him Noah."

"I call him Meanie because he's mean."

"Now Torrance," Mr. Parker chastised. "That's not nice. I'm sure you can think of something nicer to call him."

"Mikey and RieRie call him Methuselah because he's the oldest."

"I guess that's… better than Meanie… want to hear another story?"

"Okay," I said.

Mr. Parker kept me entertained with stories until Grandpa came and got me around six that evening. He was fuming.

"Damian, thank you for watching him until I could get here."

"No problem. He's a good kid."

Grandpa and Mr. Parker talked a bit more while I got in the car. After they finished, Grandpa drove me home. When we got there, Brown's car was in the driveway.

"Stay in the car," Grandpa said.

He got out, and I noticed something sticking out the back of his pants. Grandpa went it the house, and Marie came out a few minutes later.

"What's going on?" I asked.

"Grandpa is in there yelling at Mama. He told me we're going with him to his house tonight which means I get to ride in the front."

"No, you don't. I was here first!"

"Well, I'm the oldest, so yes I do."

She opened the door and unbuckled my seatbelt. I pushed her, and she pushed me back. Marie tried to pull me from the car when we heard it. A loud pop. Mama screamed, and Grandpa came out of the house.

"Get in the car...," Grandpa whispered to Marie. It was like he was in a daze.

"What happened?" Marie asked.

"Get in the car!" Grandpa yelled.

Marie got in the backseat, and Grandpa took us to his house. Jeremy-Micah later came by and told us Brown had been admitted to the hospital. Mama wouldn't tell him what happened, but she told him that Marie and I would be living with Grandpa from then on.

Chapter Fourteen

Grandpa was lonely after Grandma died. Mama rarely visited him before the incident and wouldn't speak to him at all after it. Once Marie and I came to live with him, Grandpa came alive. Us and the church were his world.

That Saturday, Grandpa prayed on the church's altar with Bishop Lionel Harrison. Grandpa prayed for forgiveness and asked that The Lord heal Brown. He asked us to pray for that too, but I only prayed that he and Mama reconciled. I didn't care what happened to Brown. Once they finished, Grandpa filled Bishop Harrison in while I played songs on the organ.

"Gabriel, what possessed you to shoot your son-in-law?"

"I was angry."

"The Bible says to be slow to wrath, for the wrath of man worketh not the righteousness of God. What if Leonard presses charges on you?"

"He won't."

"You don't know that."

"If he does, he'll have to explain why I shot him in the first place. He won't want to do that."

"Just because I call you 'The Gangster for Christ' doesn't mean you have to act like one," Bishop Harrison sighed. "You are not that man anymore. That part of you died when you gave your life to Christ. How can you expect to lead the music ministry if you're out of order? How can you expect to be a good example to your grandchildren if you're in jail?"

"I know. But that Marianne..."

"Is a grown woman who's made her choice. I wish you and my pig-headed son would get that through your thick heads and stop doing things that lead you astray. Who do you sing for? Who do you play that organ your grandson is playing on for?"

"Cut that out!" Grandpa snapped at me. "That's not a toy!"

I stopped playing.

"Don't lose sight of what's important," Bishop Harrison said as he shook Grandpa by his shoulders. "This can't happen again. Understand?"

"Yeah... Thanks Lionel."

We carried on as normally as we could. Jeremy-Micah told us that Brown said he accidentally shot himself in the leg. He had to walk with a cane for the rest of his life. Grandpa was right. Brown wouldn't press charges on him.

Church was weird that Sunday. Pastor Harrison preached a sermon that made the adults uncomfortable. Then, Marlin cornered me after church while I was waiting for Grandpa.

"Hey snitch," he sneered. He was still mad about what'd I'd told his father the previous year. "You know my dad was talking about your mama in his sermon, right?"

"No, he wasn't."

"Yes, he was. Everyone knows your mama cheated on Mr. Damian and got pregnant with your brother."

"So?"

"Word on the street is she did it again, and Mr. Damian is your dad," Marlin whispered. "Mrs. Thelma found out and that's why they broke up."

"That's not true!" I yelled.

"I bet you don't even know who your father really is," Marlin teased.

"Leave me alone!"

"Hey, don't get mad at me." Marlin threw his hands up. He hadn't noticed his father standing next to him yet. "It's not my fault your mama don't know–!"

Pastor Harrison smacked Marlin in his mouth before he finished the sentence. It grew silent enough that you could hear a pin drop on the carpet.

"Fix your face before I fix it for you," Pastor Harrison told his son as he wiped his hand on his pants. He dragged Marlin to the back of the church. Grandpa and Marie found me, and we left.

"What was that about?" Grandpa asked when we were in the car.

"Nothing."

"Now look, Derrick can be a bit rough and have a slick mouth sometimes. But he doesn't just haul off on people, especially not one of his sons, over nothing. What happened?"

"Marlin said something he didn't like."

"What'd he say?"

"Nothing," I complained. "Can you drop it, please?"

"Boy," Grandpa glared. "Don't get beat down in this car."

I released a frustrated breath and looked out the window. Not having a father sucked. Mama maintained Brown was my father, but if Marlin told the truth, it explained why Mr. Damian was always nice to me. But if Mr. Damian *was* my father, he would've already claimed me. Questions clouded my head, and no one would give me a straight answer. Everything sucked.

That same year, Terrence married Sarah. Sarah was a lawyer with average looks, and she was five years older than Terrence. They married when he was twenty-two. Jeremy-Micah was his best man, and he let me be his ring-bearer.

"When you walk up the aisle, don't walk too fast," Terrence told me as he fixed my tie. We were at Grandpa's house getting ready for the wedding. "There's a tear in the carpet near the front, so if you're not careful, you'll trip."

"I'm not going to trip," I griped.

"I'm just making sure you know."

Terrence was always hard on me for no reason. He returned to fixing himself in the mirror, and Jeremy-Micah started brushing my hair.

"Aw, lay off him, Methuselah," Jeremy-Micah laughed. "Hasn't Torrey had a hard enough year as it is without you picking with him?"

"I'm not picking with him! I want to make sure he knows what he's doing."

"Don't mind him, Torrey," Jeremy-Micah whispered as he finished my hair. He always was the better older brother in my eyes. "He's stressed."

Terrence left to check on Grandpa, leaving Jeremy-Micah and me alone.

"How are things here at Grandpa's?" Jeremy-Micah asked as he put on his tie.

"Good," I said. "It's so much better here than at Brown's."

"That's good. Mama calls me every day and tells me she misses you and Marie."

"She can always come and visit us."

"That's what I said. But she said she doesn't want to see Grandpa."

"Does Brown miss us?"

Jeremy-Micah ran his brush over his head.

"Mikey?"

"He misses his Ladybug."

My stomach knotted up. Brown only missed Marie. He didn't care that I was gone.

"Don't let that get you down," Jeremy-Micah said as he bent down in front of me. "Today is a happy day. So, let's be happy, alright?"

"Alright."

The wedding was nice. All the bridesmaids wore purple dresses. Marie was the flower girl even though she was fifteen. Mama sat with Ruth-Anne and Arnold on the left, while Grandpa sat on the right with Sarah's parents. Not even Terrence's wedding got them to talk. Mr. Parker sat in his usual spot in the back of the church near the door. Terrence tried to get him to sit up front with the rest of the family, but he refused.

My turn to go down the aisle came, and I walked slowly as Terrence suggested. He stared at me the whole time. I didn't trip over the tear in the carpet, and I heard him release a quiet, relieved sigh.

When it was time for Sarah to appear, everyone stood up and looked toward the back. The doors opened, and Sarah came down the aisle with her father. White lace covered her dark-brown skin, and a thick veil covered her face. Terrence pushed back the veil to reveal Sarah's smiling face, and Mama started weeping.

"Do you, Terrence Lee Parker, take this woman to be your lawfully wedded wife?" Pastor Harrison asked.

"I do."

"Do you, Sarah Eileen Martin, take this man to be your lawfully wedded husband?"

"I do." Sarah gazed into Terrence's eyes.

"I now pronounce you husband and wife," Pastor Harrison said. "You may kiss the bride."

Terrence locked his lips onto Sarah's, and everyone started cheering and whistling. It was the happiest I'd ever seen Terrence be, and I wished he stayed like that forever.

Chapter Fifteen

Marie and I had lived with Grandpa for one year, and his dream of us singing together ended. Ruth-Anne had a baby and would start nursing school soon. Terrence had a baby too, and Jeremy-Micah was in college. Grandpa was happy to have great-grandchildren, but he and Mama still wouldn't talk. Instead, he focused on getting Marie and me through our teenage years in one piece.

"RieRie, hurry up!" I whined as I pranced outside the bathroom door one morning. "I need to pee!"

"Give me a few minutes, Torrance!" Marie called from the other side.

"Marie!" I banged on the door. "I can't wait a few minutes!"

"What are y'all arguing now?" Grandpa sighed.

"Marie's taking forever in the bathroom, and I have to pee!"

"Marie?" Grandpa asked as he knocked on the door. "You alright in there?"

"I'm fine. I need a few minutes, Grandpa."

"Go use my bathroom," Grandpa told me.

"But–!"

"Go!"

Grandpa gave me a look that shut me up. I barely made it to his bathroom. Once I finished, I realized I was alone in his room. Temptation got the best of me, and I opened what he called his 'memory book'. It was a picture book full of old pictures and papers that belonged to Grandma Mavis. I'd never seen anything in it because Grandpa said the book made Grandma sad. Upon opening it, I saw two birth certificates.

One had the name 'Abel Joel Jones' printed on it, and the other 'Abigail Elizabeth Jones'. The parents listed were Gabriel Jones and Mavis Ellis.

"What are you doing?" someone asked, startling me. I turned to find Grandpa staring down at me.

"Grandpa, who are these people?"

"Why are you looking through that?"

"I was curious," I said. "I thought Mama was your only child."

"Lord," Grandpa sighed as he removed his glasses and rubbed his eyes. "Marianne is my third child."

"Your third child?"

"Abel and Abigail both died at birth. Marianne was the only one to survive."

"Oh... I'm sorry, Grandpa."

"This is why you stay out of people's stuff."

I put the book back and followed Grandpa to the living room.

"I don't know what to do with you," Grandpa complained as I sat with him on the couch. "First, you're fighting with your sister, then you're being nosy. Do you ever act right?"

"How come you always get mad at me?" I whined. "You never get mad at Marie. Like earlier when she hogged up the bathroom, you yelled at me and not her."

"I have twelve sisters. If I've learned anything, it's that sisters need to do certain things we don't have to. And us adding more stress on top of that only makes things worse and everybody angry."

"Hmph...," I grumbled.

"You know I'm right."

"You ready, Torrey?" Marie asked as she fluttered into the living room. Marie was sixteen and started wearing makeup and trying different hairstyles. But she was still as shy as ever.

"I'm ready," I announced as I stood up.

"Now you two be on your best behavior," Grandpa said as he saw us to the door. "Don't be out there fighting with each other."

"We'll be fine, Grandpa," I said.

"Alright," Grandpa said as he shut the door.

When Marie and I made it to the sidewalk, I looked at her.

"What?" she said.

"If you were on your period, you could've just said so," I teased.

"Torrance!" Marie gasped as she blushed.

"Last one there is a rotten egg!" I yelled as I ran before she could do anything.

"Ooooh!" Marie chased after me. "I'm going to get you!"

It was summer, and the party spirit was in Creeke's air. Leilana Allen was the queen of teen parties. She was a slim, light-brown girl that was the same age as me. Every year since we were twelve, she threw a big summer party.

The sun was out, music blasted from the boombox, and I was swum with a bunch of other kids in Leilana's pool. I loved being in the water. Something about it made me feel at ease. Marie had run off with her friends to do her own thing.

"Yo Torrance!" one of the other kids yelled when I exited the pool. "Spit a rhyme for us, man!"

"I'm at the pool in the summertime, cause it's cool to do something outside of school," I rhymed as someone played a makeshift beat with their hands. I'd taken to rap like a moth to a flame. It was a fun, new avenue of music for me to explore, and I didn't have to sing to do it.

"Alright!" someone else cheered me on.

"Everybody's here to have some fun, in the sun, the party's only just begun," I continued. "My rhymes put you in trance, while I work on my suntans. I might even do my dance and everybody around will yell–! "

"Torrance!" a voice screamed. It belonged to Marie's friend, Athena.

"Woah," I laughed when she reached me. "Perfect timing, Athena."

"Marie needs you," Athena panted.

"What's wrong?" I asked as I followed her.

"I don't know. Me and one of the other girls went to the restroom and when we came back, she was crying."

Marie sat hunched in a chair with her towel wrapped around her. Her knees hid her face, and I could hear her sniffling.

"What's the matter?" I asked as I bent down next to her.

"Marlin said I looked like a pig," Marie cried.

"He said what?!" I yelled as I stood up. "Where is he?!"

Marlin, Kasey, and Zackariah were talking to Soleya Perry and Leilana. The boys towered over the girls lounging in pool chairs. As I approached them, I could hear Zackariah trying to flirt with Soleya.

"What's up with you, Leya?" Seventeen-year-old Zackariah said to Soleya.

"Boy please." Soleya dismissed him with a handwave. I couldn't help but look at her bright orange bathing suit as she adjusted her sunglasses. "My men need to have money."

"I got money," Eighteen-year-old Kasey puffed out his chest. Soleya pulled her sunglasses down and looked him up and down.

"Girl, anyways," she giggled as she turned to Leilana.

"Man, y'all ain't even cute anyways," Kasey spat. "Bunch of gold-diggers."

"First of all." Leilana glared at the boys with her dark-brown eyes. Her kinky black hair was pulled into a ponytail behind her head, and she wore a light purple bathing suit. "Don't worry about us. Worry about Torrance standing over there with both eyes out looking like he's ready to kill y'all."

The boys turned and looked at me.

"What?" Marlin barked.

"You said my sister looked like a pig?"

"And if I did?"

"Okay." I didn't want to ruin Leilana's party, so I walked away. But one thing was certain: I *would* get him for making Marie cry.

On the walk home, I spotted Marlin and his friends ahead of us. If I approached him, they'd jump me. So, I had to make him come to me. A smile crept across my face as I looked down at my feet. Sometimes, Mama threw her shoes at Brown when she got mad at him.

"What are you doing?" Marie asked as I removed my right shoe.

"Nothing," I said as I chucked my shoe at Marlin. I understood why Mama threw them. Throwing that shoe made me feel powerful. For the first time, I felt like I was in control. It landed square in the back of Marlin's head.

"Ooooooooh!" Kasey instigated.

Marlin put his hand to his head as he looked around. His eyes landed on me.

"You threw your shoe at me?!"

"And if I did?" I repeated his words back to him.

"You're dead meat, Brown!" Marlin declared.

He ripped his shirt off, pulled his shorts up, and charged at me like a raging bull. Marlin knocked the wind out of me as he rammed me into the ground.

"Urgh!" Marlin grunted as he punched me. He was stronger and faster than I remembered. My left arm was pinned under his knee while Marlin held my other arm in his hand to keep it still. Every punch he threw was more agonizing than the last.

"Man, he's done," Zackariah laughed. "Let him up."

"Nah!" Marlin hollered. "I'm going to kill him!"

I tried to wiggle my arm free, but it wouldn't budge. Usually, Marlin would let me go once it was clear he'd won. But Marlin didn't want this fight to end. He kept swinging, and I feared he'd really kill me.

"Get him off me!" I cried.

"You wanted to fight, right?" Kasey mocked. "Fight back!"

Marlin stopped punching me. He looked down at me, and a wicked grin spread across his face.

"Yeah Torrance," he teased. "Fight back."

"Let me go," I growled.

"Aw man," Marlin laughed. It wasn't a warm laugh like his father's. His laugh was cold and cruel. "And here I was thinking we were getting along for once."

"Let me go!"

"I'll let you go," Marlin said. "If you cry."

"Yeah boy," Kasey sneered as he walked up. He kicked me in my side, and I clenched my jaw. "Cry so I can go home."

"Hurry up and cry!" Zackariah pleaded. "I can't hold her back much longer."

I turned to see Zackariah holding Marie back. She was desperately tried to get away from him.

"Daddy!" she screamed.

"Cry," Marlin snarled. He held up a fist to signal he wouldn't ask again. A scratch rested on the side of his face, and I pieced together that Marie had tried to rescue me. Instead of avenging her, I was pinned to the ground, and it made me burn with anger. Another punch crashed into my nose, and my eyes watered.

"Hey!" someone yelled. "What's going on?!"

"Bro!" Kasey panicked. "Let's go!"

"I ain't scared of him," Marlin claimed, referring to whoever was yelling.

"Get off him!" the person yelled again. They were getting closer.

"Marlin, come on!" Kasey grabbed Marlin and dragged him off me. "I can't get in trouble again!"

"Man whatever!" Marlin shoved Kasey away. He turned to Zackariah and said, "Let her go and come on!"

Marlin ran off with his friends. Marie helped me up and dusted me off. We were in front of Brown's house.

"Look at your face," Brown groaned. He squeezed the bridge of his nose and shook his head. "Everybody's going to think I did this to you. Come in the house so we can clean you up."

Brown limped toward the house with Marie right behind him. My feet stayed rooted to the ground as I stared at the brown, bricked house with white window shutters. Walking through the black bars on the screen door would be like returning to a prison I'd escaped. I didn't want to go back in that house.

"Come on boy!" Brown hollered. "Got me out here breaking up fights knowing full well I can't hardly walk!"

I took a deep breath and entered the house. Everything looked the way it did when I left. Brown led me to the kitchen and wet a rag. He put it to my face, and I winced under its sting.

"Stop moving," Brown fussed as he dabbed at my face. I sat still. Brown sucked his teeth and said, "Good grief boy. You can't start fights if you don't know how to win one."

"I've beaten him before," I grumbled.

"I couldn't tell. I'll tell you like I told Jeremy-Micah. When you fight, you do whatever you have to do to win. You don't see him losing fights out here."

"Why do you care whether I win or lose?"

"Because boy." Brown scrunched his face up. "You can't have the last name Brown and then be out here getting bullied by someone like Marlin Harrison. Browns don't lose to Harrisons."

Brown removed the eyepatch from my eye.

"Why do you still wear this thing?"

"Because I don't want people to see my scar."

Brown looked at the scar that split my eyebrow into two pieces.

"Sorry...," he muttered as he turned his face away from me.

"What for?"

"Your eye," Brown said. He still wouldn't look at me. "Sorry."

I couldn't believe it. Brown apologized to me for something.

"I have a scar too," he said.

"You do?"

"Yeah." Brown removed his sock to reveal a giant scar on the bottom of his right foot. "I slipped and cut my foot on a rock while swimming in the creek when I was around your age. When I called to my father for help, he laughed at me and said he hoped I drowned."

"Why'd he do that?"

"He's mean. My mother had to rescue me."

Hearing about Brown's childhood made me feel a little bad for him. He did many things to me, but he never told me he hoped I died. I realized I had him in front of me, and he wasn't angry at me for once. This was my chance to ask him the one thing I'd always wanted to know.

"Are you my father?"

"I don't know," Brown admitted. He stopped wiping my face. "I did my best, but you still might have some bruises."

"That's alright," I said as I slipped my eyepatch back on. "Thank you."

"You're welcome, T-Rex," Brown mumbled.

I'd heard that nickname before when I was young. A man held me and called me '*his little T-Rex*', but I couldn't remember his face. Terrence's words about how Brown was nice before I was born rang in my ears. It sucked that we didn't know the truth. Maybe if we did, our relationship would've been different.

I couldn't hide the evidence on my face from Grandpa when I got home, and he forced me to tell him about the fight. He called the Harrisons, and they agreed to have a mediation. That evening, First Lady Kiana Harrison brought Marlin to Grandpa's house.

"What happened?" First Lady Harrison asked me.

"Marlin said Marie looked like a pig," I explained. "So, I threw my shoe at his head, and we fought."

"Is this true?" First Lady Harrison asked Marlin.

"Yeah," Marlin mumbled.

"Why'd you call Marie a pig?" First Lady Harrison glared at her son, causing him to shift away from her.

"Because she had on a pink bathing suit!"

"Lord have mercy." First Lady Harrison buried her face in her hands. "Apologize! Now!"

"Sorry," Marlin grumbled.

"And you need to apologize for throwing your shoe at his head," Grandpa told me.

"But–!" I protested.

Grandpa gave me that look, and I shut up.

"Sorry," I muttered.

"Now hug and make up," First Lady Harrison said.

"Seriously Mom?!"

"What'd I say?"

"Man!" Marlin sucked his teeth and stood up. "Get up!"

I stood up and waited as Marlin approached me. A hug was the last thing I wanted from him, but I'd take it if it got him to leave faster.

"I won't forget this, Brown," Marlin whispered in my ear as he hugged me.

"Neither will I," I whispered back.

-

Chapter Sixteen

As I got older, I understood better why Mama wanted to leave Grandpa's house by any means necessary when she could. Marie left for college, and I was the only child left with Grandpa. He was strict about everything, especially the music I could listen to. Grandpa hated rap, and he lost his mind one day when he caught me listening to it.

"It's just music, Grandpa," I complained as I followed him up the hallway. He'd unplugged my radio and was carrying it away.

"It's not just music, Torrance Dean!" Grandpa yelled. "When the Devil was still an angel, he was the minister of Heaven's music. Music is the easiest way for him to influence you!"

"Grandpa, I'm seventeen. Don't you trust me to make good decisions?"

"Nope! I trusted Marianne to make good decisions and she ended up pregnant."

"But I'm not Mama," I whined.

"I don't want you listening to that devil music in my house anymore," Grandpa said as he shook his finger in my face. His brown eyes glowed with determination as his face burned red with anger. "Do you understand me?"

"Yes sir," I sighed. Sometimes Grandpa irritated me. I pictured myself flinging my shoe at the back of his head like I did Marlin. But then I felt bad. Grandpa didn't deserve that, especially since he'd rescued me from Brown.

The keywords to Grandpa's command were 'in his house.' So, I didn't listen to rap 'in his house' anymore. I listened to it outside his house. And Leilana was more than willing to help me do that. Her parents didn't care what she listened to.

"You come over here so much, people will think we're dating," she teased me one day when I was at her house doing homework.

"So? You'd probably like that anyways."

"Me date you?" Leilana laughed. "No offense but you're not my type."

"Well, you're not my type either."

"Rude!"

"You said it first."

"Whatever pirate. Are you coming to my party after the game Friday night?"

"Grandpa doesn't let me go to parties anymore after that fight I had two years ago."

"Your grandfather doesn't let you do anything."

"Even if I wanted to go, I still wouldn't. Pastor Derrick asked Pastor Hall to have someone recite a scripture for the main service this Sunday, and he chose me. I'm spending my weekend memorizing Psalms twenty-three."

"That'll be fun," Leilana snorted.

"It can't be that hard. It's only six verses."

"Good luck with that. I'll be sure to enjoy myself for the both of us."

The football game was at Preston High. It was the big rivalry game between the Creeke High Cowboys and the Preston High Pirates. Kickoff was at five-thirty that evening, and I didn't want to miss a single second of it. Grandpa never went to away games because he said they took too long, and he didn't like driving at night. My curfew was at eight because that's when he locked the front door. Sometimes, he'd make exceptions though and give me his house key.

"Here's some money to get yourself some food," Grandpa said as he handed me a ten-dollar bill. "Find someone to give you a ride home, and don't lose my key. If you do, you'll be spending the night outside."

"Yes sir," I said as I exited the car.

"Have a good time. And try not to get in any trouble."

"Okay."

Grandpa drove off, leaving me on the curb all alone. The game was exciting, and all eyes were on Marlin. As the years rolled by, he picked with me less. He'd tried to be a linebacker freshman year like his dad, but he sucked at it. However, he was a great quarterback and worked his way up to becoming the star of the team.

"RUN BOY! RUN!" Pastor Harrison hollered at his son as he ran along the front edge of the stands. First Lady Harrison sat nearby giggling at him with two women that looked like her.

The stands erupted into a roar of cheers as Marlin scored the winning touchdown. Creeke stomped Preston, and everyone filtered from the stadium after the game. I looked for somebody to give me a ride, but there weren't any familiar faces around. Before I knew it, almost everyone was gone. My only options were to walk or hitch a ride with a stranger. So, I prayed and asked The Lord to get me home.

"Yo!" Someone hollered at me as I trekked through the city. Marlin hung from the passenger window of Kasey's car. I ignored him and kept walking. The car pulled up beside me, and Marlin glared at me. "I know you hear me calling you!"

"Leave me alone, Marlin," I grumbled as I kept walking. "I'm not in the mood."

"Look," Marlin complained as the car followed me. "It's obvious you need a ride so get in the car!"

"Why would I get in a car with you?!"

"Because we're going to the same place, idiot!"

"Just leave me alone!" I yelled as I ran away from the car. There had to be a better option. The sound of footsteps behind me grew louder, and I turned to see Marlin chasing me. I tried to outrun him, but he was too fast. Marlin chased me into an alley and cornered me.

"Look here," Marlin growled as he crossed his arms. The car pulled up behind him, illuminating his imposing figure. He looked like a superhero come to life. "If my father finds out I saw you and didn't help you, he'll get mad at me. And if he gets mad at me over you *again*,

I'm going to beat you up again. So, you either get in the car or I put you in the car. Either way, you're getting in the car so we can take you back to Creeke."

I looked between the car and Marlin. Although he'd just finished playing a whole football game, he looked like he could still put up a fight.

"Alright," I grumbled.

"See?" Marlin said as he got in the car behind me. "That's all you had to do in the first place!"

"Just take me home."

"We'll get you home," Kasey laughed from the driver's seat. His eyelids drooped to the point they almost looked closed. "We just have to make a stop first."

"A stop?" I asked as I glanced at Marlin. He shrugged.

"It'll be fine," Kasey said. "I need to get something for Leilana's party, that's all. Sit back and enjoy the ride."

Kasey drove to a convenience store and went inside. Marlin and I were alone. It suffocated me to be in the car with him. He could do what he wanted to me, and no one was around to stop him. I pictured him lunging at me and pinning me down by my neck.

"You thought I forgot about what you did?" Marlin growled as he squeezed the air from my throat.

"No," I squeaked. "Please!"

"I told you I'd get you, Brown," Marlin laughed.

"No..."

"What's wrong?" he teased. "Why are you trembling?"

The car began to rotate. It was hot and my hands were sweaty. Marlin would kill me.

"H... help!" I rasped.

"Brown," Marlin said. "Breathe."

"H...huh?"

"Breathe," Marlin repeated. "You're okay."

He held me by my shoulders. It seemed like it took an eternity to calm down.

"Do you always have panic attacks?" Marlin asked.

"I was having a panic attack?"

"Yeah."

"How do you know?"

"My dad has them all the time."

"And you helped me?"

"Do I look like I want to sit next to someone having a panic attack?"

"Thanks, I guess...," I mumbled.

"Why were you walking all alone?" Marlin asked.

"Because I couldn't find anyone to give me a ride."

"Why didn't you ask my parents for a ride?"

"I couldn't find them."

"Guess it's a good thing Kasey and I were still around then."

"Why *were* you still around?"

"I didn't want to ride the bus, so I snuck away after the game and had one of my friends cover for me. I hid out in Kasey's car until the coast was clear. Any more questions?"

"Yeah," I said. "Would you have really beat me up if I didn't get in the car?"

"You got in the car, didn't you? So, don't worry about it."

"Why do you always have to be mean to me? What'd I do to you?"

"For starters, you threw a shoe at my head. You've always put your hands on me first. You lied on me and told my dad I was picking on you."

"Look, your father was asking me questions and I had to tell him something. And I hit you because you pick on me."

"I wasn't when you lied on me," Marlin grumbled. "I'd left you alone after my dad went off on me. Even got Kasey and Zack to leave you alone too. And then you lied and got us all in trouble *again* just like you did when I accidentally kicked you in the face with that kickball. So, it's like 'what's the point of behaving if I'm going to get in trouble anyways'? Because every time I try to do right, someone gets me in trouble with my parents for stuff I didn't even do!"

"That's why you've been picking with me this whole time?"

"Heck yeah!" Marlin exclaimed. "Why not tell him the truth?"

"Because...," I muttered. "Look, I'm sorry. I didn't mean to get you in trouble."

"Whatever, man," Marlin sighed. "I'm too old and got too much going on to be picking with people anyways."

"How about a truce then?" I suggested as I extended my hand to him. "You don't start with me, and I won't start with you."

"Alright," Marlin agreed. He took my hand and shook it. "Deal."

The radio ran through two songs before Kasey returned.

"Did you guys have fun?" Kasey laughed.

"Kase, we need to get Brown home," Marlin said. "He's not doing too well."

"Alright, alright," Kasey laughed. "I get it. You want to see Soleya already."

"Kasey."

"Relax, Marlin," Kasey said. "We'll get Brown home in one piece. Just sit back and enjoy the ride."

Kasey spent the whole ride chatting, laughing, and munching on the snacks he'd bought. He revealed Zackariah moved away from Creeke after graduating high school among other things. We arrived in Creeke a few minutes before ten, and Grandpa had gone to bed by the time I got home. I went to bed thinking about everything that'd happened. Marlin did right by me and made sure I got home safely. It was weird to see him be nice.

"The Lord is my shepherd, I shall not want," I recited from memory in my room the next day. "He maketh me to lie in green pastures. He leadeth me beside still waters. He restoreth my soul... He... He leadeth... ugh."

I looked down at my Bible again for the umpteenth time. Memorizing this passage turned out to be harder than I thought. I'd heard these verses used my whole life but putting them together seemed impossible.

"How's it going?" Grandpa asked.

"Horrible," I sighed. "Who knew memorizing six verses was this hard."

"You can do it," Grandpa encouraged me. "Keep practicing and you'll get it."

"I want it to be perfect. I don't want to get up there tomorrow and make a fool of myself."

"You're not going to make a fool of yourself." Grandpa put a hand on my shoulder. "Whenever I need to remember something, I make a song for it."

"A song, huh?" I said. "You use music for everything."

"Of course, I do," Grandpa chuckled. "It's my gift from The Lord and it's what I'm good at. Music is a tool that can bring people together."

"Is that why you wanted us to sing together so badly?"

"It was the only way everyone would get along. I remember the day I realized it too. Y'all were sitting in the living room, acting a plum fool. Jeremy-Micah and Marie were arguing, Terrence was running me ragged with questions, and Mavis almost burnt the house down doing Ruth-Anne's hair. You had to have been about five or six, and you were just running around the house like a maniac. Every time I tried to make you sit down, you took off somewhere."

"I don't remember this."

"Well, I do. Your grandmother had the radio playing and this one song came on and it got quiet. Then one by one, you all started singing until you all sung together. After that moment, everyone was peaceful. Except you. You just refused to sit still and eventually I had to pop you. Then that night, I had a dream you all sung together on a stage. Everyone had on these nice brown clothes but for some reason you specifically didn't have on any shoes, Torrance. After that, Marie kept messing with your grandmother's tambourine, you and Jeremy-Micah started playing with my organ, Terrence was always humming something, and Ruth-Anne danced all over the house. You all took to music and got along."

"Until Brown happened," I grumbled.

"That's alright." Grandpa ruffled my hair. "At least we had fun while it lasted."

"Yeah," I sighed. "Did you used to sing with Mama when she was young too?"

"I tried once." Grandpa made a face of pure and utter disgust. "The Lord said make a *joyful noise* unto Him. Marianne made a noise, but it wasn't joyful to listen to."

"Sounds like Mama," I giggled as I thought about the times Mama sang to us. The sound she made was indescribable. "You still haven't talked to her?"

"It's her choice." Grandpa looked down at my desk and drew a few circles on the surface. He patted my back and said, "I'll let you get back to it."

Grandpa and Mama hadn't talked to each other in three years, and it was all because of Brown. Even when I was away from him, Brown still haunted me. He was the reason my life was the way it was. The reason I'd stopped singing. My Bible sat open in front of me. I could make a song like Grandpa suggested to help me memorize this passage. Or I could do things my way. All I needed was a beat.

"Duh duh-DUH duh... duh DUH..." I hummed as I beat my hands against the desk in a steady rhythm. I added the words to it. "The Lord is my... shepherd. I duh-DUH shall... not want."

My stomach cramped up Sunday morning. I hadn't done anything in front of a congregation since I was thirteen. No wonder Marie was always nervous about singing to people. Jitters shook me as my breakfast threatened to make an appearance on the church's carpet.

"You ready?" Pastor Forrest Hall asked me as we waited off to the side. The twenty-eight-year-old had replaced Pastor Derrick as the youth pastor at Creeke Church. His dark-brown skin always shined, and he smelled like cocoa butter.

"I'm a little nervous."

"If I didn't think you could do it, I wouldn't have asked you to," Pastor Hall encouraged me. "You've got this. Okay?"

"Okay."

My time to present came. I ascended the pulpit and looked out at the church. All eyes were on me.

"The Lord is... my shepherd," I stammered. "I shall not want... He... He..."

"That's alright, baby!" One of the church mothers yelled. "Take your time!"

I'd forgotten the verses. My body froze as my worst nightmare became reality. I searched for the words that came next, but I couldn't find them. They were a jumbled, tangled mess in my brain, and I couldn't put them in the correct order. A stray piano note cut through the silence, and we all turned to the culprit.

"Sorry...," Grandpa whispered. He glanced at me before looking down. It was a signal. A reminder of what we'd talked about the night before. I had no choice. Using the song I'd created was the only way I'd get through this.

"The Lord is my... shepherd," I restarted as I closed my eyes. I patted out the beat I'd made against my leg. "I... shall... not want. He maketh me... to lie. Down... in green... pastures. He restoreth... my soul. He leadeth me... in the. Paths of righteousness. Yea though I walk... through the. Valley of the... shadow. Of death I will... fear no. Evil for thou... art with. Me, thy rod and... thy staff. Comfort me, thou preparest. A table before me. In the presence of mine. Enemies, thou anointest. My head with oil... my cup. Runneth over, surely goodness. And mercy shall follow. Me all the days... of my life. And I will dwell in the house of the Lord forever."

I opened my eyes to a silent congregation.

"Amen, amen, amen," Pastor Harrison said as he joined me on the pulpit. "Y'all give Torrance a hand. Don't be shy. It takes a *boldness* for The Lord to get up here and minister to His people."

The congregation slowly started to clap. Pastor Harrison grabbed me by my shoulder and pulled me into a side hug.

"I'm just letting you know now that your grandfather does not look happy," he whispered in my ear with a smile. He raised the microphone back to his face and said, "Thank you, Torrance. Take your seat."

As I returned to my seat, I stole a look at Grandpa. He didn't look happy at all. After service ended, I built up the courage to ask him about his thoughts.

"Grandpa, how do you feel about how I did?"

"I'm not happy with it," Grandpa admitted. "But I can't help but feel like it was the only way you were going to memorize your passage. And since Christ was still preached, I guess I'll live."

"So, you're not upset with me?"

"No, I'm not upset. I *am* disappointed though because you disobeyed me. I told you I didn't want you listening to that devil music anymore, but it's clear you didn't listen to me."

"Grandpa, this is a part of who I am."

"Who you are," Grandpa said as he cut his eyes at me. "Is a child of God."

"Isn't God the Creator of all things? Doesn't that mean He also created rap?"

"When the Lord creates, it's too glorify Him. What part of 'rap' glorifies God?"

"Christian rap exists Grandpa."

"But that's not what you're listening to, now is it?"

"You told me yesterday that music is a tool that can bring people together? Why can't rap be a tool that glorifies God?"

"Because I told you I didn't want you listening to it, and you disobeyed me. And The Lord doesn't like disobedience. You can't serve Him and be in rebellion at the same time. I'm done talking about this."

I sat back in my seat and looked out the window. There were things Grandpa and I wouldn't agree on, and I had to accept it.

-

Chapter Seventeen

I'd made it to my senior year of high school without any interest in girls. Not until Leilana. Talking to her made me nervous, yet I never wanted her to leave my side. I wanted to be around her forever. And with the prom coming up, it was the perfect time to ask her to be my girlfriend.

"Does she have a date?" Soleya repeated my question as she slammed her locker shut. "I don't know."

"Come on, Leya," I whined. "You're her best friend. How do you not know?"

"Try not to stand too close to me," Soleya said as she looked around the hallway. "I don't want people getting the wrong idea."

"Wrong idea about what?" I scrunched up my face. "Everyone knows you're dating Marlin."

"Yeah, well that doesn't stop people from letting their imaginations run wild."

"Same old Leya," I teased as I followed her up the hallway. "Always worried about what everyone else thinks."

"*My image* is very important to me," Soleya stated as she glared at me. "And if you want my help getting Leilana to go to prom with you, I suggest you don't do anything to jeopardize that."

"Alright, alright." I threw my hands up in surrender. "I won't walk too close to you."

"Thank you," Soleya said. "I'll ask her at lunch if she has a date so make sure you're paying attention because I'll give you a signal. If she has a date, I'll flick my hair like this."

Soleya paused to toss a fingerful of hair over her shoulder.

"And if she doesn't, I'll get up and walk away for a bit. That's your cue to ask her to prom because I'm only getting up once. I look too cute to be doing all that walking."

"You're wearing a school uniform though…"

"I look cute regardless of what I have on."

"Okay," I said. "Thanks, Soleya."

"Yeah, yeah," Soleya said as she waved me away so she could go to class.

The day trudged on as I waited for lunch to come. My thoughts centered on how I'd ask Leilana to prom. I replayed the scenario several times in my head, imagining the moment when Leilana would say yes.

"Leilana?" I asked as I took her soft, manicured hand in mine.

"Yes Torrance?" she whispered with her angelic voice.

"Will you go to prom with me?"

"I thought you'd never ask!" she cried. "Of course, I'll go with you! I'll be your girlfriend too!"

"You will?!"

"I will!"

Leilana leaned across the table. I watched as her face moved closer to mine. My eyes closed as I waited for our lips to touch.

"Mr. Brown!" the teacher yelled. My eyes snapped open, and I realized I was still in class. "This isn't nap time. Try to stay awake please."

"Yes ma'am," I said as I shrank in my chair. Every thought I had was about Leilana. It would crush me if she had a date. And my world would shatter if she had a boyfriend.

Lunch came, and I watched Soleya and Leilana like a hawk. I wasn't missing my chance to ask Leilana to prom. Halfway through lunch, the back of my chair took on weight.

"Is there a reason you keep staring at Soleya?" Marlin asked as he towered over me.

"She's helping me with something."

"With what?"

"None of your business."

"Look Brown," Marlin sighed. Soleya looked our way and got up from the table. She walked towards us as Marlin said, "We've been doing really good with this truce, and I'd hate to ruin it over my girlfriend. Everyone knows we're together."

"I know."

"Why do you keep looking at her then? And why are people telling me they saw y'all walking together earlier?"

"Marlin, what are you doing?" Soleya asked as she reached us.

"I'm holding up my end of our deal and having a man-to-man conversation with Brown about looking at you."

"Can you please tell your boyfriend you're helping me with something so he can leave me alone?" I complained.

"What are you helping him with?" Marlin demanded.

"I'm helping him ask Leilana to prom," Soleya explained.

"You needed help with that?" Marlin teased me.

"You're one to talk," Soleya said.

"How was I supposed to know you wanted to be together?"

"Look," Soleya said with a smile. "Torrance needed help. That's it. Now, if only he'd get with the program and go ask."

"I'm waiting for your signal," I protested.

"Hello?" Soleya said in a breathy tone like she was singing. "I'm up from the table."

"Oh!" I shot up from my chair. "Right now?"

"Lord, have mercy...," Soleya groaned. "Yes, right now!"

I'd almost missed my chance to ask because of Marlin. I flopped into the chair in front of Leilana. She blushed when she saw me.

"Um...," Leilana whispered. "Leya's sitting there."

"I'll be quick," I told her. I looked into her eyes and forgot my words. "So..."

"So...?"

"I was wondering...," I started slowly before rushing through the rest. "If you'd like to go to prom with me?"

"Huh?"

"Will you go to prom with me?" I repeated more slowly.

"Su... sure, I'll go with you," Leilana stuttered as her lips curled into a smile. My heart thumped so hard it threatened to leave my chest.

"You will?"

"Yeah. My dress is aquamarine so try to match that."

"Aquamarine? What color is that?"

"It's...," Leilana said before stopping. "Just go with black. It goes with anything."

"Okay," I agreed. I couldn't contain my excitement.

"Um...," Leilana said. "Leya's still sitting there."

"Ri...right!" I stuttered. "I... I... I... I'll go now."

That evening, I helped Grandpa with dinner. As I snapped beans, I fantasized about the wonderful time I'd have with Leilana at prom. I'd never felt this way about someone before. It was weird and exciting.

"Grandpa... how do you know if you're in love?"

"In love?" Grandpa looked up from the potato he was peeling. He eyed me. "You're eighteen. What do you know about being 'in love'?"

"I don't know," I said. "How did you know you were in love with Grandma?"

"I married her."

"Grandpa!" I whined.

"It's true. I married her because I was in love with her."

"*When* did you know you were in love with her?"

"Now that's a different question," Grandpa said with a wink. "I knew I was in love with your grandmother when I didn't see her at church one Sunday and it made me upset. Turned out she was so sick she could hardly move."

"How did you two meet?"

"Through Lionel," Grandpa told me. "It was my first time at the church and Mavis caught my eye. I'll never forget it. She was all done up and had this pretty yellow dress on."

"And you guys fell in love like that?"

"Heck no!" Grandpa laughed. "Mavis wasn't thinking about me like that at first."

"Then how'd you two end up together?"

"It was a lot of trial and error," Grandpa reminisced. "But eventually, I got Mavis to agree to a date with me and we took it from there."

"I see."

"Now what's got you so interested in romance all of a sudden?"

"No...nothing!"

"Mhmm," Grandpa said with a smile. "You've got a little crush on someone, don't you?"

"Cut it out, Grandpa!" I felt my cheeks burn.

"Aww you do!" Grandpa teased. "What's her name?"

I snapped a bean in the wrong place.

"Shoot!" I exclaimed. "Look what you made me do, Grandpa. Now, it's all messed up."

"You are such a perfectionist," Grandpa sighed. "The bean doesn't have to be evenly snapped for you to eat it."

"It would've been even if you weren't teasing me."

"Don't get beside yourself now, Torrance Dean," Grandpa warned. "I'm still your grandfather."

"Sorry sir..."

"I'll find out who your mystery girl is soon enough anyways," Grandpa chuckled. "Nothing stays hidden for long in this town."

The day of prom was a nerve-wracking one. Grandpa let me drive his station wagon. It still didn't have air conditioning, but at least I could choose to roll the window down. I'd never been as nervous as I was picking up Leilana. Her parents weren't as strict as Grandpa, but they weren't pushovers either.

"You go straight to prom, and you come straight back," Mr. Jared Allen told me as we waited for Leilana to get ready. He was light-brown with an afro.

"Yes sir."

"You look too eager," Mr. Allen said, leaning his face close to mine until our noses touched.

"Sorry sir!" I squeaked.

"Boy, you are too funny!" Mr. Allen howled. He copied my posture and mocked my voice. "Sorry sir!"

"Daddy, stop messing with him!" Leilana yelled from her room.

"Why don't you hurry up then, Buttercup?" Mr. Allen called back. "Torrance will have died and gone off to be with The Lord by the time you finish getting ready."

Leilana strode into the living room in her aquamarine dress, and her hair straightened for the occasion. She could've told me aquamarine was a shade of blue.

"You look phenomenal," Mr. Allen said. "Don't you agree, Torrance?"

"Yeah!"

"Alright, let me get my pictures!" Mrs. Ernestine Allen exclaimed as she grabbed a wind-up camera off the living room table. She looked like Leilana but older.

"Aw Mom!" Leilana protested.

"The faster she gets her pictures, the faster you can go Buttercup," Mr. Allen stated.

Mrs. Allen held us hostage long enough to use up the entire roll of film. By the time we got to prom, we'd already missed an hour of it. The food was decent, the music was great, and Soleya and Marlin won prom queen and king. After their first dance, we all joined them on the dance floor. As Leilana and I swayed to the beat of the music, I looked at her radiant face and felt my stomach knot up. This was my chance.

"Leilana?"

"Hmm...?"

"I had a nice time with you tonight."

"I had a nice time too."

"And I was wondering..."

"What's up?"

"Will you be my girlfriend?"

"Took you long enough, pirate," Leilana giggled before leaning her head against my chest. "I thought I was going to have to tie you down and force it out of you."

A feeling of celebration washed over me as my body relaxed. Leilana agreed to be my girlfriend. We were an item. My life was complete.

-

Chapter Eighteen

Leilana and I married when we were nineteen and had three kids by the time we were twenty-two. Drake Jared Brown was my oldest child born in the December that I was twenty. He looked like me. My oldest daughter, Karla Elizabeth Brown, came in January a year later, and she looked like Leilana. Then after her came Mary Ann Brown in February the following year. Mary looked like Mama, so we named her after Mama.

Despite these wonderful things, none of them reconciled Mama and Grandpa. Eight long years passed without either of them speaking to the other. Any time we had family events, they stayed as far apart as possible. They were stubborn, but I wanted to reconcile them. I first started trying with Grandpa when I was eighteen.

"Grandpa, you haven't talked to Mama in four years."

"I'm not talking to that stiff-necked little girl! Been trouble since the day she was born, and she'll be trouble till the day I die. If she wants to talk, she knows where I live."

Once I couldn't get through to Grandpa, I tried to convince Mama.

"Mama, you should talk to Grandpa. You know he's getting up there in age."

"I'm not talking to him! Since I was little, all he's done is nitpick every little thing I do!"

"It's only because he loves you Mama."

"If Daddy wants to talk, he knows where I stay. I don't want to talk about this anymore Torrance and that's final!"

It seemed more likely I'd learn who my father was before they ever talked again. I'd spent four years trying to get them to talk, and nothing I did worked. I needed a new approach. So, I took Bishop Lionel Harrison to lunch. He was Grandpa's best friend, which meant he'd have the most info on him.

"You've known Grandpa a long time, correct?" I asked.

"Since he first came to Creeke," Bishop Harrison answered. "My father and his Uncle Garland agreed that I should mentor him after he got here. That boy ran me ragged then and he still does all these years later. I still love him though."

"Do you know what his life was like before he came here?"

"Only what he's told me. I'm sure it's the same stuff he told you."

"He hasn't told me much about his younger days," I admitted. "I was hoping you could tell me something."

"I can't betray your grandfather's trust like that." Bishop Harrison took my hand in his. "I'm sure if you ask him, he'll tell you what you want to know."

"I don't think he will."

"Why not?"

"Because... it's a long story."

"I'm an old man with nothing but time," Bishop Harrison announced as he sat back in his chair.

"Well... a few years ago, I noticed Grandpa had a passage from Second Samuel highlighted in his Bible. And every time I brought it up to him, he got sad. I didn't think much of it until I found the birth certificates for his other two children. Then I noticed some similarities between the passage and Grandpa. Like how he and David both lost children, and then gave their new children the name Solomon. Granted, in Mama's case it's her middle name instead of her first name."

"That's quite a theory you've got there," Bishop Harrison said. He crossed his arms and looked down at the table. "What brought this on?"

"I'm trying to get Mama and Grandpa to talk again."

"Oh," Bishop Harrison sighed. He uncrossed his arms and sat up. "To tell you the truth, I don't know exactly what happened before your grandfather came to Creeke. But I do know Gabriel took losing Abel and Abigail hard."

"You knew their names?"

"Of course, I did," Bishop Harrison laughed, a hint of sadness in his voice. "Those babies were all Gabe talked about. He was so excited for them. Your grandparents nearly lost their minds after Abigail's death. It was to the point that Mavis didn't even want to be pregnant again. I didn't know what we were going to do if Marianne didn't make it."

"It was that bad?"

"Gabriel kept blaming himself for their deaths. No matter what I told him, he maintained it was his fault. He still does."

"Do you think that's why he's so hard on Mama?"

"That's something you'll have to ask him. Only Gabriel and God know the reasons he does the things he does."

"Thank you, Bishop."

"You're welcome," Bishop said as he picked up his fork. "Now, let's dig into this lunch. I didn't come all the way out here to starve."

Grandpa stared at the forbidden picture book when I stopped by his house after lunch. He had it open to the birth certificates.

"Grandpa."

"Yeah?" Grandpa responded without looking up from the book.

"We're going to see Mama."

"No."

"I wasn't asking."

"Who in the world...?" Grandpa began as he threw the book on his side table.

"It's been eight years since you talked to her," I said. "*Eight.*"

"So?"

"What if you dropped dead right now? Would you be okay with leaving this Earth without speaking to Mama again?"

"It's what she wanted."

"If Mama wanted to jump off a bridge, would you let her jump off the bridge?"

"No..."

"So why would you let eight years go by without talking to her?"

"Because it's–!"

"Yeah, yeah, it's what she wanted," I finished his sentence. I pulled him to his feet. "You know what I want? *I* want you and Mama to talk again. So that's what we're going to do."

"You're blessed I'm not as young as I used to be!" Grandpa complained as I led him towards the door. "Because all these smart-alecky remarks would've got you knocked in your head. I don't care if you are twenty-two!"

I dragged Grandpa over to Mama's house. He pouted the entire time, but I didn't care. These two would talk if it was the last thing I did.

"I'll go in and talk to her first," I said when we arrived. "And if I think it's okay, I'll come and get you."

"Don't take too long," Grandpa grumbled. "It's cold out here."

I grabbed Grandpa's Bible from the backseat and went inside the house. Ever since the fight I had there, I'd timed my visits to when Brown wasn't home. Seeing him in a softened state made me warier of him. It reminded me of when he'd be nice to amend the horrible things he did. Mama sat in the living room watching television.

"Torrance!" Mama cried as she hugged me. "What are you doing here?"

"I need to talk to you."

"What's going on?"

"It's about Grandpa."

"What about him?" Mama mumbled.

"I want you two to talk again."

"Didn't I tell you I didn't want to hear about this again?"

"Hear me out," I pleaded.

Mama crossed her arms and pushed an annoyed breath through her nose. I opened Grandpa's Bible to the passage and handed it to her.

"What's this?" she asked.

"It's Grandpa's Bible."

"Why are you giving this to me?"

"Did you know Grandpa and Grandma had two other children before you?"

"Yeah, Abel and Abigail," Mama said as she shifted in her seat.

"Do you know what happened to them?"

"Mommy told me they were both stillborn. What does this have to do with me talking to your grandfather?"

"Everything," I responded. "Mama, did you ever wonder why Grandpa is so hard on you?"

"Because he wants to control my life," Mama said in an 'isn't-it-obvious' tone.

"No."

"No?" Mama wrinkled her face up. "What do you mean 'no'?"

"Mama, I think Grandpa is hard on you because he's scared to lose you."

"Seriously?" Mama snorted.

"Look at his Bible." I motioned to the book in her hand. "Look at the passage he's highlighted."

"What's so special about this?" she asked.

"Well... I mean...," I stammered. "Grandpa lost two kids... and then he had you... and your middle name is Solomon..."

"Torrance, David lost his first son because he was disobedient to God."

"I know that. But why else would Grandpa have this passage highlighted?"

"Did you try asking him?"

"Several times and he always told me not to worry about it."

"Why are you worrying about it then?"

"Because I want you two to reconcile!" I complained. I rubbed my temples and headed for the door. "Wait there!"

"Where else am I going to go?" Mama called as I left the house.

I walked to Grandpa's side of the car and flung the door open.

"Boy, don't fling my door open like that!" Grandpa snapped.

"Sorry!" I huffed. "But you and Mama are making this harder than it needs to be!"

"She doesn't want to talk to me."

"Oh no," I protested. "You are going in there. We're not leaving until you two talk."

"You sure are stubborn about this," Grandpa sighed.

"I've had great role models."

I led Grandpa into the house. He stared at the back of Mama's head before going to stand before her.

"Daddy?" Mama gasped when she saw Grandpa. "What are you doing here?"

"Your son wanted us to talk." Grandpa maintained his indifferent composure as he sat on the other end of the couch. "Let's talk."

"Alright." Mama crossed her legs. "Daddy do you like me?"

"What do you mean 'do I like you'?" Grandpa scoffed.

"It's just always felt like you didn't like me. You're always yelling at me..."

"Because you do stupid things."

"...And you get mad at me all the time..."

"Only when you do stupid things."

"...And you interrupt my sentences..."

"Don't get smart, Marianne."

"So, you must not like me."

"If I didn't like you, I wouldn't be here," Grandpa argued. "I'm your father. It's my job to raise you and steer you in the right direction."

"Daddy, I'm not a little girl anymore. I'm a grandparent like you now!"

"That doesn't mean I stop being your father, girl."

"Well, you haven't been around in the past eight years."

"That's what you wanted."

"No, it isn't."

"You told me you were a grown woman and you wanted me out your life. So, I left."

"You'd just shot my husband and took my kids! I was upset and spoke out of anger!"

"Oh well," Grandpa sighed. "Can't do anything about it now."

"Do you treat me like this because of Abel and Abigail?

"Where'd that come from?"

"That's what Torrance thinks," Mama said. "And the more I think about it, the more it makes sense. You don't give me any room to have a life. It's like everything I do has to make you proud and when it doesn't, you come in and bulldoze over it all. It makes me feel like I'm just a big disappointment to you."

I understood how Mama felt. Sometimes, I felt like a disappointment to Grandpa too. He was hard to please, and it seemed like I never did anything right in his eyes. All I wanted was for him to be proud of me for once.

"You've made some disappointing decisions," Grandpa sighed. Mama's face fell, and she started crying. "But I would be a hypocrite if I didn't admit that I've made some disappointing decisions too."

Grandpa moved closer to Mama.

"Marianne, all I've ever wanted is what's best for you." Grandpa held Mama's face in his hands. "You don't know how badly I've wanted to talk to you these past eight years."

"So why didn't you?" Mama asked. She wiped a tear from her face.

"Because I was scared I'd make things worse and lose you for good."

Mama sobbed as she wrapped her arms around Grandpa. They cried and hugged until no more tears remained. I'd never felt happier than I did seeing Mama and Grandpa reunited. That feeling stayed with me as I returned home.

"Leilana?" I called for my wife. She came flying from the room with Drake in her arms.

"You're home!" she cheered. "I have to tell you something."

"What?" I joked. "Are you pregnant again or something?"

"Maybe..."

"Seriously?"

"I took a pregnancy test earlier," Leilana announced as she bounced up and down. "It came back positive."

"Another baby," I said. I would be twenty-three with four kids. And the only thing on my mind was how I would afford them all on a janitor's salary.

-

Chapter Nineteen

I was twenty-three when Grandpa died at the age of seventy-three in November. He'd gotten sick, and soon his body couldn't handle it anymore. It was hard to process. I couldn't sleep, I couldn't eat, my thoughts were all over the place, and I didn't want to go anywhere. Grandpa was gone.

Grandpa was the youngest and only boy of thirteen kids. Eleven of his sisters were dead. The only one alive was the one born before him, Aunt Leanne. Aunt Leanne was seventy-five years old. Freckles dotted her light-brown face, and she held a glint of joy in her eyes. She flew into town the day before Grandpa's funeral and would stay with Ruth-Anne for the whole weekend.

"My!" Aunt Leanne gasped as I led her into Ruth-Anne's house that evening. "This sure is a beautiful home, Ruthie. Very pristine."

"Thank you," Ruth-Anne said.

"And who is this?" Aunt Leanne gushed over the little girl watching television in the living room.

"That's my daughter, Naomi," Ruth-Anne introduced them. "Mimi, this is your Aunt Leanne."

"Hi," Naomi said as she waved.

"Why hello there," Aunt Leanne said. "How old are you, sweetie?"

"Seven."

"You sure are a pretty little girl. Just like your mother."

"Auntie!" Ruth-Anne giggled. "Mimi, tell Auntie 'Thank you'."

"Thank you." Naomi said.

"You're welcome, sweetie," Aunt Leanne responded. She followed us into the kitchen. "Such a precious little thing and she looks just like you too, Ruthie."

"Thank you, Auntie," Ruth-Anne said. "Arnie's still at work, but Mama should be here any minute."

"Wonderful! It's been a minute since I've seen Marianne."

We talked with Aunt Leanne as we waited for Mama. She told us stories about Grandpa, her sisters, and herself from when they were younger. Each story was a memory Aunt Leanne held close to her heart. After five stories, Mama came bustling into the kitchen with a rectangular pan in her hand.

"Auntie!" Mama sat the pan on the table and threw her arms around Aunt Leanne.

"Hi sweetheart!" Aunt Leanne rocked Mama back and forth in her arms.

"Sorry I took so long," Mama apologized. "I was waiting on this lasagna to get done."

"That's alright," Aunt Leanne told Mama. She looked her niece over and beamed. "You've really grown into a beautiful woman. I still remember when Gabriel brought you home to see us for the first time when you were just a cute little baby. As soon as he gave you to Susan, you spit up all over her and she didn't want to hold you no more after that."

"Aunt Susan was mean," Mama complained as she sucked her teeth. She sat at the table with us.

"Susan was just bossy because she was the eldest," Aunt Leanne giggled. "By the time Gabriel was born, Susan was already twenty and out the house. She'd get mad when we listen to Ophelia over her because Ophi was the eldest in the house when most of us were growing up."

"How was Aunt Ophi the oldest in the house if Aunt Susan was the oldest?"

"Well, Susan, Loretta, and April were already grown when Gabriel was born. Josephine said she didn't want to listen to 'no crying baby every night' so she went to live with Loretta. That left Ophi as the eldest there."

"I don't know how Grandma managed thirteen kids," Mama said. "I could barely handle five."

"That's just how it was back then," Aunt Leanne answered.

"Oh!" Mama exclaimed. "One of my aunts used to make me chocolate chip cookies every time we visited. Who was that again?"

"That was Agnes. That girl could bake like nobody's business."

"Who was the one who used to read me bedtime stories when we'd visit?"

"Charlotte. She was the smart one."

"And then there were the three Daddy used to call his 'Calendar sisters' because he said y'all's mom ran out of names."

"April, May, and June," Aunt Leanne laughed. "Lord, they used to hate when Gabriel called them that."

"Who was the one that got on everyone's nerves? Daddy would never tell me who it was."

"Josephine," Aunt Leanne grumbled. "Every time Josie came around to visit, she was always complaining about something."

"Daddy also said one of his sisters hated him."

"Louise," Aunt Leanne sighed. Her tone of voice made it clear she didn't want to discuss Aunt Louise anymore.

"Who was the one Daddy said loved rolling around in the dirt?"

"That was Cara," Aunt Leanne giggled. "She couldn't keep anything clean to save her life."

"Like Torrance," Ruth-Anne teased.

"You can see the floor in my house," I argued.

"No thanks to you," Ruth-Anne snorted. "You've probably got poor Leilana working hard to keep the house clean behind your clumsiness."

"You mean the same way you run poor Arnie ragged over leaving a single spoon in the sink?"

"Stop it you two," Mama chastised. "Your auntie's here and all you two want to do is fuss."

"I don't mind," Aunt Leanne said. "They remind me of me and Gabriel when we were younger. Tell me, is Marie still super shy?"

"As shy as she's always been," Mama grumbled. "The girl is twenty-four years old and still talking like she's a baby. I was hoping her husband would bring her out her shell, but it seems she's only gotten worse."

"Just like Ophi," Aunt Leanne laughed as she clapped her hands together. Her face became sad. "They're all gone now. It's just little old me here by myself now."

"At least my Auntie Leanne is still here," Mama said. She squeezed Aunt Leanne's hand. "Smelling just as good as she always has."

"I do always smell good, don't I?"

"You do," Mama agreed. "Today, you smell like cinnamon."

"That's my lotion," Aunt Leanne said. She stood up and reached for her purse. "I should start getting ready for bed. We've got a long day ahead of us tomorrow."

The viewing of Grandpa's body was at ten in the morning. I didn't handle it well, but at least I handled it better than Bishop Harrison did. He collapsed in a puddle of tears when he reached the casket. I'd never seen him so broken down before. Mama threw on a black skirt for the occasion. As we waited for the funeral to start, people came up to us to offer their condolences.

"Hey...," Ms. Thelma Reid greeted Mama as she approached with Mrs. Kiana Harrison.

"Thelma!" Mama cried as she embraced them. "Kiana!"

"I know," Ms. Thelma said as she rubbed Mama's back. "I know."

"We're here for you," Mrs. Kiana said as she fixed Mama's hair. "Whatever you need, we're here."

"Okay," Mama said as she wiped her face. "I'm okay."

Grandpa's funeral was unreal. A mixture of singing, laughter, and tears filled the room as the service went along. Pastor Hall ministered to us because Bishop Harrison was too upset to do it. Mr. Derrick Harrison was sat down the month before, so he couldn't do it either. He didn't even want to be called Pastor anymore. The time to read the obituary came, and I opened my program to look at the summary of Grandpa's life that Mama wrote:

'Gabriel Ray Jones was born to Rosario Jones and Lilly Harvey Jones.

Gabriel was the youngest and only boy of thirteen children. He was known to be a rowdy boy, and that rowdiness grew into a passion for The Lord as Gabriel aged. Gabriel moved to a small town called Creeke when he was fourteen and graduated from Creeke High School.

Gabriel took on a job as a sanitation worker in the city before retiring to be the music minister at Creeke Church. Gabriel took his position seriously and did his best to encourage others to walk on the right path. He married Mavis Ellis and they remained together until her death. He was preceded in death by his eleven sisters and two children, Abel and Abigail.

Gabriel is survived by his daughter, Marianne Brown; sister, Leanne Clayton; grandchildren, Terrence Parker, Ruth-Anne Green, Jeremy-Micah Brown, Marie Garza, and Torrance Brown; and a host of great-grandchildren, nieces, nephews, and friends to cherish his memory.'

I zoned out after finishing the obituary. It all became too much for me, and I needed a break. Soon, the time for remarks came, and I tuned back in.

"Gabriel was my baby brother," Aunt Leanne started off the remarks. She dabbed at her eyes with a handkerchief. "Two years younger than me. And even though I was his older sister, I looked up to him sometimes. I always admired how confident he was, especially when it came to The Lord. If Gabriel felt like it wouldn't please Jesus, he wouldn't go for it, and I loved that about him. My brother didn't let anyone run over him, and I just know he's up there right now cutting up in Heaven."

"My best friend," Bishop Harrison said during his turn. He looked down at Grandpa's casket, and his lip quivered. Bishop Harrison latched onto the podium to balance himself.

"Whew Lord," Bishop Harrison exhaled as he wiped some tears off his face. He released a sad laugh into the air. "Lord, I can hear him now: *'What you crying for?! You know where I'm at!'* If Gabe didn't do nothing else, he screamed and hollered at *all* of us. But that's what I loved most about him. You never had to question how Gabe felt, and you knew something was wrong if he wasn't fussing. And even with all that fussing, he was still one of the most patient men I knew. All the hardships this man endured in his life, he *had* to be patient. Because if he wasn't, Gabe would've been in jail. Gabe was one of the strongest men I knew, and I'm really going to miss him."

"Minister Jones did not play," Mr. Derrick said. "Especially when it came to his faith in God. Do y'all know this man came to my house in the middle of the night and whooped me on my eighteenth birthday? Because of how I chose to celebrate *my* eighteenth birthday? And then showed up on my doorstep the next day with a cherry pie like nothing happened?"

Mama bent down to pick at her heel, but I could see her trying to stifle a laugh. I couldn't imagine Grandpa whooping someone as big and strong as Mr. Derrick.

"This man scared me!" Mr. Derrick continued. "Every time I was around him, I made sure I was on point! And the older I get, the more thankful I am to him for being who he was. He could've been a 'Sundays-only Christian' and lived how he wanted to Monday through Saturday. But he didn't do that. He chose to be a good and faithful servant every single day, and he held us accountable if we didn't do the same. Things around here won't be the same now that he's gone."

"I've known Gabriel since he first moved to Creeke," First Lady Judith Harrison reminisced. "Watching him grow and change into the man he became was a sight to see. But one thing that was always consistent with Gabriel was how giving he was. He was always there to lend a helping hand if you needed it. Gabriel was a good man, and we're so blessed to have had him for as long as we did."

"Grandpa liked peace," Terrence stated when it was his turn. "He didn't allow me and my siblings to fight in his presence. If we did, I was the that got in the most trouble. He'd always say, *'you're the oldest, it's your job to keep the peace!'*. I'd always get mad because why am I the only one getting yelled at? But now as a father of three kids, I understand. Where there's peace, there's unity. Grandpa loved unity. In his home, the church, the community. He did whatever was necessary to keep the peace in his life. And he made sure we knew how to keep the peace in our lives too."

"Grandpa was kind," Ruth-Anne sniffled. "Yeah, he yelled a lot, but we knew it came from a place of love and kindness. There was never a time I couldn't go to Grandpa for anything. If I needed encouragement, I knew I could go to him because he'd always tell me the truth. It was his kind and encouraging words that got me through nursing school. I love you Grandpa, and I'm going to miss you."

"Y'all are going to look at me like I'm crazy, but Grandpa was full of joy," Jeremy-Micah laughed. "You can't get in front of a whole church and play an organ the way he did, and not be full of joy. Singing for Jesus? Ministering to the people? That brought him joy. He'd always get so excited when we'd sing with him, because he loved sharing his love for music with us. And when we started singing in front of people, you couldn't tell him *nothing*. It was always *'who are you singing for?'* and *'and what does He do?'* with him. Jesus was his joy, and even though I'll miss him, I'm happy Grandpa's finally reunited with Jesus at last."

"I... I used to think Grandpa... was mean when I was little," Marie whispered. "He'd always... get onto me for being... shy. But the older I got... the gentler he became. Grandpa knew the importance... of being just as gentle... as he was tough. I'm so thankful... I got to have him in my life."

"Do you want to say something?" Mama whispered to me after Marie sat down.

I looked at Grandpa's casket. Just beyond it sat the church's organ. As I stared at the instrument, I pictured Grandpa sitting there. He ran his fingers across the keys, and his voice rang in my ears.

"It's my gift from The Lord and it's what I'm good at."

"Torrance?" Mama asked as she tapped me.

I crumbled. Tears flowed from my eyes as I mourned the man who'd raised me. There weren't enough words to describe how he impacted my life. Grandpa was gone. Mama got up and went to the podium.

"The last words my father said to me were, *'I love you, baby girl'*," Mama sighed. "My father was a loving man. His heart was so full of love, even if I didn't always see it. We butted heads a lot, but we never stopped loving each other. I don't think I can explain how sad I am that he's gone. But I am comforted by the fact that I know he's in Heaven and that one day I'll see him again. Goodbye Daddy, I love you."

The Tuesday after the funeral, I found Terrence alone in the church, staring at the organ. He'd been appointed the new music minister and was trying to teach himself how to play. Terrence still sounded boring and dull when he sang. But since he'd helped Grandpa run the choir, he was made the music minister.

"You know, RieRie or Mikey could play for you while you teach the songs," I said as I approached him.

"I've almost got the hang of it," Terrence replied as he removed his glasses and rubbed his eyes. He'd never admit he needed help, but I could see that he was struggling. All he needed was a little nudge in the right direction.

"Do you mind if I play for a while?" I asked.

Terrence didn't say anything, but he scooted over on the bench. I sat down and removed my shoes. It felt freeing whenever I took them off. Grandpa taught me how to play by having me watch him, and I did the same with Terrence.

"You know," I said as I played slowly enough for Terrence to see what I did. "I used to think you didn't love me."

"Why on God's green earth would you think that?" Terrence asked as he looked up from my hands.

"Because you were always mean to me."

"I was not."

"You told me you wished I wasn't born."

"I was fourteen when I said that!"

"I was six."

Terrence grew quiet. I don't think it ever crossed his mind how young I was when he told me that.

"I'm sorry," he apologized. "I shouldn't have said that. It's just that Brown was nice, and he was so excited when you were born. You were like his favorite baby. He even used to call you his little T-Rex because you kept trying to bite him when you were teething."

I hit the wrong note.

"Darn it!" I exclaimed. "Now I'll have to start over."

"Why don't you just start from where you left off?" Terrence asked.

"Because it ruins the whole song."

"It's just one note."

"No, it's not," I huffed. "That one note can throw everything off. It *has* to be right."

"Okay then... where was I?"

"T-Rex."

"Oh yeah. That's what Brown called you until you were about three. Then, he flipped and started saying you were Dad's baby because of how you looked. Brown took all his frustrations out on me, and Gracie, and eventually you too, and it was scary. I didn't know how to handle it. I'm sorry."

If what Terrence said was true, then Brown was the man that called me his little T-Rex. Something stirred up inside me. A fit of intense anger. Brown might've actually been my father, and even worse, might've known and still denied me. He didn't deserve that honor in my eyes. Grandpa had been my father, and now he was gone. I hit the wrong note again and slammed my fingers against the keys.

"ARGH!" I yelled as I picked up my shoe and threw it at the wall. It seemed like the only thing I could control.

"Why'd you do that?" Terrence asked. I ignored him and walked toward the exit. Terrence called after me, saying, "Where are you going?"

Every memory I had of Brown and Grandpa replayed themselves before me. Every time Brown didn't act like a father, and every time Grandpa did. I found myself in the doorway of Grandpa's house. His cologne permeated through the walls. The sound of his voice rang in my ears.

"It's just music, Grandpa," I heard myself say as I stared at the hallway. I saw us walk down that hallway, arguing over my taste in music.

"It's not just music, Torrance Dean!" Grandpa turned to look at me. I felt the heat of his ferocious glare as he wagged his finger in my face. *"When the devil was still an angel, he was the minister of Heaven's music. Music is the easiest way for him to influence you!"*

"Grandpa, I'm seventeen. Don't you trust me to make good decisions?"

"Nope! I trusted Marianne to make good decisions and she ended up pregnant."

"But I'm not Mama."

"I don't want you listening to that devil music in my house anymore. Do you understand me?"

A lump formed in my throat as I moved through the house. I thought the kitchen would help me escape the memories. My eyes fell on the chair I sat in as I snapped beans with Grandpa before prom.

"Grandpa...," I began as I snapped a bean between my hands. *"How do you know if you're in love?"*

"In love? You're eighteen. What do you know about being 'in love'?"

"I don't know. How did you know you were in love with Grandma?"

"I married her."

"Grandpa!"

"It's true. I married her because I was in love with her."

My hands flew to my ears, and my vision blurred with tears. I ran back into the living room. Grandpa's chair stared me in the face.

"Torrance," Grandpa called my name. He looked up at me.

"Yeah?"

"I love you so much."

"What made you say that?"

"I just felt like it."

"I love you too, Grandpa."

I wrapped my arms around him and held him close.

We'd had that conversation the week before he died when I visited him. I couldn't take it anymore. The tears flooded down my face, and I ended up in the street wailing at the top of my lungs.

"Yo Brown!" someone stopped me. It was Marlin. He wore his work clothes and smelled like garbage. "What are you doing out here so late?"

"My dad is gone!" I cried. My body collapsed against Marlin's, and I let the tears out. It wasn't lost on me that Marlin finally got to see me cry. I just didn't care enough to hold it in anymore. To my surprise, Marlin didn't push me away. He stood there like a wall and let me cry on him.

"Are you done?" Marlin asked when I'd calmed down.

I couldn't speak. All I could do was nod.

"I'll take you home."

Marlin took me home, and Terrence returned my shoes the next day. I was thankful to them, even if I couldn't express it then. All I felt was anger. Anger at what I'd lost and what I'd never had.

-

Chapter Twenty

My fourth child, Andre Joel Brown, was born the March after Grandpa died. I don't know what it was, but something about this baby was different. Drake, Karla, and Mary were all pretty calm, but Andre was restless.

"Shhh," I whispered as I rocked him in my arms one night. He'd been crying all day. I didn't want him to wake anyone else up, but he wasn't trying to go back to sleep. Despite my efforts, Andre woke Mary up.

"Give him here," Leilana groaned as she stumbled into the room. I handed Andre to her and went to calm down Mary.

"It's okay," I murmured as I took Mary from her crib. I told her a story to calm her down. By the time I finished, my one-year-old was back asleep. Leilana and I crawled into bed, careful not to wake the sprawled-out three-year-old Drake that couldn't sleep because of Andre's crying.

"Torrance," Leilana whispered. "Four is enough. No more."

"Agreed."

Our agreement didn't last long. By age twenty-nine, we had six children. Two years after Andre came another girl: Adrianna Ernestine Brown. She looked like how I'd look if I were a girl. A year after her came Antoine Marvin Brown. He also looked like me but lighter. All my children had my nose, Leilana's eyes, and they all needed glasses. Regardless of how they looked, these were my kids. I wouldn't be like Brown.

As the years went by, my kids took on their own personalities. Drake was sophisticated, while Karla was bougie. Mary was reserved, while

Andre was expressive. Adrianna tended to be indecisive, while Antoine was always sure of what he wanted.

During that time, I got a college degree in music. Slowly, my professional life improved while my marriage suffered. After Antoine was born, I started to grow apart from Leilana. We argued over everything, and soon things came to a head.

One day, I decided to cook dinner for my wife on my day off. We'd been married for ten years, and I wanted to propose a fresh start for us. I made everything as romantic as I could. When she came home, Leilana looked at my gesture and shook her head.

"I can't do this anymore," she sighed.

"Aw come on," I whined as I threw my shoulder towel on the table. "I worked hard on this meal."

"I'm talking about us, Torrance. I want a divorce."

"Why?"

"Because we're not on the same page anymore," Leilana said as she went to our bedroom. "We're too different now."

"We can work through this, Leilana."

"We've tried working through it," Leilana complained as she sat a suitcase on the bed. "We did marriage counseling at the church and everything. Nothing's worked."

"You don't have to do this. I can change."

"You've already changed."

"I mean I can be better."

"I'm sure you can," Leilana stopped throwing clothes into the suitcase to look at me. "But I'm tired of waiting for it to happen. You've got a lot of built-up anger and I can't deal with it anymore."

"Where are you going to go?"

"Back to my parents'. Then I'll get my own place."

"What'll I tell the kids?"

"The truth."

Leilana left after that. We decided to keep things simple for our children's sake. I got to keep the house, and the children stayed with me because I had enough room for them. She went back to live with her parents, and we wouldn't demonize each other to our kids. It seemed like my life was coming together and falling apart at the same time, and it only made me angrier.

That following year, I completed my college degree at age thirty. The divorce had taken a toll on my kids, especially Karla. She was the closest to Leilana, and her mother's absence affected her greatly. My sweet little girl had turned sour on me, and I didn't know how to handle it.

"What am I going to do with her?" I complained to Jeremy-Micah and Marie one Saturday. Ruth-Anne had taken the kids with her to visit Mr. Parker.

"She's nine," Jeremy-Micah said. "What's the worst thing she could possibly do to you?"

"Give her a few years and we'll find out," I grumbled. "I'm telling y'all, this child has not liked me ever since the divorce."

"I think you're just stressed about finding a new job," Marie whispered.

"Well, yeah," I said. "But Karla isn't making it any better."

"You could always become a teacher," Jeremy-Micah suggested. "The schools always have positions open."

"I don't know," I sighed. "I don't think I'd make a great teacher."

"So, you're just going to spend the rest of your life being a janitor?"

"Mikey's right, Torrey," Marie agreed. "Your kids are getting older which means they're going to need you to be around more. You can't do that if you're never home when they are."

"I should go," I said as I looked at the time on my flip phone. "Ruthie will be back any minute now."

"Alright," Jeremy-Micah said. "Think about what we said."

"I will."

When I got home, Ruth-Anne was already there with the kids.

"Daddy!" five-year-old Adrianna and four-year-old Antoine cried as they ran and hugged me.

"Hi!" I patted their heads. "Did you guys have fun?"

"I had fun, Daddy," Seven-year-old Andre said.

"Good," I said. "Did y'all eat?"

"Yeah," Ruth-Anne said. "Daddy fed them."

"It was nasty," Karla complained.

"Karla, you think everything's nasty," I grumbled.

"It was nasty, Dad," ten-year-old Drake agreed with his sister. "His sandwiches didn't have mayonnaise."

"See?" Karla said. "You never believe me."

"Karla, don't start," I said. I knew Mr. Parker's sandwiches weren't good, but I couldn't allow Karla to be disrespectful. "Where's Mary?"

"She's still in the car," Ruth-Anne said. "She fell asleep on the way home."

I looked in the van. Eight-year-old Mary was sound asleep in the backseat. The book she'd been reading sat under her dangling hand. It must've fallen from her grip when she dozed off.

"Mary," I whispered. "Time to wake up."

"Mmm...," Mary whimpered.

"Drake, help your sister out the car," I said.

"Yes sir." Drake obeyed and shook Mary awake. "Come on, Mary."

"So, what did you do with your day off besides dump your kids off on me?" Ruth-Anne joked as she helped me get the kids settled. Mary snuggled herself into the couch next to us and read her book while Drake and Karla played hand games. Adrianna and Antoine played a dance video game together that Leilana had bought them. The only child I couldn't account for was Andre.

"I went over to Mikey's," I said as I scanned the room looking for my missing child. "He and Marie think I should become a teacher."

"That's not a bad idea. Arty's desperate to fill the positions at Creeke High."

"Okay but–!" I began. Andre sat next to a wall with a crayon in his hand. He had a history of practicing his art on my walls when I wasn't around. Before he could do anything, I flung my shoe at the wall beside him.

"Eek!" Andre cried. He dropped the crayon in his hand and stared at the shoe.

"Bring me my shoe!" I commanded. Andre obeyed. "What have I told you about coloring on my walls?"

"Not to."

"So, why did it look like that's what you were about to do?"

"I wasn't!"

"I'm not playing with you, Andre Joel," I warned him. "Go get a piece of paper if you want to color."

"Yes sir," Andre said before scurrying away.

"See?" Ruth-Anne teased. "You'd make a great teacher. All you have to do is keep your shoes to yourself."

"Easier said than done," I groaned.

Ruth-Anne left an hour later. I fed all my kids' dinner and put them to bed. Being a single father was not easy. It seemed that almost all my siblings agreed that I would make a great teacher and were pushing me to do that. They weren't the only ones in Creeke that believed it either.

The next day I received a visit from Arthur Lee. Arthur had become school principal at Creeke High School the previous school year. He visited me because he said he had a proposal.

"What's this proposal, Arthur?" I said as I invited him into my home.

"Call me Arty," Arthur laughed. "I want to hire you, Torrance Brown. I want the man with the eyepatch and no shoes to be my new choir teacher."

"Me?" I snorted. "I haven't sung in a *long* time."

"Oh, I know," Arthur winked. "But that doesn't mean you can't still teach others to sing."

"Why me?"

"Why not you?"

"I don't know...," I said. "I'm not sure I'd make a good teacher."

"How about you think over it?" Arthur suggested. "I'm willing to work with you to make the transition as smooth as possible."

"I'll think about it."

"That's all I ask... for now," Arthur chuckled as he headed for the front door. "I await your decision."

After Arthur left, Terrence called me. He needed help arranging a song for the church choir and asked that I meet him at the church. I headed there and found him sitting at the organ with his head buried in his hands.

"I can't figure out what's wrong with it," Terrence complained. "It sounds fine until I get to this one note. Listen."

Terrence played the song for me. He'd improved a lot in the ten years he'd spent as the church's music minister. As he said, the arrangement was great until he reached a certain note.

"It sounds wrong because that's the wrong note," I told him.

"It is?" he asked.

"Yeah," I said. I played the song for him again, making sure to press the correct note. "It's supposed to sound like this."

"Oh," Terrence sighed. "No wonder it didn't sound right. I was playing it from memory."

"Why don't you use Grandpa's hymnal?" I asked. "The song is in there."

"I gave it to a boy at the hospital."

"You gave ... my grandfather's hymnal ... to a boy at the hospital?"

"We didn't need it anymore."

"Terrence! Grandpa passed that down to you!"

"And I passed it down to a boy that needed it. Gracie was okay with it."

"You and Ruthie are two out of five grandchildren! You didn't even bother to ask me, Mikey or RieRie how we felt about it!"

"Would you have said no?"

"Well... no! But you could have asked first!"

"I'm sure Grandpa would've been okay with the decision. He always said music was meant to be shared."

"Sometimes, I just can't with you and your thought process," I huffed. "You're probably the one that told Arthur to offer me a job at Creeke High."

"I suggested you as a candidate, but so did Gracie, Mikey and RieRie."

"Why?"

"Because we all think you're the best fit for it," Terrence said. "Shoot, you taught me how to play this organ. That's something even Grandpa couldn't do."

"Anyone can learn to play if they're determined enough."

"You were also able to figure out what was wrong with this song just by listening to it once. I've played this song several times and couldn't even figure it out. You've got a good ear for music."

"I don't know," I sighed. "What if I'm horrible at it?"

"What if you're great at it?"

Terrence stood up and grabbed my shoulders.

"You held onto me telling you I wished you weren't born for seventeen years," Terrence spoke. "Now I want you to hold onto these words for the rest of your life. If no one else believes you can do it, I do. Gracie does. Mikey does. RieRie does. We all believe you can do this. Believe in yourself. And if you fail, we'll all still be here to help you. Because we're your family and that's what family does. Well, family that cares anyways..."

Terrence's words echoed in my mind as I returned home. Everyone believed I could be a great teacher, but I didn't see it. Grandpa was a great teacher. He taught me everything I knew, and I wasn't his only student. I couldn't be half as great a teacher as he was or make the impact he did.

I started making dinner for the kids. As I cooked, I heard someone play a simple song on my piano. Whoever it was, did a good job. At least until they missed a note.

"That's not right," I said.

"Okay," Drake called, revealing himself to be the player.

The piano playing began again but slower. There weren't any mess-ups during the second attempt.

"Good job," I said.

"Thank you," Mary answered, revealing herself to be the player.

Drake and Mary took turns playing the song. I could tell who played by whether there was a mistake or not. Soon, I joined them and watched. It was Drake's turn. He played, and when he reached the troubling section, he messed up again.

"Why do you keep hitting that same wrong key?" I asked.

"I don't know," he said.

"This is the right one, okay?" I said as I showed him the correct key to press. "Try it again."

Drake did as I said and played again. Sometimes he did well, and sometimes he messed up. I had him replay it several times until he could get it right.

"Dad, I'm tired of playing this," he complained.

"Don't give up yet," I said. "You can do it. If you play it right this time, I'll let you do something else, okay?"

Drake played again. It was perfect by the time he finished.

"Do you feel like you have it?" I asked.

"Yeah," he said. "Can I go now?"

"You can go," I said. "You did a good job."

"Thanks Dad."

Seeing how well Drake did after helping him showed me I could be a decent teacher after all. After our lesson was over, I made a phone call.

"Hello?" Arthur said when he answered.

"Hey Arty, it's Torrançe," I said. "About that position..."

Part 3:
Drake Brown

Chapter Twenty-One

Growing up under Dad's fiery spirit was not easy. He had a short temper, and everything had to be perfect with him. Especially music. It was because of these qualities that my siblings and I had varying relationships with him. I argued with him a lot. Karla chose to live with Mom when she turned eighteen, and Mary was indifferent towards him. Andre tried to please Dad while Adrianna and Antoine still believed Dad could change.

The only time we were all together with Dad was when he made us sing together. He claimed it 'helped us get along', but I couldn't see how because only Mary and I took to music. Adrianna enjoyed dancing more than singing, while Andre liked science. Karla leaned toward caretaking, and Antoine liked video games. But since it made Dad happy to see us all sing, we sang together sometimes.

Although Dad would be entering his tenth year as a choir teacher, he didn't sing. Instead, I helped him arrange the songs he taught and sang for him as a volunteer. It'd been our routine since I was in high school, and the upcoming school year wouldn't be any different. He'd returned from his annual teachers' teambuilding retreat energized and ready to work. I suspected it was because he left with a girlfriend and returned with a fiancée.

"Dad, this part is too high." I said as I looked at the song he was arranging. It was a muggy August Saturday afternoon. "There's not a man on earth who can sing these notes."

"I could if I wanted to. If I can, then you can. And if you can, then they can too."

"But... you don't sing and... I can't sing this."

"I'm going to tell you the same thing my grandfather told your Aunt Marie: if you can talk that high, you can sing that high." Dad pressed a key on the piano. "Now sing because we don't have all day. I need to know how this sounds so I can have it ready for the school year in two weeks."

"Why do I have to sing it though?" I complained. I looked at Antoine, who sat feet away on his phone. "Antoine's only fourteen, his voice should still be high enough for it."

"Antoine's voice has already started changing. You, on the other hand, are a twenty-year-old grown man with a voice that's still high enough to reach these notes."

"Well, I wish I wasn't," I sighed. I messed with the engraved silver cross necklace around my neck. Dad gifted each of us one the previous Christmas. Every necklace had its owner's name on the front and the words 'Psalm 31:5' on the back.

"The Lord made your voice the way it is for a reason," Dad said. "Look at it this way. At least you won't sound like a dying cat like your Uncle Mikey when he attempts high notes. Just sitting up yelling."

"I guess you're right."

"Dad's always right. Now sing."

I couldn't reach the notes as I said. Dad said I wasn't trying hard enough, I told him he should change songs, and it ended in an argument. As usual. We took a break, and I called my girlfriend, Tamela Kane.

"Tam...," I whined. "He's getting on my nerves."

"He's your dad and you're the oldest," Tamela chuckled. "You're the best equipped to deal with him."

"You know, this is not the encouragement I was hoping to hear from my you today."

"How about I buy you another cardigan to make up for it?"

"I don't want another cardigan; I want you to stay."

"And I want my degree," Tamela said. She was leaving me to start her junior year in college halfway across the country. "You'll be fine."

"No, I won't. I don't get to see you again until December."

"You know Em isn't whining as much as you are about me leaving."

"Because you get on her nerves," I teased Tamela about her younger sister, Tamara. She liked being called Em because her middle name was Emily. "I'm your boyfriend. I'm supposed to whine when you leave me here all alone."

"Anyways," Tamela said. Her tone told me she smiled through the phone. It was nice to hear considering Tamela wouldn't even be my friend when we first met. I was glad we were able to move past that part of our relationship into friendship, and eventually dating. My life wouldn't be the same without her.

"Drake," Dad interrupted. "We need to get back to work."

"Okay," I sighed. "I have to go. Bye."

"Bye."

I hung up the phone and followed Dad back to the piano. As I passed by Antoine, I glanced at his phone.

"*You're a thief, Vincent Cartwright!*" the man on his screen yelled. "*And I don't deal with thieves!*"

"Antoine, what are you watching?"

"A video about the KV and Knokout situation."

"Who?

"A rap duo. They disbanded because KV claims Knokout stole some money and jewelry from him."

"Oh," I said.

"Dria!" Andre yelled from the other end of the house. The last thing we needed was for Dad to get mad at us. I followed Andre's voice as he continued yelling at Adrianna. "Come on! I have to use the bathroom!"

"I said hold on, Andre!" Adrianna called from inside the bathroom.

"You said that five minutes ago!" Andre hollered back as he pranced in the hallway.

"Why are you guys yelling?" I asked Andre.

"Because I have to use the bathroom BUT SOMEONE'S TAKING FOREVER!"

"YOU DON'T HAVE TO GO THAT BADLY!"

"YES I DO!"

Something whizzed past my head and slammed into the bathroom door.

"What was that?!" Adrianna screamed.

I stared at the fuzzy black slipper I bought Dad last Christmas. It was too big for his foot but that didn't stop him from throwing it.

"Y'all stop all that yelling in my house!" Dad snapped as he stormed up the hallway. He snatched his slipper up and dusted it off.

"Never mind," Adrianna said. "I know what it was."

"What's the problem?" Dad asked as he slipped his slipper back on his foot. "And it better be good since y'all have me breaking my promise to Gretchen."

"Dria is hogging up the bathroom," Andre complained.

"Adrianna?" Dad said, knocking on the door. "Are you alright?"

"Yeah! I just need a few minutes!"

"Andre, go use my bathroom."

"But–!"

Dad gave Andre 'the look', and Andre shut up. 'The look' was a warning sign. It meant we needed to back down. Because what came after 'the look' was an angry father throwing more shoes and screaming. Andre scampered up the hallway towards Dad's room.

"Why were you letting them yell like that?" Dad accused me.

"How is this my fault?"

"Because you're the oldest. You're supposed to be looking after them."

"Dad, these are *your* children. Why is it my job to watch *your* children?"

"Do you like having a roof over your head? Do you like having food to eat? Do you like not having to spend your own money?"

"Here we go," I groaned.

"If you want to live here, you'll do as I say. That includes watching *my* children because you're the oldest, and it's your responsibility to look after your brothers and sisters. If you don't like it, you can get out."

I focused on Dad's scar instead of responding. He never covered it at home unless he had company. It was easier to let him have the last word than argue with him. That evening, I went to Mom's house. Her home was the perfect place for us to go when we needed a break from Dad.

Mom remarried to Pastor Forrest Hall a few years after she divorced Dad. Forrest was already Head Pastor of Creeke Church when they married, and many felt he should've stepped down after marrying a divorced woman. They accused Mom of gold-digging because of the eleven-year age difference and wouldn't acknowledge her as First Lady. But if Forrest stepped down, the only option left was Mr. Derrick. And people at the time wouldn't forgive him for whatever he did to get removed, so everyone stuck with Forrest. After a few years of Forrest's sermons though, the town changed their tune on taking Mr. Derrick back.

"And then he told me if I didn't like it, I could get out," I complained to Karla.

"And that's exactly why I moved in with Mom," Karla scoffed as she waved the crayon in her hand around. "It's a difference between helping out and pushing *every* responsibility off on us. Mom understands that difference. Dad doesn't for some reason."

"Karla," our six-year-old sister Layla Esther Hall whined. "You're supposed to be coloring."

"Sorry," Karla said.

"The crazy part is, he never asks Mary to do anything and never yells at her either," I continued.

"Are we surprised?" Karla snorted. "He can deny it all he wants but we all know Mary is his favorite."

"But don't tell Mary that because you'll know she'll have a fit."

"Well duh. Mary would rather pretend like we're all equal in that house when she knows full well, we're not."

Layla teetered over to us and inspected the coloring book pages she wanted us to fill in. We were playing school, and Karla and I were her 'students'.

"Teacher," I said as I showed her my coloring page. "Do you like my drawing?"

"No." Layla scrunched her face up. "It's supposed to be blue."

"No, it's not."

"That's it!" Layla yelled as she grabbed my hand. "You're going to time out!"

"Why?"

"For being diss speck full," Layla explained as she led me to a chair in the kitchen. She placed her hands on her hips once I sat and said, "If you get up, you're getting a whooping!"

Layla's dark-brown frame disappeared from the kitchen as she returned to tend to her classroom. A pot simmered on the stove as the last rays of sunlight filtered through the kitchen window. Mom exited the laundry room with a basket of clothes in her hand.

"Why are you in here?" she asked.

"Layla put me in time out."

"What'd you do?" Mom set her basket on the floor and sat in the chair next to mine.

"She said I was being disrespectful."

"I'm about to take Layla out of that daycare," Mom groaned. "Every time she comes home, she claims somebody is disrespectful. I was disrespectful yesterday for drinking too much of my juice... that I paid for... with my money... in my house."

"You could leave her with Dad and Mary again."

"I only ask Torrance to watch her when I have *no* other option," Mom declared. "I won't have Layla out here throwing shoes like the rest of y'all. And speaking of Torrance, what's this I heard about you getting into it with him again?"

"Dad blamed me for Andre and Adrianna arguing over the bathroom, so I asked why I was be responsible for his children."

"Lord, you were asking for an argument with that one," Mom sighed. "You know your dad goes off about any and everything so why would you ask him something like that?"

"Because it's true."

"Just because it's true doesn't mean you have to say it. You have to be wise with the hills you choose to die on."

"Why do I have to walk on eggshells around him and he gets to say whatever he wants to me?"

"Because it's his house."

"That's not right. It's like every time I talk to him now, it turns into an argument."

"It's because you both have similar personalities. Hard-headed about everything."

"I am not hard-headed."

"You sure?"

"Not like him."

"If you say so. All I'm saying is, be mindful about the conversations you have with your father while you're still living with him. One wrong word and you might find yourself out on the street with nowhere to go."

Mom picked up her basket and left. Being on time out gave me time to think. With Dad preparing to remarry, he didn't need our relationship to become more strained. I would make one last attempt to get along with Dad.

Chapter Twenty-Two

The weekend before the school year started, Karla and I met with Dad's fiancée, Gretchen Nelson, for lunch at Patty's. It would be Karla's first time meeting her. Gretchen was the shy journalism, yearbook, speech, and English teacher at Creeke High.

"Is she ugly?" Karla asked as we walked through Patty's parking lot.

"No."

"Then she's dumb, right?"

"No."

"Is she broke? Does she think he has money?"

"She's a teacher like Dad."

"Teachers can be broke."

"She's not broke."

"So... she's crazy?"

"Karla!"

"What's wrong with her then? If she's pretty, smart, sane, and has money, why is she engaged to a man who has six kids? Something has to be wrong with her."

"Why does something have to be wrong with her?"

"Because it doesn't make sense. All these options out here and the best she could do was Dad? Mom left him for a reason."

"Dad can't help that he's passionate."

"You've complained about him all month and now you're defending him?"

"He's my dad. I'm allowed to do both."

"Well, he's my dad too, but I'm still going to call things as I see them. I don't see any reason why this woman wants to marry him unless she has something to gain from it."

"I do remember Dad at some point saying he was her first boy-friend..."

"Aha! She's desperate!"

"Will you cut it out? There's nothing wrong with Gretchen."

"That we know of."

I opened the door for Karla to walk in first. Patty's was owned by the Townsend family, and it was Creeke's most popular restaurant. It looked like an old-school diner, with a black-and-white checkered tile floor and red leather booths.

"Welcome to Patty's!" Charmaine Townsend greeted us with a smile. She was the sixteen-year-old daughter of the owners, Raymond and Patricia. "What can I get you guys today?"

We placed our order and Charmaine rang us up.

"Your food will be out shortly," Charmaine said. "Have a nice day!"

"You too," I said. We left the counter and walked through the restaurant.

"Who's this wonderful woman we're looking for?" Karla grumbled.

I searched the room for Gretchen. She sat in the back with her twin sister, Greta. The Nelson twins were five years younger than Dad, and they had medium-brown skin and curly black hair. Greta was Creeke High's guidance counselor and was the reason Gretchen moved to Creeke too. Gretchen used to do marine photography, and her love of water was how she and Dad bonded.

"She's over there," I said as I pointed to them.

"There's two of them?!" Karla gasped.

"You didn't know that?"

"No! And they're pretty too!"

"I told you that..."

"You said she wasn't ugly," Karla corrected. "Which one is he marrying?"

"The one on the left."

"How can you tell?"

"I'll show you."

I led Karla to the table.

"Hi Drake," Gretchen greeted me.

"Hi," I said. I sat and looked at Greta. She raised her eyebrows at me, waiting for me to say something. We stared at each other until she got fed up.

"What?!" Greta exclaimed. "Why do you and your dad always stare at me?!"

"That's how," I said to Karla. "If she snaps, it's Greta. If she smiles, it's Gretchen."

"Who came up with that?" Karla grumbled.

"Dad."

"I should've known," Karla muttered. She looked at the twins. "I'm Karla. I'm Torrance's oldest daughter."

"So, you're the mysterious Karla I've heard so much about." Gretchen extended her hand to Karla. "Nice to meet you."

"What've you heard about me?" Karla accepted Gretchen's handshake.

"Nothing bad. Just that you're more... independent."

"That's the first time I heard that one," Karla laughed. "Dad usually calls me difficult."

"Aw, he calls you difficult too?" Greta said. "We have something in common."

"Let's get straight to it." Karla laced her hands together in front of her. "Everyone likes you, and my dad wants to marry you, so I have a question."

"Okay," Gretchen said.

"Are you aware he has anger issues?"

"Yes," Greta snorted as she sipped her drink. "I like her. She's trying to help you out."

"Shut up, Greta," Gretchen urged.

"Don't be mad at me because your man has anger issues, and his daughter is concerned about you marrying him."

"Shut... up... Greta."

"Then again, I don't have room to talk because my ex left me at the altar a decade ago and I haven't bothered with dating since."

"Karla, please continue before she says something else," Gretchen pleaded.

"I'm only asking because my dad's temper can be a bit much. If you two get married, I want to be sure you know what you're dealing with."

"She better be," Greta interjected. "Do you know how much time I had to spend with that man, putting together the perfect proposal for her? I'm exhaust- OW! Why'd you kick me, Gretchen?!"

"Because you talk too much."

"Order up!" the cook yelled.

Our food appeared in the window. It looked delicious.

"Benji!" Charmaine called. "The food is getting cold! Come on!"

"I'M COMING!" a deep voice bellowed. Seventeen-year-old Benjamin Townsend thundered through the restaurant with the scowl he always wore. He was the oldest child of the Townsend family. A short, medium-brown teenager with locs down his back, Benjamin wasn't as talkative or friendly as Charmaine.

"You don't have to get an attitude, Benji," Charmaine complained.

"You see I'm steady moving toward the window, Charmaine!" Benjamin ranted as he picked up our food. "Can I get to it before you start hollering at me?!"

Benjamin slammed our food down on the table and left.

"He needs to sort that attitude out," Karla said as she bit into a fry. "That's not cute."

Volunteering at the school was different from being a student. Many of the teachers were nicer than they were back then. They even let me call them by their first names. Dad claimed it was my perspective changing because I was grown. The students responded well to me, and some of the seniors were my friends since I'd gone to school with them. One of those seniors was Derek Harrison.

Since I was born, I'd been told to avoid the Harrisons because they didn't like us. Grandma didn't get along with Mr. Derrick, and Dad had a weird relationship with Marlin Harrison. It was a generations-old rivalry, but nobody wanted to explain how it started. Derek was different though. He was loud and goofy like his grandfather, and all he wanted to do in life was dance. I took him under my wing senior year when he was a freshman, and he'd stayed there ever since. Befriending a Harrison was never something I thought was possible before I met him.

I sat with Derek on the first Friday of the school year, waiting for Dad's sixth-period music theory class to start. Most students took music theory because they thought it was an easy class, and Derek was no different. However, Dad's classes were never easy.

"You know I've always wondered," I said as I looked at the tiger stripe tattoo on Derek's right wrist. "How did you get a tattoo?"

"It's a funny story actually," Derek laughed. "Last year, Queenie dared me to get a tattoo and if I did, she would get one too."

"Who's Queenie?"

"My cousin, Allison."

"Oh! Keep going."

"Anyways, she knew a guy through her cousin who could tattoo, and he did them for us. Queenie was just smart enough to get hers on her thigh where no one would see it."

"I assume your dad was okay with it like he always is?"

"Actually, he got mad at me for once. He smacked me upside the head and was all like 'if you think I'm going to let you throw your life away, you're wrong!'. Then he said it was stupid and dangerous and he calmed down after that."

"That's it?"

"You know how my dad is."

"Must be nice..."

"Your dad isn't that bad," Derik chimed in. He was Derek's quieter, fifteen-year-old cousin. I found it funny how they had the same name and looked similar but had opposite personalities.

"If you say so," I sighed. I looked at Derek again and smiled. "What's your grandfather's nickname for you?"

"No."

"Aw, why not?"

"It's embarrassing."

"But I want to know," I whined.

"You know what I want to know," Samiel Dow butted in. He was the other freshman I took in my senior year, and he and Derek were best friends. "What's *your* nickname, Drake?"

"I don't have one."

"Come on." Samiel gazed at me with his bright hazel eyes. The smile on his face showed off the braces in his mouth. "Everyone has a nickname."

"I don't."

"We'll give you one then," Samiel said. "You can be... Big Bro."

"Big Man," Derek chimed in.

"Big Fella."

"Big Guy."

"How about both of you shut your big mouths?" Benjamin griped.

"Look Benji," Derek protested. "You don't have to spoil our fun."

"Yeah Benji," Samiel agreed. "You don't have to be so mean about it."

"Derek. Sami." Benjamin leaned in close to their faces. "Shut up."

"Your face is going to get stuck like that," Derek chided. "Don't you ever get tired of being grumpy all the time?"

"Don't you ever get tired of being grumpy all the time?" Derik copied his cousin's voice. It was something they did with each other at random times.

"Yeah, don't you get tired of being a meanie?" Samiel said.

"Get your cousin and his annoying shadow," Benjamin said to Derik.

"Leave Benji alone, guys," Derik said.

"Alright," Derek chuckled. "But only because he's clearly having a bad day."

"Just go back to what you were talking about," Benjamin grumbled.

"Okay." Derek turned back to me. "We'll call you... Mister Dragon."

"Mister Dragon?" I laughed.

"I like that," Samiel said. "Mister Dragon the assistant. If you miss the note, he'll throw his special flaming shoes at you."

"And The only man that can defeat him is–!" Derek continued the gimmick.

"Drake, leave my students alone and come on," Dad commanded as he exited his office.

"His father, Mr. Shoe-Thrower... thrower...thrower," Derek whispered in my ear, getting quieter each time he repeated the word 'thrower'.

"You two are so silly," I giggled as I stood up.

"We know," Samiel said.

"We'll be here all period long with the grump." Derek gave me a thumbs up.

That evening, I drove to the city to visit my best friend Andrew Stone at college. I'd nicknamed him Titan because of how much taller than me he was. He loved video games, and we played them together every time we hung out. We played one of his fighting games while I caught him up on everything going on.

"Dude," Andrew said as he beat my character up. "You and your dad need some space apart from each other."

"I know," I sighed as I mashed random buttons, hoping to win by some stroke of luck. Andrew never let me win.

"HAHA!" Andrew's bulky, dark-brown frame shot up from his chair as he executed a combo that defeated my character. He patted me on my shoulder as he set his controller down. "You're getting better."

"No, I'm not."

"Trust me, you are." Andrew started a solo game while I sat and watched. "Don't let your relationship with your dad get worse than it already is."

"Easier said than done."

"True. Both of you are unapproachable balls of stress that go nuts over every little thing that goes wrong,"

"I don't get mad over *every* little thing."

"You had a meltdown once because you thought you lost your glasses, and they were in your hand."

"Glasses are expensive."

"They. Were. In. Your. Hand."

"I didn't come here to be attacked, Titan," I laughed.

"I know. You came here to vent while I whoop you in video games like in high school."

"What do you think I should do?"

"Well, me and my parents got closer after we found things to do together we all enjoyed," Andrew suggested. "Find something you and your dad would both like to do together. What do y'all have in common?"

"We both like music."

"There you go. Find something to do together that involves music. And then move out so that you both can have some space."

"Where would I move to?"

"You could move out here with me," Andrew said with a grin. "Become my roommate and cover half my rent."

"Haha, very funny."

"I'm serious," Andrew doubled down. "My old roommate moved out on me. I need somebody to cover half the rent on this apartment."

"You really want me to move in with you?"

"I'm giving you top consideration before I have to resort to desperate measures."

"Let's say I do move in," I hypothesized. "How much would I have to pay per month?"

"About three-hundred dollars a month," Andrew figured. "I'll need your decision by the end of the month."

"Okay"

Someone knocked on the door.

"Who's that?" I asked.

"I invited some people over," Andrew said as he moved toward the door.

"I guess that's my cue to leave," I said as I stood up.

"No." Andrew stopped me. "I think you'll like these people."

"How do you know?"

Andrew smirked at me and answered the door.

"I was promised a Drake," I heard Dorothea Burton say. She was a twenty-year-old, thin, dark-brown friend that kept her head shaved down to a bald fade. "Where's my Drake?"

"Yeah," I heard Philomena James agree. She was my plump, dark-brown, nineteen-year-old friend that almost always wore her hair in a single braid. Although Philomena was my friend first, she was best friends with Mary. "Where's Drake?"

"I'm in here," I called from the living room. The girls came around the couch that blocked me from view and lit up when they saw me.

"Drake!" Dorothea hollered as she rushed at me with Philomena right behind her. Before I knew it, they'd engulfed me in a group hug.

"Well, hello to you guys too," Andrew groaned.

"We see you every day, Andrew," Dorothea said as she let me go. "Drake in person is a rare treat now."

"The only thing rarer than him these days is Tamela," Philomena chimed in.

"You guys do know Creeke is down the road, right?" Andrew said. "Y'all could drive down there and see him whenever you like."

"Or he could come up here and see us like he did today," Dorothea countered. "How's my little Drake been?"

"We're the same age, Do."

"I'm older than you by three months," Dorothea teased. "So, you're my little Drake."

"Just go with it," Philomena advised. "I'm her little Phil. Andrew's her little Andy. You're her little Drake."

I've been fine. We were talking about my dad before y'all got here."

"How is the infamous Mr. Shoe-Thrower?" Dorothea asked as she sat down. "Andrew, bring me a soda please."

"Andrew, bring me a soda please," Andrew mocked her as he went to the fridge. "I'll bring you a soda, alright."

"Dad's surprisingly not throwing shoes anymore," I said. "He's only thrown one once since he came back from the teacher trip."

"Mr. Shoe-Thrower isn't throwing his shoes anymore?" Philomena gasped. "What is this world coming to?"

"Here." Andrew handed a soda to Dorothea. She peered at it and eyed Andrew.

"Open it," Dorothea said.

"Why can't you open it?"

"Because you're a little prankster," Dorothea said as she crossed her arms. "You probably shook the can, so it'd spill all over me when I open it."

"Now why would I do that?"

"Because I know you. Open it."

Andrew lifted the little metal tab on the can with his thumb. We watched to see if anything would spill. When nothing did, Andrew thrust the can at Dorothea.

"Satisfied?"

"Hmm...," Dorothea eyed him as she took the can. "Thank you."

"No problem," Andrew said with a smile.

Dorothea took a swig of the drink and immediately spat it out.

"Blech!" she wretched. "What is this?!"

"Sparkling water!" Andrew howled with laughter. "I'm trying to cut back on drinking soda."

"Andrew," Dorothea growled.

"Should've stuck to your guns," Andrew teased.

"Some things never change," Philomena sighed.

"I was telling Drake he should move out here with me," Andrew mentioned as he sat down.

"Why?" Dorothea snorted. "So, you can torture him with sparkling water too?"

"So, he can cover half my rent."

"You're not even going to try to dress it up a little?" Dorothea laughed. "Not even a 'because I want to live with my friend'? He can't even get that?"

"I already told him what it was."

"I think it would be great for Drake to move out here," Philomena suggested. "It's a lot more opportunities for music out here than there are in Creeke. You'd love it."

"Yeah, but I can't up and leave Dad," I said.

"Why not?" Dorothea asked. "He's grown, he's getting married again..."

"He has four other kids that live with him and can do what you do," Andrew added. "There's really nothing keeping you there, Drake."

"I don't want to leave while our relationship is the way it is."

"I already told you what you need to do," Andrew reminded me. "You need space apart."

"I agree," Philomena said. "My relationship with my parents improved so much when I left for college. You don't have to be under the same roof for your relationship to get better."

"Guys, this is Drake we're talking about," Dorothea objected. "Y'all know Mr. Shoe-Thrower keeps them sheltered in that house like it's the last place on Earth with breathable air. Do you really think Drake is ready to be on his own?"

"He won't be on his own," Andrew disagreed. "He'll have us."

"We are broke college students," Dorothea argued. "What help can we give him?"

"Emotional support."

"How's he supposed to pay half your rent with that?"

"Guys, I don't even know if I want to move out yet," I butted in. "I'm really just trying to get my relationship with Dad together first."

"You said y'all both like music," Andrew sighed. "What can you do with that?"

"Maybe try to get him to sing for once...," Dorothea joked.

"That's not a bad idea," I said.

"I was joking."

"I know. But it's really not a bad idea. A lot of the students complain to me about how he doesn't sing and show them himself what he wants from them."

"It is kind of hard to learn when your teacher refuses to sing the parts for you," Philomena said.

"And a lot of the older people are always talking about how they miss hearing him sing," I said.

"Have you ever heard him sing?" Andrew asked.

"I'm not sure," I said

"You've never heard his album?" Andrew asked.

"What album?" I asked.

"The one he made with his family back in the day," Andrew said.

"They made an album?" I asked. "How come I've never heard of it until now?"

"That's a question for you to ask your family," Andrew said.

"I know Althea's mom still has her copy of it," Dorothea informed me. "Maybe see if she'll let you borrow it?"

"How do you guys know about the album, and I don't?" I asked.

"Althea told us about it," Dorothea said.

"Why didn't she tell me?"

"Because you're an unapproachable ball of stress," Andrew teased.

Chapter Twenty-Three

I went to see Althea Green and her mom that Saturday. She was Aunt Ruth-Anne's sixteen-year-old niece through Uncle Arnold. Her dad was Creeke High's head football coach, Alfred Green, and her mom was Mrs. Athena. Althea had three older sisters: twenty-two-year-old Cynthia, twenty-year-old Gloria, and eighteen-year-old Diana. Every time I saw Althea, her medium-brown arms and blonde-tipped black hair stuck out from behind a book. One wouldn't know she had brown eyes or freckles like her mother because she stayed buried in a novel.

It interested me that Dad made an album when he was younger. I knew Dad loved music as I did, but it felt lonely being unable to share it with him beyond volunteering. This discovery came with many questions. The main one was why he chose to keep this a secret. Mrs. Athena Green was willing to share everything she knew about Dad's days as a singer.

"Your daddy sure could sing to be as young as he was," Mrs. Athena explained. "His voice was so angelic. It's a shame he doesn't use it anymore."

"When's the last time you heard him sing?" I asked.

"Around when he was fourteen. Of course, after he stopped singing, he started rapping."

"Dad rapped in public?"

"He used to do it all the time," Mrs. Athena laughed. "All he needed was a beat and he'd come up with little rhymes off the top of his head. I'm sure Minister Jones put an end to all that though after the Psalms twenty-three incident."

"Psalms twenty-three incident?"

"I wouldn't really call it an incident," Mrs. Athena giggled. "Your father got on the pulpit and rapped Psalms twenty-three to open Mr. Derrick's sermon. Most of us younger people at the time liked it and so did Mr. Derrick. Of course, he was still Pastor Harrison at the time. But Minister Jones and the elders were not happy. They Romans twelve and two'd that poor man to death after that."

"He's never told me any of this."

"I'm not surprised," Mrs. Athena sighed. "From the few stories Ruth-Anne and Marie shared with me about their childhood, I see why your father wouldn't want to share. It's a sore spot for all of them."

I looked at the cover of the album. In brown letters at the top read *The Brown Family Band: No Longer Lost*. A sepia-colored photo showed six smiling faces in two rows on the steps of a church. On the front row, I recognized Aunt Ruth-Anne in a floor-length dress, Aunt Marie with white gloves and black hairbows, and Dad wearing his eyepatch. The back row had Uncle Terrence with a Jheri curl, Uncle Jeremy-Micah with a big grin, and Great-Grandpa, who stood tall and proud.

Great-Grandpa died when I was four, and I only had one memory of him.

"Are you my grandpa?" I asked when I first met him. Dad had taken me to Great-Grandpa's house to visit.

"I'm your Great-Grandpa," he answered. He sat in a green recliner.

"What's a great-grandpa?"

"A grandpa that's great," he cackled. His laughter became coughing.

"Are you sick?" I asked.

"Drake!" Dad snapped.

"It's alright," Great-Grandpa told Dad. He looked at me and said, "I'm old, Drake. My day to go be with The Lord in Heaven is getting closer."

"Don't say that Grandpa" Dad said. "That won't be for a long time."

"Alright," Great-Grandpa sighed. He hugged me tight and said, "I'll just play with my great-grandson instead."

"Great-Grandpa looks like he was a nice man," I said as my memory of him ended.

"Don't let that man's sweet smile fool you," Mrs. Athena said with a shudder. "Minister Gabriel Ray Jones did not play. I can still hear him yelling and it's been almost eighteen years since he died!"

I stared at Great-Grandpa. Everyone who talked about him mentioned how much he yelled. But they also mentioned how amazing of a musician he was. Seven tracks were listed on the back of the album. One was an introduction by Great-Grandpa, and the other six were songs.

"Do you know why Dad stopped singing?"

"Because–!" Mrs. Athena started before stopping. We watched Diana enter the kitchen with a purse on her arm. She was dark-brown with shoulder-length black hair.

"Where are you going?" Althea asked, looking up from her book.

"Where I go," Diana said. "Why are you in my business?"

"Don't be mean to your sister, Diana," Mrs. Athena chastised.

"If you must know," Diana grumbled. "I'm going on my first date with Ralph Brewer. He's taking me to dinner and a movie."

"That sounds expensive."

"When you're the prettiest girl in town, men don't mind spending money on you," Diana bragged as she fluffed her hair. "Don't wait up for me. I don't know when I'll be back."

"That door will be locked by ten, so if you're not back by then, you'll be spending the night outside," Mrs. Athena called.

"Alright, alright," Diana huffed as she left.

"That sister of yours is something else," Mrs. Athena sighed. She grabbed an album off the table and showed it to me. "Where were we?"

"You were about to tell me why Dad stopped singing."

"Ruth-Anne told me it was because of Leonard Brown," Mrs. Athena griped. "He didn't want his kids singing with the group and that was the end of that."

"But how did that cause Dad to stop singing?"

"That's a question for him," Mrs. Athena said. "All I know is, this album was so good, and I would give anything to hear them sing together one more time."

"It would be nice to hear Mr. Brown sing for once," Althea said.

"Yeah, it would be nice...," I agreed, the wheels turning in my head.

I planned to ask Dad all my questions when I got home, but he wasn't there. Mary sat on the couch reading a book while Andre and Antoine played a board game in the kitchen. None of them knew where Adrianna went.

"What's that in your hand?" Mary asked as she looked up from her book. It looked like the same one Althea was reading.

"It's the album Dad and his siblings made when they were younger," I said as I handed the album to Mary.

"Album?" Mary asked. She bent the corner of the page she was on and closed it. "Is this real?"

"As real as that book in your hand."

Mary put the CD in Dad's old CD player and pressed play.

"Make a joyful noise unto the Lord, all ye lands," a gravelly voice boomed from the speakers. "Serve the Lord with gladness: come before his presence with singing. Know ye that the Lord he is God: it is he that hath made us, and not we ourselves; we are his people, and the sheep of his pasture. Enter into his gates with thanksgiving, and into his courts with praise: be thankful unto him, and bless his name.For the Lord is good; his mercy is everlasting; and his truth endureth to all generations. Psalms One-Hundred, Verses One through Five."

"Who is that?" Andre asked as he and Antoine joined us in the living room.

"It's Great-Grandpa," Mary said as she looked at the back of the CD case.

"This album was an idea The Good Lord above gave me and my grandchildren," Great-Grandpa said. "We hope you enjoy it and that it blesses you on today."

The first song began. An angelic voice filled the room. As we listened to the male singer, I realized I'd heard this song before.

"This sounds familiar," Antoine said.

"Yeah, I've heard this song before," Andre agreed.

"We all have," Mary said. "Drake sings it all the time."

Someone sang this song to me when I was younger. I always sang it randomly, and every time, I heard the same person quietly sing with me. Almost like they didn't want to be heard. It was the same voice as on this CD, but much older.

"This is Dad's voice," I whispered. I took the CD case from Mary and discovered I was right. It *was* Dad's voice.

"I never would've imagined he sounded this good," Andre gasped.

"It's like a warm hug," Antoine expressed as he wrapped his arms around himself.

"He's wasted such a beautiful voice," Mary sighed.

"It doesn't have to be wasted," I spoke up. "What if we got Dad to sing again with his siblings?"

"Get Dad to sing?" Andre asked. "*Dad*, Dad? As in 'Torrance Dean Brown' Dad? The Dad that doesn't sing?"

"Yeah."

"I don't know," Mary disagreed.

"Why not, Mary?"

"Do you think he'd even want to do something like that?"

"Why wouldn't he?"

Tires squealed outside. Andre walked over to the window.

"Guys," Andre said. "Dad's home."

Antoine cut the music off. We all walked outside to find Dad grabbing groceries from the trunk.

"What's this?" Dad joked. "My children are being useful today?"

"I can go back inside," Mary said.

"I was just kidding," Dad whined as he handed Mary some bags. He would've snapped at me if I'd said something like that. "So, your aunt called and wants me, your uncles, and your other aunt to come over–"

"Which aunt?" I perked up.

"Boy, don't interrupt me when I'm talking!" Dad snapped.

"Sorry."

"Your Aunt Ruth-Anne," Dad continued. "She called out of the blue and said she wanted to see all of us."

"Can I go too?" I asked.

"Why do you want to go?"

"I want to see my family."

"You want to see your family?" Dad repeated. He squinted at me. "What are you up to?"

"Why do I have to be up to something?"

"Because you have a car and could go see your family if you wanted to," Dad said. I'd bought a car with the money I earned from my old job. I was the only one of my siblings with a car.

"Maybe I just wanted to spend time with you."

"Now I know you're up to something," Dad laughed. "Be ready in an hour or you will get left."

Family gatherings were always interesting. Every time Dad got around his siblings, he forgot how to act. He transformed from a strict and stern father to the youngest that whined and fussed about everything. We arrived at Aunt Ruth-Anne's house, and it didn't take long for him to get into character.

"Hi Ruthie," Dad said as he waved.

"Everyone's inside already," Aunt Ruth-Anne said as she grabbed me by my shoulders. "I just want to talk to my handsome nephew for a minute."

"Alright," Dad said. He entered the house.

"Come with me to the sidewalk," Aunt Ruth-Anne whispered. She looked behind her and yelled: "Your dad looks like he wants to be nosy!"

"No, I don't!"

"How'd you hear me then?!"

"Because you're yelling!"

"And I'm going to keep yelling because it's my house!"

"Ain't nobody worried about your old raggedy house, Ruth-Anne!"

"Raggedy?!"

"Raggedy!" Dad emphasized each syllable.

"Auntie let's go to the sidewalk," I said.

"That's right! You better be glad your son is pulling me away!"

We walked to the sidewalk.

"So, I got a call from Athena earlier today, right?" Aunt Ruth-Anne said. "And she was so excited because she said my wonderful nephew Drake wanted to hear us sing, right? And I didn't know what she was talking about. Because why would my nephew want to hear me sing, right? So, she starts explaining about the little trip you made to her house, and I realize she's talking about me and my siblings singing together again."

"Auntie..."

"You don't have to explain yet. I've gathered everyone together for you so you can tell us all at once what you're planning."

"How do you know I'm planning something?"

"Because I know you. Why else would you ask about an album from way back in the day?"

"Am I that easy to read?"

"About as easy as your father staring through the window at us," Auntie Ruth-Anne said. I turned and spotted Dad peeking through the blinds. "As soon as we walk in, the first thing out of his mouth will be 'what were y'all talking about?'. Then he'll try and force you to tell him."

When we went inside, Dad cornered me in the kitchen.

"What we're y'all talking about?" he asked.

"Stuff."

"What kind of stuff?"

"Personal stuff."

"I can't know what it is?"

"Why are you in my business?"

"You don't have any business. What were you talking about out there?"

"Whoops!" I yelped. I'd dropped some food on the floor.

"Boy!" Dad groaned. "Pay more attention to what you're doing!"

"I would've been if you weren't distracting me!"

"Oh, so this is my fault?!"

"Yes!"

"Why are you yelling at me?!"

"Because you're yelling at me!"

"Y'all are always yelling at each other," Uncle Jeremy-Micah sighed as he entered the kitchen. "Why don't you both take a break for once and come in the living room so Ruthie can tell us why we're here?"

We did as he suggested.

"What's going on, Gracie?" Uncle Terrence asked.

"Your nephew here came up with a great idea, and I decided to get us all together so he could tell us all at once."

"What's this 'great' idea?" Dad asked.

I placed the album on the table. Their faces held differing emotions as they recognized it.

"Where'd you get this?" Uncle Terrence gasped.

"From Mrs. Athena."

"I haven't seen this thing in ages!" Uncle Jeremy-Micah exclaimed.

"Look at us!" Aunt Ruth-Anne gushed. "We look so young!"

"I wonder if it still works," Aunt Marie whispered.

"It does," I answered with a grin.

"I'm still waiting for the great idea," Dad muttered as he crossed his arms. He didn't seem as excited as everyone else.

"I was talking to Mrs. Athena, and she said she would give anything to hear you guys sing again. So, I thought maybe you guys could remake this album."

"You want me... to sing with them?" Dad asked.

"What's wrong with singing with us?" Uncle Jeremy-Micah said.

"Well, you don't even sing, you just holler."

"It's called letting the Spirit use you."

"It's called I-can't-reach-the-note-so-I'm-going-to-yell-instead."

"At least I'm not afraid to sing in front of people."

"At least I'd be on key if I sung in front of people."

"Will you two shut up?" Uncle Terrence interjected. "Y'all both scream, holler, and run around the building like y'all don't have sense when y'all sing. I don't know why y'all are competing over who does it better."

"Methuselah don't get involved," Dad sighed as he got up and went to the kitchen.

"I think it's a great idea, Drake," Aunt Marie whispered.

"Me too," Uncle Jeremy-Micah agreed. "And I'm sure we could get Alex to help us too. There's no way he'd say no to his old man about something like this."

"So, I've got four out of five people on board," I groaned. "Great."

Dad returned from the kitchen with a cup, and Aunt Ruth-Anne zeroed in on it.

"What is that?" she asked.

"Water."

"Why is it in my living room?"

"It's water."

"Kitchen," Aunt Ruth-Anne growled as she squinted at Dad.

"It's water!"

"Dean...!"

"Fine!" Dad huffed as he retreated into the kitchen. "I'll stay in your stupid kitchen with my cup of– oops!"

Some of the water splashed from the cup onto the tile floor.

"You see that?" Aunt Ruth-Anne said as she pointed at Dad. "That's the exact reason why!"

Silence fell over the room as Dad chugged down his cup of water. All it took was a cup of water to ruin everyone's good moods. As Dad returned to the living room, he grabbed his keys and his shoes.

"I'm not doing it," he declared.

"Why not?" Aunt Marie asked.

"Because I don't want to."

"It would mean a lot to Drake if you did it," Uncle Terrence said. "Right, Drake?"

"I...," I uttered.

"I'm not doing it and that's final," Dad cut me off. "Come on, Drake."

Dad exited the house, leaving me alone with my aunts and uncles.

"It was a nice idea while it lasted," I sighed.

"Give your dad some time," Uncle Jeremy-Micah encouraged me. "He'll come around."

"How do you know?" I asked.

"DRAKE!" Dad screeched from outside.

"Trust me, I know," Uncle Jeremy-Micah chuckled. "Don't give up on him just yet."

Uncle Jeremy-Micah's words gave me hope as I joined Dad in the car. This was important to everyone, and I'm sure Dad saw that. He just needed a nudged in the right direction.

"Dad, can I ask you something?" I asked on the car ride home.

"I don't want to talk about the album."

"I just want to know why you never told us about it."

"Because I want to leave it in the past where it belongs."

His tone of voice inferred the reason was much deeper than what he told me. Getting Dad to agree to this wouldn't be easy. But I wouldn't give up on him yet.

-

Chapter Twenty-Four

Not giving up on Dad was harder than I thought. He didn't want to sing again, and it wore on me. All I wanted was to spend quality time with my father over a common interest. Everyone was on board except him. I couldn't understand why he made it harder than it needed to be.

"Have you noticed your father acting a little... different... lately?" Gretchen asked me the following Monday during our lunch break. It was the last few days of August.

"It's okay sweetie, you can say 'acting meaner'," Greta teased.

"Greta!" Gretchen whined.

"It's not like she's lying," Jana Vaughn shrugged as she swiped her curly red hair from her bronze skin. She taught art, and her eyeliner always looked smudged around her green eyes.

"Jana, don't agree with her!"

"Face it, Gretchen," Greta said. "Your fiancé is rubbing everyone the wrong way."

"You guys talking about Mr. Brown?" Jonathan Haynes asked as he joined us at the table. He was the dark-brown dance teacher that was two years older than me. We'd gone to school together, and I didn't like him. Jonathan was the type to get people out of character. "He needs to chill out."

"Don't talk about my dad like that," I argued.

"Your dad needs to chill out," Jonathan repeated.

"You know what–!"

"One of you needs to talk to him," Greta interrupted our argument.

"Why one of us?" Gretchen asked.

"Because you accepted the ring, and he's his son," Greta explained. "That makes you two responsible for him."

"And please do it fast," Jana pleaded.

"And then he had the nerve to ask me if he could have an extension on the assignment," I heard Troy Lewis laugh as Gretchen and I entered Dad's classroom. "And I was like, 'I already gave you one'."

"That's nice, Troy," Dad said.

"You sure are out of it today," Troy sighed. He was the plump theater teacher that starred in a few regional productions before returning to Creeke to 'educate the future of theater'.

"I'm just not in a laughing mood today."

"Not even for me?" Gretchen asked as she rested her hand on Dad's shoulder.

"Y...you came to visit me for lunch today?!" Dad said, his cheeks turning red.

"I came to talk to you."

"I don't like the sound of that."

"Everyone feels like you've been a bit... mean today," Gretchen admitted as she sat next to Dad.

"Who's everyone?"

"Everyone in the department," Gretchen said.

"Should've known," Dad grumbled.

"I'll let y'all talk," Troy said as he left.

"What's the matter?" Gretchen asked.

"My family has turned on me," Dad declared as he glared at me. "And it's all Drake's fault."

"All I did was ask you to sing," I huffed.

"That doesn't sound like such a bad idea," Gretchen agreed.

"I don't want to sing."

"Why not? You were singing when we first met."

"That's different," Dad reasoned. "I didn't know anyone was around."

"So, is it that you don't like singing or you don't like singing in front of other people?" Gretchen coaxed.

"I just don't want to do it."

"Okay," Gretchen said. "You don't have to do it if you don't want to. Right Drake?"

"I guess..."

"Just as long as you don't throw your shoes anymore," Gretchen advised Dad. "Because we talked about that, right? Remember you promised you wouldn't throw them anymore when we were on the trip?"

Dad looked down at his desk.

"Right?"

"He threw a slipper," I tattled.

"Traitor!" Dad yelled.

"Torrance," Gretchen spoke. We both watched as she twisted the engagement ring on her finger. "I was serious about what I said."

"It won't happen again, I promise," Dad pleaded.

That weekend, I'd started giving up on my plan. It didn't seem likely Dad would agree to sing. I was filled with doubt as my ringing phone woke me up.

"Hello?" I yawned.

"You haven't called me in like a week," Tamela complained. "Is everything alright?"

"You do know phones work two ways, right?"

"Somebody's grouchy."

"I am not grouchy! I just have a lot going on!"

"Oh, you're in one of your dad moods," Tamela teased. 'Dad moods' was her term for when I acted like Dad. "Something's definitely up."

"I'm just trying to bond with this man I call a father and he's making it hard, okay?" I complained. I got up and looked for some clothes to throw on for the day.

"How's he making it hard?"

"He doesn't want to sing and that's the only way I can think of to bond with him." I settled on a gray t-shirt with some jeans.

"Have you asked him why he doesn't want to sing?"

"Every time I try, he gets an attitude about it."

"Sounds like someone else I know."

"What's that supposed to mean?"

"You do the same thing when I ask you to do something you don't want to do."

"It's not the same."

"I think it is. Have you tried explaining to him why this is important to you?"

"You want me to explain my feelings to my dad?"

"Yeah."

"The trumpets must be getting ready to sound for you to suggest something like that."

"So, he won't tell you why he doesn't want to sing, and you won't tell him why you want him to. Do you see the issue here?"

"Every time I try to express myself to him it ends up being an argument."

"Drake, have you heard the way you talk when you try to express yourself?" Tamela laughed.

"What's wrong with how I talk?"

"Nothing, if you think fussing and throwing shoes is normal for expressing yourself."

"That's how Dad talks and acts."

"And where's that gotten him besides being called Crazy-Man and Mr. Shoe-Thrower behind his back?" Tamela said. "All I'm saying is, maybe you should consider a different approach. One that doesn't leave shoe-sized holes in a wall."

"It was Andre who made that hole at the church."

"And it was Karla who broke the children's church window. Mary almost broke the piano. Adrianna has to attend praise dance practice barefoot, and Antoine hit me in the back of my head once. Y'all need to find a new, *healthier* way of expressing anger."

"I don't appreciate this attack on my character," I joked.

"Yeah, yeah," Tamela said. "What are you doing today?"

"I'm meeting with Alex. He's helping me with a project."

"A project?"

"Yeah, it's–!"

My phone beeped.

"I've got another call coming in."

"Well, I'll let you go then. I was just calling to see if you broke up with me and forgot to tell me."

"I love you, Tam."

"Love you too, Drakie. Bye."

Tamela hung up, and I answered the other call.

"Hello?"

"Drake!" Twenty-two-year-old Ralph Brewer laughed. He worked as a journalist under Uncle Arnold at the Creeke Courier. "Just the man I wanted to talk to."

"Hello Ralphie," I said. "What can I help you with?"

"I heard from Mr. Green that you were working on a special project," Ralph explained. "And you know I go wherever a story is brewing. Get it? Brewing? Because I'm Ralph Brewer."

"I get it," I answered as Ralph cackled at his joke. "Did you have a nice date with Diana?"

"How'd you know about that?"

"You're not the only one that goes where a story is brewing."

"Yes, I had a great time. Back to why I called."

"I'm afraid I don't have much to tell you right now."

"That's alright. It's a feature story so I have time for it to develop. I'm thinking front page of the Creeke Courier."

"Front... page?"

"This is a big deal, Drake," Ralph said. "The only thing I see topping the Brown Family Band's return is Mr. Derrick returning to pastoring."

"I see."

"Can you keep me updated on everything that happens with this?" Ralph asked. "You know I'm Mr. Green's best journalist."

"You're his only journalist."

"Not anymore," Ralph chuckled. "I'm sure you know Derik Harrison, right?"

"Which one?"

"The youngest one. I'm mentoring him, which means he also now writes for the Creeke Courier. You can share any new details with him too, and he'll give them to me to add to the story."

"Alright," I agreed. "I'll keep you both updated."

"Thanks Drake. I appreciate it."

Alexander Tanner Brown was my big cousin who was one year older than me. He produced music, which made him the perfect person to help me with my idea. I'd gone to visit him at Uncle Jeremy-Micah's house to discuss what we could do. His best friend, Matthias Harrison, sprawled across Alexander's bed with a toothpick in his mouth. Matthias had his phone at max volume, watching an interview about KV's ventures after his split from K$K.

"*So, KV,*" one of the interviewers said as the topic turned to the KV and Knokout situation. "*Knokout said he didn't steal from you. Y'all's fans are going crazy hoping this is all a joke. They've even got 'Punch Your Lights Out' back on the charts again. Do you have any response to all this?*"

"*Yeah, I got a response,*" KV laughed. "*You heard it here first straight from the mouth of Ra'Kaveon King. When I catch you Vincent, it's on sight. So, be ready. And to the fans: K and K is over. But thank y'all for listening to 'Punch Your Lights Out' and still supporting. I appreciate it.*"

"*That's how you pronounce it?*" the other interviewer gasped. "*I've been saying K dollar sign K this whole time. Why y'all ain't correct me?*"

"Matt, can you turn that down?" Alexander asked. "We're trying to work."

"Sorry," Matthias said. He lowered the volume on the phone.

"Drake, this idea of yours is going to take a lot of time and money," Alexander told me.

"I know," I agreed. "But the big picture will be worth it."

"You can't make the big picture if you can't afford it."

"Look, I've prayed about it and if The Lord wants this to happen, He'll make a way."

"You want to know what I think?" Matthias sat up. He wore a tie-dye t-shirt with a white logo on the front.

"Sure." I gestured for him to speak. "Go ahead."

"I think you guys should have a church bake sale," Matthias rasped. "If the people want to hear your family sing so much, then they can pay for it themselves."

"I don't know if that would work...," I said.

"It was only an idea," Matthias said as he left the room. "I figured you'd be in an exploring mood since you walked out the house in something other than a cardigan for once. But I know how moody y'all Browns get when stuff gets hard, so I'll go."

"Did I say something wrong?" I asked.

"I doubt it. Matthias' feelings don't get hurt that easily."

"Then, why'd he leave?"

"He probably just went outside."

"You know me so well," Matthias called from outside.

"Are you outside my window?"

"I am now," Matthias said while crunching on something. "I still wanted to hear the conversation."

"What are you eating?" Alexander asked.

"A pickle."

"You went outside to eat a pickle?"

"Of course not," Matthias yelled as he displayed an unlit cigarette in the window.

"Why'd I even ask?" Alexander sighed. "You know that stuff's not good for you, Matthias."

"Neither is all that beer your father has in the fridge."

"I'll do whatever I have to do to get this thing made," I told Alexander.

"And everyone's agreed to do it?"

"Well..."

"Who's not on board?"

"Dad..."

"He's the person you need the most."

"I know!" I groaned. "It's so hard convincing him to get on board."

"Can't help you there," Matthias said. "I don't even talk to my own dad."

"Don't be like him," Alexander referred to Matthias. "Talk to Uncle Torrey again. You can't make this project without him."

"I'll give it my best shot."

"If you get everyone on board, I'll pay for it," Matthias stated as he came into view.

"You will?" I gasped.

"How are you going to get the money?" Alexander asked.

"Never ask a man how he gets his money, Alexander," Matthias said. "Hmph."

"What do you want in return?" I asked.

"We'll talk about that another time," Matthias said with a grin. "Just focus on your little project for now."

"Thanks Matthias."

One person telling me to talk to Dad was advice. But two people telling me to talk to Dad was confirmation. I would take Tamela and Alexander's advice and give it another try. Hopefully, things would turn out differently than last time.

Dad sat in the kitchen shining his leather dress shoes when I came home. I didn't know why Dad threw shoes when he was upset, nor did I know when I'd picked up the habit. But I did know that Dad with a shoe was a dangerous combination. He may have told Gretchen he wouldn't throw them anymore, but she wasn't always around yet to make sure he kept his word.

"Dad, can we talk?"

"About?"

The brush passed back and forth across the surface of the shoe.

"I want to know why you don't like singing."

"How many times are you going to ask me that, Drake?"

"Until I get a straight answer," I said as I watched Dad rub polish and water into the tip of the shoe. "Do you even understand why I want you to do this?"

"Not really."

"Because I want to spend time with you," I said. "Doing something we both enjoy and that'll make us happy. But you don't want to sing, and you won't tell me why either. It makes me feel... rejected."

I'd laid my feelings on the table. Whatever Dad did with them after that determined the course of our relationship.

"Singing...," Dad said. "Singing was something I did with my grandpa. It was something all of us did with him because it made him happy. He always said music brought us together. But then someone made fun of my voice and I didn't want to sing anymore."

I perked up when Dad revealed this to me. Jonathan had teased me about how high my voice was, which was why I didn't like him. I'd never told Dad about the insecurities I had with my voice. Hearing Dad had similar struggles as I did made me understand him better.

"Then I started to wonder if other people felt the same way as that person did," Dad said. "Eventually, I didn't want to sing in public anymore because I felt everyone was laughing at me behind my back."

He took my hand in his and looked into my eyes.

"But if it'll make you happy, I'll do it," Dad told me. "I'll sing again."

"You will?"

"I will."

He grabbed his shoe, and I backed up.

"Why'd you flinch?" Dad asked as he placed his shoe on the floor.

"No... no reason!" I stammered. "I...I was just go...going to my room!"

"Okay..."

I hurried from the kitchen. Dad and his shoes made me nervous. But I did have something to be happy about. He'd agreed to sing for me. All that was left to do was to get it done.

-

Chapter Twenty-Five

With Dad agreeing to the project, Alexander felt it best to have something to show Matthias before he invested. He still questioned how Matthias would cover everything, but he put his worries aside for my sake. Alexander tasked Dad with song arrangement, which meant my siblings and I would be singing.

That Monday evening, we all waited for Karla. Mom and Forrest gave us special permission to use the church for our rehearsals because Karla didn't like being at Dad's house. Eventually, she came sauntering up the church aisle.

"You're late," Dad griped at her.

"You said rehearsal started at six." Karla looked at her watch. "It's six."

"If you're on time, you're late."

"If you're on time, you're on time," Karla argued. "That's why it's called 'on time'."

"Just get in line," Dad grumbled.

Karla sat her purse in a chair and joined us on the pulpit. Her relationship with Dad was more strained than mine was with him. They only saw each other once a week.

"Karla, Mary, this is your note," Dad said as he pressed a note on the organ matching to the soprano part. He repeated the process twice more with Adrianna for the alto part and with us boys for the tenor part. Once he finished, he said, "Alright, sing. And make it good."

We all sang. Or at least I thought we all did.

"Andre," Dad called to my younger brother staring off into space.

"Huh?"

"Why didn't you sing?"

"I... don't know...," Andre said, getting quieter with each word.

"Okay...," Dad said. "Let's try this again."

We all sang again.

"Oh no!" Dad covered his ears in horror. "Somebody is off! One more time."

Dad came and stood in front of us. He placed his hands on his hips and leaned forward as we sang again.

"It's you, Andre!" Dad shouted. "Why are you singing the wrong note?"

"I..."

"Wasn't paying attention as usual?" Dad accused. "Don't try to deny it either."

"Sorry sir..."

"This is the note," Dad said as he played the note for Andre again. "Don't mess it up this time. I've had a good day and I want to keep it that way."

"Yes sir."

We sang again. After two hours of singing, we got a break when Dad went to the bathroom. As soon as he exited the sanctuary, Karla turned to Mary and pointed at her.

"You need to talk to him."

"Why me?" Mary asked.

"Because you're the one he yells at the least," Antoine said.

"If anyone needs to talk to him, its Drake," Mary protested. "This was his idea."

"Look guys, we're only arranging the songs," I said. "It's not like we'll actually be singing them."

"Can someone tell *him* that?" Karla huffed.

Mary looked at Andre, who once again stared off into space.

"Andre, what are you looking at?" she asked him.

"I was thinking about Adrianna's dance recital."

"From four months ago?" Adrianna asked. "Why?"

"Because Dad said he was going to the bathroom," Andre explained. "That made me think of how you hog up the bathroom, and then that made me think of your dance recital."

"How do you go from the bathroom to a dance recital?" Adrianna tilted her head to the side.

"I don't know. I just did."

"Sometimes I wonder how you're the second highest ranked person in your class," Karla groaned.

"Excuse me," a gruff voice interrupted us. Leonard Brown hobbled up the aisle of the church. The meanest man in Creeke was coming toward us. As far as I knew, none of us had met him before. He stopped and leaned on his infamous brown cane.

"Yes?" Mary acknowledged him.

"Mary, don't talk to him!" Antoine whispered.

"I'll talk to him if I want!" Mary said. "Can we help you with something?"

"I'm looking for my son, Jeremy-Micah. Is he here?"

"No."

"Oh," Leonard Brown said. His eyes remained on Mary. "This might sound strange, but you look a lot like my mother."

"Why wouldn't I?" Mary said. "We might be related, after all."

"Why does she only speak up when she's not supposed to?" Karla whispered to me. "Any other time she's on mute."

"Who knows?" I sighed.

"What's your name?" Leonard Brown asked.

"Mary Brown."

"Mary Brown...," Leonard Brown repeated with a smile. "You must be one of my granddaughters since you have my last name. These are your brothers and sisters?"

"Yes."

"Wow," Leonard Brown said. "I have grandkids after all. Who's your parent? Jeremy-Micah? Marie?"

"Get away from my children!"

Dad charged from the back of the church and put himself between us, and Leonard Brown.

"Your children?" Leonard Brown said, his eyes growing wide.

"What are you doing here?!"

"I'm looking for Jeremy-Micah."

"He isn't here!" Dad shouted. "Get out!"

"There's no need to be hostile, T-Rex."

"Don't call me that!" Dad roared. "Stay away from my family!"

"Alright, I'm going," Leonard Brown growled. He hobbled away.

"So, that's our grandfather," Mary said when he was gone.

"No!" Dad snapped. "That man is not your grandfather! Why were you talking to him?!"

"He asked me a question."

"Stay away from him, understand me? All of you!"

"Yes sir," we all answered.

Dad couldn't focus after that. Seeing Leonard Brown in person made him tremble with rage. He was all over the place, and after a while, he ended the rehearsal.

"Can you do me a favor?" Mary said after rehearsal.

"What?"

"Can you drop this off to Mimi on your way home?" she asked as she handed me a book.

"Didn't you start this yesterday?" I said as I gawked at the thick book in my hands.

"Yeah. I finished it today. And make sure you remind Mimi to give you the book I loaned to Althea."

"Why can't you do all this yourself?"

"Because I'm going to see the movie this book is based on with Phil. She's waiting for me in the parking lot right now and we have just enough time to get there by the end of the previews."

"Alright, I'll drop your book off."

"Thanks," Mary said before running off. She called over her shoulder, "Tell Dad not to wait up for me!"

It was around eight-thirty at night when I left the church. Naomi lived with her parents while attending nursing school in the city. I always had to call her first before I visited because she was rarely home.

"Hello?" Naomi answered her phone.

"Mimi, where are you?"

"I'm at Grampa's," Naomi revealed, referring to Mr. Damian's house. "Why do you ask?"

"Mary asked me to drop off this book for her."

"What a coincidence!" Naomi laughed. "I was coming over there next to drop off a book for Althea."

"Well, I'm already in the car so I'll come to you."

"Alright, I'll stay put then," Naomi agreed. I recognized my other cousins' voices in the background, and Naomi whispered, "It's Drake."

Giggling followed the announcement of my name, and we ended our conversation. Visiting the Parker side of the family was never dull. They loved to give out hugs and generally made one feel welcome around them. All of them looked like Mr. Damian, and they'd all inherited his sharp tongue.

"It's open!" someone called from the other side when I knocked on the door. I stepped inside and was ambushed by hugs and affection.

"My baby cousin's here!" My twenty-five-year-old cousin Angela Parker gushed. She and Naomi were three months apart.

"Every time I see you, you get thinner and thinner," My twenty-two-year-old cousin Terrence Parker Jr. laughed. He jiggled his stomach. "You need to get some meat on your bones like I've got."

"Junior, if The Lord wanted Drake to be big-boned like us, He would've made him big," My nineteen-year-old cousin Michael Parker griped.

"Grampa's in the kitchen with Mimi and Mrs. Thelma," Angela informed as she grabbed my hand. She started guiding me through the house. "Come say hi."

As we got closer to the kitchen, I could hear Mr. Damian telling one of his stories.

"And I pulled that curtain back and all I saw was a big old snake just sitting in the driveway!" Mr. Damian exclaimed. "And I was like–!"

Mr. Damian paused as he spotted me. His lips curled into a sly smile as he lowered his face toward me.

"Drake...," he sang. He opened his arms wide, and I knew what was coming next. Mr. Damian's hugs were so tight it felt like he was trying to squeeze the life out of a person. I walked over to him, and he wrapped his arms tightly around me.

"Okay!" I squeaked.

"Is it only you?" he asked as he let me go.

"Yeah," I exhaled. I placed the book Mary gave me in front of Naomi. "It's only me."

"Okay, good," Mr. Damian laughed. "Because we don't have any more food."

"Damian!" Mrs. Thelma yelled from the backyard. "Come here!"

"Oh boy," Mr. Damian sighed. "What's she gotten herself into this time?"

Mr. Damian exited the kitchen.

"I didn't want to say this in front of Mr. Damian, but I met Leonard Brown today," I informed my cousins.

"Did he try to do anything to you?" Terrence Jr. asked.

"No, he was looking for Uncle Mikey," I said. "He was actually kind of... nice."

"So was the serpent in the Garden of Eden," Angela remarked. "We see how that went..."

"I don't like the idea of you talking to him," Michael stated.

"I didn't really say anything," I recounted. "It was mostly Mary that talked to him. He said she looked like his mother, and it went from there until Dad came back and freaked out."

"Well, Grandma's always maintained that Leonard Brown is Uncle Torrey's father," Naomi reminded us. She gave me the book Althea wanted her to give Mary. "So, it's not surprising that Mary would look like his mother."

"I don't understand why Grandma stayed with him," Angela huffed.

"You know how the older generations were about divorces," Naomi countered. "Grandma would've been an outcast if she got divorced again, especially in a small town like this."

"I'd rather be an outcast than let my children be abused," Angela argued. "Growing up hearing Daddy wake up screaming in the middle of the night was terrifying. And then Auntie Gracie uses cleaning as a coping mechanism."

"She likes a clean house," Naomi said.

"Do you know why your mother likes a clean house?"

"Because Uncle Torrey spilled some juice on Leonard Brown's favorite rug, and Leonard Brown beat Uncle Torrey, Mommy and Uncle Noah. I'm sure we all know this by now, Angie."

"I didn't know that," I said.

"Yeah, that's how Uncle Torrey got that scar above his eye," Terrence Jr. explained. "Leonard Brown smacked him into a table when he admitted to messing up the rug."

"Dad told us he tripped and fell into a table."

"That's the lie Grandma made them tell the doctor so Uncle Torrey wouldn't get taken away," Michael complained.

"How do y'all know all this?" I asked.

"We talked to our parents about their childhoods," Angela said. "Because some of the stuff they put *us* through growing up needed explanations."

"Shoot even Uncle Mikey and Aunt RieRie are affected," Terrence Jr. continued. "I stayed with Uncle Mikey for one week when I was a teenager, and I will never do that again. I don't know how Alex and Aunt Francine survived all these years with that man."

"Oh, we know," Angela grumbled. "Aunt RieRie letting her husband and daughters run all over her is all the proof we need. I love Grandma but what she allowed Leonard Brown to do to our parents doesn't sit right with me."

"Me either," Michael agreed.

"So, Thelma thought she saw a snake, but it was really the garden hose," Mr. Damian joked as he re-entered the kitchen. He looked at our faces and stopped smiling. "What's got y'all's faces all screwed up?"

"Nothing Grampa," Naomi said. "We were just talking."

"Oh," Mr. Damian's said. "It must've been a serious conversation to make y'all look like this."

Mr. Damian waited for someone to tell him what we were discussing. The looks in my cousins' eyes were all the same. They all silently begged me not to bring up Grandma or Leonard Brown.

"I was... telling them about rehearsal with Dad," I answered as I stood up. "Speaking of Dad, I should probably get home before he wonders where I went."

"I'll see you out," Mr. Damian offered. When we were far enough outside the house, he asked me, "What were you guys really talking about, Drake?"

"Rehearsal."

"Unless he sent one of y'all to the hospital from throwing a shoe, a rehearsal story about Torrance wouldn't cause that reaction," Mr. Damian noted. "I know there's more to it than that."

"Leonard Brown showed up to the rehearsal," I sighed. I couldn't lie to him.

"He did?" Mr. Damian's face darkened at the mention of Leonard Brown.

"He claimed Mary looked like his mother. Then Dad came back from the bathroom, and they argued until Leonard Brown left."

"That's all?"

"I didn't want to tell you because I know you don't like Leonard Brown."

"Drake, I'm an old man," Mr. Damian snorted. "I've seen and heard worse. Leonard Brown being an idiot for the umpteenth time doesn't faze me."

"I didn't want to cause any drama."

"Trust me, there won't be any drama coming from my end." Mr. Damian puffed up his chest. "I've left those days behind."

"I'm sorry."

"There's nothing to apologize for," Mr. Damian said as he patted my shoulder. "But you *should* get home before your dad wonders where you went."

"Right," I agreed as I opened my car door.

"And Drake?"

"Sir?"

"If you happen to pass by Noah's squad car on your way home, honk your horn at him to wake him up," Mr. Damian instructed. "Can't have Creeke's police chief fast asleep in his car now, can we?"

"No sir, we can't," I giggled.

Chapter Twenty-Six

"You want to know why your father acts how he does?" Mom repeated my question as we folded clothes together the next day. My cousins had inspired me to get to the root of Dad's trauma.

"He seems to have a lot of unresolved issues," I said. "I feel like it holds him back from doing what he loves."

"It's not your job to fix your father's life, Drake."

"I'm not trying to fix it. I'm trying to understand it."

"Maybe he doesn't want you to understand those things, and that's why he hasn't told you about them. *I* still don't know everything that happened to him, and I was married to him for ten years."

"Mom... my relationship with Dad is riding on this."

"It's that serious?"

"We're approaching a Karla and Dad situation."

"Oh, it *is* serious."

"Really?" Karla stopped folding to glare at us. "Y'all act like I hate the man."

"You *did* move out his house on your eighteenth birthday," Mom muttered.

"Because I needed space," Karla said. "Just because I refuse to be his emotional punching bag doesn't mean I love him any less."

"If things keep going the way they are, I'm going to need space away from him soon too," I sighed.

"Well, if you ask me, you should talk to the people who've been with him the longest to get your answers," Karla advised. "We both know Dad isn't giving up any info."

"I might do that," I figured.

"Whatever happens, I wasn't involved," Mom said. "Your father and I are in a good place, and I'm not taking the heat from him if things go wrong."

"That's why I'm here," Karla joked. "To take the heat for you."

"Mommy!" Layla yelled as she ran into the room, her face covered in glitter and face paint.

"Someone had fun at Aunt Tavia's today," Mom said.

"She sure did," Tavia answered as she followed Layla. She was Forrest's forty-seven-year-old sister and the band director at Creeke High. Tavia took off from work that day to take Layla to a doctor's appointment while Mom cleaned the house.

"Let's get you cleaned up," Karla said to Layla, leading her away.

"Girl," Tavia exhaled as she fell on the sofa. She pushed her locs from her dark-brown face. "That child has so much energy. My daughter, Brianne, wasn't even that energetic at that age."

"I know," Mom giggled. "Thanks for taking her to her appointment. Karla and I really needed time to clean the house."

"You're welcome," Tavia said as she grabbed a shirt to fold. "What's new?"

"Torrance," Mom said.

"Don't tell me he did something on the one day I'm not at work," Tavia whined.

"Drake wants to understand his past."

"I feel like the only person he'll trust that information to is Gretchen."

"It seems like she can get him to do pretty much anything just by sweet-talking him," Mom said.

"Baby, Gretchen is just as much sugar and spice as her sister is," Tavia laughed. "You should've seen the way she was going off when we were on that teambuilding trip."

"What happened?"

"All I remember is walking with Donna into our meeting area on the last day and Gretchen was going off. She calmed down after Torrance proposed to her, but I think she and him are more alike than we realized."

"I like her even more now," Mom said. "She won't let Torrance and the kids walk all over her like I thought. That's good."

"But you do have a point though," Tavia said. "Torrance seems to open up more to people that are nice to him. Maybe you should try that approach, Drake."

"Okay."

"You want to understand Torrance's anger issues?" Uncle Jeremy-Micah howled with laughter that evening. I'd gone with him to Aunt Marie's house to get answers from them both. "Do you know what you're asking, Drake?"

"Oh, come on Mikey," Aunt Marie chastised. "It can't be that hard to explain why Torrance acts the way he does."

"You do it then," Uncle Jeremy-Micah dared Aunt Marie. "You were with him the longest."

"Yeah, but you know more about what went on outside of us."

"Why don't you both combine what you know?" I suggested.

"Are you sure you want the truth?" Uncle Jeremy-Micah warned me. "Because once I start, I'm not stopping."

"Tell me everything."

"Okay," Uncle Jeremy-Micah said. "We all know Mama cheated on Mr. Damian and left him for Dad. After that drama ended, things were fine until Torrance was about three. Dad claimed Mr. Damian was Torrance's father because of how he looked, while Mama maintained Dad was the father. Then Dad tried to separate Marie and I from the other three as much as possible. He made them all sleep together in one bed, they couldn't eat with us at the table, and they were never allowed to go on family trips with us. The rug incident was the only time he hit them as far as I know."

"That whole weekend was horrifying," Aunt Marie added. "Dad took us to see his parents that weekend. He wanted to make up with his father and... it didn't go well. His father was mean... and his mother acted like nothing was wrong. When we got home, Dad saw the rug and lost it."

"And Mama was powerless against him," Uncle Jeremy-Micah grumbled. "She couldn't stop him. After that, Mr. Damian took Terrence and Ruth-Anne from the house for good. Dad didn't touch Torrance again because Grandpa threatened him. It was like a rollercoaster between them. Sometimes Dad would be nice, and then he'd switch back to being mean again."

"I think Torrance reminded Dad of himself," Aunt Marie whispered. "I think Dad didn't want to admit that he'd become like his father. And so instead of trying to do better, he pushed Torrance away instead."

"Look at you, sounding like a guidance counselor," Uncle Jeremy-Micah chuckled. "You trying to take my job at the middle school, Marie?"

"It's the only way I can explain why he tried to get rid of Torrance for good when he was fourteen."

"He tried to get rid of Dad?" I gasped.

"He tried to pawn him off on Mr. Damian," Uncle Jeremy-Micah said.

"It backfired," Aunt Marie revealed. "When Grandpa brought him back home, Grandpa said he was taking us to live with him and this big argument started. And you know I don't like loud noises, so I went outside. Torrance and I started fighting over the front seat and next thing I know Grandpa shot Dad."

"Great-Grandpa shot someone?!"

"He's shot several people," Uncle Jeremy-Micah sighed. ""You'd be surprised what people confess to when they're old and facing death. That's why Dad has to use a cane. He lied and told everyone he shot himself on accident, but I learned the truth from Mama."

"Oh wow."

"Dad wholeheartedly believed that Torrance wasn't his son," Uncle Jeremy-Micah said. "Then a year later, Dad wasn't sure about what he believed, and Torrance started saying he wished they knew the truth."

"They had a heart-to-heart after Torrance got in a fight," Aunt Marie said.

"That's what happened?" Uncle Jeremy-Micah asked.

"Yeah," Aunt Marie said. "I was eavesdropping."

"I'm surprised at you, Marie," Uncle Jeremy-Micah teased. "After that, Torrance and Dad started avoiding each other like they both had the plague. And then when Grandpa died, Torrance had this new surge of anger. Except, I don't think it's new. I think it's old anger that he refuses to deal with."

"That... explains a lot," I said.

"I believe they know they're father and son and don't want to accept it," Uncle Jeremy-Micah ranted. "Because if they do, Dad has to accept he abused his own son and accused Mama of doing something she didn't do. And Torrance would have to accept the truth that Dad *is* his father, and I don't think he's ready to do that."

"That was a lot," I sighed.

"Oh, we're not finished," Uncle Jeremy-Micah laughed. "That's only half of the truth. The other half is the feud between the Browns and the Harrisons."

"What's that got to do with this?" I asked.

"You know how Mr. Derrick and Mr. Damian are best friends?"

"Yeah."

"Well, Dad was their other best friend. It used to be the three of them. And after Mama cheated with Dad, it ruined the friendship. Dad , Mama, and Mr. Derrick stopped being friends because Mr. Derrick blames them for everything."

"That's why they're feuding?"

"Yeah," Uncle Jeremy-Micah affirmed. "Marie can explain the rest because she knows more than I do."

"The men are the ones feuding," Aunt Marie corrected. "Mama, Mrs. Kiana, and Mrs. Thelma have forgiven and moved on. Mama just doesn't fool with Mr. Derrick because of a sermon he preached against her back in the day."

"That's out of character for him," I said

"Right?" Uncle Jeremy-Micah echoed. "I was shocked."

"You weren't even there!" Aunt Marie argued.

"I heard about it!" Uncle Jeremy-Micah said. "That man smiled in my face and everything that *same day*, and the whole time he preached a sermon against us."

"Against Mama and Dad," Aunt Marie corrected. "He never came after us kids. But it explained a lot about why Marlin Harrison didn't like us. Let me ask you something, Drake. Have you ever disliked something because your dad disliked it?"

"Yeah."

"That's what I think was Marlin's problem. I believe Mr. Derrick used to complain about the situation in front of Marlin, and that caused Marlin to dislike us. Mama complained about him all the time in front of us, so that's why I believe that. Your father and Marlin used to fight all the time. My concern is, I don't think it's going to stop with them."

"I don't think we'll have to worry about Matthias," Uncle Jeremy-Micah chuckled. "He's always at my house."

"Hola Mama," My eighteen-year-old cousin Mariana Garza said as she entered the house with shopping bags.

"Stop," Aunt Marie commanded. "Where've you been, Mariana?"

"Out," Mariana answered rolled her blue eyes. They were the only thing she'd inherited from her father.

"Out?" Aunt Marie said. "What does 'out' mean?"

"It means that I was out," Mariana huffed as she turned to go to her room.

"Mariana," Uncle Jeremy-Micah warned. "Don't you walk away without giving your mother a proper answer."

"Ugh." Mariana blew air through her nostrils. "I was at the mall with my friends, okay?"

"And where is Mariella?" Aunt Marie asked, referring to her other, fourteen-year-old daughter Mariella.

"I don't know," Mariana huffed. "I'm not responsible for her. Can I go now?"

"Yeah," Aunt Marie sighed. "You can go."

Mariana stomped off to her room and slammed the door.

"You need to stop letting that little girl walk all over you," Uncle Jeremy-Micah said.

"I'm doing the best I can."

"Well maybe if Alejandro stopped letting them have their way, you wouldn't have to do your best."

"Alejandro is fifty. He can't do as much as he'd like."

"Why do you always make excuses for him?"

"Mikey, do I come into your home and criticize you?"

"That's not the point, Marie. You need to stop being a doormat."

"How about I start right now then? Get out."

"Oh yeah," Uncle Jeremy-Micah huffed. "Kick out the person trying to help you. Come on, Drake."

"Bye Auntie," I said as I stood up.

"Bye sweetie," Aunt Marie hugged me. "Talk some sense into your uncle for me, okay?"

"Whatever Marie," Uncle Jeremy-Micah said as he sucked his teeth. "You know I'm right."

Instead of going home, I asked Uncle Jeremy-Micah to drop me off at Derek's house. He didn't live far from us, so I could walk home when I finished my visit.

"I need your help," I told Derek when he opened the door.

"You need *my* help?" Derek repeated.

"Okay, more like I need your dad's help," I clarified. "You can help by taking me to him."

"Come on in." Derek stepped to the side to let me inside.

"I'm on my grown man tonight!" Mr. Malcolm hollered from the back of the house. He attempted to sing along to a song, but it didn't sound good.

"Hang on," Derek groaned. He ran to the back of the house, and I heard him yell, "YO!"

"What?" Mr. Malcolm called back as he turned down his music.

"We've got company, man! Wrap it up in there!"

"Who is it?"

"It's Drake!"

"Alright, give me a minute!"

"Sorry about that," Derek sighed. "He's getting ready for his little date tonight."

"That's alright," I said. "I'm sure if we went to my house, we'd walk in on my dad freestyling to himself."

"Torrance still freestyles?" Mr. Malcolm asked as he entered the room. A sweet scent followed him. "Aw man, I used to love when he did that."

"Lord, you've got the whole house smelling like old man body wash," Derek said as he pinched his nose.

"Can I be on my grown man in peace?"

"You can after you leave for tonight."

"Hater," Mr. Malcolm grumbled.

"What am I hating on? Soon, I won't be single like *you*."

"What brings you by Drake?" Mr. Malcolm asked as he flicked his son's ear.

"I had some questions, but I could come back another time."

"No, no, you're already here. Ask away."

"I wanted to know what you could tell me about the feud between the Harrisons and the Browns."

"Where do we even begin?"

"Well, my uncle told me the feud started because your father held my grandma and her husband accountable for their actions. Then my aunt told me your brother didn't like my dad because their parents didn't like each other and complained about each other in front of you guys."

"That's partly right," Mr. Malcolm agreed. "Dad doesn't like the Brown parents, and he did complain about them in front of us. And Marlin didn't like their kids back then, but now he's indifferent. Personally, I think he was jealous of the attention Dad showed to Torrance. He always complained that Dad treated Torrance and me better than him."

"What about you?"

"I could care less about all that mess," Mr. Malcolm said. He motioned to Derek. "I had more important things to worry about."

"I'm a thing now?" Derek teased.

"A thing that's looking to be noogied if he keeps it up," Mr. Malcolm joked as he held his fist up.

"I give noogies too," Derek said.

"Is there a way to end the feud between our families?" I interrupted their father-son moment.

"End the feud?" Mr. Malcolm said.

"The only way I see that happening is if you build a time machine and go back in time to stop it before it starts," Derek joked.

"You could try fixing the source of it, but good luck with that," Mr. Malcolm laughed. "Everyone at that level is stubborn."

"I guess you're right," I sighed.

"Well, if you'll excuse me." Mr. Malcolm stood up. "I need to finish getting ready."

"I should probably leave too," I said.

"I'll walk with you," Derek offered. I looked at his outfit. He wore a white tank top with orange shorts, dark blue socks, and black slides.

"You're going out like that?" I asked.

"Yeah?" Derek said as he put a red baseball cap on his head. "We're just going around the corner."

As we walked to my house, Derek started playing music.

"Who is this you're playing?" I asked.

"It's Knokout."

"The dude that stole from KV?"

"*Allegedly,*" Derek protested.

"You must be a fan of his," I teased him.

"Knokout's one of my favorite rappers," Derek said. "I'm waiting for him to drop his new single on Friday. Have you heard his diss track to KV?"

"He made a diss track?"

"Yeah, like a few days after KV did his interview."

"*When I catch you Vincent, it's on sight,*" KV's voice said from the phone. "*So, be ready.*"

"*Be ready?*" Knokout's voice said. "*I'm always ready, Ra'Kaveon. You know where I stay. But since you're looking for a moment, let me give it to you.*"

The beat started. It sounded like one of those old-school songs Dad listened to when he was my age.

"*You say I'm a thief and that I stole from you,*" Knokout rapped. "*But we both know that that is really far from the truth. Anything you have, just know I have it too. I don't need your stuff, so why don't you get a clue?*"

"*You should check the people that you still have around. Because they're the ones running you in the ground. Tried to keep it quiet, didn't want to make a sound. But had to clear my name before you sent me to the pound.*"

"*Now you see, I really thought that you were my brother. Even though we don't share a father or mother. I really thought our bond was thicker than water, but now I see that all we have is it out for each other.*"

Knokout stopped rapping and started talking to KV.

"*Ra'Kaveon, let me ask you a question man to man,*" Knokout ranted. "*If I really stole your watch and your money, don't you think you would've found it by now somewhere on the internet? Because if I stole it, I would've sold it. You need to check the people around you. They're the ones stealing from you not me. But since you don't believe me, why don't you consider this you being bodied by a so-called thief. Knokout knocked KV out. Night-night.*"

"I'm not going to lie, that was kind of weak," I said.

"Yeah," Derek sighed. "Knokout is better at beats and writing hooks, while KV is more of a verse guy. That's why they're old music worked. They each did what they were good at. I hope they solve their issues one day."

"Well, if it isn't Drake Brown!" Ralph called as he stopped his car beside us. "Just the man I wanted to see."

"Hello Ralphie," I said. I looked at the person in his passenger seat. "Derik."

"What are you doing in there, Dee-Three?" Derek asked.

"Chasing a story," Derik said.

"On a school night?"

"I did all my homework."

"And now the real work begins," Ralph declared. "You got something for me, Mr. Drake?"

"Everyone's on board, Alex is our producer, and we've started rehearsals," I said.

"So, this is a multi-generational thing," Ralph said, nodding his head. "I'm telling you, Drake. This'll be front page news. I can smell it."

"Ralphie, we're going to be late to our story," Derik said.

"Oh no, we won't," Ralph said. "Duty calls, gentlemen. Have a nice day."

Ralph sped off in his car.

"How's he going to make this a front-page story?" Derek asked.

"I'm sure he'll find a way," I said.

-

Chapter Twenty-Seven

The smell of bleach forced me awake as a familiar old-school beat threatened to shake the walls loose. Daylight poured into my room as bar after bar of music flowed through the house. Dad's favorite genre on a Saturday morning only meant one thing.

"No...," I groaned. I pulled the covers over my head as heavy footsteps came to my room.

"Don't act like you're asleep." Dad ripped the blanket off my head. "It's cleaning time."

"Why?" I whined.

"Do you want to live in a dirty house?"

"No."

"Then get up," Dad ordered. "Your grandmother is coming over today."

"Why?"

"She has something important to tell me, but she wanted to say it in person. I'm going to the store to get something to cook, so you're in charge until I get back."

I wiped the crust from my eyes and dragged myself from the bed. Cleaning Dad's house was never fun. Especially the warzone he called a room. We all worked hard to clean up for Grandma Marianne's visit that afternoon.

"Knock, knock," Grandma announced as she walked through the door.

"What's all this?" I asked, motioning to the bags in her hands.

"Some pies I plan to make. Where's everybody at?"

"I don't know. Adrianna's here, but she's getting ready for a date."

"A date? Who's she going on a date with at fifteen?"

"I don't know. You'll have to ask her."

"Where's your dad?"

"He's re-cleaning his room because he said we didn't do it right."

"That's like the pot calling the kettle black because he doesn't clean his room right either," Grandma said. She placed two frozen cherry pies in the oven. "Normally, I'd make these from scratch but there's too much going on right now."

"Like what?"

"I'll wait until your father gets done."

The pies finished cooking before Dad did cleaning. Grandma brought her picture book to share some memories. Adrianna entered the kitchen wearing a black sweater with a denim skirt and matching black boots.

"What smells so good in here?" she asked as she played with her cross necklace.

"Some pies," Grandma answered. "Your brother said you were going on a date today."

"Yeah, I'm going to the movies with a boy from school."

"What's his name?"

"Grandma, it's our third date. I'm still feeling him out."

"I can't know who he is?"

"Not yet."

"Does he have a job at least?"

"I don't know."

"What about a car?"

"I don't think so."

"How are you getting there then?"

"We're meeting there."

"He's not picking you up?!"

"That man looks like Dad," Adrianna said to change the subject. She pointed to a black and white photo with a smiling man. "Is that his father?"

"Yep. That's Leonard when he was younger."

"*It is?!*"

We both looked closer at the photo. The younger version of Leonard Brown resembled Dad but with darker skin.

"That's crazy," I said as I stared at the photo. "Dad told us that Leonard Brown wasn't his father."

"Torrance said that?"

"I said what, Mama?" Dad asked as he entered the kitchen.

"You told your kids Leonard wasn't your father?"

"He's not."

"Move." Grandma pushed Dad away from the oven. She wrapped the pies in aluminum foil. "Are you trying to tell me I don't know who my own child's father is?"

"He doesn't claim me."

"So, I was just with any and everybody now, huh?"

"That's not what I meant, Mama. I don't want my kids around him."

"So, say that!" Grandma yelled, slamming the aluminum foil box against the counter. She pointed the object at Dad's face. "Don't lie to them and say he's not your father!"

"Sorry Mama..."

"Yeah, you ought to be sorry," Grandma ranted as she snatched up her purse. "Accusing me of not knowing who your father is? After I spent sixteen hours pushing your big head into the world? Oh, you get on my nerves!"

She grabbed the pies and dragged me from the house with her.

"Grandma, where are we going?"

"We're delivering these pies!" Grandma huffed as she put everything in the car and drove off. She ranted the whole time about what Dad said. "The nerve of that boy! Spreading lies about me like I'm just the worst mother in the world!"

Grandma stopped the car in front of Mr. Derrick's house.

"Grab that cherry pie and come on," Grandma said.

I followed Grandma up to the front door. She knocked on the door, and Mrs. Kiana answered it.

"Marianne?" Mrs. Kiana said from the other side of the screen door. "What are you doing here?"

"I need to see your husband about some business," Grandma explained. She pointed to the pie in my hand. "We brought cherry pie."

"Cherry?" Mrs. Kiana asked, her face brightening up. She opened the screen door and ushered us inside. "Drake, take that to the kitchen while I talk to your grandmother."

"Kiki, who's at the door?" Mr. Derrick called from the kitchen.

"It's me," I answered.

"Drake!" Mr. Derrick said. "What are you doing here?"

"I brought pie," I said, holding the pie in my hand up. "It's cherry."

"Cherry?" Mr. Derrick said, licking his lips. "Let me get a slice of that."

Mr. Derrick grabbed a knife from a drawer and started cutting the pie up.

"Who made it?"

"My grandma."

"Ernestine made this? Oh, I know it's going to be good."

"My... other grandma..."

"Oh." Mr. Derrick stopped cutting and sat back down. "It's probably poisoned."

Grandma and Mrs. Kiana entered the kitchen.

"Why you ain't give him any pie?" Grandma demanded of me.

"He doesn't want any."

"Why not?" Mrs. Kiana asked. "It's cherry. Your favorite."

"I'm not eating that pie," Mr. Derrick declared. "Why are you in my house, Marianne?"

"I need your help," Grandma said as she sat down across from him.

"Why don't you ask your husband for help? The one you chose to be with, remember?"

"I don't even know why I bothered coming over here."

"I don't either."

"You just love holding stuff over people when you know full well you were out here being wild like the rest of us."

"You're the one who cheated, got pregnant and married your side-piece, not me."

"You know what your real issue is? You're just mad that I didn't sleep with you!"

"I didn't want to sleep with you, Marianne," Mr. Derrick said. He placed his hand on Mrs. Kiana's shoulder as she ate a slice of pie. "I have a wife that I'm very much in love with."

"Hold on," I interjected. Everyone looked at me. "Is this what the problem has been all these years?"

"Yep," Mrs. Kiana nodded as she took another bite of pie. "They've been fighting this whole time over who Marianne slept with."

"It's deeper than that," Mr. Derrick griped.

"Okay." I sat down at the end of the table between them. "Why don't you both explain to me why y'all are mad at each other and maybe we can fix this together."

"You're just like your daddy," Grandma groaned. "Always want to fix something."

"Grandma." I looked at her, and she quieted down. "Mr. Derrick, you go first."

"I'm mad at Marianne because she cheated on my best friend with my other *former* best friend."

"Okay. Grandma, your turn."

"I'm mad at Derrick because he likes to point out everyone else's faults but won't acknowledge his own. Last time I checked, you were sat down because you didn't have it together."

"Oh, that's where we're going now?" Mr. Derrick laughed.

"No," I said. "That's not where we're not going. Mr. Derrick, what did Grandma specifically do to you?"

"She...," Mr. Derrick stopped to think. He wrinkled his face trying to think before confirming what I already suspected. "I don't know."

"Grandma, what did he specifically do to you?"

"He embarrassed me in front of the whole church!"

"So, if he apologizes, can y'all move on?"

"I guess...," Grandma mumbled.

"I already tried to apologize, and she didn't want to hear it," Mr. Derrick protested.

"Well, now she does," Mrs. Kiana said. "So, why don't you go ahead and apologize?"

"Alright," Mr. Derrick sighed. "I'm sorry for calling you out in front of the whole church."

"And?" Grandma said.

"And hurting your feelings."

"And?"

"What else is there?"

"You said I was a bad mother."

"When did you say that?!" Mrs. Kiana exclaimed as she finished her slice of pie.

"When he came to my house interrogating me."

"Lord," Mrs. Kiana groaned. "Can't let you go nowhere by yourself."

"I still stand by what I said," Mr. Derrick declared. "You allowed that to happen to your kids."

"No, I didn't!" Grandma protested. "Do you really think I wouldn't put up a fight for them?"

"Well, you defended Leonard's actions."

"I was scared!"

"Why didn't you let me help you then?!"

"Because you jumped to conclusions and blamed me!" Grandma said. "I felt like I couldn't trust you!"

"You know I would've put our differences aside to help you in that kind of situation," Mr. Derrick said.

"How would I have known, especially after everything you did?"

"Because you know the type of person I am."

"And you know the type of person I am too, which means you know I wouldn't just willingly let my kids be hurt."

Grandma and Mr. Derrick stared at each other. They were like stubborn mules, unwilling to bend to the other.

"Y'all have both made mistakes that y'all regret," Mrs. Kiana said. "Sitting here blaming each other won't solve anything."

The pair continued staring at each other until Mr. Derrick cracked.

"Look," he sighed. "I'm sorry for everything I did. I was just hurt by what you did to Damian."

"I forgive you," Grandma said.

"Now hug and make up," Mrs. Kiana said.

Grandma and Mr. Derrick hugged.

"I still need your help," Grandma said when they sat back down.

"With what?" Mr. Derrick asked.

"Leonard has agreed to do a DNA test with Torrance."

"Look at God!" Mrs. Kiana hollered as she clapped her hands together. She leaped from her chair and started leaving the kitchen. "Yes Lord! Hallelujah! Thank you, Father! *Thank you!*"

"Where are you going?" Mr. Derrick asked.

"I'm going back to my prayer closet to thank The Lord for these blessings! He's answering my prayers today! Hallelujah!"

"What's this got to do with me, Marianne?" Mr. Derrick asked.

"I need you to read the results."

"Why me?"

"Because if you read them, they'll have no choice but to accept its the truth. If anyone else reads them, they'll both think they were tampered with in some way."

"I'll ask Kiana to do it. I don't want to be around Leonard yet."

"Good enough," Grandma agreed. "I'll let you know when we get the results."

As we left Mr. Derrick's house, I confronted Grandma about the information she'd shared.

"Um... Grandma?"

"Yeah?"

"Does Dad know he's doing a DNA test?"

"Oh no!" Grandma gasped. "I got so worked up I forgot to tell him!"

"That's okay," I said. "You can tell him when we get back."

"I left the test on the table."

"Lord have mercy."

"What are we going to do?!"

"We?"

"Yeah, you and me, little boy."

"Why am I in this?"

"Because I said so."

Our next stop was Mr. Damian's house. On our way there, I looked through my social media to see what was new. Adrianna posed next to the movie posters by herself in her post. I noticed she wore a second necklace she wasn't wearing earlier. It was a gold necklace with her name centered on its chain.

A few posts later, Derek squatted in the same area and pointed at the camera while his tongue hung from his mouth. He wore purple track pants that coordinated with the space-themed logo on his black hoodie. A black cap sat twisted to the side on his head, and he wore his usual black sneakers. But what caught my eye was the chain around his neck. It had his name on it too, and his caption was 'It cost a bag to bag her'. I found it all interesting.

"Listen to me," Grandma said as we arrived at Mr. Damian's. "Give Damian the pie as soon as he answers the door. That way he'll be distracted and won't get upset that I'm there."

"What if it's not him that answers?" I asked as I followed her up the driveway.

"Why wouldn't it be him?" Grandma asked as she knocked on the door.

"Because–!"

Before I could finish my sentence, Mrs. Thelma opened the door.

"Marianne?" she said.

"Thelma?" Grandma said. "What are you doing here?"

"I live here with my husband."

"Husband? What husband?"

"Damian."

"Damian?! I thought y'all were only dating!"

"Marianne, we've been married for like sixteen years now."

"Sixteen years?! Where was I when this happened?"

"We decided to keep it quiet."

"I still should've known! Especially since you married the father of my kids, Thelma! I could've got you a gift or...or something if I'd known!"

"Who's at the door, Honeybun?" Mr. Damian called from inside.

"It's Marianne, Sugarbear."

Mr. Damian came to the door. A grim frown sat on his face as he looked at Grandma. It wasn't the smiling man in three-piece suits I was used to seeing.

"What are you doing here?" Mr. Damian asked as he scowled at Grandma.

"We brought pie as a peace offering," I said. I handed the pie to Mr. Damian. "It's cherry."

"Thanks Drake." Mr. Damian pursed his lips as he accepted the pie. He turned back to Grandma. "What?"

"I need to talk to you."

"Unless it's about Noah or Gracie, we have nothing to talk about."

"It's about... Torrance," Grandma admitted, getting quieter when she said Dad's name.

"What about him?" Mr. Damian's demeanor softened.

"It's about who his father is."

"It's not me."

"I know that!" Grandma snapped. "Look, Leonard agreed to do a DNA test and I need you to be there when the results are read."

"Why?"

"Just come! You make things way harder than they need to be for no reason!"

Grandma walked off the porch, digging in her purse for her keys. Mr. Damian's watched her, looking at her the same way Dad looked at Leonard Brown. This wouldn't be as easy to fix.

"Okay," Grandma encouraged herself up as we sat in the car outside the house. "All we have to do is go in there and tell Torrance about the DNA test. Right?"

"Right."

"Why am I so nervous then?" Grandma's hand shook. "Are you nervous?"

"A little."

"There's nothing to be nervous about!" Grandma declared. "I'm his mother! I can go in there and tell him to take the test right now! And he'll have to listen to me, right?"

"Right!"

"I'm going to go in there and I'm going to tell Torrance he's taking that test! And you're going to back me up! Right?"

"I don't know about that, Grandma..."

"What do you mean? You're supposed to be my help!"

"Your help comes from The Lord."

"Lord, you sound like my daddy."

"As Dad's mom, you can tell him what to do. If I try to tell him what to do, I might get slapped since he's not throwing shoes anymore."

"Boy please," Grandma said. "You're with me. And as long as I'm around, none of my grandbabies are being slapped. Let's go."

Grandma led me into the house. Dad sat on the couch holding the DNA test.

"Hey Torrance...," Grandma squeaked.

"Mama," Dad held up the DNA test. He bounced his leg up and down in a steady rhythm. "Is there something you want to tell me?"

"Well... I... it's um... well... Uh..."

"Leonard Brown wants to do a DNA test with you," I spat out. "Grandma meant to tell you before we left, but she forgot."

"Why now?"

"He said he has reason to believe that you might be his son," Grandma explained, finding her words again.

"What's the reason?"

"I don't know," Grandma sighed. "He came home Monday evening muttering to himself. When I got tired of it and asked him about it, he said that he wanted to do a DNA test with you. Then he started asking me about grandkids and why he'd never met any."

Dad looked at me.

"He said Mary looked like his mom."

"And there it is," Dad laughed. "He wants to do a test because of *Mary*, not me."

"Does it matter?" Grandma cried. "It's still a test. We can settle this and y'all can stop blaming like I did something wrong when I know I didn't."

"I guess you're right," Dad grumbled. "What do I have to do?"

"We have to swab the inside of your cheek four times."

"Four times?!"

"That's what it says to do in the instructions."

"Fine," Dad sighed as he ripped the packet containing the swabs open. "Let's get this over with."

-

Chapter Twenty-Eight

The results arrived the third week of September. Grandma wanted everyone to gather at her house to hear them, and Dad chose me as his emotional support buddy. We all sat at the kitchen table that Friday, waiting for Leonard Brown.

"I guess you're all wondering why I've gathered you here for this," Grandma spoke. "I need to get some things off my chest before the results."

Grandma looked at Mr. Damian and Mrs. Thelma.

"Damian, I'm sorry that I cheated on you," Grandma apologized. "I should've told you how I felt... that I didn't love you the same way you loved me."

"You don't have to explain nothing to me," Mr. Damian said. "I'll accept your apology though."

"Thelma, take care of him," Grandma said. "He's a good man I didn't deserve."

Grandma turned to her children.

"Children," Grandma choked up. "I'm sorry... that I... that I didn't do enough to protect you."

"Mama, why did you stay with him?" Uncle Jeremy-Micah asked.

"I... I didn't want to be divorced twice," Grandma said.

"Mama, you don't owe us an explanation," Uncle Terrence said.

"I want to explain," Grandma said. "I never wanted any of you to be hurt. But I didn't want the embarrassment of having two failed marriages. And I didn't want my daddy to be ashamed of me. So, I stayed. It's all my fault and I'm sorry."

"Grandpa wasn't ashamed of you," Dad said.

"And it's not *all* your fault either," Mrs. Kiana said. "Leonard also has a huge part to play in this too."

"Yeah," Mrs. Thelma agreed. "None of this would even be necessary if it weren't for him."

"Now that, I agree with," Mr. Damian said. "Leonard is as much to blame as you are."

The front door squeaked open.

"What's with all these cars in front of my house?!" Leonard Brown complained. "Marianne!"

"I'm in the kitchen," Grandma sighed.

Leonard Brown stormed into the kitchen. He stopped when he saw everyone at the table.

"What's going on here?"

"The results came."

"They did?" Leonard Brown looked around the room. He locked onto Mr. Damian and Mrs. Thelma, then shifted to Mrs. Kiana sitting next to him. "Why are they here?"

"I asked them to come."

"For what?"

"Because I wanted them to be here."

"Woman, you got all these people I don't fool with in my house!"

"Just sit down so we can get this over with!" Dad huffed. I nudged him under the table with my foot and he settled down. Leonard Brown sat at the other end of the table.

"Go ahead, Kiana," Grandma said.

"Okay," Mrs. Kiana nodded as he held up the envelope. "These are the results. Everyone can clearly see the envelope is still sealed. I'm just here to read the results. Nothing more, nothing less."

Mrs. Kiana unsealed the envelope and removed the contents. I held Dad's hand as we waited to hear the truth.

"The possibility of paternity is... ninety-nine-point nine percent," Mrs. Kiana read. "You are father and son."

"Wow...," Uncle Terrence laughed. A single tear slid down his face. "*Wow...*"

Mrs. Kiana placed the results on the table and left. Dad picked them up and read them for himself.

"Everything you put us through, and you were the father this whole time," Aunt Ruth-Anne said.

"Ninety-nine-point nine percent?" Uncle Arnold said from a clenched jaw.

"Come on, honey," Aunt Ruth-Anne grabbed her husband's hand. "Take me home. I don't want you to go to jail today."

"Ninety-nine-point nine percent," Uncle Arnold repeated as Aunt Ruth-Anne led him from the house.

"You know you screwed up, right?" Uncle Jeremy-Micah told his father.

Dad flung the results on the table and left. I followed him up the sidewalk.

"Where are you going?" I yelled.

"I had to get out that house!" Dad ranted. "*Ninety-nine-point nine percent?!*"

"Dad, slow down!"

"Thirty-seven years!" Dad continued. "This man denied me for thirty-seven years!"

"Hello?" I called "Dad!"

"What?!"

"Here, put your shoes on."

"Man!" Dad snatched the shoes from my hand and flung them into the street. "Forget these shoes! I just found out my father is the one person I didn't want it to be, and you're worried about some shoes?!"

"I'm worried about *you*," I corrected. "You're walking down the street ranting to yourself with no shoes on. I know you're upset but I need to know where you're going."

"I'll go where I want!" Dad shouted. "I'm the father, not you! I don't have to answer to you! Why don't you mind your business?!"

"Because you brought me here for emotional support!" I argued.

"Well, you're not doing a very good job!" Dad yelled. "In fact, you never do a good job at being supportive! It's always 'Dad, why do you do this?' and 'Dad, how could you do that?'! I'm sick of it! Leave me alone!"

Dad stormed off up the street. His words stunned me, and I felt a rage build in me. Every time I tried to do something for him, he pushed me aside. As I scooped his shoes up, I realized I couldn't do it anymore. I was done with Dad.

Dad locked himself in his room the whole weekend. I told my siblings the results and ignored all their other questions. Several people came over to check on Dad that Saturday. First was Arthur.

"Torrance, can you open the door please?" Arthur said.

"I don't feel like talking right now Arty."

An hour after he left, Troy, Donna and, Tavia visited.

"You can't stay in there forever," Troy said.

"Yes, I can."

"Dude, we're your friends," Donna reasoned. "Open the door."

"You're my coworkers."

"Oh, that's how it is?" Tavia hollered. "Alright, we can go."

"That's what I want."

Then it was Jana and Jonathan.

"If you need anything, you know we're here for you," Jana said.

"I just want you guys to leave me alone."

"You don't have to be so mean about it," Jonathan complained. He was one to talk.

"Leave me alone."

Then it was Mom and Forrest. Tavia called them to rant about Dad, and they figured they'd try to get him out of his room.

"If you don't open this door, I'm suing you for full custody of our remaining kids," Mom joked.

"If that'll make you leave me alone, go ahead."

"Come on Torrance," Forrest pleaded. "Don't be like that."

"I just want to be left alone."

"He's not even going back and forth with me," Mom said to me. "This is bad."

"Seems like it," I said.

After they left, Gretchen and Greta came by.

"OPEN THE DOOR!" Greta screamed as she banged on the door.

"LEAVE ME ALONE!"

"JERK!" Greta yelled as she kicked the door.

Once Greta's approach didn't work, Gretchen tried her sweet-talking method.

"Torrance?" Gretchen knocked. "Can I come in?"

Dad didn't answer.

"Torrance?"

"I'll see you on Monday, Gretchen."

"Okay," Gretchen sighed. If she couldn't get him to come out, no one could. On her way out, she asked me, "Can you let me know if anything changes with him? I don't want to upset him more than he already is."

"Okay," I agreed.

That Sunday, we went to church without him. It wasn't my job to be his keeper.

"I want to talk about faith today," Forrest said, opening his sermon. "As Christians, our faith should be in God. But sometimes we struggle with that. Sometimes life gets a little too real, and we wonder where God is? We wonder why He lets certain things happen when we know He has the power to stop them. Our faith is tested. In those times, we must remember why we have faith: to bring us closer to God. There are five qualities of faith I want to look at today: Fruitful, Assured, Infinite, Tenacious, and Humble."

"Faith is Fruitful. It's listed as a literal fruit of the Spirit in Galatians Five. But it's just as much a producer as it is a product. Hebrews Eleven lists several examples of how God rewarded those who had faith in Him. Abel is remembered as righteous which means he made it to Heaven, Enoch and Elijah didn't experience death, Noah survived the flood, Abraham became a father of many in old age, Sarah had a baby at ninety, and the list goes on. All these people believed in God, and they're all in Heaven right now enjoying the fruit of their faith: getting to spend eternity with God.

"Faith is Assured. Second Corinthians Five and Seven tells us 'We live by faith and not by sight'. You have to be assured to believe something you can't see. And if you have doubts and questions sometimes, that's okay. All that does is leave room for God to prove His faithfulness to you and renew your faith in him. Second Corinthians Twelve, Verse Nine says God's power is made perfect in weakness. Remember, the Israelites watched God part the Red Sea *with their own eyes*, and sometimes their faith would still be weak. So, you're not the first and won't be the last to have doubts and questions. Just make sure you take those doubt and questions to God first.

"Faith is Infinite. Our faith is made strong by believing in God's faithfulness. Psalm Thirty-Six, Vere Five says 'Your love, Lord, reaches to the heavens, your faithfulness to the skies'. God's faithfulness never runs out. There are countless examples in the Bible where God proves Himself faithful, and He's still doing it to this day. Our faith will go through trials and tribulations, but if you hold fast to God, it'll never run out. Romans Eight, Verses Thirty-Seven through Thirty-Nine tells us 'In all these things we are more than conquerors through Him who loved us. For I am convinced that neither death nor life, neither angels nor demons, neither the present nor the future, nor any powers. Neither height nor depth, nor anything else in all creation, will be able to separate us from the love of God that is in Christ Jesus our Lord'. God's love and faithfulness is stronger than anything that wishes to separate us from Him. Hold onto Him.

"This leads into my next point: Faith is Tenacious. Isaiah Forty, Verse Thirty-One tells us 'But those who hope in the Lord will renew their strength. They will soar on wings like eagles; they will run and not grow weary, they will walk and not be faint'. Faith doesn't give up on God, just like God doesn't give up on us. Imagine if Jesus gave up on us and didn't go to the cross. We would still be bound to our sins. But Jesus was faithful to us and redeemed us because he wanted us to be free in

Him. And since we want to be like Jesus, we must be as tenacious in our faith as He was and is. Yes, we'll make mistakes because we're human. But no mistake is bigger than God and his ability to fix it.

Faith is Humble. It recognizes that it needs help and relies on God to provide that help. If we could do it on our own, we wouldn't need to rely on God. Philippians Four, Verse Thirteen says 'I can do all this through Him who gives me strength'. The keywords of that verse are 'through Him'. We can't do anything unless we believe that Jesus died for us and will one day return for us. And that's the reason we have faith: because we believe we are saved through Jesus Christ and will one day reunite with Him for eternity in Heaven."

Karla approached me after service ended.

"Why wasn't Dad here today?" she asked.

"I don't know."

"What do you mean 'you don't know'?"

"It's not my job to look after him."

"No," Karla rejected my answer. "It is your job."

"No, it's not," I said. "He hasn't left his room in two days, and I could care less."

"Are you telling me my father has not eaten or bathed in two days?"

"Maybe?"

"No." Karla snatched her purse off her chair. "I'm not having it."

"What's going on?" Mom asked us.

"Dad missed church, Drake has an attitude, you made me wear a dress today," Karla ranted. "The whole family is out of whack and I'm. Not. Having. It."

"Why do you have an attitude?" Mom asked.

"I can't be bothered with Dad anymore."

"This is why I told you it's not your job to fix his life," Mom sighed. "He still hasn't left his room?"

"Nope."

"I'm going over there because we're getting this resolved today," Karla declared.

"Just don't do anything drastic, Karla," Mom said. "You know how you are when you get worked up."

"It'll be fine," Karla said.

Karla stopped outside the door when we arrived at the house. She stared at it, almost as if she didn't want to walk through it.

"You don't have to go in if you don't want," I said.

"I'm going, I'm going" she huffed.

Karla inhaled and marched inside to Dad's room with us behind her. She jiggled his doorknob, and when it would budge, she knocked on his door.

"Go away!" Dad hollered.

Karla banged on the door.

"I said GO AWAY!"

"Open the door!" Karla yelled back.

I heard Dad shuffle to the door and unlock it. By the time we entered the room, he'd crawled back into bed. Karla pushed his curtains open to let light into the room. Clothes laid all over his floor, and dirty dishes sat on his dresser.

"Trifling." Karla wrinkled her nose up. "Dad, you need to get up and clean this room. So, we can do this the easy way or my way."

"I'm not getting out this bed."

"Okay." Karla slid her purse off her arm and shoved it into my chest. "Hold this."

Karla approached Dad's bed and grabbed him by his arm.

"What are you–?!" Dad said as Karla pulled on his arm. "HEY!"

Dad tumbled to the floor in a flurry of blankets and sheets. He shot up and ripped the sheets from his body.

"Have you lost your mind?! You don't drag me out my bed by my arm!"

"You can't mope around for the rest of your life over a man that didn't want you!" Karla argued. "Especially not in a dirty room like this!"

"I can mope if I want! It's my house!"

"No, you will not!" Karla said. "Not my dad! My dad screams, throws his shoes, and calls it a day. He doesn't lay in the bed all day feeling sorry for himself."

"Why are you even here?"

"I came here to get you back on track!" Karla explained. She pointed at me and my other siblings. "Lord knows they weren't going to do it. You have one, two, three, four, five, six – and yes, I'm number six whether you like it or not – people depending on you to be the father you wish you had. You have a fiancée willing to marry you despite *all* your flaws. A mother, siblings, and friends, who still care about you. You even have men in this town who aren't even your father looking out for you. Do you know how rare that is? And you're going to throw all that away over some Leonard Brown? The same Leonard Brown who up until Friday wouldn't claim you even though you look exactly like him?"

"I do look like him, don't I?" Dad asked.

"You sure do," Karla huffed. "And why doesn't Drake want to be bothered with you?"

"I don't know what's wrong with your brother."

"Whatever it is, y'all need to fix it," Karla commanded as she rummaged through Dad's drawers. "Because Drake can't be the one that can't be bothered with you. That's my job."

Karla threw some clothes on Dad's bed.

"Go shower," she continued. "Change your clothes. Eat. Do whatever you need to do to make yourself feel better. Just don't get back in that bed and start moping again, okay?"

"Okay."

"And you," Karla said to me as she left the room. "Fix it."

I was tired of trying to fix it. My limit with Dad had been reached. It was his turn to fix it.

That Monday, Dad apologized to his coworkers for his behavior. They accepted his apology and told him they understood. Despite Dad acting like he was fine, I could tell he was still upset. Something in my spirit felt off about that day, but I couldn't understand what. All day, I kept an eye on Dad. No matter how I felt, I didn't want him getting hurt. At the beginning of the sixth-period class, Dad had words with Arthur's daughter, Danielle.

"Danielle, how can you expect to learn if you're always talking?" Dad called her out.

"What do I have to learn from a man that doesn't even sing?" Danielle snorted.

"Would you like to ask your father since he's the one that hired me?"

"That's alright."

"Can't you take a joke, Uncle T?" Mariana said. She and Mariella had started hanging around Danielle a lot more.

"Some people have no class," Latasia Williams whispered to Ralph's youngest sister, Nicole Brewer. Latasia was Samiel's sister, and she and Nicole were Danielle's former best friends.

"None," Nicole agreed.

"Does the peanut gallery have something to say?" Danielle asked.

"Actually, I do," Latasia responded.

"Girls, please," Dad stopped them. "Leave the drama in theater class."

"Sorry," Latasia and Nicole apologized.

I figured that was the bad thing that would happen. Class continued after that, but I noticed Derik seemed down. His whole vibe was off, and he wasn't paying attention to the lesson. Dad redirected him several times until his patience wore thin.

"Derik!" Dad yelled. "Stop being an idiot and pay attention!"

"Mr. Brown?" Derek raised his hand.

"What?"

"Are you yelling at me or him?"

"Does it matter?! I'm yelling at both of you now!"

Derik whispered to himself.

"Do you have something to say?" Dad dared him to speak up.

"You're irritating!" Derik exclaimed, shocking everyone.

"Little boy, who are you yelling at?"

"Mr. Brown," Derik began listing off names. "Mr. Torrance, Mr. Shoe-Thrower, Mr. No-Shoes, Mr. Drake's Dad, Mr. Got-Fifty-Eleven-Kids, Mr. Crazy Man; I can keep going if you like."

Dad gave Derik 'the look'.

"I don't know who you think you're scaring with that little ugly face you're making but it ain't me."

"What's wrong with you?" Derek whispered. "Cut it out."

"I'm not going to keep getting yelled at when he's not even doing his job right! I don't want to agree with Danielle but she's right! How do you expect me to learn when you don't do what you teach?!"

"Why don't you go down to Principal Lee's office and ask him your-self?" Dad said. "And while you're down there, you can explain to him why I kicked you out my class."

"Fine." Derik gathered his stuff. "I don't want to be in here with you anyways."

Derik left the classroom.

"What is his problem?" Dad asked Derek.

"I don't... it's not...I...," Derek stammered. "Uh, uh, I'm not in this."

"Seems like I'm not the only one with no class around here," Danielle remarked.

"But you are the most annoying," Latasia grumbled.

After school ended, I approached Dad to give him my thoughts.

"Dad."

"You're talking to me now?"

"You need to apologize to him."

"Apologize for what? He disrespected me first!"

"You need to be the adult and apologize before you get fired. You can't just yell at people and expect nothing to happen."

"My grandpa yelled at everyone, and no one ever said anything to him about it."

"Was your grandpa in charge of a choir full of other people's children?"

"Yeah, sometimes."

"Was he getting paid to be in charge?"

"Yeah."

"Well...," I stuttered. I hadn't counted on my argument working against me. "You...you're not your grandpa! You can't just yell at folks for no reason. People get tired of that mess. *I know I do...*"

"What did you say?"

"Brown!" Mr. Marlin Harrison yelled at Dad as he charged into the classroom. He marched up to Dad and stuck his finger in Dad's face. "You called my son an idiot?"

"You're really going to act like you care about your son today?"

"Excuse me?!"

"Drake, leave us."

I did as Dad said and went into the hallway. I closed the door behind me and found Derik standing in the hallway.

"What happened?"

"Principal Lee called my dad and he demanded to see Mr. Brown."

"Why'd you go off like that?"

"Because I'm tired of everyone yelling at me and expecting me not to say anything back. Would you just let somebody yell in your face for no reason?"

I didn't answer him. My whole life had been Dad yelling at me for stuff that had nothing to do with me. It wasn't until I was sixteen that I'd started questioning it. Dad and Mr. Harrison started raising their voices.

"GET OUT OF MY FACE, MARLIN!"

"I'M NOT PLAYING WITH YOU, BROWN!"

I SAID GET–!"

The argument stopped. Something scraped against the floor and then there were thumping noises. I ran back into the classroom and before I knew it, was swept into their chaos. Hands flew everywhere, and a stray punch knocked the glasses off my face.

"STOP!" I yelled as I latched onto someone. I assumed it was Dad because I could feel his itchy sweater in my hands. He was trying to break free of my grasp.

"I'm going to get that–! Drake, let me go!"

For someone as old as Dad, he was pretty strong. He dragged me with him until my foot got caught on something. I tripped, and Dad escaped.

"No!" someone screamed. "Stop!"

I patted the floor, hoping to find my glasses. My hand brushed against them, and I put them on. Dad and Mr. Harrison rolled around on the hallway floor. One of the school's security guards stepped in to separate them. Derik remained in his spot by the door, unfazed by the fight. He didn't seem to care his father was fighting over him.

The guard broke up the fight and escorted Mr. Harrison away. Tavia took Dad to Arthur's office, and I followed them to find out what happened.

"He started getting closer to me, so I hit him," Dad explained as he placed a bandage on his scraped-up arm. "He wanted to act like he cared about his son and got what he was looking for."

"This is not what I signed up for when I became principal," Arthur sighed.

"Arty!" Jana said as she ran into the office. "We have a problem."

The other teachers came into the room, and Jana pointed at something outside the window. A police squad car pulled into the parking lot.

"Who called the police?" Arthur complained.

"Jana...," Jonathan grumbled.

"No, I didn't!"

"Does anyone else here have a brother on the force?"

"Yes!" Jana said, pointing at Dad.

"Y'all stop arguing," Tavia chastised.

"Tavia's right," Gretchen agreed as she stroked Dad's back. "I'm sure everything will be alright."

"Oh, It's the chief!" Troy gasped.

"Never mind." Gretchen moved away from Dad, leaving him to face Uncle Terrence alone.

I could hear Uncle Terrence's boots against the floor as he stomped up the hallway. Arthur ran to meet him and probably calm him down before he reached the office. They'd been raised like cousins, but they were really uncle and nephew.

"Noah," I heard Arthur whined. "It's not that bad."

Uncle Terrence entered the room. He scanned the room with furious eyes, and I saw the smoke coming from his ears.

"Out," he commanded through clenched teeth.

"You don't have to tell me twice," Donna said as she took my hand in her dark-brown one. "Come on y'all."

We all left the room, and Uncle Terrence slammed the door behind us.

"Psst," someone whispered. "Guys!"

Greta waved her hands at us. She led us into her office which was next to Arthur's office. I could hear Uncle Terrence going off in the other room.

"Sam gets a call, right?" He chuckled. "It's Latasia, who's panicking because her teacher and a parent are brawling in the middle of the hallway, and she's scared someone's going to get hurt! So, Sam wanted to come down here, right? Because Christine's already left and he's concerned that Sami and Latasia are in danger, right? And Bud wanted to come down here because he thinks his sister is being attacked by a parent, right? But no, something told me to come down here myself because I just *knew* it was you or Greta!"

"Now how'd I get in it?" Greta griped.

"Terrence I–!"

"SHUT UP!" Uncle Terrence yelled. "I am *this close* to sticking my boot up your behind!"

"Why are you blaming me?! You don't even know what happened!"

"I DON'T CARE WHAT HAPPENED! You're forty years old fighting in the middle of a high school hallway like you're one of the students! And now I have to come down here from my job because you don't know how to act right at yours!"

Silence.

"It wasn't my fault," Dad said.

"Get your stuff and come on! Mama brought you into this world and I'm about five seconds from taking you out of it!"

Uncle Terrence escorted Dad off the campus.

After school, I went to Antoine for information. He sat in his room playing an online game with some people named TitanDaBeast, Sweet_PatatoWato, and SuperGentleman12.

"What are you playing?" I asked.

"A game called *The Well*," Antoine said. "My character is a bard."

"A what?"

"A musician that can fight."

"Oh."

"*Who are you talking to, RobotBoy?*" TitanDaBeast asked.

"My brother."

"*Hi, RobotBoy's brother!*" Sweet_PatatoWato said.

"*What's up, bro!*" TitanDaBeast yelled.

"*Hello sir!*" SuperGentleman12 said.

"Um... hi?" I said.

"He said hi, guys," Antoine laughed. "I'll be back."

"*It's alright if you have to go, RobotBoy,*" TitanDaBeast said. "*We can explore The Well another time.*"

"That's okay," Antoine said. "This won't take too long."

Antoine muted his mic.

"RobotBoy?" I asked.

"It's part of my username, RobotBoy_Toine," Antoine explained as he took his headset off. "What's up?"

"Do you know those people?"

"TitanDaBeast is Andrew," Antoine said. "He let me join his guild when I first started playing the game. The other two are his friends. Is that what you came to ask me?"

"No," I said. "What's going on with Derik? He hasn't been himself lately."

"He has a lot going on right now," Antoine sighed. "His parents have been arguing a lot lately, and that's just adding on to the other problems they already have."

"Arguing about what?"

"He won't say. And even if he did, I wouldn't tell you."

"Why not?"

"Because it's none of your business," Antoine said. He put his head-set back on. "Now, if you'll excuse me..."

It wasn't a secret that the Harrison kids were a bit wild. Their parents were rarely home and didn't care much about what their children did. Things must've gotten bad in that house for Derik to start acting out. I could only pray that he got it together before things got worse for him.

-

Chapter Twenty-Nine

Dad and the Harrisons met with Arthur for conflict resolution the next day after he convinced Uncle Terrence not to press charges. They all apologized, and Dad and Marlin Harrison made another truce. An hour after Dad came home, Leonard Brown showed up. Part of me wanted to turn him away and protect Dad. But I knew they needed to confront each other, so I let him in, and Dad was not happy.

"What do you want?" he barked when he realized who it was.

"I know I'm the last person you want to see right now," Leonard Brown said. "I'm not here to ask you to forgive me. All I'm asking is that you hear me out."

"Hear you out?" Dad laughed. "You want me to hear you out?"

"Yes."

"Make it quick," Dad huffed. "I don't have all day."

"I know you won't believe me," Leonard Brown said after clearing his throat. "But I'm sorry for everything I did to you."

"That's it?"

"You said make it quick."

"Okay," Dad said. He removed his glasses and played with them. "I want to hear directly from you why you denied me in the first place."

"I thought your mama had cheated on me with Damian," Leonard Brown mumbled. "Had it been anyone else, I wouldn't have cared as much. But since it was Damian..."

"She didn't even cheat on you."

"Ri...right," Leonard Brown stammered. "But it's not like I didn't have reason to be suspicious."

"Do you know how stupid you sound?" Dad said. "Mary doesn't look exactly like me, and I've never denied her. My other daughter, Karla, looks almost nothing like me, but I still know she's mine. But you and me? We look just alike. I can't look in the mirror without seeing you. So, I'll ask you again. Why after a certain point, did you deny me?"

"I..."

"Don't have an answer?" Dad said as he tilted his head to the side. "Because whatever reason you give with won't be good enough. I can tell you that right now."

"I didn't know."

"Even if you weren't sure, all I wanted was for you to treat me right," Dad explained. "You couldn't even bother to do that."

"I didn't know."

"Yes, you did," Dad said. "You knew. You've always known. When you nicknamed me T-Rex, you knew. When you did this to my face, you knew. When you abandoned me at Mr. Damian's, you knew. When we sat face to face in your kitchen, and you cleaned my wounds and apologized to me, you definitely knew. Because by that point I knew, and I didn't want to accept it. You've always known that I was your son."

Leonard Brown stood stone-faced.

"And now you're going to march in here and apologize like everything's all peachy keen?" Dad continued as he pushed his finger into Leonard Brown's chest. "You hurt me, and you didn't care."

"You're right. I didn't care."

"And now I don't care," Dad said. "Get out of my house. I never want to see you again."

"I'm sorry."

Those were Leonard Brown's parting words before leaving. As soon as the door closed, Dad pounced on me.

"Why would you let him in my house?"

I shrugged.

"What is your problem?" Dad asked. "You've had this attitude since Friday, and I don't appreciate it."

"Well, I don't appreciate you sidelining me for the past month and a half."

"Why do you make everything about you?"

"Because this is about us right now. I've been trying to improve our relationship and you won't get with the program."

"What's wrong with our relationship?"

"You haven't noticed every time we talk, we argue?"

"That's because you get smart, and I have to remind you who you're talking to."

"You don't have to remind me of anything, Dad. I'm a grown man. We can have an adult conversation."

"I don't know too many grown men that still live with their fathers."

"I don't have to live here."

"So, what are you saying? Because you can't live here and have an attitude with me. That's not how that works."

"Alright," I said. "I'll move out."

"To where? And with what money?"

"I'll figure it out. I'll go anywhere but here."

"Get out then if that's how you feel."

"I will. I'm tired of dealing with you."

"Oh really? That's how you feel?"

"Yep!"

"Okay, well get up out my house ASAP!" Dad demanded. "And don't come crying to me when you need help, since you're so tired of dealing with me!"

"I won't!" I yelled as I walked out of the front door. "You won't ever have to worry about me again!"

"Good!" Dad agreed. "One less mouth to feed!"

Dad slammed the door behind me. It was really over. I was really moving out of Dad's house.

I drove through Creeke with everything I could fit in my suitcase. K$K's 'Punch Your Lights Out' blared through my car's speakers. The local stations played it a lot ever since their disbandment issue came to light.

"*Talking real tough when you got a crowd around,*" KV rapped the pre-hook. "*Got your fists balled like you want to go to town. Hope that you know this ain't what you want, cause imma give you that one two punch*!"

"*Go ahead and give me your best shot, and show me what you are really about,*" Knokout rapped the hook. Derek was right. His hooks and beats were better than his verses. "*It's probably best you swing on me first, cause when I hit you, I'm knocking you out! I'll punch your lights out, punch your lights out. Should've stayed cool, cause now you on the ground. I punched your lights out, punched your lights out. You out like a log, night-night now.*"

"*That was 'Punch Your Lights Out' by the duo formerly known as K$K,*" the radio host said when the song ended. "*Hopefully y'all are staying classy and not trying to punch anyone's lights out. Coming up...*"

I turned the radio down and dialed Tamela's number when I reached the stop sign at the church. The bullet hole in the middle of the 'O' stared me in the face.

"Hello?" Tamela said.

"Yeah, I just got into it with Dad."

"Why?"

"He said he didn't like my attitude, so I told him I was tired of him."

"You said *what*?!" Tamela yelled. "Are you stupid?! *Why would you say that*?!"

"Because it's true!"

"When I said express yourself, I didn't mean tell the man stuff that would make him put you out."

"He didn't put me out. I left."

"That's even worse!" Tamela ranted. "Where are you going to go? It's getting cold out there and you know Creeke barely has streetlights as it is."

"I'll be alright."

"I'm surprised he didn't take your phone and your car."

"I paid for those, not him."

"How were you paying for them when you quit your job at Brewer's?"

"Dad paid me to volunteer."

"You've bitten the hand that fed you."

"I'm going to be alright, Tamela," I told her as I walked up the steps to my grandparents' house. "I'll call you later, okay?"

"Alright."

I knocked on the door to my Gran Ernestine and Grandpap Jared's house. Mom didn't have any extra rooms so I couldn't stay with her. Hopefully, my grandparents would let me stay with them for the night. Because if they didn't, I had nowhere else to go.

Chapter Thirty

"Drake, you can't stay on our couch forever," Gran Ernestine told me that Saturday. It'd been at my grandparents' house all week since the argument. "Go make up with your father."

"I'm not talking to him."

"Boy, you and your dad are just alike," Grandpap Jared laughed. "Stubborn and always wanting to argue with folks. I still can't believe you told him to his face that you were tired of him."

"I am tired of him."

"You don't tell him that to his face," Gran said. "Lord knows we've all been tired of our parents at some point, but we don't admit to it. I'm sure your father gets tired of you sometimes too."

"I know he does," I griped. "He tells me all the time."

"Maybe that wasn't the best example..."

"What your grandmother is trying to say is that you and your father shouldn't be at odds like this," Grandpap added. "God forbid, what if something happened to him right now? How would you feel knowing your last conversation with him was you telling him you're tired of him?"

"I wouldn't feel great...," I admitted.

"Exactly," Grandpap said. "Go make things right. And if you're lucky enough, he'll let you move back in."

"I'm not moving back in."

"Well, where are you going to go?" Gran asked. "You can't live on our couch."

"I've already figured it out."

"I don't like the sound of that," Grandpap muttered.

"It'll be fine," I told him. "Thank you for letting me stay with you guys."

"Of course, baby." Gran hugged me. "Just don't make a habit of it."

"I won't," I giggled.

"And Drake," Grandpap advised me. "Try not to argue with your father again."

"Yes sir."

Before returning to Dad's house, I stopped at Brewer's grocery store. I used to work there, but I quit after a customer tried to attack me over a candy bar.

"Long time, no see," Twenty-one-year-old Mikayla Brewer said when she saw me. She was the middle child between Ralph and Nicole. "Come to beg for your job back?"

"Actually, I came to speak to Ralph," I said. "Is he here?"

"For once," Mikayla said. "You know where to find him."

"Thanks."

I went to the 'staff only' door and knocked on it. Ralph opened it and grinned at me.

"Just the man I hoped to see!" he laughed.

"You might not be as happy when we get through talking."

"I don't like the sound of that."

"So... the reunion isn't happening."

"I'm not surprised."

"You're not?"

"You know nothing in this town stays hidden. As soon as word got out that Leonard Brown *was* the father, I figured there'd be too much drama for a reunion. I appreciate you telling me though."

"Sorry Ralphie."

"It's alright," Ralph said. "It's not the first time this has happened to me, and I doubt it'll be the last. There'll be other stories. My main concern right now is Derik. He's been acting strange lately."

"I heard he has a lot going on at home."

"He always has a lot going on at home," Ralph complained. "I was excited to mentor him so he could have an outlet away from that house. But now I'm worried something's wrong."

"Maybe he's just having a teenage crisis."

"I hope so but something tells me it's deeper than that. I'm going to keep my eye on him for the time being."

"He's lucky to have someone like you in his life that cares about him so much."

"Yeah," Ralph sighed. "I only hope he can see that."

I felt like I would throw up as I drove to Dad's house. It would be the first time I'd been there in a week, and I didn't know if Dad was still mad at me or not.

"Let me spell out what imma do to you, I'll go real slow since I know you're new," KV rapped his verse of 'Punch Your Lights Out. *"Imma bash you straight in your dome, make it hurt so bad, you'll want to go home. But it won't end till I say so, and so you know, I put on a show. So, get prepared since you think you're tough, cause once I start, I'm beating you up! Knock you straight into a daze, put a knot straight on your face. I'm ready to throw, this the end of my flow, let's fight cause I'm ready to go!"*

I cut the radio off. The last thing I needed to hear was a song about fighting. When I got to the house, I found my key still worked. Dad hadn't changed the locks on me. He ate lunch in the kitchen when I approached him.

"Dad?"

"Yeah?"

"Can we talk?"

"Okay."

I sat down.

"Look," Dad started. "Things got heated and I'm sure we both said some things we didn't mean..."

"Oh no, I meant what I said. I'm tired of you."

"Boy!" Dad said. "We're supposed to be making up!"

"We can make up, but I'm not going to lie to you," I explained. "I'm tired of feeling like I can't express myself to you. I'm tired of living in fear of your overreactions. I'm tired of your trauma being my trauma. I'm tired."

"Why didn't you just say that instead of having an attitude?"

"Because I can't talk to you. It feels like every time we talk something goes wrong."

"I've been under a lot of stress lately."

"When Karla moved out the house, did you ever wonder why she left?"

"Because she wanted to live with her mother instead."

"Yeah, because she felt like you were taking all your anger about the divorce out on her."

"That's not true."

"Dad, it's not a secret that Mary and Karla were your favorites until the divorce happened. You started taking all the anger out on Karla because she looked like Mom. And now only Mary is your favorite. We all know it's true."

"That's crazy! I don't have a favorite! And I would never do that to Karla!"

"But you did do it though. I watched you do it. And after she left you took all your anger out on me and I'm tired of it. This is just the first time I'm telling you about it."

"Well, how can we fix this then? Because I don't want y'all feeling like I play favorites and hate y'all. That's how I felt growing up and I hated it."

"I don't know."

"Well, while we figure it out you can move back in."

"I'm not moving back in."

"Where are you going to go?"

"I already have a place figured out in the city."

"You found a place in a week?" Dad scrunched his face up. "Where did you get the money?"

"Dad, never ask a man how he gets his money."

"Now you sound like one of the Perrys."

"I'll be alright," I said as I prepared to drop the bigger bomb on Dad. "Also, we're not doing the album."

"Why not?"

"Because I know you're not up to it right now."

"I told you I'd do it, Drake," Dad said. "One little argument won't get in the way of my commitment."

"I think it's best we don't do it."

"What are you going to tell your aunts and uncles?"

"They'll understand."

"I was kind of looking forward to it though..."

"Sorry Dad," I apologized. I know it crushed him. But I couldn't go through with the project knowing we weren't in the best place. Dad had too many things to work on to worry about making an album too.

When I left Dad's house, I got a call from Tamela.

"Hello?"

"I need a favor."

"Okay."

"Can you go by my house and help Em with something?"

"What am I helping her with?"

"You'll see when you get there."

I did as Tamela asked. When I arrived at her house, Tamela's sixteen-year-old sister Tamara stood outside waiting for me. She looked like Tamela: thin and light-brown with black hair.

"Hey Em," I greeted her. "What's going on?"

"Tam told me you were coming by to help me," Tamara said. "It's in the house."

"What is it?"

"You'll see," Tamara giggled. She placed her hands over my eyes and led me. "It's a surprise."

"I'm helping you with a surprise?"

"Yep. But I need to test it out on you first."

"Okay..."

Tamara led me to where she wanted me to stand. Once I was positioned, I heard her shuffle around, giggling.

"Can I open my eyes yet?"

"Hang on," Tamara said. She moved around a bit more and then said, "Okay, go ahead."

I opened my eyes and my breath hitched in my throat. Standing in front of me was my twenty-year-old girlfriend.

"Surprise!" Tamela and Tamara yelled.

"What are you doing here?" I cried as I ran to hug her.

"After our phone call, I booked a flight to come back here to visit. You had me worried."

"You booked a flight for me?"

"Yeah, I did."

"But it's Saturday," I said. "Don't you have to go back tomorrow?"

"Nope," Tamela said. "I'll be here the whole week since my professors are going away to some conference. And when this semester ends, I'm transferring to the university Andrew, Do and Phil go to."

"You are? I thought you liked your school."

"I do. But it's more important to me that I be closer to home."

"Is it because of me and my drama?" I sighed.

"A little," Tamela answered. "But let's not worry about that. Let's enjoy our week together."

"Okay," I said. As I gazed into Tamela's eyes, I felt for the first time that things would be alright.

-

Part 4:
Derek Harrison

Chapter Thirty-One

"Dad told me the lady who gave birth to me didn't want me. Granddad held me while she and Dad argued, and she was like 'it doesn't even matter because I'm not keeping the baby anyways'. Then everybody argued, and Granddad was like 'are you sure?' and the lady's mom was like 'she's sure' and Granddad was like 'I asked her'. And she was like 'I'm not keeping the baby', and she and her mom left town for good."

"That's... interesting," Adrianna answered. I was helping her and her brothers clean their dad's garage on a Sunday. "But that doesn't explain why you and Derik have the same name."

"I'm getting there!" I said. "Dad named me after Granddad and combined their names to make my middle name. Uncle Marlin did the same thing when Derik was born, but he changed the spelling. It caused a huge fight between him and Dad."

"So, you're both named after your grandfather?"

"Yeah."

"Why would you give two babies from the same family the same name?" Andre laughed from the other side of the room.

"Andre!" Antoine slapped Andre's arm.

"What? It's not my fault Derek can't whisper!"

"And you wonder why no one tells you anything," Antoine huffed. "You can't keep a secret to save your life!"

"I guess it's a good thing Jesus saved my life for me, isn't it?"

"Don't mind them," Adrianna said. "They're just being idiots as usual."

I lifted a box and a CD case fell out onto the ground.

"What's this?" I asked as I picked it up.

"That's the CD Dad made with his family back in the day," Adrianna said. "They were supposed to remake it, but that failed."

"All because Mister Dragon couldn't get it together," I sighed. "We could've finally heard your dad sing for once."

"I know...," Adrianna grumbled. We sat silently until she brightened up. "I've got it! What if we get them to sing at the revival?"

"What revival?"

"The one at the church. Haven't you heard about it?"

"I don't go to the church that much."

"Why not?"

"Dad doesn't want to go. He said he's never stepping foot in Creeke Church again."

"Again? What does he mean again?"

"I don't know. Every time I ask, he says not to worry about it."

"Okay, one dad at a time," Adrianna said. "First we'll get my dad to sing at the revival, and then we'll get yours to go to it."

"Why would we do that?"

"Because it'll make me happy." Adrianna batted her eyes. "Don't you want me to be happy?"

"Yeah."

"Great! We can pick up where Drake left off. I know just the place to start."

Fifteen minutes later, we were at Adrianna's mom's house. Karla played with a little girl in the front yard. The little girl had dark-brown skin and a thick afro with a hairbow tied through it. As we got closer, I noticed the little girl had similar features to Adrianna.

"Dria!" the girl yelled. She wrapped herself around Adrianna's legs.

"Hi baby!" Adrianna gushed. "Dee, this is my younger sister, Layla. She's Mom's daughter with Forrest."

"Hi Mister!" Layla said.

"Hi!"

"What are you doing here?" Karla asked.

"I came to see Mom."

"You too?"

"What do you mean 'you too'?"

"You're in for a real surprise…"

"What's the surprise, Karla?"

"Go see."

"Oh Lord," Adrianna muttered. "Come on, Dee."

Adrianna led me into the house.

"Hello?" Adrianna called.

"Adrianna?" First Lady Hall asked. "You came to visit too?"

"Karla said the same thing," Adrianna said. "Who else is here?"

"Me!"

Drake grabbed us from behind and pulled us into a hug.

"Can't breathe!" Adrianna wheezed.

"Sorry," Drake apologized as he released us.

"What are you doing here?" Adrianna asked.

"I came to get the rest of my stuff. Why's Derek here?"

"Because he's my boyfriend and he's helping me with something," Adrianna explained as she patted her hair back into place.

"I KNEW IT!" Drake shouted. "I KNEW YOU TWO WERE TOGETHER!"

"We just started dating," Adrianna said as she readjusted her glasses. "Mom, we need your help."

"With what?"

"Dee and I need you to talk to Forrest about letting the Brown Family Band sing at the revival."

"Good luck with that," Drake snorted. "I tried to get him to sing too. We saw how that went."

"That's because you got in your feelings and made it about you." Adrianna wagged her finger at Drake. "I won't make that mistake."

"Why do you need my help then?" First Lady Hall asked as she dried her hands. "Seems like you've got it all figured out."

"Because you're Forrest's wife. You can get him to say yes."

"Adrianna, you're fifteen," First Lady Hall huffed. "You don't need me to do everything for you. I'm sure Forrest will say yes if you ask him yourself."

"Alright..."

"Now, about this boyfriend of yours."

"That I totally called!" Drake cheered.

"How'd you too meet?"

"We danced at the same studio...?" Adrianna reminded her mother. "You've met him several times, Mom."

"Oh!" First Lady Hall exclaimed. "You're the one that dances! The one Mr. Derrick calls D-Money, right?"

"D-Money?" Drake chuckled. "Is that the nickname that's so embarrassing?"

"Yeah...," I said, my cheeks burning. "He calls me that because he says I'm cheap."

"You are, but that's okay," Adrianna said as she patted my shoulder.

"I don't know why I thought you were the other one for some reason," First Lady Hall said. "Sorry about that."

"It's alright," I chuckled. "You're not the first person to make that mistake."

"If I'd known I'd have all these guests, I would've cooked something," First Lady Hall sighed.

"That's okay," I said. "I should probably head home anyways."

"I'll walk you out," Drake offered.

Drake led me to the porch. When the door closed, he grabbed me by my shoulders and turned me to face him.

"What are you doing, Mister Dragon?"

"Our friendship is at risk now."

"It is?"

"Yes. We'll have no choice but to fight if you hurt my sister."

"It won't have to come to that because I don't plan on hurting Adrianna," I laughed.

"Okay." Drake let me go. "I'm trusting you with her."

"Bye Drake," I continued laughing. "Don't get into too much trouble in the city, okay?"

The smell of frying chicken greeted me as I entered my house. Dad was home. Our house had two bedrooms, and one bathroom we shared. I passed by my favorite photo of me and him. Nanna took it at a family cookout when I was about six. A red fitted cap sat twisted to the side on Dad's head with a durag underneath. His tattooed arm held my sleeping body in place against his chest.

"*You out like a log, night-night now!*" Dad rapped from the kitchen.

"*Already lost to my man KV, and now you want to go and try and fight me?!*" I yelled the first line of Knokout's verse from 'Punch Your Lights Out'.

"*Are you aware your face is bleeding?*" Dad yelled back.

"*Do you know your head is leaking?*"

"*It's not wise to start a new round, cause imma stomp you into the ground.*"

"*I'm giving you your warning now, cause I won't kick you while you're down.*"

"*You must be the hard-headed type, cause you coming up to me acting real hype.*"

"*All you do is scream and shout, guess you got to learn why KV named me Knokout!*"

Dad laughed as he threw his arms around me. Since he was only fourteen years older than me, Dad was more like an older brother than he was a father. He was one of my best friends, and I don't know what I'd do without him.

"Have you ever considered I might be not your actual son?" I asked when we calmed down. "Like, we're in here having fun and we might not even be related."

"Nah," Dad chuckled. He sat down at the kitchen table, waiting for the food to cook. "We did the DNA test after you were born. Your big head is mine."

"What was the lady who gave birth to me like?"

"Why do you want to know?" Dad sipped his drink.

"Because I was talking with Adrianna about her parents, and I was curious."

"Honestly, she was a pass-around," Dad shrugged. "She was sleeping with me and three other dudes at the same time. You're lucky your mine because those other dudes sucked."

"That's all she was to you?"

"That's all she is to me now." Dad chugged his drink. "But back then, you couldn't tell me nothing. I was in love with that girl."

"What happened to her?"

"She left town with her mom after you were born. I haven't heard from her since, and I don't expect to."

"Sorry Dad."

"Don't be," Dad said. "If it wasn't for her, I wouldn't have you."

"And I wouldn't have you either," I said. "By the way, did you know the church is having a revival soon?"

"Is today open-old-wounds day or something?" Dad joked.

"Are you going?"

"The only way I'm going anywhere near that church is if your grandfather gets on the pulpit," Dad told me. "And I don't see that happening any time soon."

"Okay."

"You can go if you want," Dad continued. "Your grandparents would be thrilled."

"I don't want to go if you don't go."

"I guess we're not going then."

"I guess not."

"Let me get back to this chicken." Dad stood up and rubbed my stomach. "I just know you're going to tear a good three-fourths of it up tonight."

"Have you seen the way you eat?!" I protested as I swatted Dad's hand away. "You eat like a pig!"

"If I'm the pig, that makes you the piglet."

"Just finish the food."

"Alright piglet," Dad laughed. Most people didn't understand the relationship we had. They said it was weird for a father and son to interact with each other the way we did. But I didn't care. I loved my dad as he was, and I wouldn't change anything about him.

-

Chapter Thirty-Two

Allison turned eighteen that week. She was the highest-ranked person in our class, competing with Andre to be valedictorian. With the way school went for her, she needed this birthday to be fun.

"My parents will be out of town again this weekend," Allison explained as we walked to lunch. It was Thursday, and Allison was filling me in on her birthday plans. "Nisha's going to get my hair together, and then we're going to Sepia."

"Sepia?" I asked. "What's that?"

"A club in the city," Allison whispered. "KV's performing there this Saturday, and you know I'm not missing my man in concert. Me, Matty, and Cornbread are going, and I want you to come too."

"Won't that cause tension between Matty and Cornbread though? You know they don't like being around each other."

"I'm sure my brothers can put aside their differences for one day," Allison said. "I'm going shopping after school for my outfit. You want to come?"

"Sure."

"Hey Miss Valedictorian!" Allison's best friend, Stacy Gilbert, greeted Allison. Stacy was the light-brown senior class president with a pixie cut. "Hey Derek."

"I might not be Miss Valedictorian anymore after that AP Bio test today," Allison laughed.

"That test was ridiculous," Stacy complained. "Even with the study guide, it still didn't make any sense."

"No, for real," Allison agreed. "And the one question I didn't understand would be the one I got wrong on the study guide because I listened to Andre and put the wrong answer."

"What question was it?"

"The 'surface area to volume ratio' one."

"Yeah, no," Stacy sighed. "That question had me like 'when did we learn this?'."

"FOR REAL!" Allison exclaimed. "They put stuff on the test we barely went over!"

"I know right!" Stacy said. "We'll talk more at the table because I'm getting in the lunch line."

"We'll see you at the table, girl."

"Okay," Stacy said as she walked away.

Ms. Gretchen Nelson passed us in a bright yellow floral print dress.

"Okay Ms. Twin!" Allison cheered. "I see you looking all cute today!"

"Oh, tha ... thank you, Allison." Ms. Nelson blushed at the compliment as she kept walking.

"Ms. Twin?" I laughed. "Queenie, they have the same last name."

"How was I supposed to know?" Allison whined. "Last I heard one of them got engaged and they look exactly alike."

"They have the same...last...name."

"Not for long!" Allison huffed. "Once the one that's engaged gets married, we're going to have to know which one is which. Did you think about that? Since you're obviously the valedictorian and not me?"

"They're pretty easy to tell apart if you know what to look for. Ms. Gretchen is always with Mr. Shoe-Thrower. Ms. Greta is always *arguing* with Mr. Shoe-Thrower."

"How do you know all this?"

"They've been here for two years, Miss Valedictorian. If you can't tell them apart by this point, I don't what to tell you."

Allison rolled her eyes as we approached Adrianna and Andre.

"Speaking of shoe-throwers," Allison said. "I spy with my little eye a cute little sophomore with glasses and her annoying brother who works my last nerve."

"Allison?" Andre asked as he squinted at Allison.

"Andre."

"Oh, it is you," Andre said as he put his glasses on. "I didn't have my glasses on so I couldn't tell."

"Listen," Adrianna said as she dragged me from Allison and Andre. "I talked to Forrest, and he said he'd be okay with us reuniting the band as long as Uncle Terrence is okay with it. Mom said we have to ask him ourselves though since it's our idea. Now all we have to do is get Dad on board again."

"How are we going to do that?"

"We'll get Mary to ask Dad for us."

"Why can't you ask him?"

"Because Mary's his favorite." Adrianna clasped my hand in hers and looked at me with wishful eyes. "He'll listen to her. That's why I was hoping you'd go visit her in the library during your free period and convince her to ask him for us?"

"I'm supposed to be going with Queenie though during my free period."

"It shouldn't take that long to talk to Mary," Adrianna pleaded. "You'll be in and out. Please Derek?"

Adrianna looked at me with puppy-dog eyes and a poked-out lip.

"Okay, I'll go."

"Thank you!" Adrianna hugged me. "I have to get to Spanish. Love you. Bye!"

Mary volunteered in the school's library sometimes since she had nothing else to do. She wanted to go to college, but something kept her from doing so. I visited Mary during my free period. Derik somehow got out of class and came with me.

"Mary, I need your help," I told her when we got to the library.

"Derek, you've been at this school long enough to know where everything is," Mary said without looking up from her book. "What could you possibly need my help with?"

"Something I'm working on with Adri." I leaned over the counter.

"Can't wait to hear this," Mary sighed as she closed her book. A commotion rose from the courtyard outside, and Derik wandered over to the window be nosy. Mary looked at me and asked, "What are you two up too?"

"We're trying to get the Brown Family Band to sing at the upcoming revival."

"What does that have to do with me?"

"Adri was hoping you could talk to your dad and convince him to sing."

"Is there a reason Adrianna can't talk to him herself?" Mary asked. She returned to her book. "Last time I checked we had the same father."

"She said he'll listen to you over her because you're his favorite."

"Why would she–!" Mary slammed her book shut. "No."

"Come on Mary, please?"

"Adrianna can ask him herself."

"Okay," I sighed. I walked over to Derik who sat on the windowsill, eating an apple. He was smiling at his phone.

"What's got you all happy?" I teased.

"Nothing!" Derik blurted as he quickly locked his phone.

"Okay," I giggled. He was hiding something. "How did you convince Ms. Nelson to let you out of class?"

"I asked to go to the library to do research for an article," he said with a smirk. "I'm one of her favorite students, so she pretty much lets me do anything."

"She doesn't seem like the type to have favorites."

"Why would she make me the editor-in-chief of the Creeke High newspaper then if I wasn't her favorite?"

"No way! I'm surprised she gave you that role after your little argument with her fiancé. I'd have thought you'd be labeled a problem child by now."

"Like I said," Derik chuckled. "I'm one of her favorites."

"What's your article about?"

"I want to do something on parent-child relationships and how they play into kids running away."

Derik bit into his apple, and I mimicked his movements. He raised his other hand, and then I raised mine. Then, I moved my head to the side, and he followed. It was our 'mirror game' we made up in middle school to make fun of people who claimed they couldn't tell us apart.

"So...," Derik spoke.

"So...," I copied his voice.

"Don't you...?"

"Don't you...?"

"Have somewhere to be?"

"Have somewhere to be?" I asked as I scrunched my face up.

"Queenie," Derik said with a grin.

"Queenie?" I repeated. I realized what Derik meant. "QUEENIE!"

"Shhh!" someone shushed me.

"Sorry," I apologized as I ran out the door. Allison would kill me if I made her late.

"This is *cute*!" Allison sang as she pulled a black romper off the rack. "What do you think?"

"I think you need to buy something," I groaned. "This is the fifth store we've been to, and you still haven't bought anything."

"Maybe I'd have something by now if *someone* would've been on time."

"Buy. Some. Thing," I begged.

"I guess I could get this." Allison held up the outfit in her hand. "It's cute, right?"

"If I say yes, will you buy it?"

"Your answer doesn't determine whether I'm buying this or not."

"Queenie!" I whined.

"Why'd I even bring you?" Allison sighed as she headed to the register. After Allison bought her outfit, we went to even more stores. She needed accessories, a new purse, and a bunch of other stuff. By the time we finished, my feet were killing me. Allison looked at all the bags in her hand and said, "I think I got everything."

"I'm never shopping with you again," I complained. "My poor feet."

"Please," Allison said. "I've seen some of the choreography you do. This was nothing to you."

"My feet hurt when I do that too!"

"Look, we're done. You can go home and put your feet up."

"Yes!" I cheered as I started rushing to the exit.

"I thought your feet hurt!" Allison teased.

"They d–!" I called before stopping to admire one of the window displays. It was a pair of black and gold shoes with a purple, red, and orange sole. "Look at these shoes!"

"Do you want them?" Allison asked when she caught up to me.

"Well... I mean... I like them... but I can't get them."

"Why not?"

"They're a hundred dollars."

"And?"

"I can't afford that!"

"Did I ask if you could afford it? Do you want the shoes?"

"Queenie, I can't ask you to get those for me."

"Look, I can buy you these and wear a pair of Cornbread's shoes instead," Allison reasoned as she led me into the shoe store by my hand. "My feet are pretty much the same size as his anyways."

"Are you sure?"

"Do you want the shoes or not?"

"Yeah..."

"Okay it's settled. Now we have to get an outfit to go with them."

"What?!"

"Relax. I'll cover it."

"Queenie..."

"Dad will put the money back in my account anyways," Allison told me. "It's the one thing he's good for."

Hearing Uncle Marlin mentioned made me shudder. He was a hard person to figure out, and I'd heard about some of the things he did in his youth. I tried not to be around him as much as possible. Allison bought me the shoes, and we went back through the mall to find a matching outfit. My plan was to stick to cheaper stores so I wouldn't spend too much of Allison's money, but I still wanted to look good. A pair of half-black, half-denim jeans caught my eye in one store, and I knew I had to have them.

"I'll get these," I declared with a smile.

"*Those*?" Allison's face scrunched up. Her eyes flicked between me and the pants. "You're playing, right?"

"What's wrong with these? I like them."

"*You do*?" Allison asked. She narrowed her eyes at me, "How much are they?"

"The price doesn't determine whether I get these or not," I repeated Allison's words to her before adding at the end, "...for once."

"They're just so...," Allison said. "Are you sure?"

"Yeah," I said. "I can make them work."

"Okay then...," Allison whispered. She wouldn't fight me on this. My black hoodie with the space-themed logo would match perfectly with these pants and shoes. That's what I would wear to Allison's birthday.

-

Chapter Thirty-Three

Uncle Marlin and Aunt Soleya were away on a business trip as Allison said. She and Deidrick chilled in the living room when I got to their house for Allison's birthday celebration.

"Listen Cornbread," Allison pleaded. "It's my birthday celebration even though my birthday's already passed. Can you and Matty please get along tonight?"

"I make no promises." Deidrick reclined his chubby frame in his father's chair. Matthias and Deidrick had been fighting for seven years. It started when Aunt Soleya put Matthias out of the house. He blamed Deidrick for getting him kicked out, and they hated being around each other ever since.

"Y'all get into it every time you're together and I look too cute today to be pulling y'all apart," Allison whined. "I want a drama-free birthday. Is that too much to ask?"

"I wanted to wear my shoes today." Deidrick looked at his white sneakers on Allison's feet. He wore a maroon tracksuit with a different pair of white sneakers and a diamond stud earring in his left ear.

"They went better with my outfit."

"Just don't scuff up my shoes," Deidrick said as he brushed waved hairstyle he'd been working on since he was eighteen. I expected nothing less from one of the best barbers in town.

Someone banged on the front door.

"Who is it?" Allison called.

"The police!" a raspy voice bellowed from the other side. "Open up!"

Allison ran to the door and opened it. Matthias latched onto Allison and hugged her.

"Queenie!" he cheered.

"Matthias!" Allison yelled as she grabbed at her back-length burgundy wig. "You're going to pull my wig off!"

"Wouldn't be the first time," Matthias laughed as he let her go. He picked me up and squeezed me. "What's up D-Money?"

"Hey!" I hugged him back. "How are you?"

"Man, I'm great!" Matthias howled. He let me go and started playing with the chain around his neck. "I'm ready to have some fun!"

Matthias flopped onto the couch without speaking to Deidrick. That was his way of keeping the peace. He wore a white and gold shirt, and his favorite black designer belt held his ripped black jeans in place.

"Have you figured out how I'm getting inside yet?" I asked Allison.

"The same way we're all getting in," Matthias laughed. "Cell is working the door tonight."

"Who?"

"Our cousin Marcellus that Matthias lives with," Allison explained. "He's tall and skinny like a string bean and he does security at Sepia sometimes."

"I'm ready to go," Matthias declared as he hopped up and started dancing. "This is how I'm going to be in there all night!"

"Bro, just come on," Deidrick complained as he got up.

"Don't get dropped."

"Drop me."

"No!" I stepped between them. "There will be no dropping tonight!"

Matthias and Deidrick pushed their bodies against my hands, contemplating if they wanted to fight or not.

"Man, you're lucky D-Money's here," Matthias said.

"Whatever bro."

They left it at that, and we headed out.

"So, we're on our way to see my man perform tonight," Allison said as she recorded a video for her social media. She flipped a strand of hair behind her shoulder. "And I just felt like I needed to show y'all how good I look for my birthday celebration."

"Yeah, we're outside with it." I threw my arm around Allison as I inserted myself into her video. "And Queenie looks good, but I look better."

"What?" Allison chuckled. "Let me show y'all what this boy got on."

"Yeah, show them how good I look!" I posed for the camera. "Make sure you get the shoes, camerawoman!"

"The shoes *are* nice." Allison bent down to show off my shoes to her followers. She left out the fact she paid for them. "They match well with his space hoodie and black cap. But this man had the nerve to throw on these little two-tone pants, talking about 'he can make it work'."

"I made it work, didn't I?" I joked.

"Y'all tell me who y'all think looks better," Allison instructed. "The birthday girl or her fashion-challenged cousin?"

We joined Matthias and Deidrick in the car. Matthias was the worst driver I'd ever ridden with. His seat leaned back into my lap. He sped, swerved between, and tailgated cars, all while yelling at their drivers. One hand drove the car while the other held a lit cigarette. The car shook from the speaker in the trunk, blasting music. Allison took more videos, and I danced in the background to the music. Once the smell of smoke got too strong, I stuck my head out of the window to escape it.

"That mess stinks!" Allison whined as she covered his nose. "Matty, I thought you were quitting!"

"I am." Matthias took a long drag and puffed it out the window. "It's a process."

"Well, I can't wait for the process to finish. You've been smoking since you were fourteen."

"I can't wait either," Matthias agreed, nodding his head to the music.

We arrived at Sepia when the doors opened. The neon orange 'SEPIA' sign glowed on the roof of the building. A sea of fitted hats with polos and colored wigs with tight outfits flooded the club's sidewalk.

"It smells like something died out here," I said as we approached the line.

"It went from bad to worse," Allison groaned.

The long line didn't stop people from having fun on the sidewalk. People danced to the music that could be heard from inside. A man with a video camera walked alongside the line, filming the partyers.

"Quick!" Allison said. "Hide your face!"

"Why?" I asked as I obeyed.

"Because you need to keep a low profile," she whispered. "Try and avoid the videographers, okay?"

"Alright."

After forty minutes, we reached the door, and the bouncer started laughing. He looked how Allison described him.

"Playboy, what are you doing out here?" Marcellus asked as he dapped Matthias up.

"Shoot nothing," Matthias said. "We're just celebrating Queenie's eighteenth, that's all."

"You're finally eighteen?"

"Yep," Allison said.

"Well, how about that," Marcellus laughed. "You're all grown up now. Even got the whole crew with you. Playboy, Cornbread…"

Marcellus paused when he got to me.

"Who's this?"

"This is our cousin D-Money on our dad's side." Matthias grabbed my shoulders. "He and Queenie are two months apart."

"Say less," Marcellus said as he gave me a wristband. "Any cousin of y'all's is a cousin of mine. Y'all have a good time and don't do anything I wouldn't do. And if you do, don't get caught because I'm not getting fired behind y'all."

"Told you he had us covered," Allison whispered as we entered the club.

Sepia was a world I'd never known before. It seemed chill and low energy. Gold light shined down from octagon-shaped lights above. I took it all in. A light-brown girl with loose curly hair sauntered past, and Deidrick bit his lip. She turned and smiled at Deidrick before switching away.

"Whew," Deidrick whistled and chased after the girl, being sure to call back over his shoulder, "Y'all have fun."

"Looks like he's found his conquest for tonight," Allison sighed. "Think you can keep a low profile?"

"Sure," I said.

"I'm DJ Yip-Yap and I'm here to make sure y'all have a good time tonight, so don't mess it up!" the bald, round, dark-brown DJ with a long black beard hollered over the microphone. "We've got the city's born-and-raised superstar KV coming to the stage later, so try not to get thrown out before then. It's a bunch of pretty ladies in here tonight having a good time and I'd like to keep it that way!"

DJ Yip-Yap's playlist was great, but the energy remained low. No one danced on the packed dance floor. Instead, everyone posed and showed off for the cell phone screens and videographers capturing every moment. It was different from the parties I was used to.

"Excuse me!" a pretty girl yelled as she carried a sparkling bottle through the floor. She took it to a group sitting on black leather couches sectioned off by a wooden beam. I noticed about four other areas like it around Sepia.

"What are those couches?" I asked Allison.

"A waste of money," Allison snorted. "Matty wanted to buy one for me for tonight and I told him no."

DJ Yip-Yap played a song that never failed to get me in a partying mood. The drums and synths hyped me up as the beat vibrated through my body. Although Sepia's energy was low, I wasn't missing my chance to dance to this song.

"Move back!" I told Allison. "This is my song!"

"I've got to see this!" Allison said as she pulled out her phone.

She cleared a space for me as I jogged back. I alternated shaking each leg, then transitioned into shaking my shoulders. My dance instructor wouldn't like my freestyle, but this wasn't dance class. The beat encouraged me as I moved under the blue lights. After jiggling my legs, I dipped and slowly came back up.

"Okay legs!" Allison cheered as she recorded me flowing through my choreography. I jumped around in a circle, pumping my arms in the air. Allison scrunched up her face and asked, "This is what you learn in dance class?"

"Nope!" I laughed. I hopped on each foot while twisting my body to the beat. "I'm just having fun!"

"I was about to say," Allison joked.

I hit several more dips, spins, and foot shuffles until the song ended.

"Have fun?" Allison asked.

"Heck yeah!" I declared. "You're not uploading that video, right?"

"Of course not," Allison said. "I'll send it to you though."

"Alright."

"Let's go!" DJ Yip-Yap hyped everyone up. He transitioned into 'Punch Your Lights Out'. "Rep your hood!"

"'Fighting spirit' song!" Allison echoed Granddad's words. "Let's move!"

"Yeah" I agreed.

Allison and I maneuvered around various sweaty bodies as we moved closer to the wall. Purple light filled the club as people jumped around and threw up signs.

"*Talking real tough when you got a crowd around*!" everyone yelled. "*Got your fists balled like you want to go to town*!"

"Y'all better not start fighting!" DJ Yip-Yap said. "Because I'll shut all this down. Y'all ain't about to tear this club up again."

We found Matthias standing near the bar with a plate of chicken wings. The wood on the bar's surface was chipped and eroded in several places.

"D-Money," Matthias said. "You've got to try these wings."

"Are they good?"

"Try it and see," Matthias said as he handed me a wing. I bit it, and it was crispy and well-seasoned.

"Well?" Matthias asked.

"It's good."

"I told you."

The three of us walked around the club. A slow, funky beat boomed from the speakers. Red light covered Sepia, and it smelled like must and cheap fragrances. I spotted Deidrick on a couch with his arm wrapped around the girl-from-earlier's waist. He whispered in her ear, and she started giggling.

"Who is she?" I asked Allison.

"Sharon," Allison answered as she rejected a dude's attempt to dance with her. "She used to work at the salon."

"Used to?"

"Mother fired her a few weeks ago."

"Why?"

"I don't know. All I know is whatever she did has been causing Mom and Dad to argue and it's annoying."

"I'm about to lose this shirt because it's hot!" DJ Yip-Yap joked as he tugged at the collar of his shirt. He observed the crowd on the dancefloor. "Some of y'all need a baby wipe and a cup of water!"

Sepia filled to the brim with people as the concert time neared. We moved closer to the stage for a good view. A few feet from me, a girl danced with a slow and steady rhythm. Her dance seemed to put me in a trance that was only broken by a red nail-polished hand landing on my shoulder. I spun around and made out the shape of Dorothea's head against the flashing lights.

"What are you doing here?!" she shouted.

"What are *you* doing here?!"

"Boy, I'm old enough to be here! Last time I checked you don't turn eighteen for another two months!"

"Shhhhh!"

"Come with me!"

Dorothea grabbed my hand and led me toward the lighted bathroom area. Marcellus perked up when he saw us and ran over to us.

"What's going on here?" he barked.

"It's fine," I told him. "This is my friend."

"Alright." Marcellus eyed Dorothea. "Just holler if you need me."

Marcellus left us alone, and Dorothea crossed her arms. Her face was caked in makeup. The fire alarm above her head was broken and hung on by a single wire.

"Why are you here?" Dorothea asked.

"We're celebrating Allison's eighteenth birthday and she wanted to do something fun."

"Y'all couldn't have a dance party at the house?" Dorothea asked. "What would your dad say if he saw you here?"

"I doubt he'd care as long as I don't drink or smoke anything."

"What about your grandparents?" Dorothea griped. "Would they care?"

"I didn't think about that..."

"Of course you di–!" Dorothea stopped mid-sentence and looked down at my pants. "What...?"

I opened my mouth to respond, but no words came out. All I could do was shrug.

"You know what, if you like it, I love it," Dorothea said. "I'll let you enjoy the concert tonight. But don't let me catch you out here again before you turn eighteen. Understand?"

"Alright," I agreed. "I'm going to use the bathroom real quick."

"I'll wait for you here," Dorothea said. She leaned against the wall to show she wasn't going anywhere.

I pushed my way into the men's bathroom and looked at myself in the mirror. A plump, medium-brown man stood at the sink next to me.

"I hope you ain't trying to wash your face," he slurred. "The hot water doesn't work."

"Oh. Thank you."

"Welcome." He blew a trail of smoke out the side of his mouth. "What's your name?"

"CJ," I told him a fake name.

"CJ...," he repeated. "I'm Malik."

"Nice to meet you...?"

"I came here to check on my girl because she got fired from her job," Malik ranted. "But she's spent the whole night wrapped up in some big head fat dude's arms!"

"Why are you in here then?" I asked. "If I was you, I'd go out there and confront them."

"Nah," Malik said. "She wouldn't be messing with old boy unless he had money anyways."

"Why'd she get fired from her job?"

"She tried to sleep with her boss and the wife found out and fired her!"

"So, she tried to sleep with her boss... and now she's in the club wrapped up in some dude's arms... and you're in here?"

"Look man, I don't care what my girl does as long as she doesn't bring home any diseases or a baby," Malik said. However, his tone of voice indicated he *was* bothered by his girlfriend's actions. But it wasn't any of my business.

"Alright then...," I said as I slowly backed away. "It was nice talking to you."

"You too," Malik sent a puff of smoke into the air.

I exited the bathroom and returned to Dorothea.

"What took you so long?"

"I was talking to someone."

"This is why you don't need to be here! Why are you talking to strangers?!"

"He talked to me first!"

"I hope you didn't tell him anything personal!"

"Of course not!"

Dorothea took me back to Allison as the last song ended. Everyone crowded around the stage for the concert.

"Where were you?" Allison asked me.

"The bathroom."

"Coming to the stage, we've got a local artist who'll give us a little something while we wait for KV," DJ Yip-Yap announced. "Give a big Sepia welcome to Bennito!"

Allison and I looked at each other as we recognized the name. Benjamin ran onto the stage. I knew he was a rapper, but I didn't expect to see him at Sepia. Although he was already eighteen, we were still in high school.

"Everybody put your hands up!" Benjamin yelled as his first song started.

"Alright!" I cheered. "Go Bennito!"

Benjamin danced around the stage and performed two songs. As his last song ended, his eyes landed on me. He stared at me for a second before scurrying off the stage.

"Give it up for Bennito!" DJ Yip-Yap hyped Benjamin up. "That was good man. Now, y'all been waiting for him all night and he's finally here. KV!"

"WOOOOOO!" Allison cheered. "KV!"

"What up, what up!" KV yelled as he ran to the stage. "Say man, somebody get Bennito's info and tell him to holler at me because I need him on a track ASAP."

"Yeah Bennito!" Allison hollered with the rest of the crowd.

"What's up y'all?" KV asked as he flashed his bejeweled grill at us. "I'm here to have a good time. Y'all want to have a good time with KV?"

"YES!" Allison screamed along with several other fans.

"That's what's up," KV said. He turned to his DJ. "Mousie, you ready?"

"You know, I'm ready," DJ Mousie said as she flipped her long black hair. KV's personal DJ had taken over the booth from DJ Yip-Yap.

"Alright then. Spin that first record and let's turn the crowd up then."

"Let's get it!" DJ Mousie agreed.

KV started his concert off with his new single, 'Party Starter'.

"*Don't underestimate the power that I have!*" he rapped. "*I can get your hands up, cuz you know I'm the man! Imma get the party jumpin and you know that's the plan! Get everybody hype cuz I know that I can!*"

"*You ain't nothing next to me!*" Allison rapped along to the song. "*Nothing in life come free!*"

"*Being the best, it ain't cheap*!" I rapped the next line back to her matching her energy. "*I'm lucky, I'm MVP! Most Valuable Party Starter, baby*!"

"Aye! Aye! Aye!" Allison threw her arms around me, and we jumped around yelling the lyrics to the first verse. The hyper energy flowed between us. "*Snatch you up and make you mine! Just by looking in my eyes! Spin that record round and round! Make you listen to my sound*!"

"*Make them hands clap*!" I shouted as I clapped my hands to the beat. "*Clap! Clap! Give me my applause! Make them hands clap! Clap! Clap! Cuz I got the sauce*!"

"*Put them hands up*!" Allison threw her hands in the air. "*Ladies if you know you bad*!"

"*Throw them hands up*!" I crossed my arms. "*Fellas cuz I know you mad*!"

"*That KV got every eye on him in this mug*!" KV yelled into the microphone. He bounced around on the stage. "*Turn that frown upside down! Make sure that you can hang! Imma turn this party up! We going out with a bang*!"

The crowd went crazy as the chorus started up again. After Party Starter, KV performed three more songs and tore the stage up with his performance. As he prepared for the final song, KV looked out over the crowd and smirked.

"I need the baddest female in here on stage with me right now!"

"Ooh me!" Allison jumped up and down. "Pick me!"

"I want the tall one in the black." KV pointed at Allison. "With the red wig on."

"Oh, that's me!" Allison cried.

One of KV's entourage pulled Allison onstage, and she did a little happy dance as she stood in front of KV.

"What's your name?" KV asked.

"Allison...," Allison giggled.

"How you doing tonight, Allison?"

"I'm good," Allison tucked her hair behind her ear. "I'm celebrating my birthday."

"Oh, it's your birthday," KV said. He turned to the crowd. "It's her birthday y'all. Let's sing happy birthday to her and then we're going to celebrate. That sound good to y'all?"

The crowd cheered in agreement. I pulled out my phone to record the moment for her.

"Happy birthday to you," KV sang to Allison. "Happy birthday to you. Happy birthday dear Allison. Happy birthday to you."

"Do 'Punch Your Lights Out'!" a fan yelled.

"Don't do that!" KV hollered. "Don't disrespect me like that! I ain't performing anything I put out with that thief! It'll be your fault that Allison's birthday got ruined because I'll end this concert right here! And I don't think you want that, because Allison look like she can fight!"

"This man is crazy!" Matthias laughed.

"Y'all getting me out of character!" KV ranted. He turned to Allison. "What do you want to hear since it's your birthday?"

"It's your concert," Allison said. "Play whatever you want."

"Alright. Yo Mousie, drop something!"

"I can't believe it!" Allison cheered as she danced around after the concert was over. "KV really brought me onstage and sang happy birthday to me. My life is complete."

"I guess this means you enjoyed your birthday?" Matthias laughed.

"I had the time of my life!" Allison declared.

"I'm still stuck on Deidrick leaving with that girl," I said. "I think I met her boyfriend in the bathroom."

"Boyfriend?" Allison choked. "The way she was all over Deidrick in there, you'd think she was single."

"Her boyfriend claims he doesn't care," I said. "According to him, Aunt Leya fired her for trying to sleep with Uncle Marlin."

"There's no way he slept with her," Matthias snorted. "He's too dedicated to upholding Mom's stupid perfect image to even consider sleeping with someone else."

"Why are they arguing then?" Allison grumbled.

"I don't know," Matthias said. "I don't live there or talk to those people."

"Allison!" Marcellus laughed as he approached us. "Why'd you make that face when KV was ranting?"

"Because," Allison whined. "Why am I in it?"

"Queenie, you might go viral from this," I said. "Knokout already responded to it with a shrugging emoji and the words 'Poor Allison' on his social media."

"This is the last thing I need," Allison sighed.

"So, what y'all still doing out here?" Marcellus asked.

"You know we couldn't leave without stopping by to see my favorite TiTi," Matthias said.

"Boy please," TiTi, the food truck owner, giggled.

"You know you love seeing me," Matthias joked.

"About as much as a cat loves seeing a bath."

"Why'd you do me like that?"

"Because you're in the way of my paying customers," TiTi teased. She handed a bag to Marcellus. "Here you go, Cell."

"Thank you, ma'am," Marcellus said.

"WHAT'D YOU CALL ME?!" someone yelled in the distance.

"There they go," Matthias groaned.

"Man, they do this mess every week," Marcellus grumbled.

"You not going to stop them, Mr. Security Guard?" Matthias asked Marcellus.

"Heck nah!" Marcellus exclaimed. "I'm off the clock now. I suggest you call it a night too Miss TiTi because you know how these people get. Especially at Sepia."

"I'm already ahead of you." TiTi cut the lights off and exited her truck. "Y'all get home safely, alright?"

"You too, TiTi," Matthias called. "See you later."

I entered the house to find Granddad Derrick reading a book at the kitchen table.

"Granddad!" I yelped.

"Your nanna would have a fit if she saw you in those pants," Granddad laughed. "Those are ugly."

"I like them," I protested. "What are you doing here so late?"

"Well...," Granddad said as he scratched his forehead. "Your nanna and I went to check on your cousins, but Dee-Three told us y'all left and he was hungry. So, Kiana stayed over there and made him dinner while I came over here to see if this was where y'all were. Nobody was here so I figured I'd watch the house till somebody got back."

"We went out to celebrate Queenie's birthday," I sighed as I sat across from him.

"I know," Granddad said. "You smell like smoke, sweat and sin."

"I didn't do anything."

"I didn't say you did," Granddad said. "But last time I checked, you were still seventeen."

"Am I in trouble?"

"Someone once told me that I am not without sin, therefore I can't cast the first stone."

"What does that mean?"

"It means you're not in trouble... this time," Granddad laughed. "I snuck out to party with my friends when I turned eighteen. It didn't end well..."

"What happened?"

"Minister Jones happened," Granddad chuckled. His eyes hazed over as he reflected on his younger years. "Of course, I don't regret it because that's how I met your grandmother."

"Out partying?"

"Your grandmother was a wild girl," Granddad giggled. "Boy, do I have some stories. We'll save those for when you're older."

"Okay."

"I doubt Malcolm will be upset with you. But don't do something like this again. You never know what types of problems can come from doing stuff like that."

-

Chapter Thirty-Four

Monday morning, Derik and I sat in the cafeteria, waiting for school to start.

"When did you know you liked Adrianna?" he asked.

"Why do you ask?"

"I'm curious."

"She was always on my mind," I said as I looked at his neck. "Do you have a necklace on?"

"You can see it?"

"Not unless you're really close. Let me see it."

"Let me see it," Derik copied me.

"Come on," I whined.

"Come on."

"Stop it."

"I can't show it to you here," Derik whispered, looking around. "One of the teachers might take it."

"It's not against dress code for guys to wear jewelry."

"It is when it's Matty's poker chip necklace."

"The black-and-white one Cornbread gave him as a gift?"

"He said I could have it last Friday," Derik said with a smirk. "You thought I stole it, didn't you?"

"Well, you do have a history of taking things that aren't yours..."

"That's when I was younger," Derik complained. "I'm fifteen now. I've outgrown that phase in my life."

"I'm glad that you've grown," I complimented him as I patted his shoulder.

Benjamin walked through the cafeteria with Charmaine. He spotted me and made a beeline for me.

"Hey Ben–!" I started before Benjamin covered my mouth.

"Don't tell anyone anything you saw Saturday or else," he threatened. I looked into his eyes and licked his hand. Benjamin wiped his hand on my shirt in disgust. "Why would you do that?!"

"Because what do you mean 'or else'?" I asked. "Do you really think I'd risk getting myself in trouble?"

"How am I supposed to know what you'd do?" Benjamin griped as he sat down.

"You knew me well enough to put your hand over my mouth and hope I wouldn't bite it."

"Just don't mention what you saw."

"What are you so worried about anyways?" I asked. "You just turned eighteen a few weeks ago."

"My parents don't exactly agree with me being a rapper yet. I need to make a name for myself to convince them to get with the program."

"Well, if you ever need a backup dancer, I'm available."

Samiel sat down at the table and buried his head in his arms.

"And Sami can sing background vocals," I added. "Right Sami?"

Samiel didn't speak.

"Sami?" When he didn't lift his head, I asked, "What's the matter?"

"Why didn't anyone tell me I was weird?"

"Who told you that?"

"Danielle."

"Sami don't listen to her," Benjamin groaned. "You're not weird. There are plenty of people who are adopted."

"That's not what I'm not talking about!" Samiel cried. "I'm so embarrassed!"

"You know what makes me feel better when I'm upset?" I said. "Food. Especially food from Patty's."

"Seriously?" Benjamin snorted.

"Your parents make good food," I said. "What do you say, Sami?"

"I'm not hungry!"

"Not even if I pay for it?"

"You're going to spend *money*?" Derik whispered. "Like, *real money*? Sami don't pass this up. He never spends money."

Samiel lifted his head and looked at me.

"I guess a small meal couldn't hurt then," he said. "But only a small one."

Benjamin stifled a laugh.

"What's funny?" I asked.

"Nothing...," Benjamin said with a smile.

"Okay...," I stared at him. "We'll go after school, Sami."

Benjamin doubled over with laughter.

"What is so funny?"

"Nothing!" Benjamin told me. "I promise."

"I just want to rip her head off," Latasia said from behind me. She and Althea sat down at the table. "Is that too much to ask?"

"Unfortunately, you can't rip Danielle's head off, Lala," Althea informed Latasia.

"Weren't you her best friend at one point?" Benjamin asked Latasia. "What happened?"

"She was cool until we got to high school," Latasia complained. "Then, she started feeling herself because 'her daddy is the principal'. This year's cheerleading tryouts was my last straw with her."

"What happened at tryouts?" I asked.

"We had an interview stage at tryouts this year, and Danielle failed hers because of her stank attitude," Latasia said. "She claims Coach Nelson added them on purpose to get her off the team. So, Danielle wanted me, Nicki, and Prissy to quit the team to back her up."

"She wanted you to give up cheer captain because *she* didn't make the team?" I asked in shock.

"She sure did," Latasia agreed. "Prissy was the only one dumb enough to do that because she can't think for herself. Me and Nicki stayed, so Danielle called us fake and that was that. I didn't care since I was already distancing myself from Danielle because Coach Nelson warned us about associating with her. But now she wants to pick on my brother, and I want to rip her head off!"

"I understand you're upset with her, but you can't retaliate," Althea said. "You could get suspended and kicked off the cheer team."

"It would be worth it if it meant I could punch Danielle," Latasia sighed.

"You want to punch her too?" Adrianna asked as she came up behind me.

"Too?" I grabbed her hand. "What do you mean 'too'?"

"Dad took me with him to visit Arty over the weekend, and Danielle and her little idiot sidekicks got on my nerves the whole time. I know Principal Lee is his best friend and all, but I can't. All those girls do is gossip and make slick comments. And now Danielle's roped Mariana and Mariella in as if those two weren't already annoying enough on their own."

"Of course, she did," Latasia laughed. "She can't do anything without a clique to back her up."

"Is there anyone that *does* like her?" I asked.

"Priscella," Derik said. "Maybe Charmaine?"

"Charmaine doesn't like her either," Benjamin said.

"You know it's a problem when Charmaine doesn't like you," Adrianna said. "She likes everybody."

"Well, well, well," a nasally, high-pitched voice joined the conversation. Danielle Lee stood at the end of our table. Her hands sat on her hips as her brown eyes peered at us through the oval-shaped eyes in her medium-brown face. Behind her stood her clique consisting of Priscella Payne and the Garza sisters. "If it isn't the less fortunate... and Derik."

"Because he has money," Priscella whispered behind her light-brown hand.

"Thank you, Captain Obvious," Danielle said.

"You're welcome," Priscella answered with a grin.

"Did you want something?" Althea politely asked.

"Actually, I did," Danielle explained. "I wanted to apologize to Sami."

"You do?" Samiel lifted his head.

"Of course, I do," Danielle gasped with fake surprise. "I didn't think about how much my words might hurt your feelings. I mean your life must already be so miserable since your parents forced Latasia on you by adopting her."

"Isn't your dad also adopted, dummy?" Latasia protested. She'd been adopted out of the foster care system by the Dows when she was four. "Do you think before you talk?"

"My dad was adopted out of love," Danielle declared. "You were adopted out of pity."

"If that's the version of your father's story you want to believe, then okay," Latasia snorted.

"Lala is my sister, period," Samiel defended his sister. "It doesn't matter how it happened."

"How sad." Danielle dabbed at her eyes. "They even make you stick up for her."

"So sad," Priscella mimicked.

"Very sad," Mariana added.

"Very, very said," Mariella said.

"Honestly, I'm surprised they kept you Latasia considering they have Kameryn now," Danielle said, referring to Samiel and Latasia's fourteen-year-old sister. Kameryn was the Dows only biological child.

"It's alright, Lala," Adrianna said. "If you ignore them, they'll go away."

"Funny, I think your dad said the same thing to your mom," Danielle giggled. "That's probably how they ended up divorced."

"And it won't surprise me if he ends up divorced again," Mariana said.

Adrianna looked at her nails, then played with her hair. It became clear she wouldn't respond.

"Now what?" Priscella asked.

"I guess there's no response," Danielle guffawed. "Come along girls."

Danielle left with her three minions trailing behind her.

"Told you they'd go away if you ignored them," Adrianna smirked.

"Girl, you are too much!" Latasia exclaimed. "The way you sat there looking at your nails."

"And did you see her face?" Adrianna laughed. "She was like 'uh okay'."

"Well, with cousins like those, who needs enemies?" I complained.

"It's alright," Adrianna said. "They won't last long with Danielle anyways. Eventually, they'll all turn on each other because they're all too self-centered."

After school, Samiel and I went to Patty's. Benjamin stood behind the counter, taking orders.

"Welcome to Patty's," he said with a bored, monotone voice. "How may I help you?"

"That's how you greet customers?" I laughed.

"People come for the food, not me."

"You could at least smile."

"Are you going to order or not?"

"Benjamin!" Mr. Raymond Townsend yelled. "That is not how I trained you to talk to the customers!"

"What would you like to order?" Benjamin said forcefully with a smile.

"I'll take a chicken tender meal and then whatever Sami wants."

"A chicken tender meal and–!" Benjamin asked before he started laughing. "And a Sami Special?"

"Sami Special? What's that?"

"Chicken and catfish with fries, greens, mac and cheese, cornbread, a large lemonade, and a peach cobbler made specially for Sami."

"*That's* a small meal for you?" I turned to look at Samiel.

"And it cost fifteen dollars," Benjamin chuckled.

"Fifteen dollars?!" I exclaimed. "Is that why you've been laughing at me all day? You knew and you said *nothing*!"

"You said you'd pay for the man's meal."

"I thought we were friends, Benji."

"Hey, Sami ordered the meal," Benjamin teased. "I only charged you the twenty-two dollars and twenty-seven cents for it."

"My heart," I groaned as I clutched at my chest. "Twenty-two dollars?!"

"And twenty-seven cents," Benjamin added.

"Y'all set me up," I grumbled as I forked over the money.

"All I did was charge you," Benjamin joked. "Take your grievances up with Sami. Have a nice day."

"Sami Special," I muttered as I snatched my receipt from Benjamin's hand.

"I'm a growing boy...," Samiel said as he followed me to our table.

"Growing, schmowing," I complained as we sat down. "You better tell me every single detail about this Danielle issue since you made me pay fifteen dollars. She said you were weird out of nowhere?"

"No," Samiel sighed. "I was talking to Nicki in our science class last Friday about my favorite band because she asked me about it. Danielle overheard our conversation and said I was weird for knowing so much about them. Then, Priscella joined in and started teasing me too. I didn't want to tell Latasia, but I think Nicki told her and now she's all worked up."

"Sami, you shouldn't worry about what some mean girls think. There's nothing wrong with knowing stuff about your favorite band."

"It's not just that," Samiel said. "I think my dad is embarrassed by my singing."

"Did he tell you he was embarrassed?"

"Not to my face."

"Did he tell anyone else he was embarrassed?"

"I overheard him on the phone talking about it."

"What did he say?"

"I heard him say my name and then he said, 'his singing is so weird' after that."

"That doesn't sound good."

"If he's embarrassed about my singing, who knows what else about me embarrasses him?" Samiel rested his head on the table and looked at the floor. "What if he regrets adopting me because I'm not the son he hoped I would be?

"Sami, the man named you after himself."

"But he kept the misspelling in my name that the nurse made on my birth certificate. What if it was because he didn't want me to be fully named after him?"

"Okay, now you're overthinking it. You told me he kept the misspelling because he liked how it looked, right?"

"Yeah... but–!"

"But nothing. Are you sure it's not a misunderstanding?"

"I don't know anymore. But if he doesn't like my singing then I won't sing anymore."

"And then what?" I joked. "You're going to start throwing shoes next?"

"This is serious!" Samiel whined. "You don't understand because your dad always supports you. He's not ashamed of you."

"And I don't think your dad is ashamed of you either. I think you're insecure."

"That's not true!" Samiel argued.

"Why'd you start singing in the first place?"

"When I was in the hospital Chief Parker came and sang for us back when he was still a regular officer. His sister was my nurse and she told him I liked to sing, so he came to my room, gave me his hymnal, and told me to never stop singing."

"Do you still have the hymnal he gave you?"

"No."

"What happened to it?"

"I left it on Mr. Shoe-Thrower's piano at the school."

"Why'd you do that?"

"Because I don't want to sing anymore."

"All this is does is prove you're insecure."

"I am not!"

"Then prove it! I'll get the hymnal back for you and then you'll sing in front of the whole church at the revival. Do that and I'll leave you alone."

"What good will that do?"

"It'll prove you're not insecure and your dad will be there, so you'll be able to see if he's really embarrassed of you or not. Plus, don't you want to see Danielle's face when you sing in front of the whole town, and show her she had no effect on you?"

"That would be funny to see..."

"There you go! We've got to get that hymnal back."

"And if this doesn't work out, Derek," Samiel warned me. "It'll be all your fault."

"I'll take that risk since I know I'm right."

Once again, I was in the library to talk with Mary the next day.

"Mary, I need your help again."

"Once again, you've been at this school long enough to know where everything is," Mary said without looking up from her book. "What could you possibly need my help with this time?"

"I need your help with Sami. He wants to quit singing and I'm trying to convince him not to."

"What does that have to do with me?"

"I was hoping you could put me in contact with Chief Parker."

"You couldn't ask Adrianna to do that?"

"Mary, are you going to help me or not?"

"Give me a minute," Mary sighed as she dialed a number on her phone.

"Hello?"

"Hey Uncle Thusi," Mary answered in a bright and chipper voice. "I need a favor. One of the students here at the school says he needs to talk to you and it's important."

Chief Parker said something. Mary nodded a few times, then covered the phone receiver.

"He wants to know if it's an emergency?"

"No."

"No, it's not," Mary told her uncle. She nodded a few more times and smiled. "Okay. Thanks Uncle Thusi. Bye."

Mary hung up the phone and looked at me.

"He said stop by the station after school and ask for him at the front desk."

After sixth period ended, I went to the police station to see Chief Parker. It was a Tuesday, which meant my visit needed to be quick because I had dance practice that evening.

"Derek," Officer Bud Vaughn greeted me. He looked like his sister, Ms. Jana Vaughn. "What are you doing here?"

"I need to speak with Chief Parker. He told me to ask for him at the front desk."

"Oh, you're who he's expecting," Officer Vaughn said. "Let me go see if he's awake."

Officer Vaughn disappeared, and I looked around the station. Only three officers worked at Creeke's police station. Chief Terrence Parker, Officer Bud Vaughn, and Officer Samuel Dow. Apparently, Chief Parker fired everyone except Officer Dow when he took over. Mayor Perry brought Officer Vaughn from one of the neighboring towns.

"The chief's awake, and he'll see you now," Officer Vaughn said when he returned. "I'll escort you to his office."

"Okay, thank you."

I followed behind Officer Vaughn to Chief Parker's office. Chief Parker never let him leave the station. Officer Dow liked to 'circle the airport and never land the plane' as Granddad put it, and Samiel was the same way. His never-ending lectures were a big reason why crime in Creeke was low.

"Here we are," Officer Vaughn announced.

"Hey Derek," Chief Parker greeted me as he wiped what looked like drool from his desk. "What's going on?"

"Hi, Chief Parker." I sat down in the chair across from him.

Chief Parker looked at Officer Vaughn.

"You can go now," he said.

"Ri...right!" Officer Vaughn hurriedly shut the door and left.

"Every day I wonder why Bernard hired him...," Chief Parker muttered under his breath. He regained his composure. "What can I help you with?"

"I wanted to speak with you about Sami."

"Sami? Should I call his dad?"

"No, it's fine."

"Okay...," Chief Parker sat back down. "What is it then?"

"Sami is considering quitting singing."

"Ah," Chief Parker said. "He told you the hospital story and that's why you wanted to talk to me."

"Yeah... he said he overheard his dad talking about his singing and now he thinks his dad is embarrassed of him. Then, a girl made fun of him at school and that only made it worse."

"Unfortunately, there's not much I can do," Chief Parker sighed. "If I talk to him, then Sami will know you told me, and he'll be mad at you. Then Sam will be mad at me because I didn't tell him his son was having issues. And *Torrance* will be mad at all of us for not including him in anything when he's the choir teacher. Granted, I can handle Torrance being mad at me because he's been mad at me his whole life, but you don't need that kind of stress. My suggestion would be to let Sami and Sam work it out on their own."

"Okay," I said. "I do have one more thing to discuss. Adrianna and I are trying to get the Brown Family Band to sing at the revival and Pastor Hall told her that since you're the music minster, it's your decision."

"When was Pastor Hall going to tell *me* this?"

"First Lady Hall said since it was our idea, it was our responsibility to ask."

"She would say that," Chief Parker grumbled. "Drake tried to get us to sing together too, and it failed. I'm not too sure if this time will work either."

"It's because he got in his feelings," I repeated Adrianna's words. "We won't make that mistake."

"That sounds like something Adrianna would say right before questioning if she made the right decision," Chief Parker laughed. "Y'all are already started to rub off on each other."

"How about we make a deal?" I asked. "If I convince Sami to sing at the revival, then the Brown Family Band will also sing."

"If you can convince Sami to sing *and* get your Granddad to preach, I'll ask my siblings to sing. That way you won't have to worry about getting Torrance on board."

"Get my Granddad to preach? Won't that cause drama?"

"Probably," Chief Parker figured. "But I know it'll make my Papa happy. Do we have a deal?"

I thought about Chief Parker's offer. Granddad hadn't preached since before I was born. He said when The Lord saw fit, He'd return Granddad to preaching. Maybe this was the opportunity he waited for.

"Deal," I said.

That night, I called Adrianna to tell her the big news.

"Everything's riding on you getting Sami to sing?" she asked me.

"And getting my Granddad to preach," I said. "Why is this hymnal so important?"

"Because it belonged to Great-Grandpa," Adrianna explained. "It's the only thing left of his we had, and Dad was really upset when Uncle Terrence gave it away."

"Oh. Speaking of your family, I'm really surprised you didn't take off on your cousins for what they said."

"I wanted to, but I'm not getting suspended over them."

"How do you feel though?"

"About the situation?"

"Yeah."

"Look, I believe my dad and Gretchen are going to have a good marriage. And I also believe The Lord will deal with those idiots on my behalf. So, I'm not going to worry about it."

"Okay."

"It's weird," Adrianna said. "Nobody's ever really asked me how *I* felt before."

"They haven't?"

"No. When you have a lot of siblings sometimes it's easy to feel... forgotten."

"You're not forgotten."

"I know," Adrianna sighed. "The Bible says The Lord doesn't forget us but sometimes I just feel... forgotten, I guess."

"Oh, I meant I haven't forgotten you, but that's even better."

"You know what, you're going to the revival because this is ridiculous," Adrianna giggled. "How does a preacher's grandson not think of that first?"

"Look ma'am, not all of us can just quote the Bible off the top of our heads," I joked.

"The more you read it, the more familiar it becomes," Adrianna giggled. "You should try it sometime. In fact, I'll let you start right now."

Before I could respond, Adrianna hung up the phone. The bible Granddad and Nanna gave me as a child sat in my nightstand drawer. It was a King James Version Bible, and I couldn't understand a single word in it. Still, I had nothing better to do since my homework was done. I retrieved the Bible and opened it to a random page.

"How long, ye simple ones, will ye love simplicity?" I read the first verse I laid my eyes on. It was from Proverbs One. "Huh?"

The passage was hard to understand, so I closed the book and went to bed. That night I had a strange dream.

I stood in Derik's room. In the mirror, I saw I was on fire. My reflection twisted himself into strange positions, writhing in pain. He looked at me.

"How long?!" he cried.

I woke up. Seeing myself on fire creeped me out, and I couldn't sleep for the rest of the night.

Chapter Thirty-Five

Convincing Granddad to preach at the revival wouldn't be easy. From what Dad told me, almost the whole town turned on Granddad when I came into the picture. It amazed me he still attended the church after all that. But attending and preaching were two different things, and I wasn't sure if Granddad would be up to the latter.

Then, there was the hymnal issue. It was a good thing Samiel was my best friend because I was doing a lot for him to regain his confidence. Getting the hymnal back from Mr. Brown wouldn't be easy, but I had to do it.

"Are you sure you want to go with me?" I asked Derik as we walked to Mr. Brown's classroom during lunch that Wednesday. "I mean, you both did have a big argument at the beginning of the year."

"It's been almost a month since then," Derik said. "We're good."

"Here goes nothing," I exhaled when we reached the classroom.

"Why are you so nervous?" Derik asked.

"Because we're about to rip Mr. Brown's heart out."

"We are?"

"Yeah," I said. "We're about to ask him to give us his dead grandfather's hymnal."

"Dead grandfather?" Derik whispered as he covered his mouth with his hand. "I wouldn't want to be in your position right now."

We entered the classroom. Mr. Brown messily slurped noodles into his mouth.

"Hey Mr. Brown," I greeted. "I need to talk to you about something."

"Oh!" Mr. Brown coughed. He wiped his mouth on his arm. "Wha... What can I help you guys with?"

"I don't know how to say this but...," I said as I scratched the back of my neck. "Um... I need your hymnal back..."

Mr. Brown stopped chewing.

"What hymnal?" he uttered through a mouthful of food.

"The one Sami left on your piano yesterday..."

"I didn't see a hymnal yesterday..."

"You didn't?" Derik gasped.

"Um." Mr. Brown stopped to swallow his food. "Why did Sami leave a hymnal on my piano?"

"It may have been your grandfather's and he may have been giving it back because he wants to quit singing."

"I don't even know which problem to start with," Mr. Brown mumbled.

"If you don't have it, then where is it?" I asked.

"I would like to know too," Mr. Brown agreed.

"I'm sure it'll turn up," Derik said. "Just... just give it some time."

"I have good news and I have bad news," I told Samiel in Mrs. Garza's fifth-period pre-calculus class. We were working on a group assignment with Latasia and Althea.

"What's the bad news?" Samiel sighed.

"Mr. Shoe-Thrower never got the hymnal, and he doesn't know where it is."

"What?" Samiel shrieked.

"Inside voices, Sami," Mrs. Garza said.

"Sorry," Samiel whispered. "What do you mean he never got it?"

"He said he never got it."

"So what? A ghost took it? It sprouted legs and walked away? What happened?"

A set of jingling keys interrupted our conversation. Samiel and Latasia's mother, Vice Principal Christine Dow entered the room. Vice

Principal Dow glided across the room like the former beauty queen that was. She went to Mrs. Garza and started talking to her.

"I still can't believe what Danielle, Priscella, Mariana and Mariella said the other day," Latasia said loudly.

"Why are you bringing this back up?" Samiel whispered. "Adrianna said not to worry about it."

"Well, sometimes a sister needs help," Latasia whispered. She raised her voice again and said, "I can't believe they told Adrianna that Mr. Brown and Ms. Nelson wouldn't last."

"And then the way Danielle teased you about being adopted?" I added, deciding to help Latasia with her scheme. "Not to mention her saying they should've gotten rid of you once they had Kameryn."

"Oh, you've gone and done it now," Samiel fretted.

Vice Principal Dow approached our group.

"Sami, Lala, can I see you two outside?" she asked.

"What's the matter, Mom?" Latasia asked.

"Nothing," Vice Principal Dow said. "I just need to see you two real quick, that's all."

"Okay."

Samiel and Latasia followed their mother from the classroom.

"Y'all are treacherous," Althea giggled.

"Those girls need to get what they deserve," I whispered.

"What was the good news you were going to tell Sami?"

"The good news...," I began before stopping to look at Mrs. Garza. I placed my hand over my mouth and whispered, "Chief Parker said he'll get his siblings to sing at the revival if I get Sami to sing and get my granddad to preach."

The whispers and murmurs in the classroom got louder.

"The Brown Family Band and Mr. Derrick at the revival?" Althea gasped. "My mother is definitely going to fall out on the floor that night."

"But I can't get Sami to sing without the hymnal first."

"Just ask Benji to perform with him."

"Why Benji?"

"He and Benji used to sing together all the time when they were younger," Althea explained. "If Benji's onstage, I guarantee you Sami will get onstage too."

"I didn't know that."

"Because you barely go to church," Althea said. "It's ironic how your family founded the church and the only ones who show up now are Mr. Derrick and Mrs. Kiana."

Samiel and Latasia returned from their meeting with their mom.

"What'd she say?" I asked.

"To use our inside voices and that she'll talk to Principal Lee about the girls," Samiel explained. "What were you two talking about?"

"Derek told us if you sing at the revival, then the Brown Family Band will also perform and Mr. Derrick will preach," Althea caught Samiel up.

"Really?" Samiel asked as he looked at Mrs. Garza. "Does she know about this?"

"She knows now," Mrs. Garza answered. "One day we'll work on your inside voices."

"Oops," I groaned.

"I can't believe y'all got those girls in trouble," Samiel laughed as we walked to sixth period. "I can't wait for them to get what they deserve."

"Poor Mrs. Garza though," I said. "Imagine having daughters like Mariana and Mariella."

"I would be so embarrassed."

Benjamin exited the cafeteria, and I caught him by his arm.

"Why do you do stuff like this?" he griped. "You almost tore my whole arm off!"

"I need a favor," I said.

"What?"

"I need you to sing at the revival with Sami."

"Huh?" Samiel said. "You want Benji to sing with me?"

"Yeah," I said. "You won't be as nervous if Benji sings with you. I'll do anything you want if you do this for me, Benji."

"Anything?" Benjamin asked.

"As long as its legal and won't bankrupt me."

"Alright, deal."

"Thanks, Benji."

"No problem."

After school, I went to Althea's house for help solving the missing hymnal mystery. Althea read mysteries like they would go out of style, so if anyone could help, it'd be her. She lived across the street from my cousins, so Allison tagged along. We sat at her kitchen table while Diana watched television in the living room.

"We need to establish a means, motive, and opportunity," Althea told us.

"And that'll help us figure out who took the hymnal?" I asked.

"It should."

"Sami told me he left the hymnal on the piano after sixth period on Monday. Almost all the seniors have seventh period off, and Mr. Brown doesn't have a class that period either. That means it had to be taken during passing period because otherwise he would've seen it."

"That's a really short period of time," Allison said. "Whoever took it would've had to know how important it was to Mr. Shoe-Thrower."

"They also probably snagged it while everyone was leaving the room," Althea figured. "So, someone took the hymnal during passing period between sixth and seventh period. Why?"

"That's the only part I can't figure out," I groaned. "If Allison's right, then the only people in the class who knew it's importance are Sami and Mariana."

"I have an idea," Allison said. She dialed Andre's number on her phone and put it on speakerphone for everyone to hear.

"Yellow?" Andre greeted.

"Andre, we have a problem," Allison informed him.

"Look, I already told you I was sorry about our study guide in Biology," Andre griped. "What more do you want from me?"

"You're lucky I passed that test," Allison huffed. "But that's not why I'm calling. Did Mariana take your dad's hymnal? We've compiled the evidence and all roads lead to her taking it."

"Why would I know if she took it?" Andre argued. "I don't talk to her."

"She's your cousin."

"Not everyone is best friends with their cousins like you are, Allison," Andre said.

"Look, this is about your dad's hymnal."

"I didn't even know Dad *had* a hymnal. Who even uses hymnals anymore when they put the lyrics up on the screen for you at church?"

"Hello!" Diana hollered her agreement. "That's a good point!"

"You know what, bye," Allison said as she hung up the phone. "He wasn't any help."

"Why don't you guys call Sami and ask him if he told anyone else about the hymnal?" Diana suggested. "Then maybe I'll be able to hear my show."

"It's worth a shot," Althea said.

We dialed Samiel's number next.

"Hello?" Samiel said.

"Sami, I have a question," I told him.

"I might have an answer."

"Did you tell anyone else about the hymnal? Like the story of how you got it?"

"Hmm...," Samiel muttered. "I remember telling Benji about it one day... Speaking of Benji, why did you ask him to sing with me at the revival? Because it's all he'll talk about now and, his ideas make my head hurt. And–!"

"Focus," I said to cut off his rambling. "Is Benji the only person you told?"

"I think... No wait! Derik was there too! He was sitting right behind Benji listening to the story. And..."

"Ah," I said, looking at Allison. Samiel was still talking, so I cut him off again. "Thanks Sami."

"You're welcome. I hope you find it because I don't think I can sing without it."

"What do you mean?" I asked as I took him off speakerphone and exited the kitchen.

"I like to have it in front of me, so I don't have to look at everyone's faces."

"You mean so you don't have to look at your dad's reaction to you sing," I called him out.

"Just find the hymnal, okay?" Samiel said.

"Don't worry, I will." I hung up the phone and returned to the kitchen.

"I know who took it," I announced. I gave Allison her phone back. "Thanks for your help, Althea."

"No problem."

"I'm going to stay over here for a bit," Allison said.

"Alright," I answered. As I passed Diana, I told her, "Enjoy your show."

"I'll try."

When I reached the front door, I found Ralph Brewer standing on the other side.

"Derek!" he said. "What a wonderful surprise!"

"Hey Ralphie," I said. "What's up?"

"I heard through the grapevine that you and Adrianna were continuing Drake's work," Ralph said. "Is that true?"

"We're trying," I laughed.

"So, I might still have a front-page story after all!" Ralph cheered. His eyes glittered with excitement.

Diana appeared next to me and glared at Ralph.

"If you don't get your butt in this house, and leave that poor boy alone," she threatened.

"We'll talk," Ralph whispered to me before following Diana into the house.

No one was home except Derik. His room was upstairs at the back of the house. I knocked twice at the top of his door and waited for him to repeat it back. When he did, I repeated the process at the bottom of his door. Then we knocked in the shape of the cross at the same time. It was our special passcode. Derik pulled the door open and leaned against the doorframe.

"To what do I owe the pleasure?" he asked with a smile.

"I know you have it," I told him. "Where is it?"

"In my desk drawer," Derik sighed as he led me into his room.

I opened the desk drawer and removed the brown book with the word 'hymnal' engraved on the front in gold letters.

"Why'd you steal it?"

"I wanted to see if I still had it," Derik admitted, referring to his past thefts. "I didn't know it was Mr. Shoe-Thrower's dead grandfather's hymnal though. When we found he didn't know he even had it, I felt bad and was going to return it tomorrow."

"So, you let me run around like a chicken with my head cut off today, and you had it the whole time?"

"Sorry."

"Sorry," I mocked. "I should chop you in your throat."

"But you're not going to."

"You're right." I waved the hymnal around. "I'm going to hold onto this for now."

"You're not going to give it to Sami?"

"Not yet. I want him to develop confidence apart from this."

I'd found the hymnal. Only one step remained to get Adrianna's revival plan underway. I had to convince Granddad to preach again. That night I had the creepy dream again.

I stood in Derik's room. In the mirror, I saw I was on fire. My reflection twisted himself into strange positions, writhing in pain. He looked at me.

"How long?!" he cried.

"What do you mean?" I asked.

"How long?!"

I woke up covered in sweat, hoping it would be my last time having that dream.

-

Chapter Thirty-Six

That Saturday, I visited Granddad and Nanna at their house. Their house had five bedrooms with wood-paneled walls and brown carpet. My cousins and I sat in their kitchen eating lunch. Allison held Derik's phone in her hands, tapping on the screen.

"Why isn't this working?" she grumbled.

Derik strolled into the kitchen wearing a black and white striped baseball jersey.

"Did you change your passcode?" Allison asked him.

"Yeah," Derik said as he sat next to me.

"Why?"

"Because it's my phone and I can."

"Taking a break from your polos?" I teased him.

"Matty gave it to me along with some of his other clothes," Derik said.

"It looks good on you," I complimented.

"Thanks," Derik said. He whispered, "Do you ever wonder what your mom is like?"

"Not really."

"Would you ever consider meeting her?"

"Why would I want to meet someone that didn't want me?"

"That's okay," Derik said, patting my shoulder. "Our dad didn't want kids either."

"Is that supposed to make him feel better?" Deidrick snorted.

"No, but it's true," Allison grumbled. "Dad didn't even remember my birthday."

"It could be worse," Deidrick said. "We could've had Mr. Shoe-Thrower as a father."

"I'd rather walk into oncoming traffic," Derik muttered.

"I thought y'all were good," I said.

"We are," Derik said. "But I'd still rather walk into oncoming traffic than have him as a father."

"Derik Tremaine, what have I told you about speaking like that?" Granddad chastised as he entered the kitchen. "The power of life and death is in the tongue."

"Sorry Granddad," Derik said.

"Granddad," I asked. "How would you feel about preaching at the revival?"

"Preach at the revival? What brought this up?"

"I told Chief Parker I'd get you to preach at the revival if he got the original Brown Family Band to sing."

"Why would you commit to something on my behalf?!"

"It was his idea. He said it would make his dad happy."

"Of course, he did," Granddad groaned. "Making big commitments like that without thinking is how Jephthah's daughter got killed!"

"Who?"

"Judges eleven, boy," Granddad sighed. "Read your Bible."

"I tried... it was hard to understand."

"Find a version you do understand. Don't they have an app for that?"

"So, you won't preach at the revival?" I asked.

Granddad crossed his arms over his chest and closed his eyes. The clock's hand ticked by as I waited for Granddad's response.

"I'll pray about it," Granddad decided. "And if the good Lord above allows, I'll do it."

The Lord must've said yes because Granddad told me he would preach at the revival the next day. It was all Creeke talked about that week. Everyone couldn't wait to have an 'old-school, fire-filled revival', as the adults called it. Some hoped that Granddad and Nanna would run the church again.

"I think Dee-Three has a secret girlfriend," I told Allison as we played a card game in Granddad's living room that Saturday.

"What makes you say that?"

"Think about it. Wearing new clothes, changing the passcode on his phone, and he's always smiling at his phone, then hides it when one of us gets near him. What else could it be?"

"Now that I think about it, he did ask Cornbread for advice on talking to girls too," Allison said.

"I hope he doesn't use that advice," I laughed.

"Whether we like it or not, Cornbread has been successful at getting girls," Allison said. "Now, if he'd just commit to one. Preferably Nisha so she'll stop complaining to me about him not committing to her."

"Let's not focus on Cornbread and his fifty-gazillion flings," I said. "This is about Dee-Three and his obvious secret girlfriend."

"But who would his girlfriend be?"

"It's has to be someone we know. Why else would he keep it a secret?"

"I bet it's Charmaine," Allison giggled.

"Would he hide it if it was Charmaine though?" I asked. "I think it's an older girl. Probably Stacy."

"Stacy would've said something by now if it was her," Allison said. Her face became one of disgust. "What if it's Danielle or one of her minions?"

"I don't think it's them. We'd know if it was one of them because they would flaunt it to everyone."

"True. Who is it then?"

"Knock, knock!" a light, playful voice called from outside the front door.

"Who is it?" Nanna called back as she approached the door.

"Open it and see!" another warm, loud voice answered.

Nanna opened the door and started screaming. Lots of excited screaming, hugs, and kisses as Nanna embraced her two younger sisters at the door.

"What are y'all doing here?" Nanna asked when the excitement died down.

"You can't just tell me my brother-in-law is going to preach again and expect me not to show up!" Aunt Nancy guffawed as she strolled into the living room. She set her suitcase down and held her arms open for us. "Come give auntie some love!"

We took turns hugging Aunt Nancy and Aunt Paulette.

"Nancy, the revival's not until next week," Nanna said.

"Girl, we're old and retired," Aunt Nancy laughed. "My son is grown, my grandsons are grown, my husband is dead and gone, Paulette divorced her sorry excuse of a husband. What else do we have to do?"

"Paulette!" Nanna whined.

"Uh, uh, Danette," Aunt Paulette said. "I get her year-round. You can handle her for two weeks."

"But...but...!" Nanna argued. "My house isn't ready to have guests yet!"

"So, we'll help you clean it," Aunt Nancy said. "Honestly Danette, we lived with you until you were twenty-six. It's not like you have anything we haven't already seen."

"Nancy!" Nanna turned red in the face. "Derrick, sa...say something!"

"I don't mind," Granddad said.

"Well... fine!" Nanna reluctantly agreed. "I don't like people showing up unannounced, but if Derrick's okay with it, you can stay."

"What was the alternative?" Aunt Nancy joked. "Let me get a look at my wonderful niece and nephews. Wow... y'all have grown up."

"They sure have," Aunt Paulette agreed. She bent down to put a hand near her knee. "I still remember when they were this big, running around covered in chocolate and peanut butter."

"Whew, Soleya sure had a fit that day," Aunt Nancy howled. "That poor girl was so embarrassed. And then Marlin just sat there staring like he didn't know what to do."

"Sounds like someone else I know," Nanna said as she nudged Granddad.

"Hey!" Granddad whined. "Come on Derek. It's too many women in here now and you're Nanna's acting up."

"You're the one that said they could stay," Nanna teased.

Granddad drove to the church. The Brown Family Band rehearsed in the main sanctuary, while Samiel and Benjamin rehearsed in the children's church. I wanted to see the growing fruits of Adrianna and my labor.

"Why doesn't Nanna want her sisters to stay?" I asked Granddad as we stood in the foyer.

"It's not that she doesn't want them to stay. They just didn't announce they were coming."

"But they've done that before and she's never had a problem with it. What's different about this time?"

"Do you really want to know? You can't get mad afterwards since you asked."

"I can handle it."

"We were going to enjoy each other's company tonight," Granddad whispered in my ear.

"Oh."

"That is not the note!" someone yelled from inside.

"Lord, that sounds like how Minister Jones used to yell at the choir," Granddad giggled. "I wonder who's hollering like that."

"There's too many possible answers to that question," I sighed.

Granddad and I entered the sanctuary to find everyone staring at Mr. Torrance.

"Why y'all looking at me?" Mr. Torrance asked. "Methuselah is the one yelling."

"Because he wouldn't be yelling if you'd sing right," Mr. Jeremy-Micah griped.

As they continued arguing amongst themselves, I sat down next to Adrianna.

"How's the rehearsal?"

"Here, take these." Adrianna slid her shoes off and handed them to me. "I don't want to get in trouble for using them."

"It's that bad?"

"I'm starting to question whether Drake was right," Adrianna huffed. "They're not focused, especially Dad."

"Hey!" Granddad yelled. Everyone in the room got quiet and looked at him. "Y'all come down here! I want to talk to y'all."

"Granddad, what are you doing?"

"Hush," he said.

"What is it, Mr. Derrick?" Mrs. Garza asked.

"Sit down." Granddad motioned to the pews.

"Now, if I sit down, I'm not going to be able to get back up," Mr. Jeremy-Micah laughed.

"Jeremy-Micah," Granddad growled.

"Yes sir." Mr. Jeremy-Micah sat down.

"I heard that y'all aren't focused."

"Who said that?" Mr. Brown asked as he swiveled around.

"It doesn't matter who said it, Torrance. Y'all are acting like y'all don't want to be here after the Lord worked through these children to bring y'all back together. What would your grandfather say if he saw y'all behaving like this?"

"He wouldn't be happy," Mrs. Ruth-Anne sighed.

"You're right," Granddad said. "He wouldn't be happy. Who are you singing for?"

"The Lord...," they all mumbled.

"Louder."

"The Lord!"

"And what does he do, Marie?"

"He gives us strength to do it," Mrs. Garza squeaked.

"So, if you're singing for him and he's giving y'all strength to do it, shouldn't you be doing your best?"

"Yes...," Chief Parker said.

"Then what's the problem?"

"Torrance!" Mrs. Ruth-Anne griped.

"Why do y'all always blame me?!"

"Because you're always the problem!"

"That is not true!"

"It is kind of true...," Mrs. Garza whispered.

"Y'all are just blaming me because I'm the youngest."

"No, we're blaming you because you're the problem," Chief Parker argued.

"Am not!"

"Are too!" Mr. Jeremy-Micah hollered. "You're up there barely singing!"

"I haven't sung in public in a long time!" Mr. Brown said. "I'm still adjusting."

"That doesn't give you an excuse to do the bare minimum."

"Hey!" Granddad shouted at them. "Y'all can spend all your time arguing, or you can get up there and practice like you have some sense. The choice is yours."

The siblings got back on the pulpit.

"Do you think they'll pull it off?" I asked.

"We'll see," Adrianna grumbled.

I left the sanctuary to go spy on Samiel and Benjamin's practice. They experienced a rougher time than the Parker and Brown siblings were. As I stood outside the room, I listened to their conversation after their latest attempt at singing.

"Come on, Sami," Benjamin said. "It's not like you to sing this badly."

"You think I sound bad?" Samiel worried.

"Oh boy," Benjamin muttered. "That's not what I meant. I just meant you should try harder."

"I am but... what if I get up there and embarrass myself in front of the whole town?"

"You sing in front of them all the time with the youth choir."

"That's different. I'm with a group when I do that, and I had the hymnal so I could just look down if I got nervous. This time I don't have it and it's only us up there. Everyone will be able to hear me and..."

Samiel's insecurities were starting to annoy me. It was like he always had an excuse ready at every moment. I needed outside help, so I made a phone call.

"Hello?" Drake said when he answered the phone.

"I need your help," I said.

"That didn't take long to come full circle," Drake joked. "What do you need help with?"

"It's Sami," I complained. "He's insecure about his singing and I need you to talk to him because I know you went through the same thing."

"I'm all the way in the city," Drake said. "Ask my dad to help."

"How can Mr. Brown help Sami with this?"

"Trust me," Drake said. "He'll be a big help."

"Okay."

I ended our conversation and returned to the sanctuary. The Brown Family Band was taking a break from rehearsing.

"Mr. Brown?" I asked.

"Yeah?" Mr. Torrance and Mr. Jeremy-Micah answered.

"Oh... I get it now," I gasped. It dawned on me why people got annoyed when they called my name, and Derik, Granddad, and I all answered. I pointed to Mr. Torrance and said, "That one."

"What is it?" he asked.

"Can you come with me real quick? One of my friends needs help."

"Sure."

Mr. Brown came with me to the children's church. Samiel and Benjamin were still talking.

"Who am I helping?" he asked.

"Just listen," I said.

"Okay..."

"Sami, it's one song," Benjamin said.

"In front of the whole town, Benji!"

"Say what you really mean, Sami," Benjamin said. "In front of your dad."

"That too," Samiel whispered. "I don't think I can do this. Especially not without the hymnal."

"You don't need that hymnal to sing, Sami."

"This sucks," Samiel complained. "My dad thinks I sound weird when I sing, and now the whole town will think so too."

"Oh," Mr. Brown sighed. "You called Drake, didn't you?"

"Yeah," I said. "He said you could help."

"Yeah, I can."

Mr. Brown knocked on the door as he entered the room.

"Knock, knock," he said. "Can I come in?"

"Mr. Brown?" Samiel said. "I thought you were in the sanctuary rehearsing."

"I was. But someone told me you needed help."

"Who said that?"

"Hi guys...," I chuckled as I entered the room.

"Why is it always you, Derek?" Samiel said.

"Sami," Mr. Brown spoke. "I understand what you're going through."

"You do?" Samiel said.

"It's no secret I don't like singing in front of people anymore. The reason why is because someone made fun of my singing when I was thirteen, and I became insecure."

"But you're singing at the revival."

"Because I have a lot of people supporting me and telling me I can do it. I'm sure you have people in your life doing that too."

"I do...," Samiel grumbled as he looked at me, causing me to laugh.

"The best advice I can give you is not to let what people said get to you. You know you're a great singer, and if you remember that, what other people say won't matter."

"Okay," Samiel said. "Can I ask you a question?"

"Sure."

"Who made fun of you?"

Mr. Brown pursed his lips.

"Leonard Brown," Mr. Brown answered. I realized why Drake said Mr. Brown would be a better help. He experienced the exact same thing Samiel did: having his own father make fun of him. We watched him leave the room.

"Okay," Samiel exhaled. "Did you find the hymnal yet?"

"I'll have it for you by the time you sing at the revival," I promised.

"Alright," Samiel said. "Benji, it's time to get serious! We've got work to do!"

"And he's back...," Benjamin mumbled.

-

Chapter Thirty-Seven

Dancing was my passion, and if I couldn't do it anymore, my world would end. I'd danced since I was ten. Before that, I did tumbling. Dad took me to a college game when I was four, and I pointed at the dancers and told him I wanted to do that. He misunderstood me and thought I wanted to cheer, so he enrolled me in tumbling. It wasn't until I was ten when I told him I actually wanted to dance.

Dad usually left me to my own devices. He was my biggest supporter, and he trusted me enough to make the right decision. The only time he intervened in my life was if he felt I was in over my head with something. That Thursday, I had the news on in the background while I did my homework when a story caught my attention.

"Administrators at a local high school are speaking out after they say one rapper's performance started an on-campus brawl," the news anchor said. *"Here's our reporter with more on the story."*

"Preston High School's homecoming activities last Friday were going normally until an unplanned concert changed everything," The reporter said. *"Students were excited to see twenty-two-year-old rapper Ra'Kaveon King, known professionally as KV, at their homecoming pep rally. But Preston High's Principal says KV was not supposed to perform."*

"From my understanding, he was there to speak to some of the English classes and that's it," Preston High's principal said. She was an older Black woman. *"He was not supposed to be at the pep rally at all."*

"King is an alumnus of Preston High and was invited by a teacher as a guest speaker for her classes," The reporter continued with her report. *"Administrators aren't sure how he gained entrance to the pep rally. But*

one student who witnessed the altercation says King's performance of his latest song 'Thief Slayer' started the incident."

"One guy was provoking the other one by rapping the lyrics to the song at him and then as soon as KV said 'when I catch you, it's on sight,' all I saw was hands start flying," a student recounted.

" 'Thief Slayer' is a diss track King aimed at his former K and K partner Vincent Cartwright, known professionally as Knokout," The reporter explained. *"The song's lyrics express King's desire to harm Cartwright for allegedly robbing him. Video footage that went viral on social media today shows King halfway through the song before the camera turns to capture the fight in the bleachers. Two male students are seen punching each other as other students run away. Preston High Principal says the students' actions are unacceptable."*

"Any violence or misconduct from our students simply is not tolerated or encouraged, period," the principal said.

"Administrators say that disciplinary action has been taken against both students involved," the reporter said. *"Back to you in the studio."*

"Uh... Derek?" Dad said as he entered the house.

"Hey," I said. "Didn't Nanna and her sisters go to Preston?"

"Yeah. Why?"

"They just did a story on how KV caused a fight there."

"It's always some mess at Preston," Dad grumbled. "Anyways, people keep telling about things you've done all over town and I want to know what's going on."

"What'd I do?"

"*You* didn't do anything," Dad groaned. "One of these 'concerned people' sent me a photo of 'you' picking a lock at one of the abandoned buildings, and when I looked at it, it was Dee-Three. What's going on with him?"

"It might be something to do with his secret girlfriend," I chuckled.

"Secret girlfriend?"

"It's a theory I have. But it's really insulting that the people of this town can't tell us apart. We're not twins, and we don't even have the same parents."

"Well, you do look a lot alike," Dad reasoned. "And you both have the same name."

"And who's fault is that?"

"Marlin's!" Dad huffed. "I picked the name first and he just had to be difficult."

"This is why I dance," I said. "It's the only way people seem to be able to tell us apart."

"Speaking of dance, I hope you've decided what you're going to do about college. It's almost admissions season."

"I told you, I want to major in dance."

"I still don't think it's a good idea," Dad cautioned me. We'd disagreed over my college major choice ever since I'd told him about it. "My advice is to choose something more stable."

"You said you'd support whatever I chose to do. This is what I want to do."

"I do support you, but what if you get hurt? Then what?"

"Did you think about me getting hurt when you signed me up for tumbling classes at four years old?"

"All the time."

"But you still let me do it for six years."

"Because you liked it, and your grandma was super excited about it. But I still had the same concerns then that I have now."

"College will always be there, my dance ability won't. All I'm asking is for you to trust me."

"Well, if this is what you want to do, then I guess we need to get you to dance practice."

My dance classes were twice a week in the city. Every Tuesday and Thursday for a few hours, I put my all into dance and perfected my craft. When class ended, I sat in the park across from the studio, waiting for my ride. I listened to music and scrolled through social media to pass the time. Knokout had responded to KV's situation at Preston High, calling him an 'idiotic attention seeker'. It didn't seem like their issue would end any time soon.

"It cost a bag to bag her, and I don't know what to do," Knokout rapped the hook along to the funky beat of his new single 'Baby Bag'. *"Spending up my money, buying clothes, hair, nails, and shoes. My baby's in my bag, so she can look how I want her to. She put that pressure on me, got me wrapped up like a fool."*

"How long?!" a hoarse voice cut through the song. I paused my music and looked around. A woman stood in the park's center, screaming at people walking past her. She wore a white t-shirt with the word 'WISDOM' written on it in black permanent marker. "How long will you who are simple love your simple ways?! How long will mockers delight in mockery and fools hate knowledge?! Repent at my rebuke!"

Our eyes met, and my stomach knotted up.

"Then I will pour out my thoughts to you!" the woman continued. "I will make known to you my teachings!"

A hand rested on my shoulder. I followed the red fingernails up to Nanna's head, illuminated by a streetlight. She clutched a jacket in her other hand. Nanna motioned for me to follow her, and we approached the woman.

"Sister, please take this," Nanna handed the woman a jacket. "It's getting cold, and we can't have you out here getting sick."

"Thank you," the woman accepted the jacket. "May God bless you."

"You too."

Nanna led me to her car.

"Nanna, what are you doing here?"

"Your aunts wanted to go shopping for new church dresses and your grandfather was too busy interviewing with Ralphie Brewer to take them. I told Malcolm I'd pick you up since I was coming out here. When I was leaving the house, The Lord told me to grab an extra jacket. I'm so glad I listened too because that poor thing looked like she's out there freezing."

"It sure did take you long enough," Aunt Nancy complained when we got in the car. "By the time we get to the store, it'll be closed."

"Why can't y'all wear something y'all already have?" Nanna argued.

"We can't be at the church looking raggedy, Danette," Aunt Paulette said.

"No one will be paying attention to y'all!"

"You guys haven't shopped yet?" I asked.

"No."

"*No*," I whined. Shopping with Nanna took longer than shopping with Allison.

"You will be alright," Nanna said. "It won't take that long... I think."

It took almost two hours for Aunt Nancy and Aunt Paulette to find dresses for the revival. Aunt Nancy wanted something that went with her blonde wig, while Aunt Paulette wanted something that wouldn't draw too much attention to her. Once they found what they wanted, we returned to Creeke, and my phone rang.

"Hello?"

"Dude," Samiel said. "You're not going to believe this."

"What?"

"Danielle and her minions didn't get in trouble."

"How do you know?"

"My mom told me earlier Principal Lee gave the girls a warning and that's it."

"Are you serious?" I complained. "All that horrible stuff they said, and they only got a warning?"

"Yup."

"That's some bull."

"I know. Lala is pissed."

"I am too. How could he let them get away with that?"

"You know he's got a blind spot when it comes to Danielle."

"He needs to fix it because this is ridiculous."

"I know. I'll let you go, man."

"Alright, goodnight."

It upset me that Danielle and her minions weren't punished for their actions. I went to bed angry and had the strange dream again.

I stood in Derik's room. In the mirror, I saw I was on fire. My reflection twisted himself into strange positions, writhing in pain. He looked at me.

"How long?!" he cried.

"What do you mean?" I asked.

"How long?!"

"How long until what?"

"HOW LONG?!"

The dream reminded me of the woman I saw in the park when I awoke. She kept repeating the words 'how long' in her questions, and I wondered if it related to my dream. I stared at the ceiling, trying to figure out what it all meant.

Chapter Thirty-Eight

Granddad, The Brown Family Band, and Samiel and Benjamin were all scheduled for Saturday, the final day of the revival. Dad and Uncle Marlin would only attend that service. I heard great things about how the revival went as the week progressed. Friday's service was short so everyone could attend the big football game between Creeke High and Preston High.

"Gray and maroon is the way to go!" Latasia chanted as she led the cheerleaders on the sideline. "Come on team, let's go for the goal! Woo!"

The cheerleaders lifted Nicole and another girl into the air as Stacy did flips in front of them. Danielle and her minions glared at them from the stands. I was still mad that they weren't punished for what they did.

"Creeke High runs it in for a touchdown, but there's a flag on the play," Granddad said over the PA system. He'd announced for Creeke High's football games since I was little.

"Seriously, ref?!" Allison shouted as she shot from her seat. "A flag?!"

"A lady doesn't do that, Allison," Aunt Soleya said.

"This is why I didn't want to sit with you!" Allison huffed. "It's a football game!"

"You should still act like a lady," Aunt Soleya whispered.

"Nanna's a lady and she yells at the refs."

"Marlin, please talk to your daughter," Aunt Soleya said to Uncle Marlin.

"I'm trying to watch the game, Leya," Uncle Marlin said, his harsh brown eyes remaining on the field. Those eyes were almost never happy. Dad told me if I stared into them for too long, I'd become unhappy too.

"Alright, Marlin," Aunt Soleya sighed. "Watch your game."

"And this is why I didn't want to sit with them," Dad whispered in my ear, causing me to laugh.

Creeke High beat Preston High. The win filled the town with energy and excitement for the revival's conclusion that Saturday. Friday night, I had the dream again.

I stood in Derik's room. In the mirror, I saw I was on fire. My reflection twisted himself into strange positions, writhing in pain. He looked at me.

"How long?!" he cried.

"What do you mean?" I asked.

"How long?!"

"How long until what?"

"HOW LONG?!"

The mirror shattered. Flames spread from the broken glass across the floor. They converged on me, and I caught on fire. It felt horrible. Creeke burned outside the window. I fell to the floor, as the flames tortured me.

"How long will this last?!" I yelled.

The fire never ended. It seemed it would torture me forever.

Saturday morning, I went with Allison to Granddad's to watch college football with him. Dad had arranged a surprise for Granddad, and I had to make sure it arrived at his house. Granddad would be distracted either cheering or screaming at his alma mater's team. I read Derik's article in the school newspaper to pass the time. His headline was 'Improving parent-child relationships, lowering runaway children cases'.

"YOU IDIOT!" Granddad hollered when a player dropped a pass. It was the fourth quarter, and Granddad's team was losing.

"HOW'D YOU DROP THAT?" Allison yelled.

Someone knocked on the front door.

"Go answer that," Granddad said to me.

I got up and did as he asked. If it was Dad's surprise, then it arrived earlier than I expected. Leonard Brown stood on the other side of the front door when I opened it. Seeing him at Granddad's house shocked me.

"Are you going to stand there looking stupid or are you going to let me in?" he said.

"Excuse you?" I asked.

"Did I stutter?"

I tilted my head to the side and slammed the door in his face. It didn't matter if he was the infamous Leonard Brown or not. He wouldn't disrespect me.

"Who was at the door?" Granddad asked.

"Leonard Brown."

"You didn't let him in?"

"He got smart with me, so I slammed the door in his face."

"Kids these days...," Granddad sighed. He got up and went to the front door.

"Your grandson slammed the door in my face!" Leonard Brown yelled. "You're going to let him get away with that?!"

"That's my business, not yours," Granddad said as he went to the kitchen with Leonard Brown behind him.

"Why am I here?" Leonard Brown huffed. He glared at me as he sat down at the kitchen table.

"I'm preaching tonight at the revival, and I can't in good conscience get on that pulpit unless I've made peace with you."

"They're letting you preach again."

"I just want to know why you did what you did."

"You want to talk about this with your grandkids this close to us?"

"They're old enough."

"Okay then," Leonard Brown sighed as he placed his elbow on the table with his hand in the air.

"Seriously?"

"Do you want to know or not?" Leonard Brown looked at him expectantly.

Granddad shook his head as he placed his hand in Leonard Brown's. It looked like they would arm wrestle.

"Where do I begin?" Leonard Brown said. He nodded, and the two old men began arm wrestling with what strength they still had. "I've had a crush on Marianne since we were young, but you already knew that. While you guys were off fighting in the war, I was here watching as she got lonelier by the day."

"So, you saw an opportunity and went for it?" Granddad glared at his opponent. He didn't seem to be struggling in the match. "You took advantage of Marianne's loneliness and seduced her."

"You could say that," Leonard Brown answered as he tried to push Granddad's arm. "I was having fun. But then she got pregnant, and she couldn't pretend it was Damian's."

"How could you do that to Damian?"

"He had everything I wanted: normal parents, the girl I liked, friends..."

"I was your friend."

"I know. One of my biggest regrets is losing you as a friend. If I could take everything I did back..."

"Well, you can't," Granddad answered as he banged Leonard Brown's hand against the kitchen table. "It hurt me to see what you became. You were my brother and I'd be lying if I said I didn't still care about you."

"I regret everything."

"Regretting it won't change that you did it. You hurt Damian and his kids because you were jealous of him. But why did you hurt Torrance too?"

"I didn't believe he was mine. I thought he looked like Damian and..."

"What?!" Granddad laughed coldly and mockingly like it was the only thing keeping him sane. I saw Uncle Marlin for the first time when I looked at Granddad. "That boy looks like you! This is what I tried to warn you about, Leonard! Look at what your jealous spirit has cost you!"

"I know!" Leonard Brown grumbled. "I just want to make it right!"

"Some things you can't fix yourself," Granddad said. "You have to leave it up to God."

"I never thought I'd say this, but I missed hearing your biblical crap."

"What you did was horrible, and I won't pretend you didn't do it."

"So, you won't forgive me?"

"That's not what I said. I'll forgive you for what you did to me, but I can't absolve you in the kids' place. It's up to them to forgive you for what you did to them."

"What does this mean for us then?"

"It means that I don't hate you, Leonard Brown. But I'm not your friend either. I'll always hold you accountable."

"I understand."

Leonard Brown left, and Granddad returned to the living room.

"Don't y'all slam that door in anybody else's face," he said. "Because my belt still works and y'all aren't too old to get beat."

"Yes sir," Allison and I answered, giggling when he turned around.

When the game ended, Granddad went to the kitchen to make lunch. While he was there, someone knocked on the door again. Granddad walked back into the living room to answer it.

"I'll get it this time since y'all like to slam doors," he said. Once he reached the door, he said, "Who is it?"

"It's me!"

"Who is me?"

"Richard!"

"*Rick?!*" Granddad shouted as he flung the door open. "It is you! Here in Creeke!"

"It is!" Mr. Richard said. His face sported a few wrinkles, and his blond hair was gray.

"What are you doing here?" Granddad asked.

"I came to hear you preach, kid. I'm not missing it this time."

"How'd you know I was preaching?"

"Malcolm told me. He wanted me to come down and surprise you."

"Did you know about this?" Granddad asked me.

"Maybe...," I chuckled.

"I can't believe you're really here," Granddad said.

"Yeah," Mr. Richard said. "I came early, but Kate and Kaitlyn will be here tonight."

"You're bringing your whole family to hear me preach?" Granddad said. He hugged Mr. Richard. "I'm so happy you're here."

"Me too," Mr. Richard said. "I'm sure you'll do a great job tonight."

"I hope so."

-

Chapter Thirty-Nine

Dad and I entered the church with Aunt Nancy and Aunt Paulette. Uncle Marlin and his family sat near the front of the church. They all wore nice, bright-colored clothes. Matthias sat apart from them, instead choosing to sit with Alexander.

"Malcolm!" Mr. Damian yelled when he saw us. "Malcolm Harrison is that you?! In church again?!"

"Yeah," Dad laughed. "I came to hear Dad preach."

"God is good!" Mr. Damian said. "You even brought my little Derek with you! Granted, he's not little anymore, but still!"

Mr. Damian squeezed me against his chest.

"So, Damian," Mr. Richard said as he approached us. "I guess you'll have to admit I'm the better godfather now. My godson has returned to the church."

"Not so fast, Anderson," Mr. Damian said. "My godson has returned too."

"Y'all still debating about that?" Aunt Nancy asked. "Why can't y'all accept that Derrick chose both of you to be a godfather and call it a day?"

"Seriously," Aunt Paulette agreed. "It's old. Both of your godsons have made mistakes and bounced back from them. Move on."

"Thanks Auntie...," Dad grumbled.

"I guess we can call a truce for now since it's Derrick's big night," Mr. Damian said.

"But after this is over, he has to pick one of us," Mr. Richard said.

The men shook hands to signal their truce. Mr. Richard returned to the front to sit with his family.

"Do you need me to find you a seat?" Mr. Damian said.

"We'll sit in the back with you and Mrs. Thelma if that's alright," Dad said to Mr. Damian.

"Fine by me," Mr. Damian said.

As we waited for the service to start, I looked around. Almost the whole town was at the church.

"I'm so excited for this," Mrs. Thelma said. "You know I put together the outfit your mother's wearing tonight, right?"

"That's interesting," Dad said. "I thought she would've pulled something together herself."

"She wanted to, but I told her I'd create a look specifically for her tonight. This is a special occasion, and she needs to look her best."

"I'm glad she has a best friend like you, Mrs. Thelma."

"Thanks Falcon," Mrs. Thelma giggled. "And to think, your parents wouldn't even be together if I hadn't notice her giving your father the eye."

"The eye?"

"The way she looked at him to show she was interested," Mrs. Thelma explained. "I looked at Damian the same way for a while, but he never noticed me, so I stopped."

"I did notice you, Honeybun," Mr. Damian said. "But your look creeped me out."

"Oh well," Mrs. Thelma sighed. She rested her head on Mr. Damian's shoulder. "In the end, you still ended up by my side. That's all that matters to me now."

"We didn't miss anything, did we?" someone whispered in my ear from behind me. I turned around to see Drake, Andrew, Philomena, Dorothea, and Tamela behind me.

"You guys came too?" I gasped. "Even Tamela?"

"You thought I would miss this?" Tamela laughed. "No, I caught a flight."

"Yeah, there's no way we would miss this," Andrew said.

"Especially after weeks of listening to Mary and Drake complain," Philomena said.

"I'm excited to see it," Dorothea said.

"Plus, I have to see the fruit of the seed I planted," Drake said. "I'm so glad you guys pulled this off."

"Me too," I said.

Drake and his friends went to find seats. I spotted Samiel enter the church. His eyes grew wide when he saw how many people there were. Samiel turned around and walked out.

"I'll be right back," I told Dad. I found Samiel standing outside. "What's wrong now?"

"The whole town is in there."

"But you already knew that. You said yourself the whole town would be here."

"Yeah, but *the whole town is in there*!" Samiel repeated. "I can't do this!"

"Yes, you can!" I said. "I've done everything I can to encourage you! But if you don't get up there and sing, Benji will get mad at us for wasting his time. Do you want to deal with an angry Benji?"

"No..."

"Exactly! Stop being scared and kill this like we know you can!"

"Why are you yelling at me?"

"To light a fire under you!" I grabbed Samiel's shoulders and pushed him toward the door. "Now get in there!"

"Okay, okay!" Samiel said.

The service started. After a long introduction by Pastor Hall, it was Samiel and Benjamin's turn to sing. Samiel was supposed to start the song with a solo, but he just stared at the congregation.

"Uh...," Samiel murmured.

"Oh no," I sighed as I buried my head in my hands.

A stray note sounded through the room. We all looked at Chief Parker sitting at the organ. He quietly apologized, but his stray note snapped Samiel from his trance. Samiel started singing, and then Benjamin joined him. Soon, the whole church sang. I watched as Samiel regained his confidence on stage. By the time the song ended, Samiel and Benjamin had everyone on their feet.

"Amen," Pastor Hall said as he ascended the pulpit. "Thank you, Sami and Benji for that wonderful ministry. We've got a group of people coming up that we've waited *years* to return. All five members of The Brown Family Band are in the building y'all!"

"Hallelujah!" someone yelled.

The Brown Family Band took their places on the pulpit. They wore brown suits and dresses.

"Good evening, everyone," Mr. Jeremy-Micah said. "We're so glad to be here to minister to you tonight. We've got three songs for y'all and then we'll get out y'all's way. I'm sure we're all excited to hear Mr. Derrick preach again."

"Take your time, baby!" someone hollered.

"Alright then," Mr. Jeremy-Micah laughed. "Who's ready to worship tonight?"

Everybody screamed. The Brown Family Band ran through their first two songs. Everything I'd heard about them was true. Their voices were amazing. Mrs. Marie's soft soprano rang out as she played her tambourine, while Mrs. Ruth-Anne's sweet voice disappeared at times during her shouting dances. Mr. Jeremy-Micah yelled his notes out, while Mr. Terrence's mellow voice made his brother's sound better. Mr. Brown's voice was a bit rough, but I could hear that angelic tone that all the older townspeople gushed about. He still had it.

"It's the last song," Mr. Jeremy-Micah said when they reached the final song. "I hope you all brought your shouting shoes because we're going to let little Torrey here have at it."

Mr. Brown nodded and removed his mic from its stand.

"Come on and put your hands together now!" he yelled. Mr. Brown kicked his shoes off and danced as he sang.

Everyone danced. Mr. Damian danced in the aisle, and I saw where Mrs. Ruth-Anne got her moves from. I felt moved to dance too. The more I danced, the more I felt something stir in me. It was an indescribable feeling.

"Hallelujah!" Mrs. Marianne yelled. She stood at the front with her arms outstretched above her and tears streaming down her face.

"Alright!" Pastor Hall exhaled as he got on the pulpit. "Alright, y'all. I know we can praise all night, but we still have to get to The Word."

Everyone settled down and returned to their seats.

"The Spirit of The Lord is in here tonight!" Pastor Hall exclaimed. "I can feel His fire in this room, and I know our next guest will preach the house down. This man has been a big part of my life since I was a kid in his Sunday School classes. I'm so honored to be able to announce his return. We've waited all week for him, and now the time is here. Pastor Derrick Harrison, everyone."

The building erupted into cheers, and Granddad took his place on the pulpit. He looked at the congregation with a face full of emotion as they applauded him.

"Amen, amen, amen," Granddad said. "Y'all know how when a football player gets injured, they train and come back the next season better than ever? That's how it feels to be back up here after eighteen years."

"We love you, Pastor!" Mr. Richard yelled.

"I love you too," Granddad laughed. "I love all of y–!"

Granddad froze. Something at the back of the church had his attention. One by one, the rows of the church turned to look at what caught Granddad's eye. Leonard Brown sat in the row opposite of us, looking at Granddad. Silence hung in the air as the congregation looked between the two men. For the first time in a long time, every single resident in Creeke was at the church.

"Who here needs to be revived?" Granddad asked as he raised his hand. "I know I do."

"Amen!" the congregation agreed.

"Before I begin, I want to thank God for blessing me with this opportunity," Granddad said. "I also want to acknowledge Pastor and First Lady Hall and thank them for asking me to preach tonight. They've done a great job leading this church so far, and I'm excited to see them continue leading it for years to come. Don't y'all agree?"

The congregation clapped for Pastor and First Lady Hall.

"I also want to acknowledge my beautiful wife, Kiana," Granddad said as he looked at Nanna. "She's stood by me through thick and thin and I couldn't have asked for a better partner through it all. And my sons and grandchildren too, for teaching me to be a responsible father, grandfather, and man. Thank you, Marlin, Malcolm, Matthias, Deidrick, Allison, and Dee-Three."

Dad nodded at Granddad. But I noticed Granddad hadn't called my name.

"If you'll notice, I left out a grandson," Granddad said. "There's a reason for that. This grandson was the straw that broke the camel's back and led to me being sat down. This grandson caused the whole town to turn on me and hold me accountable for my actions, just like I did to others. But it was also this specific grandson that God used to return me to this pulpit. God used this specific grandson to get me together. If it was not for him, I wouldn't have a message tonight."

My heart raced.

"Derek Drumaine Harrison and all the people that helped him make this possible," Granddad said as he looked at me. "Thank you. This couldn't have happened without you all."

I smiled at Granddad as everyone looked at me.

"So," Granddad said. "Revival. The dictionary defines revival as a reviving of interest. Let's break that down. When we look at the word 'revive', the definition is 'to bring back or come back to life, consciousness, or activity. To make or become fresh or strong again. To bring back into use'. Interest in this context is defined as 'readiness to be concerned with or moved by something'. So, let's put it together: revival is 'bringing back to life, consciousness, or activity a readiness to be concerned with or moved by something'."

"Yes!" someone yelled.

"Most of y'all know this story, but when I turned eighteen, I went out partying with my friends to celebrate. They're all here tonight too. Anyways, I got in trouble and the next day, my Grandpapa basically rebuked me in front of the whole church. The question he asked in that sermon was 'how long'?"

My stomach tightened up.

"How long ye simple ones will ye love simplicity?" Granddad asked. "That's the question he asked. It's the question The Lord asks us when we don't turn to him. The Lord calls for a revival amongst His people. But what does revival in The Lord look like? I'm glad y'all asked."

Granddad opened his Bible.

"The answer can be found several places in the Bible, but I'm going to the King James Version of Zechariah One, Verse Two," Granddad asked. "Whether you use a Bible, phone, tablet, it doesn't matter. The Word is The Word. Say 'amen' when you get there."

I turned in my Bible to where Granddad said he would be.

"Amen," everyone said.

"Amen," Granddad repeated. "So, a little backstory. The Israelites got exiled from the Promised Land because they weren't doing right. Then after about ninety years in Babylon, they were allowed to return to Jerusalem to rebuild their temple to The Lord. That's where our story begins. Verse two, 'The Lord hath been sore displeased with your fathers. Therefore say thou unto them, Thus saith the Lord of hosts; Turn ye unto me, saith the Lord of hosts, and I will turn unto you, saith the Lord of hosts'.

"We see here that The Lord hasn't been happy with the Israelites actions up to that point. But He's promised that he will redeem them if they turn their hearts back to Him. In our day in age, turning your heart to God means accepting Jesus as your Lord and Savior and believing in his sacrifice. But at this point in the Bible, Jesus hadn't come yet. Let's keep reading.

"Verse Four, 'be ye not as your fathers, unto whom the former prophets have cried, saying, Thus saith the Lord of hosts; Turn ye now from your evil ways, and from your evil doings: but they did not hear, nor hearken unto me, saith the Lord'. Verse Five, 'Your fathers, where are they? and the prophets, do they live for ever'? Verse Six, 'But my words and my statutes, which I commanded my servants the prophets, did they not take hold of your fathers? and they returned and said, Like as the Lord of hosts thought to do unto us, according to our ways, and according to our doings, so hath he dealt with us'.

"So here, The Lord tells the Israelites don't be like those that came before you. I've warned them and they didn't listen. I'm giving you that same warning, so choose correctly. How many of us have been warned by God, and we didn't listen? I have and we all saw how that went. So, because the Israelites didn't listen, he let them experience the consequences of their actions which was being exiled. When you don't listen to God, He will remove things from your life that distract you until you get yourself together. Trust me, I've been there and experienced it for myself. Now we'll skip down to Verse Twelve.

"Verse Twelve, 'Then the angel of the Lord answered and said, O Lord of hosts, how long wilt thou not have mercy on Jerusalem and on the cities of Judah, against which thou hast had indignation these threescore and ten years?' Thirteen, 'And the Lord answered the angel that talked with me with good words and comfortable words'. Fourteen, 'So the angel that communed with me said unto me, Cry thou, saying, Thus saith the Lord of hosts; I am jealous for Jerusalem and for Zion with a great jealousy'. Fifteen, 'And I am very sore displeased with the heathen that are at ease: for I was but a little displeased, and they helped forward the affliction'. Sixteen, 'Therefore thus saith the Lord; I am returned to Jerusalem with mercies: my house shall be built in it, saith the Lord of hosts, and a line shall be stretched forth upon Jerusalem'. Seventeen, 'Cry yet, saying, Thus saith the Lord of hosts; My cities through prosperity shall yet be spread abroad; and the Lord shall yet comfort Zion, and shall yet choose Jerusalem.'"

"We see that The Lord is not pleased with the state of the world," Granddad preached. He placed his hand to his ear and said, "And the angel of the Lord asked what question?"

"How long?" the congregation answered.

"That's right," Granddad said. "How long? How long will The Lord punish the Israelites for their sins? And The Lord is like 'even though I'm upset with my children, I still love them and am still for them. I'm upset with how they've been treated because the mistreatment has gone too far. So, I'm going to return them to me and establish a standard among them. Spoiler alert: the standard was and still is Jesus Christ. And The Lord declares that he will comfort and choose his people. Now, how does that relate to us? I'm glad you asked."

"See, it upsets God when you live a life apart from Him," Granddad said. "He knows how much better your life would be if you let Him in, so He asks, 'how long until you turn to me'? Because when you accept Jesus into your heart, you become part of his chosen people. Therefore, The Lord's promise to comfort and choose his people now includes you. But you can't experience that if you're not living for Him."

"But say you are living for Him. Sometimes as Christians, life wears our spirits down, and we forget to be fruitful, assured, infinite, tenacious and humble in our walks with God. Thank you, Pastor Hall for that."

"You're welcome!" Pastor Hall yelled.

"Those moments when our spirits are weakened is when The Lord ushers in a spirit of revival. A spirit of renewed interest in serving him. A reminder to show us what we're striving for. Revival with God is to remember His promises to us. To comfort and choose us and be faithful to us even when our faith in Him falters. The promise of eternal salvation and an eternity with Him if we choose Him and His way. Because let's be honest the alternative is Hell. A place of weeping and gnashing of teeth. Who wants to experience that for all eternity?"

I thought about the dream I kept having. Everything was on fire, and I was always in pain in the dream. Maybe I'd dreamt about being in Hell.

"But Hell is never an option when you choose life with Christ. So, I encourage you today to revive your interest in serving God. The first place to start is to accept Jesus into your heart or recommit yourself to him. Everyone, bow your heads and close your eyes.

We did as Granddad asked. He led us in a prayer of salvation, and I prayed along with him. Once we finished, I felt light. I couldn't explain the feeling other than it was a good one. After service ended, Allison and I found Samiel standing with his family.

"And then you were like 'Uh...'," Kameryn teased Samiel about his solo.

"Cut it out, Kamie," Samiel grumbled.

"Sami," I called.

"Dude," Samiel said. "You told me you'd have the hymnal by tonight. What happened?"

"I have it right here," I chuckled. I handed the hymnal to Samiel. "Tonight isn't over yet so I'm still good."

"Where'd you find it?" Samiel gasped.

"I have a confession to make," I said. "I've had it for some time now."

"Why didn't you give it back sooner?"

"Because I wanted to prove to you that you didn't need it to sing. And I was right. You killed it up there."

"He's right," Officer Dow agreed. "You did a great job, Sami."

"Thanks Dad," Samiel said, his cheeks turning red.

"See?" I said. "I told you he wasn't ashamed of you."

"Shhh!" Samiel said.

"Ashamed?" Officer Dow repeated. "Why would I be ashamed of you, Sami?"

"I may have heard you on the phone...," Samiel said. "When you were talking about my singing and said I sounded weird."

"Oh Sami." Officer Dow hugged his son. "I wasn't talking about you, son."

"You weren't?"

"No. I was talking to Bud about Terrence."

"*What?!*" Chief Parker shrieked. "You think I sound weird, Sam?!"

"I mean...," Officer Dow said. "Well..."

"Someone's getting fired," Kameryn giggled.

"Don't say that," Vice Principal Dow laughed.

"Oh wait!" Samiel exclaimed. He went up to Mr. Brown with the hymnal and said, "Here."

"What's this?" Mr. Brown asked.

"Your grandfather's hymnal," Samiel said. "I don't need it anymore. Thank you for helping me."

"You're welcome, Sami," Mr. Brown said with a smile.

Samiel returned to us with a triumphant grin. He'd overcome his trouble like I knew he would.

"Did you see Danielle and her minions' faces when you guys sung?" Latasia cheered as she ran up to us with the rest of our friends. "This totally makes up for that slap on the wrist Principal Lee gave them."

"No, it doesn't," Allison grumbled.

Danielle and Priscella walked past us.

"Did you enjoy the show, ladies?" I asked.

"It was nice," Priscella answered.

"Hmph!" Danielle huffed. "I've seen better."

"You didn't like it?" Allison teased. "How sad."

"So sad," Latasia said as she dabbed at her eyes.

"Very sad," Adrianna said

"I think they're mocking us," Priscella whispered.

"I'm not surprised, Prissy," Danielle complained. "They have to feel like they won somehow, since their plan to get us in trouble failed. Let's not waste any more time on these losers."

Danielle led Priscella away.

"What plan is she talking about?" Adrianna asked me.

"Lala and I may have repeated what they said in front of Vice Principal Dow to get them in trouble...," I said. "And it may have failed..."

"That's what happens when you try and take matters into your own hands," Adrianna chastised. "I told you let The Lord handle it. Notice how your grandfather let The Lord handle everything, and now he's back preaching again. The Lord will handle Danielle."

"Alright," I sighed.

Chapter Forty

Creeke Church revival sees return of The Brown Family Band, Pastor Derrick Harrison

by Ralph Brewer, senior staff writer, and Derik Harrison, staff writer

The conclusion to Creeke Church's revival saw the return of six beloved figures Saturday evening.

The Brown Family Band, a singing group made up of five siblings, reunited on the church's pulpit to minister three songs. Their members consist of Terrence Parker, Ruth-Anne Green, Jeremy-Micah Brown, Marie Garza, and Torrance Brown. After their performance, Pastor Derrick Harrison returned to preach on Creeke's pulpit for the first time in eighteen years.

"It was a wonderful event filled with the Holy Ghost," Creeke Church's Head Pastor Forrest Hall said. "I couldn't have asked for anything better."

Pastor Harrison was sat down from the Head Pastor position of Creeke Church due to missteps during his tenure. He was succeeded by then-Youth Pastor Hall. The Brown Family Band disbanded twenty-six years ago after releasing one album. Saturday evening was a special moment for all of them.

"None of this would've been possible without my children, their friends and even my grandfather even though he's passed on," The Brown Family Band member Torrance Brown said. "I'm very grateful to all of them for uniting us. My siblings and I hope to keep singing together from now on."

As for Pastor Harrison, his time as a pastor will not end with the revival.

"I'm proud to say I will be the new Youth Pastor at Creeke Church," Former Creeke Head Pastor Derrick Harrison said. "I believe it's a fresh start The Lord has blessed me with."

"Looks like Ralphie's story made it to the front page after all," I said.

"Sure has," Granddad agreed. Dad and I were visiting him and Nanna for Sunday dinner. "Marianne talked my head off all afternoon about how well everything went."

"I'm glad you guys are back on good terms," Dad said.

"Me too," Granddad said.

"I liked your message too," I said. "I still don't know if it related to my nightmares though."

"What nightmares?" Dad asked.

"I kept having same this nightmare about everything being on fire including me."

"I had a recurring dream like that once," Granddad said. "My skin melted in it, and my blood turned into a man made of rotten wood that made everything around him rot."

"What kind of dream...?" I said.

"It was a nightmare," Granddad said. "I believe it was a prophetic dream from The Lord, and I didn't listen to it right away. I didn't realize I was the rotten man in my dream until I made up with Marianne."

"Interesting," I said.

"You said you've dreamt multiple times of Creeke being on fire, right?"

"Yeah. It always started with Uncle Marlin's house on fire and ended with the whole town burning."

"We should pray about it then," Granddad said. "Just promise me you won't burn the town down."

"I don't plan on it."

"The food's almost finished," Nanna announced as she entered the living room. "Once Marlin and his family get here, we can eat."

"I asked Matty if he wanted to come and he said no," Granddad sighed. "He can't avoid his parents forever."

"I wouldn't want to talk to my parents either if they kicked me out at fourteen," Dad said.

"You came close," Nanna laughed. "God's grace and Etta's ignorance saved you."

"Who's Etta?" I asked.

"No one," Dad said.

"Lord have mercy," Aunt Nancy said as she entered the room. She'd been outside on the phone with her grandson, James. "James said his brother has disappeared again."

"Jordan can't ever stay put," Nanna complained.

"As long as my grandson's not dead in a ditch somewhere, he can always turn it around," Aunt Nancy said.

"But Jordan has been getting in a lot of trouble lately," Aunt Paulette said. "He needs to wise up now that he's eighteen."

"He'll get it together," Aunt Nancy said. "I know he will."

"We'll be praying for it," Nanna said.

Uncle Marlin arrived with his wife and three of their children. We sat down to the meal Nanna prepared, and Granddad said grace.

"How's the salon doing, Soleya?" Nanna asked.

"It's doing well, ma'am," Aunt Soleya said. Uncle Marlin laughed at her answer, and Aunt Soleya glared at him. "Business is great."

"Does your mother still think you shouldn't own a business?" Granddad joked.

"Yes sir," Aunt Soleya said. "My shop has been open for ten years now, and she hasn't stepped foot in it once."

"Oh dear," Granddad stopped laughing. "I... uh... forgive me for that."

"How's your tech business, Marlin?" Nanna asked.

"Great," Uncle Marlin answered. Aunt Soleya rolled her eyes at him.

"Okay then," Granddad said, pursing his lips. "Kids, how's life?"

"It's great," Deidrick said. "I'm still the best barber in Creeke."

"And I'm still the highest-ranked person in my class," Allison said.

"Good," Granddad said. "How about you, Dee-Three? The first person in this family to skip a grade must have something good to say."

"I'm fine," Derik said.

"That's all we get?" Granddad asked. "Just fine?"

"Just fine," Derik repeated.

"That was a wonderful word you preached yesterday, Derrick," Aunt Paulette said.

"Thank you."

"Also, can you pick the better godfather already?" Aunt Nancy complained.

"God is the best Father," Granddad said. "That's my decision."

"Child...," Aunt Nancy groaned.

"Can I be excused?" Derik asked.

"Me too," I said.

"Me three," Allison said.

"Me four," Deidrick said.

"That's almost half the table," Granddad said.

"You chased them away with your bad jokes," Aunt Nancy laughed.

"Now Nancy."

"Yes, y'all can be excused," Nanna said.

Derik went outside to sit on the porch, and Allison and I followed him. We watched Deidrick sneak off down the sidewalk.

"Where's he going?" I asked.

"Probably to Nisha's," Allison said.

"How's your secret girlfriend?" I asked Derik.

"My what?"

"We know you have one," Allison teased.

"No, I don't."

"You don't have to hide it," I said.

"I don't have a secret girlfriend!"

"Okay, okay," I said. "We were just kidding."

"Y'all play too much, then wonder why no one wants to be around y'all."

"First of all, who are you talking to?" Allison asked.

"No, for real," I agreed. "Don't get chopped in your throat."

"Don't get chopped in your throat," Derik mocked me. "Always saying that but don't ever d–!"

I chopped Derik in his throat.

"Oop!" Allison gasped.

Derik stared at me in disbelief. Then, he chopped me in my throat. I chopped him back. We went back and forth, chopping each other until Allison stopped us.

"Alright y'all, that's enough," she said. "Let's stop before y'all start fighting for real."

"I would never fight my family members," I declared. "That's what Browns do, not Harrisons."

"You're going to throw your girlfriend under the bus like that?" Allison giggled.

"She knows it's true."

"But you're right," Allison said. "Harrisons are family through thick and thin."

"It's definitely thin right now," Derik muttered.

"It won't always be though," I encouraged him. "We'll always be here for you, just like I'm sure you'll always be here for us. Because that's what our family does. We stick together."

"If you say so," Derik said.

Creeke is my family's legacy, and this is our genealogy. Abraham was the father of Nathaniel and Laverne, and he founded Creeke Church. Nathaniel died young while Laverne married Franklin Harrison. Franklin was the father of Lionel, who married Judith Morris. Lionel was the father of Derrick, who apparently met Kiana in a nightclub and married her afterward. Derrick was the father of Marlin and Malcolm and lost the family church because of his actions. Marlin married Soleya and was the father of Matthias, Deidrick, Allison, and Derik. Malcolm got Monique pregnant when he was fourteen and was the father of Derek. The Harrisons were restored to the family church in Derek's generation. And all I could do now was wonder what was next for us.